I t... ...orch, soaked ... dark hair, and he brushed it out of his face then removed my weapon from my shaking hand.

"Mind if I come in?" he asked.

"Someone called." How ridiculous that sounded. Like I expected the suspect to reach through the phone and grab me. "At first I thought it was Scolari, but I couldn't tell."

He showed no emotion in his face. It was strong being on this side of the fence. I'd overreacted. It shook me to think how quickly I'd lost control.

"Sorry I got you out of your car," I finished.

He didn't quite smile, but almost, and I expected it was probably an effort. "Don't worry about—" He stopped. This time there was someone on the steps. Then a knock. Had the caller dared to come over anyway?

Torrance wasn't taking any chances. He stood to the side of the door, drew his weapon from his shoulder holster and motioned me to answer. . . .

Books by
Robin Burcell

DEADLY LEGACY
EVERY MOVE SHE MAKES
FATAL TRUTH

Coming Soon
COLD CASE

EVERY MOVE SHE MAKES

ROBIN BURCELL

AVON BOOKS
An Imprint of HarperCollinsPublishers

This is a work of fiction. Names, characters, places, and incidents are products of the author's imagination or are used fictitiously and are not to be construed as real. Any resemblance to actual events, locales, organizations, or persons, living or dead, is entirely coincidental.

AVON BOOKS
An Imprint of HarperCollins*Publishers*
10 East 53rd Street
New York, New York 10022-5299

First Avon Books paperback printing: July 2003
First HarperPaperbacks printing: December 1999

Avon Trademark Reg. U.S. Pat. Off. and in Other Countries, Marca Registrada, Hecho en U.S.A.
HarperCollins® is a trademark of HarperCollins Publishers Inc.

Printed in the U.S.A.

10 9 8 7 6 5 4

In memory of Rick Charles Cromwell 1963–1998

Killed in the line of duty, December 9

Fellow officer, and friend, we will never forget you

EVERY MOVE
SHE MAKES

1

Ask any homicide inspector and he—or she—will tell you the same. Just before the end of shift on any given Friday, Murphy's Law prevails. If you have plans, you might as well cancel them, because someone's bound to find a body. Such is the life of a cop. Mine at San Francisco PD was no different.

On this particular Friday in early November, I got the call precisely twenty minutes before I was due to leave on a weekend trip to Napa. My ex-husband, DA Investigator Reid Bettencourt, intended the trip as a means to bring us back together, though God only knew where he was getting the money—he still owed me three thousand dollars for bills I was left with after our divorce. I, having no intention of getting back together with him, agreed to go—Dutch, of course—and was dressed for the occasion in a winter-white cashmere sweater, tan plaid wool skirt, and soft leather boots. I wore my shoulder-length brown hair pulled back in a clip, leaving a few trendy strands loose to frame my face and bring out the brown in my eyes. It was a gray, windy day, and I was en route to Reid's North Beach flat when my pager went off, alerting me to the homicide out by Pier 24. I telephoned Reid from the car.

"Why can't Scolari take it?" he asked.

"I'm sure he will. Once he gets there." Sam Scolari,

my partner, knew I was on my way out of town and had
promised to cover for me. So far he had yet to answer his
page, which left me no choice. "I have to respond. You
know the routine." Reid should. It was one of the reasons
we divorced. I was at the beck and call of fate, and he didn't
like it. "Drive on up. If I get off in time, I'll meet you for
dinner," I said. "If not, we'll make it breakfast. Hopefully
they'll hold my room."

"How are we supposed to make this work if you're
not there?"

"Short of making the body come back to life, I don't
have much choice." Come to think of it, I'd had the same
problem with our marriage.

"Scolari's doing this on purpose."

"Gotta go," I said, having no wish to get into it with
him about my partner. "I'll call you."

I drove inland, past Pier 24, parking behind two
patrol cars in front of a single-story brick warehouse that
occupied one full block, making sure I kept my Irish-
Italian temper in check. It was not the weekend away with
Reid I was sore about missing. It was the weekend away,
period. I wanted to go anyplace where I didn't have to
look at dead bodies.

An officer stood sentinel at the door, and as I
approached I did a double take. The officer, like me, had
dark eyes and chestnut hair, reminding me of my older
brother—until he spoke. It was not my brother's voice.
That I would never hear again.

I composed myself, and showed my gold inspector's
star. "Kate Gillespie. Homicide."

"Body's inside," he said. "Medical Examiner's investigator hasn't gotten here yet."

I pulled a small spiral notebook from my overcoat

pocket. A gust of wind tore at the pages, made it difficult to write. I glanced at the officer's nameplate to copy it. Robertson. Star 3632. "Who's the reporting party?"

"Officer O'Sullivan."

"Sully?" Kyle O'Sullivan was a senior officer assigned to Mission Station. He liked the action, and I couldn't picture him working this area. Too quiet. "What's he doing out here?"

"Working security next door."

"Next door?" I looked up from my notebook, but didn't see another entrance.

"Hilliard Pharmaceutical. Entrance is around the corner. The warehouse is split in half. Cinder block right down the middle. From what Sully says, it's just a storage facility. No pharmaceuticals."

"Didn't know they had a facility out this far," I commented, jotting the information down. Hilliard Pharmaceutical was probably one of the single largest employers of off-duty San Francisco cops. My father had worked security there while he was an officer at the department, and I'd heard that's where my partner, Scolari, had earned his extra money, too, putting his wife through medical school.

"Where's Sully at?" I asked.

"Left as soon as Fisk and I got here and secured the crime scene. Said he was going to Tahoe for the weekend."

"Must be nice." Had I wanted to get off on time ever again, I would have remained a patrol officer. Even then you rolled the dice.

"And the morgue gave a ten-minute ETA for their investigators. That was five minutes ago. Oh, and I got a statement from Sully before he took off. Said he was driving around the premises in a Hilliard Pharmaceutical security truck. Saw some kids climbing in that window over there." Robertson indicated a broken window at the east end, and a Dumpster below it. "They told him they broke in on a dare. Heard the place was haunted."

"Where're they at now?"

"Got 'em separated. One in my radio car, the other in Fisk's. He's inside with the body."

I looked over at the black and whites parked nearby. Sure enough, the kids, maybe about ten years old, peered out the window of each car, their frightened gazes watching my every move. Probably scared about being blamed for the murder.

"Let's get them transported to the Hall, put a couple volunteers with them, hot chocolate, the works." "The Hall" was what we called the Hall of Justice, a one-stop-shopping of county facilities housed in a seven-story building that included not only the police department and most of its investigative units, but the courts, the jail, the District Attorney's office, and nearly every other county agency you could think of.

I pushed open the warehouse door, stepped into the musty darkness, still harboring the hope that this would turn out to be a simple homicide, something that wouldn't take more than a couple hours of my time, max. I'd be on the road to Napa by seven tonight at the latest. Plenty of time for dinner and a bottle of wine, preferably something heavy, red. Cabernet sauvignon, reserve.

Above me, timbers creaked from the force of the wind. What little light there was came from the same broken windows the kids had apparently climbed through, that and the beam of the other officer's flashlight. Fisk, I presumed, eyeing his uniformed figure standing in the northwest corner next to several stacks of wooden pallets in the otherwise empty building. My footsteps echoed across the concrete flooring, and as I neared, I could make out something large and white between the stacked slats of wood. Not until my sight had adjusted to the dim light could I see what the pallets hid, a chest freezer—and any thoughts of dining in a four-star Napa restaurant were replaced by visions of fast food eaten at my desk. In my experience, simple homicides rarely involved corpses hidden in freezers.

"Body in there?" I asked.

He eyed my gold inspector's star, nodded, and lifted the freezer lid. A fog of cold air swirled up from the interior. It dissipated, and I looked in to see a man curled in a fetal position. I drew latex gloves out of my pocket, put them on, reached in to lift his arm. It didn't budge. He was either in full rigor, frozen solid, or both. His clothes were covered with ice crystals. Apparently the freezer wasn't frost-free.

Pulling my mini Streamlight from my coat pocket, I turned it on and took a look around, noticing the cobwebs behind the appliance, the buildup of dust on the enameled surface. I aimed the beam onto the corpse's face, the ice particles lighting up like diamonds. His hair, whatever color beneath the ice, was short, neatly cut, straight, and parted to the side.

Scolari showed about ten minutes later. I glanced up from my note taking when I heard him enter. At six-three, he towered over me by a good eight inches. As usual, his tan sport coat and navy pants were rumpled, but still he was an imposing figure, even with his slight paunch and graying hair.

We'd been partners for about a year, working

together daily, yet never becoming close. At thirty-six, I was the first female homicide inspector SFPD ever had, and although Scolari never came out and said it, I suspected that he resented not only the notoriety I'd received from the position, but also being partnered with me. Even so, I respected him. He was an outstanding homicide inspector—maybe even one of the best. And he'd saved my life once in a shooting incident. These past few weeks, though, things had been even more tense between us, and I had yet to discover why.

"Gillespie," he said by way of greeting, his voice sounding hollow in the cavernous space. "A little over-dressed for the occasion?"

Normally I let his comments bounce right off, but I was more than irritated. Had he answered his page in a timely manner, I wouldn't be here right now. "You getting your calls by carrier pigeon?"

"Yeah. It got lost on the way." He gave a pointed look to the uniformed officer, and I let drop the subject about him being late. Judging by the expression on Scolari's face, he was in a worse mood than I. "What'dya got?" he asked.

"The lonely repairman." I stood aside to let him view the body.

He put on a latex glove and peered in. "Yeah, he's lookin' pretty lonely right now. Sort of like the ice sculpture for the policeman's ball," Scolari said. He allowed Officer Fisk to have a look, then lowered the freezer lid. Careful not to disturb any possible prints, Scolari inspected the handle and the exterior of the appliance. "Been looking for one of these things. What'dya figure it holds?"

"You mean how many frozen dinners?" I asked.

"Pot pies are real cheap right now. Think it'll fit in my apartment?"

"Sure. You can stick it in your living room. Use it for a TV stand."

"No lock." He eyed the pallets. I knew how his mind worked, that he'd come to the same conclusion I had. With no way to secure the freezer lid, the guy had to be dead or unconscious going in, unless someone weighted the top to keep him from escaping. The pallets, however, were full of cobwebs, the dust undisturbed. They didn't appear to have been moved in a while. "How long you figure he's been in there?" Scolari asked.

"Twelve hours, fifteen minutes and . . ." I glanced at my watch, "thirty-nine seconds." Fisk's gaze widened slightly, as though he might be taking me seriously. "Amazing what they teach you in homicide school," I said, since Scolari's question was purely rhetorical. Neither of us would know until the autopsy was performed, and even then it would be a guess.

The most the pathologist would be able to determine was an approximate time of death before the body had been placed in the freezer, assuming he was dead when he was put in. His fetal position and his closed eyes suggested he may have been put in alive. Hypothermia, suffocation?

Before I could speculate, the Coroner's investigators and then the crime scene investigators arrived. They did their bloodhound routine, videotaped the scene, snapped their photos, dusted the outside of the freezer for prints, and looked for further clues in the vacant warehouse. Scolari and I also made a search, but found nothing that stood out. Scolari left to do a premise history. All that remained was the transportation of the body, the arrangements having been made by the Coroner's investigators. Unsure what evidence might be disturbed should the ice crystals melt, they called for a crew to move the freezer, body and all, straight to the morgue.

It wasn't until after the freezer was moved that I wondered what power source had been used to run the appliance. I strode over to the dust-free square where the freezer had once sat. The power cord had made a line in the dust that disappeared behind the pallets. I followed it, trying to find where the cord had been plugged in.

Scolari returned right about that time. "The last tenants were evicted six months ago," he said. "It's been vacant ever since. You'll never guess who."

"Okay, Scolari." I admit I was annoyed. I wanted to be on the road to Napa, not here at a homicide playing twenty questions with my partner, despite that it was only Reid waiting for me. "Tell me."

"Your dear friend. Nick Paolini."

I hoped like hell Scolari was joking, but even in the worst of moods, I didn't think he'd do that to me. Nicholas Paolini was an affluent businessman who specialized in soliciting donations for a worthy cause—namely, Nicholas Paolini. Over a year ago, when I was assigned to the Narcotics detail, I'd arrested Paolini on drug charges.

Had that been the end of it, hearing his name wouldn't have bothered me, but I'd received numerous death threats since then, all attempts to keep me from testifying at his trial.

"You okay?" Scolari asked, watching me carefully.·

"Yeah, fine." I was determined not to let him see how much the very mention of Paolini's name bothered me. Shining the light at the corner where the two walls met the floor, I saw the receptacle end of a black extension cord dangling about an inch off the floor. I ran the beam of light up the cloth-covered cord, revealing its frayed and tattered length; the thing must have been as old as the building. It disappeared into the ceiling, presumably over to the other side of the common wall of the warehouse next door.

"Wonder if Hilliard Pharmaceutical knows their electricity's being sucked to store a frozen corpse," I said.

Scolari didn't answer. He shuffled out, and I wondered what was up with him. It wasn't like him to let me get in the last word.

I followed, squinting in the afternoon glare. Thinking of Paolini, I shivered, feeling as cold as the body we'd found.

Scolari called the main Hilliard Pharmaceutical facility to get someone to let us in next door. While we waited, I leaned against the side of the building, watching Scolari pace. At one point he paused beneath the Hilliard Pharmaceutical sign above the entrance. "Who would have guessed?"

"Guessed what?"

"That Hilliard's nickel and dime stock would take off like it did." His gaze narrowed as he stared up at the sign. A vein in his temple pulsed. "Wish I'd bought some."

You and me both. I kept my thought to myself, however, since at the moment, Scolari seemed to be suffering from a major case of sour grapes. Hilliard Pharmaceutical researchers had taken the pharmaceutical world by storm. What started with an expedition in the jungle to find ingredients for Hilliard's wife's environmental project, Lost Forest Shampoo, ended with the discovery of a rare plant that had the potential to cure a number of cancers.

Suddenly they were converged upon by Fortune 500 conglomerates eager to assimilate the moderate-sized company. I imagine those who had missed the boat with Apple computers, Microsoft, and California Cooler felt the same way.

"Why were you late?" I asked, figuring from his mood that he didn't want to talk about Hilliard.

"Signing loan papers."

"For what?"

"New car for the wife."

Then again, maybe the subject change wasn't so good an idea. "The wife," as Scolari so eloquently put it, was Doctor Patricia Mead-Scolari, a pathologist at the morgue. She'd recently booted Scolari from the house after allegedly walking in on him with his pants down around his ankles and a records clerk beneath him. "I don't think a car's gonna do it," I said.

He stopped his pacing long enough to give me a sarcastically paternal look he felt was his right to bestow. "I'm supposed to take advice from you? A woman whose marriage lasted all of what, five, six months? Hell, you've barely been divorced six months. Come back and talk to me after you been married twenty years."

I didn't comment. I knew better. Scolari made it a point to voice his disapproval of Reid as well as my failed marriage, though what made him an authority, I didn't know. Reid and my brother Sean had been college friends, up until the time Sean died of a drug overdose twelve years ago. Their friendship played a small part in why I married Reid, mostly because Sean had always been the biggest influence in my life. In fact, Sean's overdose was what made me want to follow in my father's footsteps and become a cop—to fight the ravages of drugs.

The arrival of a gray Nissan pickup put a halt to any further conversation about my marriage, which was just as well. A man exited the truck, and as he approached, his sport coat blew open in the wind, revealing a gold pen in the pocket of his white shirt. Something about his craggy face and pale blue eyes looked familiar, though it wasn't until he held out his hand that I placed him.

"I'm Dexter Kermgard," he said. "Chief security officer for the lab."

"Dex?" Dex Kermgard, a regular in my father's late-night poker games, used to be an officer, before circumstances and opportunity led him to the more lucrative job at Hilliard Pharmaceutical.

He gave me a searching look. "Son of a gun. Kate Gillespie. How are you?"

"Fine," I said.

"Haven't seen you since—well, forever."

Since my brother's funeral. Dex had left SFPD under a cloud about twelve years ago, right after my brother died. He'd killed a man in a narcotics-related offense, and his use of deadly force as well as some missing drug money had been brought under scrutiny.

"I hear you made Homicide," he said. He reached into his left coat pocket, pulling out a pack of cigarettes. He held the pack out in silent offer; I shook my head. "So, how do you like it?"

"Not bad. You remember my partner, Sam Scolari?"

Their gazes locked. Dex broke contact to light a cigarette. "We go way back," he said on the exhale. Scolari simply stared, the vein in his temple pulsing again. Although Dex had been absolved of any wrongdoing, his reputation as an officer had suffered—there were still those in the department who believed him guilty. Scolari, apparently, was one of them. For a moment I thought Scolari intended to ignore Dex's outstretched hand. Finally he gave it a gruff shake.

"You better be taking good care of this girl, here," Dexter said, seemingly unfazed by Scolari's reaction. And then, as if he suddenly realized the significance of our presence, he tensed. "Anything I should be worried about?"

"Hopefully not," I said. "At the moment, we can't release any details—but if possible, we would like to get inside the warehouse. Have a look around."

After Dexter tossed his cigarette into the gutter, he unlocked the door to let us in. "It's used primarily to store old research files. They're scanned into the computer banks, then boxed up and sent here."

Row upon row of metal shelves revealed just what he said. File boxes. Thousands of them.

The place smelled of dust, but even so, appeared sterile. Fluorescent lights overhead and the cement floor painted white below made it seem as though we'd stepped into a different world from that on the other side of the wall. We walked down one aisle toward the back, past neatly stacked boxes, each dated and labeled with unpronounceable compounds. I suspected the company gave them those convoluted names to keep the public in the dark as to why one simple prescription for the newest antibiotic could possibly cost twenty-five dollars a pill.

Dex gave us a running narrative, probably to avoid direct conversation with Scolari, who was pointedly not making eye contact with him.

"I don't know who occupied the place before Hilliard Pharmaceutical," Dex said, looking back at me over his shoulder as he led us to that end of the building, "but I understand it was built in the forties, and was retrofitted in the sixties with cinder block separating this side from the other. The electrical on this side has all been reworked, and is self-contained, if that's what you're wondering. Since we were using it to store files, we had a sprinkler system installed, and the lights put in . . ."

Personally I found the file boxes more fascinating, especially as I began to recognize a few of the brand names I read on some of the labels. Some had color names. Project Yellow, and Red. Others were more scientific sounding, such as Virunex, the plant derivative that was supposedly the promising cure for some cancers. There must have been three dozen file boxes on this drug alone.

Scolari wandered about, looking for any hint of the power cord. False ceiling panels impeded our visual inspection, and we couldn't tell if the cord made it to this side of the building.

I looked around and saw a ladder on wheels. It reminded me of something you'd use to board an airplane with, only on a smaller scale. "How about this?" I asked.

I wheeled it toward them, and the cardboard lid of a file box fell to the floor. I picked up the top, but the file box it belonged to, labeled "Project Green," was just out of reach.

"I'll put it back later," Dex told me, so I set it against the bottom row of shelves, out of the way.

Scolari climbed to the top platform of the ladder. He lifted a ceiling panel, then shined his flashlight, eventually discovering the power source. "Got a mouse condo sittin' on top of it," he called down. "Looks like it's been here forever."

He climbed down while Dex related more of the

building's history. Hilliard Pharmaceutical bought the
warehouse after the earthquake of '89 damaged their storage facility. They leased out the other half, which had had
two tenants since then, most recently an export business—undoubtedly Paolini's front.

After Dex locked up, he took my hand in his, shaking
it warmly. "It was good to see you again, Kate. Give my
regards to your aunt."

"I will."

Scolari took my spiral notebook from me, scrawling
something in it as though taking copious notes of our
visit. He managed a curt nod when Dex left, never looking up from the paper. The moment Dex got into his car,
Scolari quit writing.

"What was that all about?" I asked.

"Don't like the guy. He was a bad cop."

"He was cleared."

"Was he?" With that, Scolari returned my notebook.
Without another word, he headed to his car, leaving me
to wonder what had crawled under his skin.

At the Hall, Scolari and I interviewed the two boys, but
learned nothing more than what we were told at the
scene. Their parents arrived about twenty minutes later,
and we released the kids with a stern warning about tres-
passing on private property.

"Whoever stuck that freezer in there knew that
power cord had juice," I said after they left.

Scolari didn't answer. He took his mug and poured
himself a cup of day-old coffee. I found his quiet as unset-
tling as the thought that Paolini might be involved in this
latest homicide. It was well after eight P.M.

Outside, the wind had died, allowing the fog to slip

in. I wanted nothing to do with Paolini, except to see him in jail. I'd settled that part of my life. "Let's see if we can get a lead on the last two tenants," I said, "make a connection to the deceased."

Scolari grunted something sounding like a response. He swallowed the sludge he'd poured, then sat to type his daily report.

We were alone in the office, and after finishing my own report, I felt compelled to say something. We'd just viewed a corpse together. Sometimes we tended to forget how much the dead really affected us. I thought about the car he'd bought.

"What'd you end up getting? For your wife?" I asked, pulling on my coat.

"Range Rover. Dark green. Might as well have bought her a Ford Pinto for all it worked. She told me I should've donated the money to the Save the Rain Forest Foundation. She's gone all environmental these days." He eyed the empty coffeepot. Several seconds of silence were broken when a police siren wailed outside our window, fading in the distance. Finally he said, "She still wants a divorce."

"So what'd you do?"

"Gave her the damn key and left."

He didn't look at me. Didn't even move. There wasn't much I could say or offer. I didn't know him well enough. I gathered the report from the printer, put it in the lieutenant's in-basket, then headed for the door. "See you tomorrow," I said.

"Yeah." He was still staring at the coffeepot when I left for home.

The fog was heavy, even in Berkeley, where I lived. I loved the Berkeley hills, the trees, the vine-covered

houses, the deer that wandered down from the eucalyp-
tus groves and the valley beyond. I rented a small apartment with a minuscule view of the bay, if I stood just so
to the left of my bedroom window. It was situated on the
second story of a house built in the 1920s, accessed by a
mossy brick walk along the north side that led to stairs at
the rear. It was set on the hillside, so the backyard was
nearly nonexistent, filled with ivy and trees, giving an
illusion of privacy from the houses on each side and
directly below.

Tonight there was no view as I looked out my window. Muffled wet gray obscured all traces of life on earth,
and I thought of my partner, and how I'd left him there,
alone, watching the coffeepot. I'd assisted in suicide cases
while working on the Hostage Negotiation Team. I don't
know why I hadn't seen it earlier, but Scolari had that
same lost look, his voice devoid of all emotion.

I called his desk, his cell phone, and the apartment he'd
been staying at ever since his wife kicked him out. No
answer. I left messages on his voice mail and his answering
machine, telling him to contact me the moment he came in.
Finally I paged him, typing "URGENT" at the end of my
computer message to call me immediately at home.

I slept fitfully that night, dreaming of Scolari holding
a gun to his mouth. The vision of a bloodied corpse was
so vivid that I awoke with a start. My alarm clock went off
simultaneously, five-thirty, and I had no idea if it was the
alarm or my dream that had sent my heart drilling
through my chest. I pictured the headline: SFPD HOMI-
CIDE INSPECTOR COMMITS SUICIDE, and knew I couldn't
leave for Napa until I assured myself that Scolari was
okay. I showered, dressed in jeans and a sweatshirt, and
headed back to the city. I should have stuck around the

office last night, talked to him. Halfway there, I realized I'd forgotten to let Reid know I wasn't coming. I used my car phone and called his cellular.

"Bettencourt," he answered. I heard a woman's voice in the background, thought it sounded familiar.

"Are you with someone?"

"Yeah, room service and the morning news. Where are you?"

"Still in the city. Something came up. Sorry I didn't make it there last night, but I'm going to have to cancel. Do me a favor. Let the hotel know, so I won't have to pay for tonight's room."

There was a hesitation. "Yeah," he said tersely. "Don't worry about it. I know these things happen. I'll see you Monday."

Surprised by his mature response, despite the tone that said he was annoyed, I was glad he wasn't going to wait around. It gave me the freedom to check up on Scolari without feeling guilty for standing Reid up.

At Scolari's apartment, the Saturday newspaper was on his front step. When he didn't answer his door, I got the manager to let me in.

"Sam?" I called, tossing the newspaper onto his couch. His apartment smelled like a dive bar in the red-light district—so much for him being on the wagon—and wherever I looked, there were empty beer bottles and ashtrays filled with cigarette butts. On the TV, on the coffee table next to a half-eaten TV dinner of fried chicken, on the kitchen counter next to a sink full of dirty dishes, in the bathroom on the edge of the mildewed tub, and on a nightstand next to his rumpled bed. My heart thudded when I saw the lump on the floor beneath the comforter. I must have stared at it for several seconds before finally lifting it, certain I'd find Scolari, thankful to see it was only pillows, no body. I scrawled out a note, taped it to his TV, then locked the door after me, fully intending to give him hell for drinking again.

After I left there, I checked a few of the bars he used to frequent before he gave up drinking. I fully expected to find him at Murphy's Law, despite that it was only mid-morning. The bartender, named Murphy, was an ex-cop; the patrons, for the most part, current cops. On the wall of the dimly lit bar was a poster listing the various things that could run amok according to the proverbial Murphy's Law. Years ago some officer whose investigation had gotten screwed up had scrawled one of his own right on the wall below the poster. "If your case hinges on a pertinent piece of evidence, you can guarantee that the property clerk will lose it when you're due to testify in court."

Apparently the clerk in question had written one of his own below that. "If Property can't find the evidence, you can guarantee the officer booked it under the wrong case number." The tradition continued, and there were at least thirty or more additions, all pertaining to "what could go wrong, will go wrong" in police work.

No one at the bar, however, had seen Scolari. I was at a dead end, and didn't know where to turn.

Scolari didn't call that night or Sunday either, and Monday, I was definitely worried when I came to work. Gypsy, the division secretary, looked up from her typing long enough to hand me a manila folder on a new case. In her mid-forties, she was tall, redheaded, and had a figure more lethal than the weapons we carried. She was the real boss, regardless of our supervisor's title. "Scolari called in sick, so the lieutenant wants you to get back on the Slasher cases ASAP."

After my weekend from hell, I wasn't sure what to think about her news, delivered so matter-of-factly. File in hand, I wandered to my desk and sat down.

My phone rang. I answered it, thinking more about Scolari than who was on the other end.

"You're dead, Gillespie."

I sat upright at the muffled voice. "Who is this?"

"Testify, and you're dead."

"Testify to what?" I asked, even though I knew. I wanted to keep him talking, hoped to hear something that would tell me who was making the call, or where it was made from. "Hello?" I prodded. There was merely silence.

I hung up, wondering if it was a coincidence that the threats had started up again, now that I was involved in yet another case with a connection to Paolini. He stood to lose a lot when his drug case came up for appeal; namely, three million dollars in assets that were seized along with several pounds of cocaine taken from his Nob Hill home in a search. He blamed me directly because I had posed as the sister of a man, a fellow Narcotics officer, interested in buying a large quantity of cocaine. We'd clicked, Paolini and I. I'd been able to slip past his defenses and gain his trust.

I phoned the DA's office to let them know of this latest threat. They had their own investigators working the case—my ex was one of them—but I knew better than to expect miracles.

Forcing the matter to the back of my mind, I opened the file folder. I read the report Gypsy gave me, a basic drunk-in-public arrest, wondering how it had found its way to Homicide, until I read the drunk's statement to the officer. He said he'd witnessed a murder of a woman about a year ago, but couldn't remember where the body was. The MO he'd described matched that of five other female murder victims—all were found with their throats slashed.

The press had dubbed the suspect the SoMa Slasher, because the murders occurred in the SoMa district, short for South of Market Street. The victims were all brunettes, but their common link seemed to stop there. They ran the gamut from businesswoman to housewife, and even included a prostitute I'd known during my days in Vice.

I interviewed my alleged witness when he came out of the drunk tank, but his memory was even worse now that his blood alcohol content was reaching normal levels. More important, the victim he described, if there was one—his facts became more skewed the longer we spoke— happened to be blond.

"Kick him loose," I told the jailer. There was nothing more he could offer.

In the meantime I decided to stop by Scolari's apartment again. If he was sick, he wasn't staying at home. My note was still taped to his TV.

I returned to work, spoke with our boss, Lieutenant Harry Andrews. Andrews, a former college quarterback, had opted for a career in law enforcement instead of pro football. There were those who said he had been promoted because he was black. After working for him, I knew otherwise. I told him about my fears and the unusual condition of Scolari's apartment. "This is beyond falling off the wagon," I finished.

"I agree," he said. "Do you know where else he might be?"

"No, sir."

"I'll look into it, Gillespie."

I left, knowing he would do his best, but still I worried about Scolari committing suicide.

I couldn't shake the feeling that maybe I should have done more, sooner.

2

On Tuesday morning Scolari again called in sick. The secretary assured me she had spoken to him personally, so I convinced myself that any thoughts of him committing suicide were strictly in my mind, not his. With Scolari gone, however, I was the one who had to pick up the evidence from our frozen homicide victim's autopsy at the morgue, located directly behind the Hall of Justice. I half suspected Scolari had called in sick to avoid running into his wife.

Not only was Dr. Patricia Mead-Scolari present, but she was doing the autopsy herself. She was a handsome woman in her fifties with short gray hair. Her commanding presence had nothing to do with the way she wielded the Stryker saw to cut into the chest cavity of my latest John Doe, or the Ice Man, as I'd dubbed him.

Send me to any murder scene, I'm usually fine as long as the body is fresh. Autopsies are a different story. I hate the morgue, the refrigerated stench of death that can't be masked by any amount of antiseptic deodorizers. The smell lingers in the crevices of the drain and grout in the tiled floor, in the green paint on the walls, in the chilled air of the refrigerated drawers that store the bodies, even on the stainless steel of the gurneys and white porcelain of the autopsy tables.

The memory of those smells assaulted my nostrils for hours after I left, even more so than the visual impact of watching the autopsies themselves—which, thanks to Cal-OSHA, California's Occupational Safety and Health Administration watchdogs, we rarely had to do anymore because of all the protective gear they require us to wear. Which is why I stayed in the doorway. I didn't want to put on a respirator, another Cal-OSHA requirement. I merely wanted to collect my evidence.

"Have you heard from Sam?" I asked the doctor. "I hear he's been pretty sick."

She barely paused in her examination of the victim's heart and lungs, making notes as to their size, weight, and condition to her assistant, a short, wiry man with curly red hair, who wrote down everything even though a tape recorder also picked up the doctor's observations.

She rattled off a few more details for her report, finished examining the remainder of the victim's organs before cutting into his skullcap. She finally answered over the whir of the saw, but I couldn't hear.

"What?" I called out precisely at the moment the saw shut off. My question echoed across the room.

"I said we're supposed to meet at seven tonight for dinner. Finalize things." This was uttered with the same matter-of-factness with which she peeled away the scalp and face from the victim's skull.

She adjusted her protective goggles with the back of her hand and wiped her brow with the sleeve of her green surgeon's jacket before turning her attention back to the macabre procedure of removing his brain.

Thawed out, the Ice Man seemed to be a normal-looking Caucasian subject, unremarkable in appearance except for some slight freezer burn, a now misplaced face, and the fact he was lying naked on a porcelain table that reminded me of a three-inch-deep bathtub.

They say dead men tell no tales. Perhaps not to the ordinary person, but the doctor could coax a story out of any corpse. She's as much a detective when it comes to dead bodies as we are when it comes to crime scenes. While she was busy weighing the Ice Man's gray matter, I turned my attention to the items found on his person once he had been brought to a normal level of refrigeration. His tan slacks, light blue shirt, and brown oxfords (no coat, no wallet) were marked and ready to be booked into evidence. There was also a wide gold wedding band in a clear plastic bag, along with something else. Seven very small brownish-green seeds. "What are these from?" I asked, holding up the bag.

"Look here," she told her assistant. He bent over and eyed something in the vicinity of the Ice Man's right ear.

"Find something?" I asked.

"Hard to say. It may indicate that a blow to the head caused his death." She glanced up, saw the bag I was holding. "Those were tucked beneath his wedding band, between the metal and his skin."

I was intrigued. What was so important about the seeds that he'd hide them? And from whom? His murderer? Had they searched him, and then, unable to find the seeds, killed him? Or had he known he was about to die, and so had hidden them to help identify the killer? Or had he been digging around in a bunch of seeds, unaware they were caught in the concave interior of his ring?

I gathered the victim's clothing, belongings, and fingerprint cards at the conclusion of the autopsy, or at least my part in it, to take back to the PD to book into evidence. Pending toxicology tests, Dr. Mead-Scolari had not determined the cause of death.

I stepped out the morgue door, looking at the seeds, only to hear the doctor calling me. She glanced behind her, then motioned me away from the doors. "You have a moment?"

"Sure."

"I was wondering if you couldn't do me a favor?" She dug into her lab coat pocket and removed a single key, which dangled from a ring. "Could you give this to Sam?" She held it out, and I knew before I even read the name on the key that it belonged to the Range Rover that Sam bought.

I gave her a hesitant smile.

"Look," she said, "I know you and Sam aren't close—"

"To say the least."

"But he is your partner. I was hoping you could convey to him that I don't under any circumstances want the car."

"I'm not sure it's my place." Politically correct for find someone else.

She dropped the key back in her pocket. "You're right. I guess I thought he might listen to you. Sort of a neutral third party. I just wasn't sure how he'd react when I tried to give it back to him when I see him tonight."

"Hey, Doc?" A coroner's investigator poked his head out of the doorway. "That FBI guy you been waitin' for? He's on the line, now. Says he can't wait."

"Damn it," she said, glancing back at him before returning her attention to me. "Look," she said with some urgency. "I want to talk to you about this before it's too late. I'll call you later."

Before I could utter a word, she hurried into the morgue, leaving me standing alone on the north terrace to contemplate her mercurial behavior. I returned to the Hall, running into my ex at the entrance. Tall, blond, and cerebrally handsome in a navy suit, he could have stepped from the cover of *GQ*.

"I called your office," he said. "They told me I'd find you down here."

He undoubtedly wanted to know what had happened to our failed Napa trip, and at the moment, I wasn't sure I wanted to discuss Scolari. I'd intentionally not told Reid. Any harsh feelings Scolari held for Reid were reciprocated tenfold.

"How'd the autopsy go?" he asked.

"Typical."

"Let me guess. He died from a blow to the head."

"Doesn't it bother you that we discuss dead bodies like normal people discuss the weather?"

"No. How'd he die?"

And he wonders why we divorced. "Actually, I didn't stay that long. I came to get the evidence." I tucked the large paper bag beneath my arm as we walked.

"Any leads?"

"Not yet." Reid opened the door for me. So far, no mention of Napa. I was on a roll. "Sort of a strange case, though," I said, deciding to run it by him. As a DA investigator, he was involved in a number of homicide cases. "The pathologist found some seeds tucked between his ring and finger."

"What sort of seeds?"

"I'm not sure yet. There's a professor out at UC Berkeley I've used before. I may take them out to him." The ground floor of the Hall was its usual sea of people, all on their way somewhere, the importance of their own agendas apparent in the speed with which they walked. We waded through them to the elevator.

"Up or down?" Reid asked.

"Property."

He pressed the DOWN button. "You look pretty serious today."

I attempted a smile. "Sorry. Got a lot on my mind. What'd you need?"

The doors opened. We stepped in.

"I was wondering if you wanted to go to lunch?"

His invitation threw me, and my first inclination was to decline. The elevator descended, opened, and we stepped into the basement, toward the Property room. I stopped in the doorway, looked at him. "Was there something you wanted to discuss?"

"Not really," he said. "I just haven't talked to you for a couple of days. Well, not since Napa." He shoved his hands in his pants pockets, his expression hopeful. He did not lack in the charm department.

"Look, Reid. I'm sorry about standing you up. It's just something I can't discuss right now."

"I'm not asking you."

"Wait here while I book this. I'll get back to you in a sec."

I moved past him into the Property room, where I signed the log, my mind telling me to steer clear, despite the maturity with which he seemed to be handling this. Why was I even considering it? Had Scolari been here, he would have sarcastically pointed out that we got divorced for a reason. And he would have been right.

One of the clerks approached, smiled when he saw me.

"Hey, Martin," I said.

"Gillespie. Bringing me more stuff?" He handed me a property sheet, and I filled it out, writing "seven seeds" for item number two. Under "Description" I included "Found with item number one," which was the wedding band.

"How's Joey?" I asked while I wrote. His grandson had been hospitalized with meningitis.

"You'd never guess he was sick." Martin beamed. "My daughter's sending me pictures of his first haircut."

I handed him the property sheet and the evidence, which I marked with my initials, the date, and the case number. "Call me when you get the pictures. I'd like to see them."

I signed out on the log book, then rejoined Reid, who had been watching from the doorway. "About lunch," he said.

"Pizza," I replied, my stomach making the decision for me. It wasn't a date. He was my ex.

We walked the two blocks to Giovanni's Italian deli, talking about nothing in particular, a refreshing change from our usual conversations about cops and cases.

The restaurant was dimly lit, with dark paneling and smoked mirrors lining the walls. For a pizza parlor it was upscale, serving more of a business clientele, which was reflected in the higher prices and white tablecloths throughout.

We sat in a corner booth, where a busboy brought us water and fresh garlic bread.

"You'll never guess who just walked in," Reid said, handing me the bread basket. The scent of butter and roasted garlic filled the air. "Look in the mirror. Sitting two booths behind you."

I took a slice of bread, still warm, as I glanced up into the bronzed glass. "Who?" Then I saw exactly who he meant.

Nicholas Paolini.

Seeing him in person had a more profound effect than any of the numerous phone threats I'd received since his arrest. Post-traumatic stress, I'm sure the department shrink would tell me.

I was well versed with the term, being the victim of a shooting—something I blamed Paolini for. Several months after his arrest and the ensuing phone threats, I was shot while assisting in another drug bust in one of the buildings Paolini owned. It was never proven that he'd been behind the threats or the attempt on my life. And once he had posted bail, he had managed to maintain his reputation as an upstanding, concerned citizen, while I'd attempted to pick up the pieces of my life.

For the several seconds that I watched him in the mirror, I told myself that I was fine. And I was, until he looked up, the reflection of his jet gaze locking with mine.

At forty-two, Paolini had dark hair and a Mediter-ranean complexion, giving him an air of mystery that only added to his looks. I recalled having been attracted to him during my assignment, something I'm sure he also felt. The knowledge of his crimes, and my good sense, how-ever, gave me the advantage and kept me on the straight and narrow. I remember wondering at his arrest if he felt that I'd betrayed him. After I was shot, I was certain that he had.

Not that it mattered now, I thought, as he nodded and lifted his water glass in a mock toast.

Sitting opposite Paolini was a man of similar color-ing, at least from the back. I couldn't see his face and was curious as to his identity. "Who's that with him?" I asked, ignoring Paolini completely.

"Antonio Foust."

"Hail, hail, the gang's all here." I dropped my gaze, turning my attention back to Reid. Foust was reputed to be Paolini's hit man, the suspected shooter in my case.

"You want to go somewhere else?"

"No. I'm fine." And I meant it. I was not going to let Paolini run my life. I bit into the bread, focused on the delicate crunch, the melted butter, not the man sitting behind me.

Reid eyed me for a moment, as if making sure I could handle the stress of being in the same room as Paolini. "Where's Scolari?" he suddenly asked. "I've probably left him half a dozen messages since Friday on the SoMa Slasher cases."

"Called in sick."

"You say that like you think something else is up."

Reid wasn't stupid. I still didn't want to voice my concerns about Scolari, but he'd suspect something if I brushed him off completely. "Have you ever known him to call in sick?"

"Maybe it's stress," he suggested. "Between his divorce and the fifteen-hour days you've both been putting in working the Slasher cases, who can blame him for calling in sick? Give him a couple of days."

"You're probably right," I said, though I wasn't convinced this was something that would pass. Not after the strange conversation I'd just had with Scolari's wife. Even so, I managed to guide the subject to more neutral topics, Paolini not included. By the time we finished our meal, he and Foust had already left.

* * *

At precisely six that evening, I paged Scolari from the office, and typed in a message about the seeds as a ruse to check on him. I was curious as well as concerned. How could I not be? Unable to shake the image of him committing suicide, I told him I was coming over to discuss the case before he left to meet his wife. I hoped he was at his apartment, and figured he'd have to come back sometime to change.

It was raining, and as I drove, my windshield wipers kept beat to the steady downpour, like dual metronomes. About halfway to Scolari's my pager went off. Certain it was from him, I pulled it from my belt and read the message.

"HOMICIDE, SACRAMENTO ST. RESPOND CODE TWO." I called dispatch and got the address. Right on the edge of Chinatown.

I pulled up to the scene about fifteen minutes later. Several marked units had the roads blocked off, their emergency lights flashing blue and red, their strobes making the raindrops appear frozen in place each instant the white lights flashed. I put on a hooded raincoat I kept in my trunk for just such occasions, and I parked my vehicle about a block away, behind several radio cars and in front of a dark-colored sedan with a smashed headlight on the driver's side. The antenna on top gave it away as an undercover cop car. I didn't recognize the car as belonging to anyone in Homicide.

I showed my star to the officer on the perimeter. I'd seen him around the Hall, but didn't know him. "Who's the OIC?" I asked.

"Majors," he said. He nodded toward a parking lot on the corner, lit up with police cruiser spotlights. About half a dozen uniformed officers, all wearing hooded yellow slickers, stood around a dark-colored sports utility vehicle, boxy-looking and high off the ground, the ever popular four-wheel drive. I owned a normal two-wheel drive Honda sedan, opting for mileage over trends.

I headed in that direction. Lieutenant Majors I knew from my days on patrol. He ran the Night Owls, the Night Investigation Unit. Their responsibility was to start the preliminary investigation on any major crime that occurred at night. It was supposed to save on overtime. Majors was about a head shorter than the other officers, easy to pick out even with his back to me. He stood near the rear of the vehicle. "What's up?" I asked when I reached his side.

"Hello to you, too, Gillespie," he said, shaking my hand. "Actually, the reason we paged you is my guys are tied up on a double homicide in the Mission district. You were it. Hope we didn't interrupt anything?"

"No. What do you have?"

"Looks like the SoMa Slasher, though I didn't think he's ever struck north of Market. Victim's in the front seat," he said. "Pretty bloody. We haven't touched anything. We don't even know who it is. Vehicle's just how we found it. Engine running, lights on. No record of VIN," he said, referring to the vehicle identification number. "Car's too new, not registered yet."

I eyed the paper plates that read CITYWIDE FOREIGN CAR SALES. The hairs prickled on the back of my neck as I saw RANGE ROVER emblazoned across the tailgate. Between the rain and the glare of all the police lights, I still couldn't tell the vehicle's color. All I knew was that I didn't want it to be green. Please, Lord, any color but green.

I approached the driver's side window and looked in.

The glass was smeared with blood, so I went around and looked through the windshield. It too was blood-splattered, but in a split second of light, I could make out the victim's profile.

Bile rose to my throat. Like a surrealistic dream, each flash of the police unit's strobe burned into my mind the lifeless face of Dr. Patricia Mead-Scolari.

3

Her head hung limply, her forehead and nose pressed against the glass of the driver's side window. With her throat slit, she was barely recognizable, and if Scolari and I hadn't talked about the new Range Rover, I never would have made the connection and identified her.

Majors started toward me, moving as if in slow motion across a disco dance floor, except it was raining and we were staring at a dead body. "Turn off the lights," I said.

"What?"

"The damn three-sixties. Turn them off."

Majors gave the order, and a moment later normalcy returned to a scene that was far from normal. No more strobe, no more red and blue flashing lights. Only the steady spotlights and rain sluicing down. I felt sick to my stomach, dizzy. I looked around. All eyes were on me, and I knew a number of them expected me to lose it—as they had from the day I entered Homicide. I took a breath, pulled myself together, pushed back the urge to cry from the unfairness of the doctor's death.

"You okay?" Majors asked.

"Where's Scolari?"

Majors raised a brow at my curt tone. "He should've been paged the same time as you."

"It's Patricia," I said. "His wife."

Majors stilled, disbelief filled his gaze. He took his Streamlight and shined it into the windshield at her head. "Son of a . . ." He backed up a step, looking as sick as I felt.

"You need to call the Op Center. I can't investigate this case," I said. "Scolari's my partner." Lord, don't let him be a suspect, I thought. Please let this be some random thing. But I recalled the way he'd stared at the coffeepot, so emotionless, like he'd given up.

Suicide, I'd thought.

Murder never entered my mind.

The lieutenant pulled his radio from his duty belt. "Three-David two-hundred," he said into it.

"Three-David two-hundred," came the response.

"You got an ETA on Scolari?"

"Negative." There were a few seconds of silence, then, "No answer to the page or land line."

Majors keyed the radio, and ordered dispatch to notify the Operation Center. "Advise them we'll need Management Control out here. And the Medical Examiner. Code Two."

"Ten four."

The Op Center would notify everyone necessary, including my boss, the crime scene investigators, Management Control, and the DA's office, who would send out their own investigators.

That done, Majors retreated to his patrol car. Dr. Mead-Scolari had been a longtime family friend of his wife, a nurse at San Francisco General Hospital. I saw him on the phone, and I suspected his wife was on the other end. He brushed his eyes, and I turned away, giving him the privacy I wished for myself.

"You," I said to an officer standing openmouthed at the sight of his lieutenant's vulnerability. "Get on the air. I need tarps, Code Two. After that, start a crime scene log. I want the name and division of every person who shows up or who's been here."

"Me?" His face registered momentary surprise at my orders.

"Yes, officer. You." He looked back at the lieutenant, then me, before nodding and heading to his patrol car to make the necessary calls. I could understand his confusion. Majors should be out here doing this. But until he composed himself, and until I was relieved, I would do it for him.

The news of the doctor's death spread quickly, and it wasn't long before the press arrived, their cameras capturing our every move. One or two reporters at the scene was understandable, they monitored the scanners. But the sheer numbers of reporters present told me they were aware that this was no simple homicide. I wondered who had notified them.

Immediately I enlarged the perimeter of my crime scene, calling for additional units to cordon off the area with yellow tape, keeping the reporters at bay.

Surveying the area, I realized there were still two officers standing in the midst of the taped-off area. I wanted the parking lot empty of all officers. I didn't want the scene contaminated. Coming up behind them, I tapped each on the shoulder, indicated they should follow me. Rookies. The taller of the two didn't even look old enough to shave. I recognized him from the warehouse. Robertson, the officer who reminded me of my brother. "Weren't you working day shift?" I asked him when I'd gotten them away from the Range Rover and out of sight of the cameras.

"Overtime."

Judging from the pallor of his face, I was surprised he got that much out. Seeing a frozen body was one thing, a fresh murder another, especially to the uninitiated. It wasn't that experience brought immunity; rather, that I'd learned to shift into autopilot. I figured what he needed was a task to keep busy, keep from picturing the morbid scene. He'd see it enough when he went to bed.

"I want each of you to get your notebooks, canvass the area, and write down every license number and VIN on every vehicle within a two-block radius. That means every driveway, parking lot, alley, and anywhere else a car is parked."

Robertson's hand went to his back pocket, feeling for his notebook. "VINs too?" he questioned, undoubtedly thinking of the extra time.

"If the suspect vehicle's out there, they could've changed plates. We won't know until we run them all."

I glanced across the lot to a narrow, dark walkway that led to Yen King's, a Chinese restaurant Scolari frequented. At the autopsy, his wife had mentioned they were meeting for dinner. Knowing it would be done anyway, I assigned two more officers to canvass each of the surrounding businesses, including Yen King's. It wasn't long before they came back with the news that Scolari had been there, and ordered take-out dinner for two. As a result, Majors deployed several radio cars to swing by Scolari's apartment to see if he'd been there.

After they left, and while I waited for the crime scene investigators, I turned on my Streamlight and began a search of the parking lot for anything that might have evidentiary value. I found a beer bottle beside a Dumpster at the back of the building. Closer to the car a rain-soaked cigarette butt lay on the ground about four feet from the front passenger door. I left both items where they were. The CSIs would videotape them first, then take photos.

Inch by inch I went over the parking lot, then turned my attention to the car. On tiptoes, I aimed the beam on the vehicle's roof. Clean and wet. The hood as well. I circled the car. On my first round, I noticed that the lens for the left rear turn signal was broken. Scolari always said his wife couldn't drive worth a damn.

As I circled again, it came to me that if the situation weren't so horrific, at her wake someone ought to mention her driving. Here she was with a car three days old, and it was already damaged. Even she had once joked about it. "The traffic division keeps a whole file drawer dedicated to my fender benders alone," she told me.

The memory caused me to look up at her through the window, as if that would bring her back to life. It was then I discovered that the door was locked. All the doors, I realized, shining my light at each one in turn.

Why would someone bother to lock all the doors after they'd just committed murder? It would take a conscious act. Murder, then pause to hit the lock button? It didn't fit.

The first investigators arrived, and I was more than ready to relinquish the scene. The tarps were nearly in place. Sergeant Kent Mathis from Management Control approached with my ex-husband. "Are you okay?" Reid asked. "Do you think you can talk about this right now?"

I told him I could, and Mathis questioned me while Reid looked on. He asked how I recognized Dr. Mead-Scolari, where Sam was. All routine questions. If Reid guessed that any of this had something to do with me canceling out on our Napa trip, he said nothing. When the interview was over, Reid handed me a cup of coffee and walked me toward my car. "You need a ride home?"

"No."

"I'm sorry," he said, his hand on my shoulder. "Go get some sleep. We'll finish tomorrow."

My fingers were frozen, my clothing soaked through, and I clutched my coffee cup, moving it to my numb lips, trying to sip the tasteless brew. I could see the news cameras on the other side of the tape near where my car was parked, and again I wondered who had tipped them off. There was nothing for it but to wade through them. I turned back to say good-bye to Reid, but he had already disappeared. I wanted to go home, to mourn in the privacy of my own room, not before thousands of viewers eager to see what dirty laundry was waved their way.

I tossed my cup into a trash bag one of the evidence techs had set up, then I strode down the street. As I lifted the tape and stepped beneath it, cameras pointed in my direction while reporters surrounded me.

"You're Inspector Gillespie," a petite woman said, holding her microphone in front of me.

I paused, surprised anyone would recognize me. She must have sensed it because she said, "Beth Skyler, Channel Two. I did that story on you. First female homicide inspector?"

"Yes," I said. "I remember." What I recalled is that she seemed to know about the transfer before I'd even made it public. At the time, I figured the mayor or chief had clued her in for publicity reasons.

"Is it true that the deceased is a pathologist at the Medical Examiner's office? Doctor Patricia Mead-Scolari?"

It seemed that everyone there was waiting on my

answer. "It's not my case. You'll have to speak to the Press Officer."

"But isn't it true you made an identification?" Skyler continued.

Now, that smacked of definite leaking. I wanted to ask who had told her that, but to do so would almost confirm her question. "No comment," I said, trying to move past her.

"Inspector," she said, scooting around until she was in front of me again, her microphone inches from my face. "Can you tell us if there's a connection between this case and the SoMa Slasher? I understand Dr. Mead-Scolari's throat was slit. Isn't that the same MO?"

Several flashes went off as photographers snapped their pictures. "No comment," I said, forcing my way to my car. I didn't know how they came by that information, and I certainly didn't want to be seen on TV or quoted in the paper confirming or denying anything.

As I unlocked and opened my car door, Skyler continued her pursuit. I kept my back to her.

"Inspector," she said. "Is it true that Dr. Mead-Scolari's husband is the suspect in her death? That he's being looked at as the SoMa Slasher?"

Her question shocked me more than anything I'd seen tonight. Speechless, I turned to face her, trying to keep my expression neutral. I had to know where she came by that information, and how. She was lost in a sea of cameras, microphones, rain and blinding lights. "At this time, we are not aware of any connection between Dr. Mead-Scolari's death and the SoMa Slasher victims."

"But what about her husband? Inspector Scolari?" another reporter shouted. "Hasn't he been investigating the Slasher cases? If he is the suspect, maybe his wife found something in the autopsies."

I never hated the press more than I did in that one moment. I hurried into my car, then slammed the door, shutting out the voices with the turn of my engine. I maneuvered out, in my hurried attempt nearly smashing the other headlight of the car behind mine. I had no desire to be filmed running over every cameraman and reporter in sight, despite the overwhelming urge.

I couldn't wait to get home, and it was close to dawn when I stepped into my apartment. The moment I did, the phone rang. I picked up. "Hello?" Silence. "Sam?" Dial tone.

I dropped it in the cradle. Stared at it. Rain drummed against the roof. I was cold, wet. My partner's wife was dead . . .

I stripped down, took a scalding shower, then buried myself in bed, too tired to cry or do much of anything else but fall into a deep sleep, haunted by fragmented dreams of strobe lights and dead bodies.

Everyone needs a vice, especially working Homicide, and mine happened to be caffeine. The expensive kind. It helped that I lived in Berkeley, since there's a coffeehouse on every corner and in every nook, which is how I spent my mornings off. It was no different this Wednesday, though a bit later than usual, as I sat down with the paper, my double latte, and a jalapeño bagel. I took a bite, but the moment I read the headlines, I tasted nothing.

PATHOLOGIST MURDERED. HOMICIDE INSPECTOR WANTED FOR QUESTIONING.

There was a photo of the officers setting up a tarp over the Range Rover. Even now, it was hard to believe.

Scolari's wife dead—murdered. The article went on to say that her husband, my partner, was wanted for questioning. They might as well have come out and said he did it. What else was the reader to think when one of SFPD's own happened to be AWOL in the face of his wife's death? Not to mention their pending divorce.

I hadn't finished the article when my pager went off: REPORT TO MANAGEMENT CONTROL. CODE TWO.

I still thought of them by their older and less-than-politically-correct name, Internal Affairs, since that was their main function. IA was not where I wanted to be this morning, but Code Two meant now, so I got a bag for my bagel and dumped my latte into a cup to go. Forty-five minutes later I deposited my breakfast on my desk, then headed up to IA, wishing I'd had the presence of mind to drink my latte, while somehow ignoring my roiling stomach. My brain was on a different plateau, somewhere between numb and la la land. I could have used the caffeine.

When I stepped off the elevator, I thought I saw Scolari turning the corner at the end of the hall. Not until I rounded the corner myself did I realize it wasn't Scolari, but his former partner, Ed Zimmerman. The two were similar in build, and with their graying hair, from behind were often mistaken for each other. Zimmerman, however, had a ruddy complexion that made him look as though his blood pressure was about to boil over any minute. It usually was.

He stood a few doors down from IA, and after glancing in the direction of their office, he stopped me. It was probably the first time he'd made any attempt to contact me since I'd transferred into the division, his displeasure at being replaced by a woman more than apparent. Never mind that I was a damn good cop. A number of peers, including Zimmerman and my partner, felt I was a political pawn, placed in my position as a token by the mayor.

"Don't screw him over," Zimmerman told me, his voice low, menacing.

"Meaning what?"

"Meaning if you know something, you keep your goddamn mouth shut."

I said nothing. His comment deserved no response.

He moved past me without another word, and I continued on toward IA. The door opened as I approached, and I was greeted by Lieutenant Mike Torrance, a man as enigmatic as the division he headed. Internal Affairs was to the officers as the CIA was to the public. Everything was done on a need-to-know basis. They needed to know, we didn't.

"Inspector Gillespie," he said, his brown gaze holding mine. I'd heard some of the women in the department called him "Lieutenant Torrid" behind his back, speculating on what he might be like in bed, and hoping to lure him to theirs. Tall, sable-haired, and dangerously good looking, he was rumored to be gay. I rarely kept up on office politics or bedmates, being careful to date outside the PD. Aside from his looks, I couldn't figure out what all the fuss was over the man. He never smiled—an IA thing, I presumed.

Torrance directed me to a chair that faced a long table. On the opposite side were three chairs, two filled by IA inspectors. Sergeant Mathis I recognized from last night, and Torrance whispered something in his ear just before taking a seat beside him. The third inspector was a woman, Sergeant Linda Perkins.

Usually in these interviews, one inspector did the

talking and the other took notes, depending on the severity of the case. Torrance's presence alone told me they considered this severe.

The interview began. After I repeated the events of last night, they took turns asking me what I knew about Scolari's whereabouts the past few days.

I told them I had no idea where he was.

"When's the last time you saw him, Inspector? And where?"

"Here," I answered. "Last Friday night. We'd just finished the preliminary on a new homicide."

"Did he talk to you about his home life? Did he seem upset?"

Scolari's emotionless voice haunted me. "He mentioned that his wife wanted a divorce."

"Did he seem upset?" Torrance repeated.

"Scolari didn't reveal his feelings to me."

"Why then did you leave a message on his answering machine to call you?"

"I thought he might need someone to talk to."

"And did he get back to you?"

"No."

"Is there anything else you wish to add, Inspector?"

I recalled my conversation with Patricia at the autopsy. My guess was they already had a copy of that tape, and knew very well what I had learned. "Dr. Mead-Scolari had mentioned that Sam was going to meet her last night to discuss their divorce. I gathered that she was concerned about his unstable emotional state."

Torrance and the other two investigators stood. "Thank you, Inspector," he told me. "We'll be in touch if there's anything further."

As I left I heard Lieutenant Torrance say, "Lunch?"

"Yeah," Sergeant Mathis returned. "But you gotta drive. My car's out at the Corp yard getting the headlight fixed. Someone backed into me last night."

My throat felt parched. When I got back to my desk, I downed my cold latte, then dumped the bagel in the trash. I couldn't help feeling like I'd thrown my partner to the wolves, even though I did nothing but tell the truth. Zimmerman's warning not to screw Scolari over echoed in my subconscious. What if they hadn't discovered the tape of the autopsy? Unlikely as it seemed, it was possible.

I looked around the vacant office. While my coworkers weren't as blatant in their distrust of me as Zimmerman was, the undercurrent was there just the same, had been ever since our very liberal mayor insisted that SFPD would have its first female homicide inspector for the millennium, and that I should be the one—all because I arrested Nicholas Paolini.

Would my fellow officers in Homicide support me? I didn't want to know. Or rather, I never wanted to be in such a predicament that I'd have to find out.

Knowing my lieutenant would be in shortly, if he wasn't here already, I decided to leave. With IA involved, the place would be crawling with investigators shortly, each being assigned a different task.

I didn't leave soon enough. Andrews strode in with the team trailing behind him, two from IA, as well as Reid, bearing a search warrant to access Scolari's desk, locker, and voice mail.

Andrews stood watching over the investigators, presumably to protect Scolari's interests, but I knew as well as anyone else that in a case such as this, the only interests being looked after were those of the department and the city. In this age of multimillion dollar lawsuits, when you crossed the blue line and got caught, you were offered for sacrifice—the more blood, the better.

"Excuse us, Gillespie," the lieutenant ordered.

I grabbed my purse and left without a word, catching the look in my ex-husband's eye. A man on the hunt.

Outside in the parking lot, I ran into Zimmerman. He stood between me and my car. I tried to move around him, but like a cobra on the attack, his hand struck out, grabbed me. My shoulder still hurt from my gunshot wound, which had never quite healed right, but I'd be damned if I let him know.

"Unless you're interested in a full body cast," I said through gritted teeth, "you can remove your hand from my arm."

We stood there, eye to eye, for an eternal second, the challenge clear. His normally red face took on a purplish hue. Finally he let go. "I just want to know where Sam is."

"What makes you think I know?"

"You're his partner. He respects you."

"Since when?" I asked, but he didn't answer. I pushed past him to my car. Opening the door, I threw in my purse before facing him. "I'll tell you the same thing I told them. I haven't seen Scolari since last Friday night, nor do I have any idea where he's at."

"He didn't do it."

"Then he better show up and start explaining." I got into my car, slammed the door, and sped off.

I didn't like Zimmerman, and his feelings were more than clear about me. I'd probably have a bruise on my arm where he'd grabbed me, and my shoulder felt stiff.

• • •

A half hour later, my arm still hurt, and I rubbed it as I picked my way carefully across the moss-covered walk to the back stairs of my apartment.

My landlord's gargantuan orange tabby had parked himself on the bottom stair, and I scooped him up, all eighteen plus pounds, scratching him under the chin just to feel him purr. I let him go at my door. "Sorry, Dinky. No milk today," I said, careful not to let him in. Besides being overweight, Dinky was spoiled. I often harbored him in my own apartment for his company, but if he didn't get his bowl of milk first, he'd meow up a storm.

After tossing my keys on the counter, then stashing my purse in the cupboard, I turned, only to run into the cat. "How'd you get in?"

He meowed for milk and hopped up onto the kitchen counter, landing quietly on the white hexagonal tiles, where he rubbed his back on the empty dish rack. It was then I noticed the kitchen window open, the yellow curtains floating with the breeze. A mockingbird's song drifted in from the branches outside.

I continued talking with the cat, keeping my voice light. I'd checked that window before I'd left. I was almost phobic about doors and windows. "You want some milk?" I reached into the cupboard, and into my purse. My fingers grasped the rubber grips of my Smith and Wesson. I pulled it out. "I don't know if I have any."

I moved through the kitchen, silent as the feline.

Long shadows filled the living room. The mockingbird's song stopped. My heart pounded against my ribs like a Stryker saw.

"I'm not armed."

I spun toward the low voice. Kept my gun pointed. It took a moment for my eyes to adjust. "Scolari?"

He remained seated, in my favorite overstuffed arm chair.

I didn't lower my weapon. I didn't ask how he got in. "What are you doing here?"

He raised both hands palms out. They shook slightly, and I saw a bandage on his left index finger. "I just need to know what's going on."

"Why come to me? Why not Zim?"

"I don't trust him."

That made two of us. "What happened?"

"I don't know. She was already dead."

His unshaven face was pale. Drawn. I had no idea if he was telling the truth.

"She mentioned something to me at the autopsy. What did she tell you that set you off?"

"I didn't kill her!" He shot to his feet, his fists clenched at his sides.

His movement shocked me, sent my adrenaline racing. I backed toward the sofa, left my finger at the trigger guard, my meaning explicit. He was a suspect, and I was a cop. He'd do the same, and I sensed he expected nothing less.

"I got called into IA," I said. "They were searching your desk when I left. Turn yourself in."

He stared right through me, unseeing. Slowly he turned toward the kitchen. Then he left.

I don't know why I didn't move. I heard the kitchen door open, then close, and then his footsteps on the stairs outside. What had he hoped to accomplish by coming here? Had he committed murder? Was he so in shock that he didn't recall the event? He was, had been, a good cop—not that good cops didn't make mistakes. Most major departments had a history checkered with good cops gone bad.

I called the PD, wondering if my father would approve. In his day, partners stood by their partners, no matter what.

"He was here," I told Torrance when he answered. I gave him the details of the visit, telling him Scolari had just left the house and that I had no idea where he was headed. What I didn't include was my earlier conversation with Zimmerman. The fact that he had concluded Scolari would tell me his whereabouts weighed on me, and I wasn't sure what to make of it.

Perhaps that was why I wasn't surprised to discover when I left the house later in the evening that I was being tailed.

4

I didn't notice the car right away, at least not until I'd turned off University down one of the side streets on my way to a secluded Thai restaurant. I was meeting my ex. He'd called, wanting to know if I wanted to have dinner, and I decided I would, mostly because I had no desire to sit in my apartment alone with nothing better to do than relive the past two days' events in my head.

When I glanced in my rearview mirror, I noticed that the headlights on the car behind me were out of adjustment. I didn't give it much thought, except they were still behind me when I turned down another street. Since I was taking a shortcut to the restaurant via the residential area, I figured it was some local on his way home. But then I missed my street—easy to do watching your mirrors instead of the road—and made a U-turn, which is when I realized I was being followed. The question was, who? Not to mention, why?

One possibility was Ed Zimmerman. I decided to find out.

Instead of continuing on to the restaurant, I headed back out to University and pulled into the parking lot of a mini market I frequented. I removed my wallet from my black evening bag and replaced it with my Smith and Wesson from the glove box before getting out. Since the shoulder strap wasn't strong enough to support the weight of the gun, I tucked the purse beneath my arm and strode toward the mini mart doors, my high heels clicking across the pavement. Just before I reached the entrance, I stopped, opened up my purse, and pulled out my lipstick, which I applied using the small mirror on the lipstick case.

I nearly froze standing there; I'd left my coat behind. The car following me, a dark sedan, turned into the lot, its headlights shining in my small mirror, so I couldn't see who was at the wheel. It parked well away from where I stood, almost out of sight around the side of the store. Confident that it wasn't going anywhere for the moment, at least not until I was, I entered the store and picked up a pack of gum from the candy aisle and placed it on the counter. "Hey, Rosalie," I said to the clerk, a Latina woman in her twenties.

"Hot date tonight?" she asked, eyeing my black sheath.

"One can only hope." I paid for the gum with change I dug out of the bottom of my purse. "Listen, I think someone's following me. Mind if I go out your back door?"

"Suit yourself," she said with a shrug, then rang up the next customer. I started toward the back of the store when she called out, "Hey. You want me to phone the cops?"

"Only if you hear gunshots."

At the back of the store, I slipped out of my shoes and carried them in one hand, the pavement ice-cold beneath my feet. The predicted rain started to fall, but I barely noticed. With my free hand I slung my purse strap over my shoulder, reached into the purse, and grasped the butt of my gun, careful not to reveal it, then proceeded around the corner where the car was parked. If not for the two working headlights, I'd swear it was the same car I'd parked in front of last night at the doctor's homicide scene. We probably had half a dozen like it at any one time in the Hall of Justice parking garage. It was a late model, blue or black, I couldn't tell in the dark. I knew a cop car when I saw one, but had no idea what sort of car Zimmerman had been given once he was transferred out of Homicide. I wasn't taking any chances.

Staying in the shadows of the building, I made my way to the car, my hand gripped tightly on my weapon. It wasn't Ed Zimmerman at all.

It was Torrance from IA.

"Son of a bitch," came his sharp oath. He nearly jumped from his seat when he discovered me at his window. His gaze dropped to the gun I partly concealed.

"Get in the car," he ordered. He leaned over, opened the passenger door.

He outranked me. I was close to hypothermia. But just to show I wasn't intimidated, first I dropped my shoes and put them on. The interior of his car was warm, but my teeth chattered uncontrollably, and I was grateful when he blasted the heater.

His gaze swept over me. "It occur to you, Inspector, that it's the middle of winter?"

"Forget the weather report. What are you doing here?"

"Continuing my investigation."

"Am I a suspect now?"

"You said that Scolari broke into your house. We thought it possible he might return. You could be in danger."

"Great," I said. "Just how long do you plan to baby-sit me?"

"Depends on how long it takes to apprehend Scolari."

"Have you considered that he might not be guilty?"

Torrance watched the traffic on University for several moments, then said softly, "Patricia's throat was slit. She was sitting in the Range Rover he'd just bought."

"You forget. I was there." A car pulled into the parking lot, its headlights flashing in my window, bringing with it Patricia Mead-Scolari's image as I saw her last night. Though I didn't know her as well as I knew Scolari, the thought of her so violently murdered—I fought to control the prick of tears. Then, without warning, a vision of her on a porcelain table flashed in my mind, somebody else performing the autopsy. I couldn't shake the cruelly ironic image, and nausea twisted my stomach. I stared out the window. Scattered raindrops dotted the glass.

"His thumbprint was on the inside passenger door handle," Torrance said softly.

"Look," I finally said when I thought I could talk without having my voice crack. "He owned the car. His prints were bound to be all over it."

"It wasn't your basic latent, Gillespie. It was a patent print."

"In what?" I asked, the evidence against Scolari mounting. A patent print—versus the more familiar latent found by dusting and lifting with tape—is made by touching something, like paint, or grease, then touching something else, leaving behind an impression of a print formed of that same substance. I'd solved a homicide after finding a so-called patent print in a tub of margarine, and knew sometimes patents were more compelling evidence than the latents. This was enough to keep me silent, waiting for what he had to say next.

"Patricia's blood," he continued. "His thumbprint was in her blood."

I didn't want to think about it. "He told me she was already dead when he found her."

"Why didn't he call us? And why did he try to hide his bloody clothes?"

I hadn't heard about the clothes, and so couldn't answer. I wanted to believe Scolari didn't do it, but I wasn't sure why. Because he was my partner? Because he was a cop, and the thought that one of our own could commit murder was too horrific? Or was it simply that I'd found him sitting in my apartment, and I didn't like to think I was that vulnerable? Despite the heat pouring into the car, I felt chilled to the bone.

"What now?" I asked.

"Now we put you to bed at night, and we get up with you in the morning. No one knows why Scolari visited you, but we do know you were the last one to see him, and you were one of the last to talk to his wife. Until he's apprehended, we're not taking any chances."

"I love IA—"

"Management Control."

"Next time, cut the subterfuge. Pick up a phone, call me. I'm not that difficult to work with." I didn't say good-bye, just got out and slammed the door. About halfway across the parking lot, I heard him call out, and thought about ignoring him until I realized I'd left my purse in his car. When I looked back, he was holding it out his window.

I retrieved my purse, turned, and made as graceful an exit as I could.

Not until I got in my car did I realize I'd shredded my nylons walking barefoot to sneak up on him. I bought a new pair at the mini mart, then drove through the rain to the restaurant with Torrance shadowing me. I figured I knew what the First Lady felt like, dogged by Secret Service every step. In fact, the more I thought about Torrance following me—was he even now aware I was sitting in my car, changing my nylons in the restaurant parking lot?—the madder I got. I crumpled up my ruined nylons, stormed to his parked car, and tossed them on his rain-spattered windshield.

Now that I was bundled up in my coat, I felt somewhat smug as he rolled down his window. "Was there something you wanted?" he had the nerve to ask.

"Don't freeze your tail off on my account." With that I left, promising that Mike Torrance would have the most uneventful and, I hoped, cold evening of his life.

Reid was seated at the bar when I got in, drinking his usual vodka and tonic. He stood when he saw me.

"Sorry I'm late," I said, allowing him to take my damp coat. "Something came up at work."

"Dr. Mead-Scolari's case?" he asked. "You hear anything more about the investigation?"

"Um, no. Not really. Mind if we talk about something else?"

"Of course not. Sorry." His cellular rang. After a brief conversation, he ordered me a glass of white wine. Even after being married, he still didn't know what I liked to drink.

I know I wasn't the best company during our leisurely dinner, but I attempted to appear interested while Reid told me about his latest investigation, an embezzlement case at Hilliard Pharmaceutical, of all places. Thirty minutes together, and we were already talking shop. It was well after eleven and pouring rain when we strolled out arm in arm. I scanned the parking lot, searched for Torrance's car. He wasn't where I'd left him. He'd taken a position of advantage in the back corner of the lot, where he could keep an eye on the front and back doors of the restaurant. My nylons were no longer on his windshield, to my relief, and I suffered a bout of delayed embarrassment for my impulsive action.

Reid and I rushed through the rain to my car. I got in, and, after waving good-bye, I watched him through the wet windshield. I was surprised when he headed toward a gold Lexus so new it still didn't have license plates. Reid generally used a county car instead of his Toyota Camry, more because it cost him nothing in gas. I drove up beside him as he opened his driver's door.

"New car?" I asked.

"Got it just before our Napa trip. I was hoping you'd be able to ride up in it."

I didn't ask how he could afford it. Money was not an issue I cared to get into with him, having learned quickly in our short marriage that he was a walking financial disaster. The car only confirmed what I already knew about our relationship. I was smart to get out with a still decent credit rating.

"Nice," I said. "Well, I've got to get up early tomorrow."

"I'll call you?"

Without committing myself, I waved again.

I drove back to the house, and saw Torrance following. I pulled into the drive while he parked farther up the hill. By the time I reached the top of the stairs, it had started pouring again, the rain came down cold as sleet.

My hands were frozen and I blew into them, thinking about him sitting down there in the car all night. I'd done a number of stakeouts myself, knew firsthand how miserable it was. Reasoning that he wasn't watching me as a suspect, but protecting me, I now felt sorry for him. Normally he'd have a partner, someone to talk to, but IA was a strange lot. Kind of reminded me of the last of the Lone Rangers.

I changed into sweats and started the hot water for tea, telling myself to mind my own business. When I glanced out the window, I saw he was still there. Without thinking, I retrieved my umbrella, trudged back down the steps and over to his car. He rolled down his window a few inches at the sight of me. "No gun this time?" he asked, his breath visible in the chilly night air. He tucked his hands beneath his armpits.

"Look, Torrance. I want you here about as much as you want to be here, so let's call a truce. If you're going to sit up all night and watch over me, you might as well do it where it's warm and dry."

I was almost grateful when he refused my offer, but found myself trying to convince him just the same. "What if something happens? And I need you?"

"Light a candle in your window."

"One if by land, two if by sea?"

"Something like that."

"Don't forget I offered," I said.

"I won't."

He gave me such an odd look, I wasn't sure how he meant that last comment, but in truth I forgot about it when I got back inside. As I kicked off my wet shoes and shrugged out of my wet coat, the phone started ringing. It was well after midnight. I couldn't think of anyone who would call at such an hour.

"Hello?"

Silence. I hung up. Thought nothing of it. A minute later it rang again. I picked up, gave a curt, "What?"

Hesitation. Then, "You alone?"

"Who is this?" I asked, not recognizing the voice through the static of the bad connection. Zimmerman? Why would he call me?

"I need to talk . . . you. I want to know what . . . now." The line was scratchy, like he was on a cellular. ". . . you alone?" I glanced at my kitchen door. Had I locked it?

Something thumped on my stairs. Briefly I wondered if Reid had returned. Forgotten something. My gaze flew to the east window, to Torrance's car. "Um, no," I said, my voice sounding strange even to my ears. I thought of all the evidence stacked against my partner. If it was Scolari, he could be standing outside my door on his phone as we spoke. But what if it wasn't? What if it was Paolini or one of his men? Was this the same caller who had threatened me about testifying in his case?

"No," I repeated, looking around for a candle, flash-light, anything. "Who is this?" I demanded. There was a junk drawer in the end table by the couch. Matches. The phone cord stretched taut, I reached into the drawer, searched blindly for the book of matches I hoped was there.

"Sam, if it's you, you need to turn yourself in," I said, trying to sound the voice of reason. Keep him talking. Away from my door. I found the matches. Rushed to the window. I lit the whole damn book. The thick, blue-yellow flame danced in the glass. Heat seared my fingers. I dropped the book into a ceramic dish on the windowsill. Had Torrance seen it? Something crashed on the stairs. I spun toward the kitchen. My gun. It was in my purse. I heard the cat scream, as if someone had stepped on its tail.

"IA's watching the place," I said, my gaze riveting on the kitchen door. If it was Scolari, he'd leave. If it wasn't Scolari, I didn't know what he'd do. Could I reach my purse before whoever was there got in? "They're outside now."

The phone disconnected. My stomach clenched.

Was I only imagining that someone was rattling the doorknob? That my kitchen door was shaking?

God, let it be the wind.

5

G oddammit. Open up!"
    I stared at the door. I didn't want to know who was there, not without reinforcements. I grabbed my gun, pointed it toward the kitchen, called 911. My heart bolted in my chest.

The pounding on the door continued. "Gillespie? You okay?"

"Torrance?" I called out. The 911 operator came on the line. I ignored her, waiting to hear it was Torrance out there. That I hadn't imagined his voice.

"Gillespie." The knob turned. Rattled. "Unlock this thing."

I slammed the phone in the receiver, then rushed into the kitchen. "Torrance?" I asked again, my hand on the lock.

"What's going on in there?"

I tore open the door. He stood on my porch, soaked to the bone. Rivulets of water ran down his dark hair and he brushed it off of his face, then removed my weapon from my shaking hand. "Mind if I come in?" he asked.

Not waiting for my answer, he entered, set my gun on the counter. I sank into one of two kitchen chairs, numbly watching while he locked the door and turned to study me.

The water from his raincoat flooded the linoleum floor, but neither of us paid much attention. "I saw your light," he said.

"Someone called." How ridiculous that sounded. Like I expected the suspect to reach through the phone and grab me. "At first I thought it was Scolari, but I couldn't tell."

"What did he say?" His voice was calm, and he showed no emotion in his face. Just as I would, were I facing a hysterical woman who cried wolf. Just as I had done many times on patrol myself. It was strange being on this side of the fence. I'd overreacted. It shook me to think how quickly I'd lost control.

"I panicked when I heard a noise on the steps. I thought he was on a cellular. I didn't recognize the voice. Thought whoever it was might have come here looking for me."

"I didn't see anyone. Maybe it was the wind."

"No. I definitely heard something . . . although I guess it could have been Dinky."

"Dinky?"

"My landlord's cat."

"The cat I saw on your porch is named Dinky? As in small?"

"Believe it or not, Dinky was the runt of the litter. He lives on my steps."

"What did Scolari say?"

"I don't think it was him," I said. Torrance leaned against the kitchen counter, his expression telling me he believed otherwise. I recounted the phone conversation. "Sorry I got you out of your car," I finished.

He didn't quite smile, but almost, and I expected it

was probably an effort. "Don't worry about—" He stopped. This time there was someone on the steps. Then a knock. Had the caller dared to come over anyway? Torrance wasn't taking any chances. He stood to the side of the door, drew his weapon from his shoulder holster, motioned for me to answer.

"Who is it?" I called out.

"Police. We got a 911 call?"

"Just a moment," I said.

Torrance backed to the kitchen window over the sink, lifted the curtain a fraction to peek out. "It's okay," he said, holstering his weapon.

I pointed to my Smith and Wesson on the counter beside him. Weapons of any sort tend to make a cop on the beat nervous, justifiably so. "The drawer," I mouthed. He nodded, pulled open the silverware drawer, and rested my gun on top of the forks and knives before sliding it shut.

I opened the door to two of Berkeley's finest, the porch light reflecting off their wet slickers. Neither seemed happy about being out in the rain.

The taller and heavier of the two peered past me, assessing the likelihood of imminent threat, while his partner spoke. "Is everything okay, ma'am?"

"Fine. Now. I thought I heard someone trying to break into my kitchen. My friend, um, Lieutenant Torrance, SFPD, happened to be stopping by, and already checked it out for me."

A look of respect and wariness, one cop sizing up another, passed over both officers' faces as they regarded Torrance. "Lieutenant," one said.

Torrance, looking very much the detective in his London Fog, nodded.

"I appreciate your coming out here," I put in. "Hope you weren't too inconvenienced."

"No problem. You want us to check the place out?" the first officer asked.

Torrance shrugged as though he didn't care, more for their benefit than mine.

"No, thanks," I said. "We're fine."

"Evening." They turned down the steps, and I heard one say "Code Four" into the radio, letting their dispatch know it was a false alarm.

"I guess I'll get back to my car," Torrance said.

"Coffee?"

"Sure."

As I pulled the kettle from the burner, I heard the crackle of the police radio outside, followed by a knock. Exchanging glances with Torrance, I stopped what I was doing to answer the door.

"Officers?"

"Sorry to disturb you, ma'am," the shorter officer said, "but dispatch says we got a second call on a prowler. Apparently your neighbor says she's pretty sure someone's hiding in her backyard."

Torrance and I stood in the living room, watching through the window, though by the time a canine officer arrived, the suspect, if there was one, had plenty of opportunity to get away. Even so, we found our noses glued to the cold windowpane. Raindrops sliced through the night, piercing the light from the porch before splatting on the shiny ivy leaves beneath my partially open window. Suddenly the dog crashed through the hedge that separated my yard from the neighbor's. It barked at something below my landing.

An officer called out a command. The dog halted, gave a low growl.

A laugh drifted up, then I heard the word "cat."

"Dinky gets around," Torrance commented to me.

I can't imagine the creature was too thrilled with the dog running about. I said nothing, just watched with interest, wondering when they'd end the search.

"Hey, Brooks," I heard an officer call out sharply, "look at this." A flashlight beam swung toward the ivy below my porch, but I couldn't see what they were looking at. Another officer parted the hedge as he stepped through to my backyard. "Looks like a stocking cap."

One of them held up something dark, and from where I stood, unidentifiable. "Yep," someone answered. "Must be the suspect's."

That was enough for me. I glanced at Torrance, who still watched the officers. "You can do your baby-sitting from the couch. I've had too much excitement for one night."

He didn't answer right off, but after a moment he nodded. "I'm going down to see what they've got."

Ten minutes later he returned, told me it was definitely a stocking cap.

Part of me hoped like hell it was Scolari's cap, lost when he was on my porch talking to me on his cellular. I felt I could handle Scolari. I didn't want to think there was someone else out there. A suspect I didn't know about.

Torrance called his partner, Mathis, explained what had occurred and where he was spending the night. I got a blanket and tossed it on the couch. I lived in a one bedroom apartment, so he really didn't have a choice about where to sleep. I called out good-night, and as I stepped into my bedroom and closed the door, I caught a glimpse

of him lifting his shirt over his head, the hard contours of
his chest silhouetted by the kitchen light behind him.
Torrid Torrance, I thought, and found myself wondering
for the first time if he really was gay, and what the hell
he'd done with my pantyhose.

That night I had dreams that my father disowned me
for my part in the IA investigation, even though I tried to
tell him I wasn't the one responsible for what happened.
As usual, the alarm woke me far earlier than my body
wanted to get up, and I dragged myself into the shower
after checking on Torrance. He had already dressed and
was sitting at the kitchen table, speaking to someone on
his cellular. I sat on my bed, towel-drying my hair, when
my Aunt Molly called.

"You're in the *Chronicle*, dear," she said, her speech so
close to normal, it was difficult to believe she'd only
recently recovered from a stroke. "But I can't say I like the
photo very much. I think you looked better when you
were near that Dumpster in last week's paper. They don't
really think your partner's that Slasher person, do they?"

"No. Of course not." I hated talking shop with my
aunt, because she tended to follow up the conversation
with a lecture on safety.

"Somebody must think so."

"Read it to me," I said. With only a towel wrapped
around me, I wasn't about to go out and get my copy
while Torrance was parked in my kitchen.

"Kevin, honey, get me the paper, please. It's on the
kitchen table." Since my aunt had near photographic memory, I assumed that retrieving the newspaper wasn't the real
reason she wanted my nephew out of the room. "I was wondering if you could call Leslie," she said a second later,
referring to a friend of mine who worked the Domestic

Violence detail at SFPD. "I thought of the perfect birthday gift for Kevin's thirteenth birthday. Forty-Niner tickets."

Kevin was my late brother's son. My father had wanted nothing to do with the child, because he never forgave my brother Sean for overdosing. It was my spinster aunt who stepped in, immediately taking custody of Kevin when the boy's mother, a suspected dealer, skipped town for fear she'd be blamed for Sean's overdose.

My aunt doted on the boy. Then again, so did I. I suppose we tried in our own way to overcompensate for the loss of his parents. Kevin's middle school coaches had long since learned to ignore my presence in the stands, and I'm sure I mortified Kevin more often than not with my cheering.

"You can get those tickets anywhere," I said.

"Yes. But not those wonderful box seats Leslie always manages to get. She has connections. Quiet. Here he comes."

I smiled at her warning, and heard the rustle of the paper just before my aunt said, "Right here beneath your photo, it says you're the investigating officer in Dr. Mead-Scolari's murder. 'Inspector Gillespie neither confirms nor denies that the department suspects Sam Scolari is the SoMa Slasher, nor would she comment on the coincidence of the similarities of Dr. Mead-Scolari's fatal injuries and those of the other victims killed by the SoMa Slasher.' I wasn't aware your partner was married to a doctor."

"She was a pathologist. And don't pay any attention to what you read," I said, knowing that this was only the beginning of what would surely turn into a media frenzy, the sharks waiting for Scolari to step foot in the water.

"I want you to promise me you'll be careful out there—"

"Promise. Hugs to Kevin. I'll see you soon." I hung up before she had a chance to start in. Dressing in gray slacks and blazer, I went out to find my copy of the *Chronicle* so that I could assess the damage to my career and Scolari's life.

When I walked into my kitchen, I fully expected to find Torrance sitting at my table, reading my paper. I found Mathis instead. He was sorting through his brief-case. Several inches shorter than Torrance, Mathis was a body builder, with broad shoulders and a muscular torso accentuated by narrow hips. And while Torrance's coloring was dark, his expression closed, Mathis was more the golden Adonis, with a broken nose that saved him from being too pretty.

"Where's Torrance?" I figured that was more polite than "What the hell are you doing in my apartment?" and would net me the same results.

"He had to leave early." That was all he said. I digested this while I went out to get the paper. The land-lady usually tossed it up for me when she picked up hers first thing every morning. I couldn't find it anywhere. Not under the steps, not in the ivy, not in the driveway. When I returned to the kitchen, I stopped, looking at Mathis sorting through his reports. Something seemed odd, but my brain wasn't totally functioning. No caffeine.

"Lose something?" he asked.

"You see the paper when you came in?"

"No," he said. "Maybe Torrance grabbed it on his way out."

I'd find it later. In the meantime, I had to leave for work. I assumed Mathis and Torrance had changed places sometime during the night. I also assumed he was leaving when I was.

I fished my keys from my purse and opened the kitchen door, waiting expectantly for Mathis to rise from his seat at the kitchen table. "Ready?" I finally asked. And that's when it struck me. He was sitting there, doing paperwork like he owned the place. He wasn't leaving

"Change of plans," he responded. "We thought it might be better to keep someone posted inside your house in case Scolari breaks in again."

I gave him a smile that I hoped spoke volumes.

"You won't even know I'm here. Promise."

"I already know you're here. Why wasn't I included on this decision?"

He shrugged. "Talk to Torrance."

Give IA an inch, they'll take a goddamn mile. "Do me a favor, try not to burn dinner."

Somehow I managed not to slam the door in his face. Torrance outranked him, so I couldn't very well take my anger out on Mathis. But I could on Torrance, and by the time I paid the toll on the Bay Bridge, I was fuming. I punched in his office number on my cellular. His secretary answered, advising me, "Lieutenant Torrance will be coming in late, if at all." He'd already put in a full twelve hours playing bodyguard.

Once in my office, I poured myself a cup of coffee, disguising it with as much creamer as I could stir in without turning it into nondairy mud. It would do in a pinch. I called Leslie's extension. She wasn't at her desk, so I left a message about the Forty-Niner tickets on her voice mail.

I hung up as the secretary poked her head in the doorway. "Andrews wants to see you, ASAP."

I walked into the lieutenant's office. The door was

open, the morning paper on his desk. Behind him, football trophies glinted under the fluorescent lights. I hated being called in here.

"What is this?" he asked softly, a bad sign. The hotter his temper, the quieter his voice. I told myself it was okay. Nothing to worry about. But when he didn't look at the newspaper, just at me, my throat tightened. I was an emotional person, and hiding that particular vulnerability from those around me did not come easy, especially when taken to task by those I respected and admired. I'm sure there was something Freudian about the whole thing, but when it came down to it, I'd rather face a man with a gun. Now was not the time to bring up the suspected press leak. Not without proof. He had every right to be upset that I spoke to Beth Skyler, and bringing up my unverified suspicions about that leak would make it appear as though I was trying to focus his attention elsewhere.

"I blew it. I should have kept my mouth shut."

"We have a Press Officer, Gillespie. Let him do his job. You understand?" This last was said so softly, I had to strain to hear him, which was precisely why he did it.

"Yes, sir."

"I understand that before all this went down, Scolari was about to canvass the Twin Palms Motel for potential witnesses in the drug ODs. You need a partner. Call Zimmerman."

"What?"

"He's experienced. I'll have him temporarily reassigned to Homicide," he said, speaking at a normal level now. His abrupt change stunned me, but I tried not to let it show. "They're hounding the Press Officer for info on the drug ODs," he said, referring to the report the department intended to release on the rash of fatal overdoses Narcotics and Homicide were jointly investigating. "Apparently one of the last victims was a nephew of Councilman Yearwood. Get me something solid by tomorrow at four. I've got a press conference scheduled for then. *You* will not be in shouting distance of a microphone. Do I make myself clear?"

"Yes."

"And I want an update on the Slasher cases."

His phone rang. He picked it up, thereby signaling the end of our conversation. Which was just as well. The Twin Palms Motel was one of the buildings owned by Paolini—the building where I had been shot. Scolari was supposed to have already canvassed it. He knew how I felt about that place. And now I had to take Zimmerman? The irony as well as the prospect of being partnered with someone who blamed me for losing his position wasn't the least bit amusing.

Reluctantly I telephoned Zim's office down in Property. He wasn't there, and I left a message on his voice mail for him to contact me. Hanging up the phone, I glanced at my case file. Twelve unsolved homicides, not including the drug ODs or the Slasher cases. Those were on Scolari's desk, since he'd been the primary investigator. I knew I'd have to read the reports again to see if I could turn up something Scolari had missed. I'd do that while I waited for Zimmerman to return my call.

I found the reports stacked on Scolari's desk beneath the clutter left by the special homicide team, who'd rifled through everything, looking for something that might indicate Scolari had killed his wife. Scolari had worked

Homicide for eight years. He'd been a cop for twenty-five. I couldn't imagine he'd be stupid enough to leave anything incriminatory behind.

I glanced up at the poster taped on the file cabinet by his phone. Two vultures sat in a twisted, bare-limbed tree. The caption read, "Our day begins when yours ends." The Homicide detail's motto. Scolari loved working Homicide. Had it finally gotten to him? Had he finally snapped?

My chair backed up to his. My desk was just as cluttered, even without IA's help. Sinking into Scolari's chair, I cleared a space on his desk, started deciphering his notes on the drug cases. After an hour of straight reading, I had yet to turn up a clue on any of them, though not for lack of trying. There just weren't any witnesses to be found. I pulled out the first Slasher case, not looking forward to reviewing something that Scolari and I had been over several dozen times already.

In frustration I stared at the phone, wondering why the hell Zimmerman was taking so long in getting back to me. Although I wasn't looking forward to going to the Twin Palms, I wanted to get it over with.

Felix Shipley and Rocky Markowski strolled in, laughing. They were partners, their desks were on the opposite side of the room from mine and Scolari's.

Markowski slapped Shipley's back. "Hell, wouldn't you do the same if you found out that your wife was . . ." He saw me and stopped, his smile fading as he ran his fingers along his mustache. Another reminder that I would never be one of the guys. I returned to my work, ignoring them both, almost grateful when Reid wandered in.

He dropped today's *Chronicle* on my desk. "You have guests?"

I stared at the newspaper, then at him. "Excuse me?"

"This is your paper. I came by to give it to you this morning, but you had someone over. I heard you talking."

I didn't care for this side of Reid. Aside from my job getting in the way, his possessiveness was one of the major reasons our marriage ended as quickly as it did. Had I actually entertained the idea of spending an entire weekend in Napa with him?

I bit my tongue for the simple reason that I was aware of just how many sets of ears now listened intently for my response. At the moment, I didn't feel it was anyone's business that IA was camped out in my apartment, and I certainly didn't owe my ex-husband any explanation.

"Hey, Gillespie," came a sarcastic male voice. "You called?"

I slid my chair back to see a red-faced Zimmerman leering at me from the secretary's office. He wasn't wearing a jacket, and his shoulder holster neatly framed the sweat stains beneath his armpits. He approached, his hand resting on the knife case on his belt. "Heard we're gonna be partners."

I chose to ignore him. Reid gave me that I-told-you-you-shouldn't-be-in-law-enforcement look, then started to say something more about the paper. I dropped it in the trash, thereby ending that conversation. Reid looked ready to protest, apparently thought better of it, and left without a word.

Zim immediately filled the space Reid vacated. "Heard you were a regular block of ice out there. Didn't even faze you to find your partner's wife dead."

"Better watch yourself, Zim," Markowski quipped from his desk. "She touches you, you won't even need a freezer like that guy she found in the warehouse."

I opened my briefcase, shoved all the drug ODs and the SoMa Slasher files into it. Abruptly the laughter stopped. I looked up, expecting the lieutenant had walked in, putting an end to their fun. Instead I saw Torrance at the doorway, his expression unreadable. "Mind if I see you a minute, Gillespie?"

I followed him from the office, only to hear Zimmerman say, "There goes the perfect couple. The ice queen and the polar prince."

"Slither back down to your basement," I said over my shoulder.

When I first transferred to Homicide a year ago, the guys waited to see me fall apart at the sight of my first floater. It was the rite of passage for every new inspector, but because I was a woman, it seemed my trial went on forever. I'd become expert at hiding my feelings, just as they'd all had to do. The male double standard. On them, it was masculine. Me, I was considered cold, unfeeling.

I silently fumed as I accompanied Torrance to his office on the next floor. He held the door open, I stepped in.

"Doesn't anything get to you?" I asked after he shut the door and took a seat on the edge of his desk. I remained standing.

"Zimmerman gets off on knowing he can make you angry."

I was mad that I'd let Zim upset me. "What do guys like you get off on?"

"Pantyhose," he said without missing a beat.

I shouldn't have asked such a question. More important, I couldn't believe he'd answered. The shock I felt must have registered on my face.

"Sorry," he said. "I couldn't resist."

That dark gaze of his, usually so intense, reflected a

sparkle of amusement, and I found myself smiling in return. "Was there something you wanted?"

The hesitation that followed was palpable, the look in his eye unmistakable. Finally, "I wanted to go over the details of Scolari's call one more time. If you don't mind." He indicated the laptop on his desk, moving aside to let me read the screen. All amusement faded from his expression.

He had it pretty much verbatim, and so I gave him my okay, for whatever it was worth. "You didn't happen to read the paper this morning, did you?" I asked.

"Not to mention seeing you on the morning news."

His face remained as impassive as his computer screen. I was beginning to wonder if he had Vulcan blood running through his veins.

"It doesn't look good," he said.

"That Scolari's considered a suspect."

"That the MO's the same."

I watched the cursor on his screen blink on and off. "Hardly the same," I heard myself say. "Patricia Mead-Scolari was sitting in a luxury car blocks away from the SoMa area."

"You might want to read Dr. Mead-Scolari's autopsy report."

His words shocked me, and I met his gaze, but couldn't tell what, if anything, he was after. Was he telling me for my benefit? Scolari's? Or was he fishing to see what I knew?

He handed me a manila envelope. "Figured I'd save you a trip to the morgue."

I opened the envelope, wondering why he'd felt the need to give me the autopsy file in private. Inside was the report, as well as some black-and-white photos. I closed it, not wanting to look at the pictures just yet. Not ever, really. "Thanks, but I have to go there anyway."

He regarded me closely, looking for what, I had no idea. I figured now was as good a time as any to discuss the surveillance he was conducting on my apartment. "How long are you planning on camping out on my doorstep?"

"As long as necessary."

As if I had a choice. "Have at it," I replied as I left, not meaning it in the least. I didn't bother with good-byes, I didn't see the point. I headed back to Homicide, and my new partner. When I got there, Zimmerman was gone.

"Zimwit told me to tell you he was on a detail that couldn't wait," Markowski said. "He'll get back to you when he's done."

As fortuitous as that sounded, I still needed a partner to canvass the Twin Palms. "Either of you busy?"

"Sorry," Shipley said. "Me and Rocky got a couple of appointments that can't wait."

Great. If I couldn't come up with a temporary partner, I'd have to take a uniform for backup. Which meant the luck of the draw, anything from slick sleeve rookie to jaded veteran. I'd try elsewhere. Perhaps Narco. Might as well. I was working some of the same overdose cases. The only difference was the status of those involved. If the overdose victims lived, Narco got them, and tried to get the name of their suppliers. If the victims died, they came to me.

The Narcotics detail was one of the few facilities not housed in the Hall of Justice. I could have called, but the truth was, I needed a break and a latte, and decided that the drive would give me both. Outside, a light, salty breeze swept through the courtyard, and I took my time walking to the parking garage.

As I drove, from the crest of a hill I caught a glimpse of the Bay Bridge crowned by cumulus clouds. Postcard perfect. A great day for camera-toting tourists who flocked here, ignorant and untouched by the crime, the death, the inner-city life that occurred beyond their wide-angled lenses.

I parked, and walked the half block to the Narcotics office. Betty Ramirez was sitting at her desk talking on the phone when I strolled in. She could have been a model, tall and thin with short, dark, wavy hair, but she had a thing for law enforcement. We were partners up until a year ago, when the mayor decided to make me Homicide's poster girl.

"Hey, Kate," she said, covering the mouthpiece. "Have a seat. Be done in a sec."

I took the chair at the desk next to hers, watched the goings-on, not really missing it. Like Betty, I'd been assigned working the street dealers, a dirty business, day-in and day-out with the scum of society. If you stayed too long, it rubbed off on you, as evidenced by many of the officers who worked there. If not for the necessity of photo IDs hanging around their necks while they were in the building, one wouldn't be able to tell them from the hookers and crack dealers on the street.

George Jamison wandered through the door, brown hair down the middle of his back, a scraggly beard and mustache. He looked much different now than when he had taken on the role of my brother when we went after Paolini. He patted me on my shoulder. "Gillespie. You aren't really thinking Sam Scolari's the SoMa Slasher, are you? Word is, the Slasher's who killed Doc Scolari."

"Let me know when word on the street gets me a viable witness. Then I'll listen."

Betty hung up the phone and turned to me. "Haven't seen you down here in a while. What's up?"

"You got anything substantial on the drug ODs?"

"Nothing new."

"Andrews wants a full report. Press conference tomorrow. If you're not busy, I need to go out and do a few knock-and-talks."

"Busy isn't the word," she said, nodding toward several file boxes on the floor, each filled with manila folders. "Between the ODs and the Scott Forrest cluster, we're all running around with our heads cut off. Makes me wish I was back on patrol."

Cluster, a cop euphemism for major mess, was putting it mildly. Forrest, a lab tech, had recently been arrested by the Narcotics detail for falsifying evidence and stealing drugs sent in for testing. To the city's embarrassment, his case was brought to light by an investigative reporter for the *Chronicle*. The reporter, Maxwell Cameron, had already made his claim to fame over the exposure of scandal in the mayor's office.

"We have to go through every one of those," Betty continued. "See if Forrest was involved in any way. There's gonna be a lot of dismissals coming up on appeal. The DA's screaming, and I'm due in court in ten minutes." She looked at her watch. "A prelim for the city manager's kid on a possession for sales. His father's hired some attorney from LA. He could have saved the money. Forrest tested the drugs. It'll be dismissed, just like the rest of them." She pulled a case folder from her desk, then motioned for me to accompany her out. "You do realize what this means?"

She handed me the folder. It contained the case I'd worked against Paolini. I met her gaze. "Tell me you're kidding."

"DA called right before you got here. Paolini's attorney got his appeal moved up on the calendar. Less than a week."

The renewed phone threats I'd received now made a lot more sense. I told Betty about them. "It's got to be the reason why they've started up."

Betty gave me a searching look. "You seem sort of nonchalant about the whole thing."

"I've got enough crap to worry about besides Paolini." Actually, I couldn't dwell on it. Not with everything else going on. I'd go crazy. "So, how about it? Can you go?"

Betty knew me well enough to let the matter drop about Paolini and the calls. "I'll be in court all day. Jury trial. I don't suppose it could wait till tomorrow morning?"

"Tomorrow's fine. Let's say, nine?"

"Nine's good. We'll meet in front of the bail room."

"Thanks. I'll be there," I said.

After I got my latte, I made my next stop the morgue. I wanted every coroner's case that might fit the Slasher profile. As I pushed open the door, I thought how odd it was to be there and not see Patricia, and I couldn't help thinking about my partner as a result. Did he do it? Where was he? And why? Simple questions, but no simple answers.

"Hey, Inspector."

Mary Whitman offered something close to a smile. A black woman in her forties, she was Patricia's secretary. She stood on the other side of a long counter that separated the lobby area from the Coroner investigators' work area. Their desks were empty, the office deserted by all but us.

"Thought you might take a few days off. You holding up okay?" I asked.

"Damn place would fall apart if I weren't here."

Patricia had said so many times. I tried not to glance into her office, but I looked just the same, shivering at the images of the last time I'd seen her, in her car.

Mary saw the direction of my gaze. "Keep doing it myself. It's like I expect her to say, 'Mary! Where the hell's that toxicology report I asked for?' Lab was always late, for all they're in the same damn building. Used to grate on her nerves." She turned around, her dark eyes filled with sadness as she eyed Patricia's door. Her voice cracked as she said, "Can't seem to get around to emptying her things. Won't let nobody else touch it, neither. Bad enough your guys searched through everything after her murder. None of their damn business. At least wait until the funeral."

"You know they couldn't," I offered, though it was of little consolation. Death did not end the violation of the victim. Every person they saw, every move they made, every breath they took would be scrutinized, picked apart, reassembled piece by piece until the final appeal of the suspect was over and done. There was no peace for the dead by homicide.

She opened the top drawer of her desk, looking for something I suspected wasn't really there. When she seemed in control again, I asked her for the autopsy reports.

"How far back did you want to go?"

"Six months—no, make it a year."

"A year?"

"I'm working on a hunch. A shot in the dark, but what the hell."

"Better be a good one. It'll take me a while. In the meantime, I've got that hit-and-run you were looking for the other day," she said, digging the report out of the current file to let me read.

I scanned over it. Nothing stood out other than the usual sorts of injuries one might expect from a hit-and-run victim. Crushed skull, blunt force trauma to his entire torso, some brown paint transfer on his Levi's. Not a lot to go on.

"And toxicology came back on your last OD." She dropped that file on the counter as well. "Say hello to victim number nine. Same tainted stuff as the other eight. Patricia was pretty upset. She made sure the lab ran it twice. Sort of strange, like she was getting personally involved."

"How could she not," I said. "He was just some clean-cut kid. Things like this aren't supposed to happen to kids like him."

"You're probably right. This one got to her. She wanted Doc Meyers to finish the case for her."

I didn't open the file, since I recalled it well. Freshman at University of San Francisco. Frat party. No one admitted where the drug came from, no one recalled him taking it. Parents well-to-do, not knowing where they went wrong, mourning the loss of their only son. Their devastation, my helplessness, promises to find the killer, not knowing if I could, knowing I never wanted to bring a child into this world. Not to face that.

"How about that last case Patricia worked?" I asked, putting the file beneath the others. "The frozen John Doe?"

"Ice Man? Waiting on toxicology."

"There's a surprise. Any changes? When I left her, she didn't have any idea about the cause of death."

"That's how it was when I typed it. Just a frozen guy. Could have been in there a week, could have been a month," Mary said, as if that were commonplace. I guess in the morgue anything was possible. "I sent the preliminary report to you about ten minutes ago."

"I was out of the building. Must have missed it. Thanks, Mary," I said. I turned to leave, stopped, and eyed her. "Did she talk to you about meeting Sam that night?"

"Your folks from IA asked me that. I told them no. Can't remember the last time she talked about Sam."

"She never mentioned about Sam cheating on her?"

"Honey," she said with a laugh, "that woman couldn't have cared less. Their marriage was for appearance's sake only."

Appearance's sake only? What on earth did she mean by that?

"They—" She stopped when a group of doctors walked in, young, scrubbed fresh and clean, in surgical greens. "Oh, hello," she told them as they lined up along the counter. "Doctor Meyers is tied up, but asked if you wouldn't mind waiting in his office."

They filed past, all five.

"Teaching class," Mary whispered. "Get back to me later when we won't be overheard."

"Sure," I said, leaving her. I was curious to find out what she knew. Why would Scolari buy Patricia a Range Rover to get back in her good graces if their marriage was one of convenience? And what about the records clerk he'd dated, and gotten booted out of the house for? What was her name, Allison? Was that for appearance's sake, too?

No time like the present to find out. I still had half an hour to kill before lunch—not that I had plans—but what better way to spend the time than talking to the little number Scolari had dated in Records?

6

The Records division of the San Francisco Police Department was a hub of activity, filled with officers and citizens alike. I couldn't simply walk in and say, "Hey, Allison, mind if we talk?"—mostly because I didn't want anyone to know I was going to question her about Scolari's case. IA didn't take kindly to anyone stepping on their toes. After considerable thought, I knew I needed a good cover.

Cops are great at ad-libbing. We have to be. Like car salesmen and politicians, we law enforcement officers are in a profession where we must make people believe we know what we're talking about, even if we haven't got a clue.

"Hi," I said to the clerk in the window, thinking I was off to a great start. Ready for an Oscar. "I've been waiting for a report on a homicide I'm working."

The clerk, Sue by her ID badge, smiled. "You have a case number?"

"Um, no. I called it in, though. It's pretty confidential. The press and everything. I think I spoke with Allison?"

She looked around the counter. "No, I don't see anything. How long ago did you call for it?"

I shrugged. "Maybe an hour or two?"

Sue looked under papers, thumbed through a few file folders. "Not here. Hold on, I'll go get Allison. You can ask her yourself."

I kept my Cheshire cat smile to myself. A few moments later, Allison strolled up to the window. The second she saw me, she immediately turned away.

"Wait. Please."

She hesitated, her back to me.

"It'll only take a minute."

She didn't move.

"For Sam?" I continued softly.

Slowly she turned. Her voice was low as she approached the window. "I've already given a full report to IA."

"So have I. But what I'm looking for is answers that might be overlooked."

Allison regarded me as though she wasn't sure what to believe. I stared right back, trying to see what a woman like her saw in a man like Scolari. Allison was in her early twenties, petite, with a face that might grace the cover of *Cosmopolitan*. She could have her choice of any man. Why him?

"Okay," she said. "But I'd rather not be seen talking to you out here. Meet me in the locker room by the showers in five minutes."

"I'm there," I said.

She leaned down, grabbed something from a drawer under the counter, then handed me an empty routing envelope, I guess to make it look as though she were turning over the nonexistent report I'd asked for.

"Thanks," I said. She didn't respond, just gave a harried glance side to side, then got back to her station. That was a girl with something on her mind. Something I definitely wanted to know.

Five minutes later she appeared in the locker room, motioning me to the showers. Following her, I was surprised when she turned one on, then peeked into each of the stalls to make sure we were alone. Now I was truly curious.

"Well?" she asked.

"Isn't this sort of overkill?"

"Sam told me this entire place is bugged."

"Maybe with roaches."

"Well, you can think what you want, but Sam's wife is dead, IA is all over my butt, and I'm not taking any chances. Now, what did you want?"

"Tell me about Sam."

She tucked a strand of perfect hair behind her ear, then eyed the tile in the shower stall as though it took her entire concentration. Maybe it did. Finally she said, "I don't think he killed his wife, if that's what you mean."

"Why not?" I prodded.

"I don't know. Something he told me about the night she was killed."

"You were with Sam that night?" I asked, incredulous.

"He came to say he couldn't see me anymore. That his wife wanted a divorce, and he was going to try to fix it." Fix a marriage that was for appearance's sake only? Allison bit her manicured thumbnail, neon pink to match her lips.

"And?"

She started, looked at me as though she'd forgotten our conversation. "I can't remember. I'm thinking."

I wondered if IA had gotten any further. Maybe a gentle reminder. "He was telling you something the night she got killed . . ."

"I don't know. Something about the frozen guy. I can't think with all this water on."

I reached over and shut off the faucet, then regretted my action when she threw me a dark look.

"I can't remember," she said, her expression telling me she'd closed me off.

"Do me a favor," I said, reaching into my black shoulder bag and pulling out a business card. "When you remember? Call me. It's important. For Sam," I said, since that had seemed to break the ice the first time.

She took the card and left. I stayed a minute longer, to preserve her air of secrecy, for all it was worth. She'd been spooked about something, that much was apparent, but what? And what had she felt was so important, the shower needed to be on? All that to tell me that Scolari didn't kill his wife?

I was missing something. *She* was missing something. A few brain cells, is what I thought at first, until I recalled the way she handed me the empty envelope. Was she an airhead? Or was it all an act? Scolari had left her with the impression of his innocence, because of their last conversation. Because Scolari had spoken to her about the "frozen guy." The Ice Man?

I sank onto the wooden slats of the bench, stymied, wondering if she wasn't feeding me a line. Scolari wasn't even at the Ice Man's autopsy. As far as I knew, and according to the report, Patricia hadn't found anything significant. Had she called Scolari after the autopsy? Spoken to him about it before they were to meet that night?

Whatever it was, it still didn't explain why Allison

was so sure of Scolari's innocence, but at least it was something to go on. I decided to take another look at the Ice Man's case.

Back at my desk, I found the autopsy report. I hadn't turned the first page when I was called out to a homicide at Golden Gate Park near the tea garden. The victim was a man, late twenties, suspected of a drug overdose. The rest of my afternoon was spent out at the scene, as we tried to determine if it was related to the other OD cases. I didn't get back to the Ice Man case at all, returning to the office just long enough to check my messages before heading home for the day.

Mathis was still at my apartment when I got there, and I refrained from asking if Scolari had bothered to show. Torrance arrived at eight that night, and I decided to organize my closet, my goal to avoid him completely. I sorted through clothes I would never fit into again, and things I hadn't worn in years. I neatly stacked and labeled my shoe boxes on the top shelf, getting downright anal about it. All that was left was a cardboard box on the floor, dust covered and sealed with masking tape. My aunt had packed it after my father died. I'd avoided it for eleven years. Too many painful reminders of my brother's life. And of my father's broken heart. He never seemed to recover from the hurt and humiliation of his son's tragic death.

It didn't matter that I had become an officer.

My brother's death made me want to right the wrongs in the world. It killed my father. He died of a heart attack almost a year to the day after he found out that the son he'd cherished, the son who'd followed in his footsteps to become an officer of the San Francisco Police Department, had overdosed on heroin.

I almost left the box there, unopened, but heard the sound of Torrance typing away on his laptop. I suppose that's what made me open it. One more reason not to go out there, face the man who'd invaded my apartment, my life, thought my partner was guilty.

I tore off the tape, dry and brittle from years of neglect, and pulled out books smelling of dust. There was a Barbie case, with a Ken doll I recalled being curiously disappointed over, when with prurient interest I had unclothed him, hoping for some hint as to the mystique of the male anatomy, certain that what I found was not what it was all about. Beneath the Barbie case was a photo album that I didn't open, containing pictures of my mother, who ran off with an insurance salesman when I was two, pictures of Sean, who looked so much like his son did now, and pictures of my father. I put it aside. At the bottom of the box was a Fisher-Price clock, the battered remnant of Sean's and my childhood. I wound it, held it to my chest, listened to the steady ticktock and the familiar tune bringing forth memories long buried of warm breezes, summer days. I opened the album, turning to a time when death was a word that held no meaning for a five-year-old girl.

The following morning Mathis greeted me at my kitchen table, and I found myself smiling at his offer to share his McMuffin breakfast. "What? No bagels?" I asked him.

"Next time," he said.

Back to the Hall. Different day, same murder. I reviewed the Ice Man's case while I waited for nine o'clock to roll around. Pending toxicology results, the only thing that stood out on the autopsy report was a small contusion behind the subject's ear. The preliminary findings suggested that he died of a blow to the head, just as Reid had guessed. I recalled saying something to Patricia right before she interrupted me to point something out on the Ice Man's head to her assistant. What were we talking about? The seeds. I'd picked up the bag, and she was telling me about them. She'd found them tucked in the band of his wedding ring. Seven seeds. Unidentified.

Which reminded me that I'd intended to have a botanist look at them.

Worth a try, I thought, pulling out my directory, then calling UC Berkeley's Professor Rocklin. I made an appointment to bring by the seeds that afternoon, then went down to the Property section to remove them from evidence. The place smelled of sawdust.

"Got the stuff right here," Martin said. He stepped over a coil of orange extension cord lying next to a circular saw. "And I got that picture of my grandson." He took a packet of photos from his desk, handed them to me, then took my request form.

I flipped through the photos, each showing a tearful, chubby, towheaded little boy sitting in a barber's chair. In the last picture he clung to his mother, his tear-streaked face pressed into her neck, his silken hair neatly cut.

Sometimes I wondered what it would be like to have a kid of my own, especially when I accompanied my aunt to Kevin's football games. But whenever the thought set my biological clock to ticking, I immediately hit the snooze button. I didn't want my kids growing up to be drug addicts or cops, or just kids without parents like my nephew. Being a cop and having children didn't mix. It hadn't worked for my father or my brother, and it wouldn't work for me.

"Pretty cute, huh?" Martin said, lifting a box from beneath the counter that separated us.

"As a button," I said, reluctantly replacing the photos in the envelope. I set them on the countertop, surprised to see Martin pulling the seeds from the box, then handing them to me. I'd often had to wait ten, fifteen minutes for evidence—and that was considered expedient. "Talk about service."

"Hey, you call, we deliver."

"I didn't call."

"Someone did. That was about fifteen minutes ago. Hey, Smitty!" he shouted toward the back of the office. A toilet flushed.

Bill Smith wandered to the front, tucking in the shirt of his uniform over his protruding stomach. In his early sixties, he'd been working Property for as long as I'd been at the PD. "What's the matter," Smith drawled. "It ain't the right stuff?"

"It's fine," I said. "I just wanted to know who asked you to release it."

"Let's see. . .was it before or after Bettencourt called? Something about the defense disputin' the tests run on the drugs. That was your case, too. Paol—" He thumbed through the property reports to look up the name.

"Paolini," I supplied.

"Yeah. Didn't think much of it, since I knew he'd have to come down, sign for it. But he gave me the impression he was workin' on the case with you. Told him I'd bring the stuff out as soon as I got back, have it here waitin'. Figured it was Scolari."

"Scolari?" I asked in disbelief. Considering he was AWOL, I didn't think he'd be within miles of the Hall.

"Well, it was noisy. Maintenance is puttin' up some

new shelves, and their saws were goin'. Truthfully, I didn't pay much attention. I just assumed it was Scolari."

I removed four of the seeds, placed them in a Ziploc bag. "Do me a favor," I said, handing him my card. "Flag the evidence. If anyone else makes inquiries about the case, I want you to call or page me, immediately."

"Sure thing." He gathered the remaining evidence, replaced it in the container, and placed that on a cart with other items intended to be put away.

In the hallway a sensation of being watched hit me, and I glanced at the open elevator door as it slid shut. I couldn't swear, but I thought it was Zimmerman's ruddy face I caught a glimpse of. Zim's office was down here—at least it was before he was temporarily reassigned as my partner. I didn't trust him, didn't trust why he was avoiding me. I wanted to know if he knew who called about the evidence. And why.

I stuffed the seeds into my fanny pack and raced to the stairwell door and up the steps two at a time, dodging a uniformed evidence tech with black hair slicked back off his pale forehead. He was kneeling on the landing by his briefcase. Graveyard man, I thought, just as my foot scuffed the briefcase and I heard something clatter. I didn't stop.

"Sorry," I called out. Then I burst through the door onto the ground floor. Markowski and Shipley were waiting for the elevator.

Shipley jabbed his finger several times on the DOWN button. "What's taking this thing so long?"

Markowski paid him little heed, regarding me intently while I watched the elevator, my chest heaving from exertion. Finally the elevator chimed, and the door opened.

Empty.

"You okay?" Markowski asked.

"Yeah," I said, drawing my gaze from the vacant portal. "You haven't seen Zim, have you?"

"Not since he left Homicide yesterday. Why, you anxious to work with him?"

I refused to grab the bait. Shipley stepped into the elevator, holding the door for Markowski. "You coming, Rocky? Or you gonna stand there and yak all day?"

"Keep your gun belt on. I'm coming."

I walked off, wondering what had happened to Zimmerman. Had he been the one to call Property trying to get the evidence from my case? Had he seen me and hit the STOP button because he'd guessed I'd be racing up the stairs to catch him? That would explain why the elevator took so long getting up here. If so, he was probably in the basement, hiding out somewhere to avoid me.

My pager went off. I pulled it from my belt to read it, saw Betty's employee number. I was fifteen minutes late.

"Damn." Zimmerman could wait. I had to trust that Smith or Martin would notify me if he or anyone else tried to secure my evidence. In the meantime, I had some hookers to wake up.

"Where do you want to start?" Betty asked.

"Twin Palms Motel."

Had Betty not been driving, she would have been staring at me, her jaw hanging open. As it was, I felt her intense glance. "You sure?" she asked, pulling onto I-80.

"Yes," I said. I kept my gaze fixed out my window. Anywhere but on her. I didn't want to lose my momentum. I'd made up my mind.

Several seconds of silence, then, "Have you been back there ... ?" She let the question hang, the word "since" unspoken.

It echoed in my mind. I watched the guardrail stream past, melting into the freeway exit as she slowed the vehicle. I took a breath, finally said, "No."

She made a right two blocks later, pulling up in front of a two-story yellow stucco building with a green and purple neon sign shaped like two palm trees surrounding the word MOTEL. We both sat there and stared up at the sign, remembering. Automatically my right elbow pressed against the butt of my holstered semiauto, the familiar feel of it bringing me little comfort. The neon sign flickered.

"Did I tell you I went out with Bettencourt?" I asked suddenly, in no hurry to get out of the car.

"Divorce wasn't good enough for the two of you?"

"A lapse of judgment."

"He improve any in the last six months?"

"About the same," was all I said. Ignoring the stiffness in my shoulder, I reached for the door handle. "Let's do it."

Twin Palms probably had more hookers per capita in its twenty-nine rooms than any other dive this side of Market Street. One of the drug overdose victims had lived in room twelve. According to Scolari's notes, everyone denied knowing anything about her. I was hoping that now, with the press coverage and others having overdosed, the working girls here at Twin Palms might be more inclined to recall details that had slipped their attention when they originally thought it couldn't happen to them.

"How do you want to do this?" Betty asked when we got out of the car.

"How about I do one side of the hallway, you do the other."

"Fine by me." She clipped her star on a chain around her neck. We both turned our radios down, knowing most of the hookers wouldn't open if they heard them. "Ready when you are."

Side by side we strode up the walk. I opened the door, and she stepped in first. I followed. The hallway, long and narrow, was lit by a single tenement bulb. Threadbare carpet, worn through to the wood subflooring at the center, was gray, gritty with dirt and cigarette butts. The walls were an unidentifiable color, more a canvas for smudges, stains, and smashed cockroaches. Betty took the right side, while I took the left. I told myself I could do this. There was no horror left in this building. I had almost convinced myself when, a half hour later, we both stood at the opposite end, near the back entrance.

"You get anything?" I asked.

"Nothing. You?"

"Yeah, a lot of curses for coming at such an ungodly hour."

"Like we want to be here?"

"My fondest dreams," I said, eyeing the stairwell. Betty saw the direction of my gaze. Neither of us moved.

"So," she said, and I guessed she was allowing me to get up my nerve. "How'd it go with IA?"

"I don't know. You can never tell with those guys. They think Scolari's guilty." My throat felt constricted, and it had nothing to do with her question or my answer. I moved to the bottom step, avoiding the crushed malt liquor can and the used condom. Just climb to the top. "What do you know about Torrance? You think he's gay?"

"Torrid Torrance? What makes you ask that?"

Because I needed to talk about something. Anything besides what's at the top of the stairs. "No reason," I said, my voice sounding calm but slightly higher than normal. "He might have my pantyhose."

"You mind running that by me again?"

I neared the top, not answering her right away, my heart pounding, but not from the exertion of climbing the stairs. My lungs wouldn't fill, and I refused to look at the wall near the top step to see if it had been painted over, afraid I'd see the smeared stain of dried blood. My blood. My elbow again sought the reassurance of my weapon holstered snugly at my waist. Unconsciously I reached up, rubbed the ache from my left shoulder. January twenty-fourth. Thirteen months ago, someone had shot me right there at the top of the stairs. A drug raid. Paolini's building. Though never proven, word on the street was that his man, Foust, was responsible. The suspect was still at large, however, and I thought of the rumor that some SFPD inspectors were on Paolini's payroll. I refused to believe it. Scolari had dragged me from the hallway and down the stairs that night . . . He alone had helped me, when no one else had.

I decided the pantyhose story would be a good distraction right about now, and told Betty how that particular piece of clothing ended up on Torrance's windshield the night he was following me, and then what he said yesterday in his office.

Betty laughed, and I found myself smiling in return. "Not one of your better moves," she said, guiding me deeper into the hallway, away from the stairs. I appreciated her subtlety.

"Yeah, well, it still doesn't answer my question. Is he or isn't he?"

Betty regarded me seriously. "What do you want him to be?"

"I'm not sure I care. It just helps talking about something else."

"Then let him remain a mystery. More fun that way."

"For who?" I asked, turning to a new page in my notebook. I'd gotten past the worst of it. I was ready to move on.

"Everyone in the department who's lusting after him. You ever watch them? They practically drool when he walks past. I suppose if I weren't happily married, I'd drool right along with them."

I knocked on door number fourteen. "The guy's a cold fish."

"An act," Betty said, knocking on door fifteen on the opposite side of the hall. "My brother's the same way. Macho cop thing. If I had to bet money on it, I'd say Torrance was straight as an arrow."

Door fourteen opened about two inches. I flashed my star. "Inspector Gillespie. Homicide."

"Someone else get killed?" a sleepy voice asked. I saw only her nose and one eye, she refused to open the door farther.

"Not yet. I was wondering if you might know anything about the girl who OD'd downstairs. Who she was with the night she died. Her supplier." As if anyone here would give up that piece of information.

"I ain't seen nothing."

She tried to shut the door, but I wedged my foot in the crack.

"Look, if anyone you know is using, it could be them next."

"Hey, no one's holding a gun to them people's heads. Seems to me you'd be more worried about someone what gets murdered like Tanya in number eighteen, not someone what takes some bad shit." She kicked my foot from the door and slammed it shut.

As far as I knew, apartment eighteen wasn't listed on any of Scolari's notes or the reports. Neither was the name Tanya. While Betty spoke to the resident in fifteen, I knocked on door eighteen. No one answered. I knocked again, heard a click behind me. I spun, drew my weapon.

In seconds, I realized I'd drawn on an unarmed woman peeking from apartment nineteen. She stood frozen, her wide gaze focused on my gun.

"Christ," I said. I lowered my firearm, holstered it. In my peripheral vision I saw Betty, her weapon drawn in response to mine. She holstered hers, came to my side. "I'm sorry," I told the woman.

"What happened?" Betty asked.

"I thought I heard a weapon cocking. I guess it was the door."

"It sticks," the woman said. Her voice sounded as shaky as my hands were at the moment. Betty leaned down, picked up my notebook, handed it to me.

"I'm sorry," I said again. "Are you okay?"

She nodded, as if being at the wrong end of a gun were commonplace for her, a possibility in this neighborhood. She opened her door, looked up and down the hallway before stepping out, clutching her tattered blue terry robe. "No one's there." She indicated the apartment door I'd knocked on. "It's been vacant for a few weeks now."

"The girl that lived there, Tanya, did you know her?" I showed her my star. "Inspector Gillespie, Homicide."

She eyed the shield, then me, as though unsure what she should do. Reluctantly, "Not really. I pretty much keep to myself. I've got a kid," she said, as if that explained everything.

"Did you ever hear or talk to her?"

"Passing in the hallway. She wasn't over that often. It was her boyfriend's apartment."

"What was his name?" I asked. I didn't bother writing anything down. Couldn't. Adrenaline pricked at my wrists, my hands were shaking.

Again she looked up and down the hallway. "Everyone 'round here called him Spider."

"He still live there?"

"Moved out a few months ago. But I might have his address somewhere. He left it in case he got any mail. You have a card?" she asked softly. "A number where I could call you, later, private-like?"

I gave her one, willing my hand to be still as I handed it to her. She took it, and like a frightened doe hurried back into her apartment, shutting and locking the door behind her.

I stood there in the hallway, trying to calm my shattered nerves. "Hell. I thought I could do this."

"You did. No one got hurt. That's all that counts," Betty said.

Hardly, but there was little to be done about the matter now, other than get through the last few apartments without blowing someone's head off. As expected, we turned up little else from the other residents, and decided to call it a day. I needed a drink, but let Betty convince me a shot of caffeine would be more in order, and allowed her to drive me to a coffeehouse instead of a bar. Neither of us talked about the incident. I couldn't, not yet, and she was too much of a friend to do so. But I knew she would, eventually, and I was grateful for the temporary break she gave me.

We were silent on the trip back to the Hall of Justice. Betty dropped me off out front, then headed on to her afternoon appointment. I saw Reid coming down the front steps, and having no wish to converse with him, made a beeline to the side entrance. As I turned the corner, I noticed a black limo pulling up to the curb and saw Reid approach it. The rear tinted window came down, and he leaned inside, spoke to the occupant.

I used my key to get in the side entrance. A crowd had gathered by the elevators. After what happened at the Twin Palms, I wasn't ready to face anyone just yet, and I bypassed them in favor of the solitude of four flights of stairs in which I could try to compose myself. On I went to Homicide, only vaguely aware of the unusual silence, the empty office. My mind was churning, piecing together what had happened with the woman in nineteen, how I'd drawn down on her, thinking I heard a gun cocking. Maybe I should make an appointment with the department shrink.

I could have killed her. It was a damn door opening. How had I ever thought it was a gun?

The shrill ring of the phone sent my heart into my throat. I was a mess. I took a breath, answered it. "Gillespie—"

"You're dead. Just like the other two."

I slammed the receiver home, stared at the phone. I sank into my chair. *The other two? What other two?*

Five, maybe ten minutes passed. How was I going to get through my day? I needed to do something, anything. A mindless task until I composed myself. Voice mail. I could do that. I picked up the receiver and pressed in my code, listening to the beginning of each message and fast-forwarding through the ones that could wait.

"Hi, this is Martha over at Social Services . . ."

"Kate? This is Reid. I was wondering if you wanted to go to the Black and White Ball . . ."

"Hey, Kate. Leslie. I've got those Forty-Niner tickets for your aunt . . ."

"Um, this is Martin. You told me to call if—"

I fast-forwarded before remembering that I'd told the guys in Property to call. I depressed the number four button again, and the message started over. "Um, this is Martin. You told me to call if anyone came to get the evidence on your cases . . . ? Um, I think you better get down—" I heard a pop. Then, "Oh, shit. Oh, God." The sound of the phone being dropped. Another pop. Approaching footsteps, and then the phone disconnected.

7

I flew from the office. My footsteps echoed down the hall. Or was it my blood pounding in my ears? Only then did it occur to me why Homicide was empty, why there was a crowd at the elevators on the ground floor. Even here on the fourth floor, a yellow crime scene tape hung across the four elevator doors. I pushed past the spectators, mostly SFPD support staff who had gathered around, some crying, others standing in shock. If I let myself, I'd be one of them, useless in my grief. The temptation beckoned.

"Gillespie!"

Lieutenant Andrews's voice carried over the hushed murmur. He was the epitome of calm, a true commander in the face of a crisis. It gave me the focus I needed, and I clung to it.

When I reached his side he said, "We've been trying to raise you on the air."

Now was not the time to go into my lapse at the Twin Palms. No one gave a rat's tail about my current mental state, as long as I could be counted on to provide support and investigative expertise. "Where do you need me?" I asked.

"In the basement to assist Markowski and Shipley. They'll brief you. You can take the back elevator."

"Yes, sir."

"One other thing, Gillespie," he said, stopping me when I was about to leave. "Scolari was seen in the building."

Whatever my heart had been doing a few moments before, it stopped cold at the implication of the lieutenant's words.

Somehow I made it to the basement, my thoughts tumbling as I surveyed the scene, identified the faint but acrid smell of smoke. I could have sworn it was Zimmerman I had seen this morning in the elevator after I picked up my evidence in Property, but I had to admit that as short a glimpse as I had, it could've been Scolari. They were frequently mistaken for each other on the street, though always by outsiders. Had I done the same?

I thought of my earlier conversation with Allison, the records clerk. How she said Scolari had spoken with her just before his wife was killed, and how he mentioned something about the frozen guy, my Ice Man. A connection, perhaps, to the mysterious inquiry into my evidence on the case? Had Scolari been the one to call, to try to pick up the evidence?

I stopped to give my name to the officer on the perimeter who kept the crime scene log, then waited on the fringes. The CSIs brought in sheets of plastic to conduct an electrostatic charge. They'd used this technique successfully in the past, picking up footprints in the otherwise invisible dust layer on the concrete floor. When that was through, and after they picked up any remaining trace evidence, I headed to the Property room. The burnt smell grew stronger.

The forewarning of Martin's phone call could not have prepared me for what I saw. Though my mind had conjured up all sorts of images, subconsciously I knew I kept alive the hope that I was wrong about what I'd heard on my voice mail. It was like reading an article in the paper, or hearing the news broadcast on TV. No matter how aptly described, unless you were directly involved, what you learned was always something that happened to someone else.

As I stepped through the doorway, the horror of what I'd heard on the phone crashed with the nightmarish reality of what I saw now. Bill Smith, Smitty, was slumped over the counter, a pool of blood beneath his head, dripping red onto the cold and unforgiving floor. I closed my eyes, every nerve in my body screaming for me to get out before I saw more. I fought for autopilot, the mode I needed to go into this case with my sanity intact, to stay removed from the scene; but Martin's phone call kept echoing in my head.

"Hey, Gillespie," Markowski called out when he saw me. "Glad you're here. We can use your help."

"What happened?" I managed, eyeing Smitty's body again. Rigor had yet to settle in, but probably would before the body was ever moved. Unlike other crimes, there was no rush in homicide.

I forced my gaze back to Markowski's.

"We're trying to piece it together. Far as I can tell, someone came down, shot them, lit those containers on fire, then left. Traced them to three cases. One belongs to Betty Ramirez, a drug case she went to court on. The others are yours." He showed me the case numbers. "Ring a bell?"

I glanced at the evidence boxes, both partially melted, the contents a blackened lump at the bottom. I recognized my case number from the Ice Man. A chill crawled up my spine.

Rocky guided me past the burnt evidence. I didn't want to look, but knew I had to. Beyond was Martin splayed on the floor, his blue eyes fixed forever in an unseeing stare at the ceiling, a single bullet hole centered on his forehead. A few inches from his hand was the packet of photos, as though he had just pulled them out to show someone but had dropped them when he fell. I thought of his grandson. His first haircut. My biological clock ticked a notch at the reminder of my own mortality. "He called me," I heard myself say.

"What?"

"I left my card. Told him and Smitty to call if someone tried to pick up any of my evidence. The murder's on my voice mail."

"Jesus Effing Christ."

A little politer than the vernacular I would've used, but apt.

Shipley walked in from the back of the room with another property clerk. "She says it doesn't look like anything else has been touched," he said, indicating the clerk, "but she can't be sure till they start an inventory."

"Gillespie heard the murder go down," Rocky said.

"*What?*"

"On her voice mail. Martin called her."

"Soon as the CSIs finish, get started on the inventory," Shipley told the clerk. To me he said, "Let's go find a phone. I want to hear it. Might as well get your statement at the same time. You were down here earlier, right?"

He knew it as well as I, since we ran into each other at the elevator. Momentarily I wondered if he suspected me of being the killer, but nothing in his manner indicated this, and I couldn't imagine he or Markowski would let me down here if they thought such a thing.

We returned to Homicide. Using the phone at my desk, I accessed my voice mail and handed Shipley the phone.

His face, impassive on taking the receiver, tensed, and I figured he'd heard the first shot. He hit the number four button, listened again, then slowly lowered the receiver. "Do me a favor. Go get something to record this thing," he said, pulling out his notebook.

I retrieved a telephonic recording device from a cabinet. Shipley was sitting, making notes. It took me a couple of minutes to set it up, my fingers still shaking. I accessed the message, recorded it. "I'm going to send it to my archives," I said when I'd finished.

He nodded, wrote something else. "Tell me what that was all about."

I explained briefly about the frozen John Doe case, how I'd gone down to check out some evidence, only to discover someone had requested it before me. "Martin must have called when this guy came to get it," I finished. Then I remembered the last threatening call I'd received. "Someone called up and said I was dead, just like the other two. I didn't know what he meant, then. Now I do."

"Same caller as on the other phone threats?"

"I think so."

He made a notation on his pad. "What time was it when you went down to Property to collect the seeds?"

"I didn't really pay attention. I do know it was several minutes before I ran into you and Rocky. I thought I'd seen Zimmerman in the elevator, and wondered if he was the one who'd requested my evidence."

"Why would he do that? He works down there."

That was a point I hadn't considered at the time.

What I believed I saw was Zimmerman trying to avoid me when he was stepping off the elevator. If it was him. Of course, he'd been avoiding me for days. But if it was Scolari, he certainly would have tried to avoid me under those circumstances as well. "I just thought it looked like Zim," I said.

"Could it have been Scolari?"

I hesitated. "I couldn't say for certain it wasn't."

"One of the property clerks said he saw Scolari in the basement."

"But it could have been Zimmerman," I pointed out in Scolari's defense.

"Where's the motive?"

I hadn't a clue. I wanted to say Zimmerman hated me, that he was setting up me and Scolari for his being banished from Homicide, but I couldn't see him killing someone just because he got caught. Then I thought of the evidence in Betty's case being destroyed too. Everyone knew the city manager had political aspirations, right along with the chief of police. Both wanted to be mayor. It was to the city manager's benefit to have his son's case dismissed. "What about Ramirez's possession case?" I asked. "What if some political bigwig came in and had the case taken care of ?"

"We're already looking at that angle," he said. "On the QT, mind you. I like my job. And if you like yours, you'll keep quiet. But back to your case. What I don't understand is, if it was Scolari, what's the connection between his wife and that box of evidence? What the hell was in there?"

"Clothes, a wedding ring, some seeds."

"What kind of seeds?"

"I don't know." But even as I said it, my gut instinct

told me that I'd better find out. I showed him the seeds, told him I planned on taking them to UC Berkeley for identification. He eyed them, nodding.

When Shipley had finished taking my statement, he told me they had everything under control, that I wasn't needed. He knew as well as I that at the moment I was too close to the case, the victims. My objectivity couldn't be relied on. I'd gone from investigator status to witness, at least in his mind. In light of everything, I knew what I needed to do despite this latest turn of events. Get those seeds to the university. If Martin's and Smith's murders were related to my case, then the possibility existed that the seeds I was carrying around in my fanny pack were pertinent. I logged out on the board in the office, then headed for my car.

No sooner had I turned the key when someone rapped on my window. My heart slammed into my sternum. My hand flew to my gun. It was Torrance. "Son of a bitch," I said to myself, when I could breathe again. At least I hadn't drawn down on him. "You ever take any time off?" I asked after rolling down my window, hoping to sound calmer than my actions indicated. I failed.

"When I'm allowed to." His gaze narrowed and seemed to penetrate through me. "I was paged for the homicides in Property by the DA. Their office called and said you got another call from one of Paolini's pawns. They're worried he'll make good on his threat. That this might be part of it."

"Alleged threat, don't you mean? It's never been proven." I knew it sounded like I was defending the man, but what I was really doing was defending my independence. I could feel it slipping away at the speed of light.

"Gillespie. Are you aware of exactly what evidence was destroyed down there?"

"Yes," I said, thinking of the seeds in my pouch, wondering what the connection was. "I was there."

"From Paolini's case. All of it's gone. His attorneys are already filing for dismissal."

I stared, shocked, the weight of it all not lost on me. I'd been so worried about my little seeds, seeing Zimmerman, and wondering who had called for that evidence, I'd forgotten the very significant fact that someone had also called for Paolini's evidence to be brought up.

Coincidence?

"Where're you off to?"

"UC Berkeley," I said absently. I thought about the night I'd been shot. All the death threats since then, threats that I'd apparently too easily dismissed when they'd stopped several months ago. They'd started up again, and now this.

I didn't move for a long while, and Torrance patiently waited. Finally he said, "I've always found that getting back on the horse helps."

I looked at him.

"Work," he clarified. "Immerse yourself."

He was right.

"I'm going to Professor Rocklin's office," I said. "Botany."

"Mind if I tag along?"

"No." At the moment, I could use the company, even his. I reached over and unlocked the door.

"Why the botany department?"

"Trying to identify a John Doe." I pulled out of the parking garage.

"What was he, tiptoeing through the tulips?"

In no mood for his attempt at humor, I glanced over at him, curious about his break in solemnity but not willing to delve into the reason for it. "Seeds," I said, patting my fanny pack. "My John Doe was the last autopsy Patricia performed. He hid some seeds on his person before he died. She found them."

Professor Rocklin was younger than I expected, maybe late thirties, about my height, with sandy hair and a scholarly goatee that went well with his turtleneck and wire-framed glasses. We shook hands, and he introduced us to his assistant, Kay, a pretty graduate student whose admiration for the professor was obvious. She watched his every move, her eyes alight—with first love? I wondered if he knew.

"So tell me, Inspector," he said after Torrance and I were seated at a table in his lab. "What can I do for you?" Around us, I recognized a few of the numerous plants growing in pots on shelves and in hanging baskets. Spider plants, pothos, a sago palm. The laughter of students on their way to classes drifted in from outside through an open window. I envied them their innocence, longed for my own college days when I thought I knew everything, but knew so little.

"I was hoping you might be able to tell me what these seeds are," I said, pulling the tiny plastic bag from my fanny pack. The bag was no more than an inch by two, the seeds grouped in one small corner.

He took them, holding the bag close. "Hmmm, right off, I'd guess Phytolacca americana."

"Which would be?" Torrance asked.

"Your garden variety pokeweed, but if you care to leave them with me, I can look them up in a catalog, do some checking. If all else fails, we can try to grow a couple, see what sprouts up."

"They're evidence," I said, disappointed by his tentative ID in some ways, yet even more curious in others. I suppose it had something to do with the fact that a man was dead, and knowing he had your basic pokeweed seeds on him did nothing to tell me why he was killed. "It's imperative that strict control be maintained as to their location at all times."

"Yes, the chain of custody. I like to watch *Quincy* reruns."

Torrance and I exchanged glances. I said, "Is there some way you can assure me they'll be locked up?"

"I'll keep them in the safe in my office."

He knitted his brows, fingering the mottled seeds in their bag. "I'll try to grow two, use the others for ID. Kay, get me a sterile jar from the cupboard, please."

Kay retrieved the jar, and Professor Rocklin, with all the care of a pharmacist doling out pills, separated the four seeds from the bag.

He walked us to the door, we shook hands, and he said, "I'll call you, Inspector, the moment I learn something."

"Thank you," I said, leaving him with my card.

We were out the door when he asked, "What sort of case is this?"

"Homicide," I said.

"So what happens next?" Torrance asked me when we'd gotten back to the car. "How's that going to solve your John Doe's murder?"

"It's not. I guess I was hoping the seeds would turn out to be something rare. I don't know. At the moment, all I want to know is why. It may turn out to be nothing, but it's the only piece of evidence remaining, with the exception of the body in the morgue."

"That was all the evidence?"

"What was booked is now a melted lump. Had I not gotten the remaining seeds out, they'd be gone too."

"Are you telling me those seeds are somehow related to the murder down in the Property room?"

"Actually, I checked them out of evidence before the arson." I couldn't say "murder." It made it all too real. Concentrating on the seeds was better. I could almost pretend that I'd never been involved with Paolini, or that he'd never threatened me, never tried to have me killed— never had the evidence destroyed.

It had to be Paolini, because the alternative was unthinkable. That Scolari . . .

I stopped myself from finishing the thought. Drive. Look out the window. Watch the road.

The day was clear, the wind having swept the clouds from the sky, and when I pulled onto the 80 from University, San Francisco's famous cityscape beckoned from across the calm bay. I couldn't help feeling that it was all an illusion, like the calm before the storm. I wondered if Torrance thought the same, because like me, he was silent, staring out the windshield as though interested in the passing scenery.

The traffic at the Bay Bridge tollbooth was surprisingly light, and we made it back to the city in record time. As we neared our exit, he asked, "The seeds aside, you have any theories on your John Doe?"

"Nothing yet. I still need to do backgrounds on the businesses that occupied the warehouse before it became vacant. Scolari had started the background, found out that Paolini was somehow involved. That's all I know."

"You mind driving past there?"

"No."

Several minutes later we pulled up to the vacant side of the warehouse. I parked in front of it. The door had been padlocked, and a remnant of yellow crime scene tape tied to the handle fluttered in the wind. Torrance eyed the windows near the roof line. "What were the businesses?" he asked.

With the events of the past few days crowding my thoughts, the exact names escaped me, but I was grateful for what Torrance was doing for both of us. Giving us a task to occupy ourselves, and keep us from remembering. "Some import place and a leather goods company."

"Shaw Imports?"

"Might have been. I'd have to look it up."

"They were being investigated by the DA for money laundering," he said. "Bettencourt was telling me about it yesterday. Nicholas Paolini and Antonio Foust. If I'm not mistaken, Foust continued the operation after Paolini was arrested in your drug sting last year."

"I'll definitely look into it," I said, wondering if the man in the freezer was a Mafia hit. Paolini had definite Mafia ties, as did Foust. If so, it shed a whole new light on the homicide of my John Doe. But why, then, would they hide the body in a warehouse that could be traced back to them?

Granted, they were not exactly the tenants at the time the body was found, but Paolini had connections to Hilliard Pharmaceutical in addition to the warehouse. Before I arrested him, his last venture was a thousand-dollar-a-plate dinner, underwritten by Hilliard Pharmaceutical, benefiting the Save the Rain Forest Foundation, a cause near and dear to Hilliard's wife's heart—since she was using the Foundation to promote her Lost Forest Shampoo. She apparently had no idea that Paolini was a major drug runner with ties to the

Mafia and that he was using the Foundation party as part of his operation.

The black tie event saw the majority of San Francisco's elite in attendance. It was a night I doubted Paolini would ever forget, for the simple reason that I was his date and as a result gathered enough evidence to conduct a search warrant served the following day that netted three million dollars of drug money he had not yet had a chance to launder.

"I think we should run the John Doe case by Bettencourt," he said.

"I'll let you handle that."

"Thought you two were working on a reconciliation." He pulled out his cellular and punched in a number.

"Where'd you hear that?" I asked, surprised. I wasn't sure that I liked my private business made public, even if there wasn't any truth to it, and wondered how much of that Torrance had dug up as an IA investigator.

"Your ex told me," he said, then talked into the phone. "Bettencourt? Mike Torrance here."

While he spoke to Reid via cellular, I drove down the street and turned right, past the entrance to Hilliard Pharmaceutical. A gray pickup with HILLIARD PHARMACEUTICAL. A COMPANY YOU CAN TRUST emblazoned on the door panels was parked out in front. Dexter Kermgard. "I can't imagine they were too thrilled to find a corpse in their backyard," I said, nodding at the pickup.

Torrance covered the receiver. "I'm sorry. What did you say?"

From my rearview mirror, I saw Dex, wearing a white lab coat, step out the door carrying a file box. I pulled to the curb and parked. "Nothing. I need to talk to this guy."

If Torrance heard me, he gave no indication. I left him in the car and strode up the street. "Dex?"

He put the file box in the back of his pickup, looked up, smiled. "Kate. What can I do for you?"

"I'm in somewhat of a bind. I'm sure you heard about my partner."

His smile faded. He said nothing.

"The DA's requested that I reinvestigate each of my homicides. To preserve the integrity of the cases." Not yet, but no need to let Dex know. "I'd like to see where the power cord was attached."

He hesitated, his jaw clenched. "Sure."

He pulled out the keys and unlocked the door. We hadn't taken two steps within when I heard a car screech to a halt outside. He eyed the white Lincoln angled against the curb out front.

"Someone you know?" I asked.

"That would be Josephine Hilliard. I wasn't expecting her." He moved on, but I hesitated, catching a glimpse of a woman exiting the car. She walked into the building, her high heels clicking on the cement floor.

I put her in her late thirties, tall, thin, and as cultured and commanding as her voice. Her entire being, from the top of her blond French twist to her woolen cream-colored swing coat and matching boots, spoke money. Lots of it. She was just as I remembered, though our contact had been brief. She'd been the hostess of the fund-raiser put on by Paolini to save the rain forests. I recalled her standing at the door, saying to everyone who entered, "How do you do? A pleasure to meet you," as she clasped their hand. I was one of several hundred guests that night to receive her plastic greeting.

"Dexter? What are you doing here?" The woman held him in her cool gaze.

Dex returned her stare, not backing down an iota. "This is Inspector Gillespie. Her father and I were on the force together."

"Inspector," she said, sparing me a glance.

"Inspector Gillespie would like to take a look at the dividing wall. For her investigation."

She sized me up. I met her gaze, never allowing her the chance to dismiss me, something at which she was practiced, I knew, from experience. Finally I said, "Undoubtedly you're aware of my investigation."

"Of course. Dexter informed me the moment he learned of it. It is his job, after all."

"Then you are aware I need to look in your building."

"I've been advised not to allow that." She brushed a speck from the sleeve of her impeccable coat.

"By whom?"

"Our legal department. You need a search warrant, I believe they said."

"Only if you refuse. I was hoping we could do this peaceably."

"Be that as it may, Inspector. You will leave the building at once. We will be more than happy to cooperate. Once you have obtained a search warrant. We have a reputation to protect."

"Gillespie."

I looked beyond her to see Torrance in the doorway, a determined expression on his face. I ignored him. I was mad, at a dead end, and needing to score a point, despite Josephine Hilliard's momentary triumph. I advanced on her until I stood inches away. "I'd think because of your company's reputation, you'd want to cooperate. But I'll be more than happy to get a warrant."

I moved past her until I reached Torrance and the door. Then I turned. "Oh, yes. There is one thing. I'll need to interview you. At my office. This afternoon." She opened her mouth, undoubtedly to object, but I hurried on. "Your husband owns this building. The entire building, from what I understand. Our department is investigating the death of a man found in the vacant side. I'm sure you understand why it's important that we get a statement from you?"

"I'll speak to our attorneys. I'm not sure if they'll allow it."

"Feel free, Mrs. Hilliard. But think about this. Everything I do is a matter of public record. All my conversations will be documented, and notes made on who does and does not cooperate. The press eats up little details like that."

Apparently I struck a chord. She clenched her delicate fists. "I'm afraid I can't. I'm under heavy medication. I shouldn't be driving."

Judging from her parking job, she could very well have been telling me the truth. "Have your attorneys drive you. This afternoon, Mrs. Hilliard. Before five." At that, I exited the building.

Dex followed me out. He glanced back in at Mrs. Hilliard, then closed the door to keep her from hearing. "Let me see if I can talk to her for you, Inspector."

His words took me by surprise. "Thank you."

Torrance took my arm and led me to the car. I had to double my pace to keep up with him. "What the hell was that about?" he asked. "Attitude adjustment?"

"I find it odd that a company that allegedly has no

connection to a homicide wouldn't cooperate in the investigation."

Torrance never slowed his pace.

"What's the hurry?" I asked.

"Get in the car." His tone was all business, his mouth set in a firm line. "We need to get to the morgue. Code Two and a Half."

"Seriously?" Code Two and a Half was lights, no siren—something that most agencies frowned on. We got in, I started the engine.

"Move it."

The all too familiar prick of adrenaline shot to my hands as I flicked a switch on the dash, activating the emergency lights in the front grill of my car. It was a dangerous way to drive, without a siren on, but I figured if an IA investigator wanted me to break the rules, then he had damn good reason for it. At the bottom of the hill, I came to a stop sign. The intersection was clear. I rolled through it.

"What's going on?" I asked.

"Your partner's at the morgue."

8

I panicked at his words. Doctor Mead-Scolari's face burned across my vision. In her Range Rover, her head hanging at an odd tilt against the bloody glass, her throat slit. Like a movie reel, the next scene flashed before me. In Property, Smith slumped over the counter, his life dripping onto the dirty concrete. And Martin . . . Martin staring at the ceiling. . . . Images. Images I wanted to forget. Images I'd remember forever.

My pulse drummed in my ears. I rolled down my window, took a deep breath against the nausea. I didn't want Scolari to end up that way, to see him that way. "What do you mean, at the morgue?" I forced myself to ask. "Is he dead?"

"No." Torrance's firm, quiet voice brought sanity with it. I took another deep breath and concentrated on my driving. "Dr. Mead-Scolari's secretary said she saw him in his wife's office. She called 911, then left the building. SWAT's setting up a perimeter."

"He's going to get himself killed."

"Not if he gives up."

I stopped for a red light, made a right turn instead, then went down an alley. I knew several shortcuts to the morgue, back streets that would avoid the congestion of city traffic. "I can't believe he killed those guys," I said, thinking of the times we were down in Property booking items from various cases we'd worked. "A man doesn't joke around with guys, ask about their wives, how their grandkids are doing, only to kill them. That's something Paolini would do."

"And Paolini's still a viable suspect," Torrance replied. "In *that* homicide."

"But not in the doctor's homicide," I said, finishing for him. "Do you think Scolari did it?"

Silence. I stole a glance, saw his dark, unfathomable gaze. Finally he said, "He's left me no choice."

"Is that the departmentally correct answer?" I regretted the question as soon as I said it, the attack on his integrity, but it was too late. The words were out, and I wanted to hear the answer.

"You mean, why didn't I come out and say yes, I think he's guilty?" His voice nearly frosted my windshield. "Unlike the opinion you and the rest of the department have about IA, our sole purpose in life is not to screw you over."

"I never said it was."

"Maybe not directly, but can you tell me you've never thought that?"

Having been at the forefront of two IA investigations myself—nothing as serious as this, and exonerated in both—I clearly recalled thinking that very thing. It occurred to me then that because of his position, the way he was treated by others, we were in a sense really more alike than I'd realized. Those in IA were looked upon by many officers as pariahs. Women officers were about one step below that. "Look," I said, evading the issue, "I'm just worried about my partner."

"Do *you* think he did it?"

"I can't think that."

"But do you?"

My grip on the steering wheel tightened, my knuckles white. Damn you, Scolari. How could you do this? How could you let me down, not give up, and let all this happen? "I don't know," I said.

We neared the Hall of Justice and the morgue, and I stopped at the outer perimeter a block away, our progress impeded by a patrol car in the road, its three-sixties flashing. Torrance showed his star to the officer nearby, who then waved us through. I didn't want Scolari to die. As I drove around the patrol car toward the inner perimeter, I could see SWAT personnel running from a van, carrying their high-powered weapons like commandos in a war zone. Ninja turtles, Scolari always called them.

"Park here," Torrance said, indicating a spot on the north side of the jail near a different van used by the Hostage Negotiation Team. At least that was a good sign, that they were willing to try to talk him from the building before sending in the heavy artillery.

We got out, and Torrance went off to talk with the Incident Commander. I saw Patricia's secretary sitting at the command post. Her hand shook as she lifted a Styrofoam cup to her mouth.

"Hey, Mary," I said, taking a seat beside her.

"Honey, you better tell me you didn't send him here," she said, shocking me.

"No. Why would I?"

"He came looking for that file you asked about this morning."

"Which file?"

"John Doe." She rattled off the number.

The Ice Man? This case was popping up far too often

for my comfort, and I wondered why. Suddenly I remembered the conversation Mary and I had had about Scolari's marriage. I worried that if Mary believed I had something to do with Scolari's appearance in her office, she'd refuse to tell me whatever it was she'd started to divulge. "I have no idea why he showed up here."

Mary regarded me thoroughly. Apparently satisfied of my innocence, she said, "Can't imagine why he came, either. Not when the whole damn force is looking for him."

Unless there's something about that case I was missing. Was it related to the SoMa Slasher? Paolini? Had Patricia somehow made a connection? I didn't know where to find the answers, but figured her death was a good place to start.

"Mary? I was wondering . . ." I stopped upon seeing the direction of her fixed gaze: the SWAT van, the snipers jumping from the back, a man handing out AK 47s to his team.

"Heaven help him," she whispered, then shivered. She wrapped her arms about her.

Too emotionally wound up to be cold, I took off my jacket, draped it over her shoulders. "Better?" I asked, grateful for the distraction of helping someone else.

She nodded. "I'm sorry. You were saying?"

I looked around, saw Torrance talking with the Incident Commander near the SWAT van. I motioned her away from the area. "What was it you were about to tell me this morning? About the Scolaris' marriage?"

As we strolled away from the command center, Torrance looked up, tensing as though worried I'd leave. But then I saw him look from me to Mary, undoubtedly eyeing my coat on her shoulders. I guessed he thought I wouldn't be going far without my coat, because he went on with what he was doing. I had a feeling he wouldn't let me wander off for too long. Not if Scolari was suspected of being around.

"It's not on the grapevine yet," she said, "but Patricia was going to leave him."

"She'd already booted him out."

"Honey, what I'm talking about was before he got caught with that little bit of a records clerk. Patricia told me she thought he did that to make her jealous." This was not the earthshaking news I'd expected. "The way I see it," Mary continued, "he killed her after he realized she was going through with the divorce."

"The PD's a regular gossip mill. What made this divorce so different?"

"Oh, it wasn't the divorce, let me tell you."

"What then?" I asked.

"Like I told your Lieutenant Torrance, it was *who* she was divorcing him for. I think he couldn't take it."

I waited for the announcement, wondering who Scolari would most be upset by. Zimmerman, his former partner? Scolari mentioned he didn't trust him. He'd certainly believe it the ultimate betrayal, but I couldn't picture Patricia falling for a man like Zim. "Well?" I prompted.

"None other than Josie Hilliard."

My jaw dropped. I stared openmouthed, but her face remained serious.

"As in Hilliard Pharmaceutical?" I asked in disbelief. I'd stood inches away from this woman, Josephine, Josie Hilliard. She'd never said a thing. Not a damned thing. Except for her comment about being heavily medicated.

I barely heard Mary's words after that. Something

about Patricia meeting Josephine over cancer research. A million thoughts raced through my head, the foremost being that Josie Hilliard was one more strike against Scolari—and that Torrance would consider it a major factor in his investigation. Hell, I would. Though I told myself that this was San Francisco, and the scenario was far from unheard of, the fact was that I knew Scolari. He was a macho cop and a man's man. He took it hard just being partnered with a woman. To have his wife leave him for a woman would devastate and humiliate him. He'd take it as a direct attack on his manhood. Especially when considering how very feminine Josephine appeared.

She was not a woman I would place as a lesbian. If anything, she was the epitome of a trophy wife. I clearly recalled her husband, Evan Hilliard, that night of Paolini's fund-raiser. Handsome, fifties, a good twenty years older than she. Society courtship, marriage. Did he have an inkling?

Josephine Hilliard. Another nail in Scolari's motivation-filled coffin. He politely respected the gay officers, but would rather be dead than have anything to do with the gay lifestyle. I still couldn't see him killing his wife.

I took a deep breath, thinking of all the weight Scolari had shouldered me with, whether he knew it or not. If it was true that he had killed his gay wife—and I didn't want to think it was—then I could see why Torrance might consider him a suspect in the SoMa Slasher slayings. The MOs were the same.

We waited, but the Hostage Negotiation Team's attempt to contact anyone in the evacuated building apparently wasn't successful. If Scolari was in there, I could do nothing to help him. Still, I needed to know he was okay, and I stood riveted to the spot, unable to turn away even as the SWAT team tossed in flash bangs before they entered. On the leader's signal, they moved. Smoke drifted from the entrance, swirled about their feet.

I knew the drill, having trained with them when I was on the Hostage Negotiation Team. In my mind, I saw them rushing in, the point man swinging his gun toward the first door, crouching. Behind him, the second man would follow, stand. One high, one low. The remainder of the team would race in at their sign of all clear. They'd do this with each door they came to, each desk, every obstacle . . .

I didn't want Scolari to die. Not like this.

"Gillespie?" I jumped at Torrance's touch on my arm. I hadn't heard him approach. "It's over."

"Was it—" I cleared my throat. I'd completely lost track of time. I'd been thinking about Scolari as my partner, not as a suspect. Figured if I looked at the evidence, surely I'd feel differently. "Was it him?"

"We don't know. They didn't find anybody."

I exhaled slowly and told myself this wasn't happening. I'd been in a robbery once—in a liquor store, off duty—and recalled how disjointed my thought process was when it went down, that it was not real, a test. I was going through the same thing now, except unlike the robbery that had lasted all of three minutes, this surrealistic nightmare seemed to go on forever.

"Why would he come here?" I pondered aloud.

"We were hoping you could tell us."

I drew my gaze from the morgue doors. "How would I know?"

"Partners . . ."

"Not by choice, I'm sure he'd tell you." I suddenly wondered why Torrance failed to mention the relationship between Scolari's wife and Josephine Hilliard. Mary had said she'd told him about it, so it wasn't as if he hadn't known. True, the drive over here hadn't exactly facilitated the atmosphere for conversation. I suppose he could have slipped it in between his "Watch out for that car," and "Go, go, it's green." All he had to do was say, "Oh, by the way, did you realize that the woman you were speaking to back there was having an affair with your partner's wife?"

"I have no idea why he came," I said. My composure was slipping. "Not at the moment."

"Has he contacted you at all? Since the other night?"

"Were you going to tell me about her? Josephine Hilliard?"

"Has he contacted you since then?" His expression never wavered as he enunciated each syllable. Obviously that subject was off-limits.

"No," I said, looking away. The SWAT team wandered past us back to their van, weapons slung muzzle down over their shoulders, their black masks pulled off.

I wanted to leave, to get away from the static of the radios, the after-adrenaline shoptalk of the men, the faces that glanced my way, making me wonder if they thought I knew where Scolari was hiding.

"I need to get to the office," I said, my patience running thin. "The lieutenant's got a press conference. I was supposed to report to him on what I found on the drug overdoses and the Slasher case."

"I doubt he'll miss you at the moment."

I refused to acknowledge the truth of his statement. With a double homicide that had occurred in the very bowels of the Hall of Justice, the lieutenant wasn't thinking about me.

"Buy you coffee?" Torrance asked.

I didn't answer right away, for the simple fact I was still mad. He'd made it perfectly clear by what he wasn't telling me that I wasn't a part of Patricia's homicide investigation. To hell with him. I'd find out what I needed on my own. Even so, I couldn't afford to make enemies with the man—not if I wanted to help Scolari—which is why I attempted a smile. I'm pretty sure I failed. "Okay. Just as long as it's away from here."

"I'll drive."

The farther from the morgue we got, the more I knew I couldn't return to work. Not yet. I didn't want to see the TV crews and press gathered on the Hall of Justice steps, calling out for more of Scolari's blood.

He pulled into the parking garage at Fifth and Minna, and we strolled into the Starbucks. The aroma of freshly ground coffee was comforting, and I hoped like hell the caffeine might give me the strength to go on.

Despite his friendly offer, inside he seemed distant, and I figured he was still angry over my questioning his integrity when it came to Scolari's guilt. "How about I buy you a cup," I said. "A truce."

"It'll cost you." He surveyed the coffee shop with practiced ease. "I'm ordering a double."

Torrance was a cheap date, his double merely black coffee. We sat at the table, our backs to the wall, an eye on both doors. Even without the murders we would have done the same, officer safety ingrained in us since our early academy days.

"You ever wish you could just go into a joint, sit anywhere, and not think about where your back is?" I asked. We both knew what I meant: You ever wish you weren't a cop?

He sipped his coffee, watched the heavy pedestrian traffic gathering at the corner, waiting for the light to turn green. A horn honked. Tires screeched somewhere in the distance. "Sometimes," he said.

We drank in silence, perhaps both contemplating what life outside of law enforcement might be like. About halfway through my latte, my pager went off. I pulled it from my belt, glanced at the number, then replaced it. I sipped my drink, pleased to see my hand remained steady.

"Anything important?" Torrance asked.

"Just my aunt. She's probably calling to remind me about some errand I promised to run for her."

"Would you like to use my phone?"

I smiled. It took all my effort. "My phone's in my car. She can wait."

"I don't mind." Torrance handed me his cellular. I held it in my hand for an eternal second, wondering what to do.

"It's a personal call," I said in a teasing voice. "You sure IA won't come down on you?"

"I'll take my chances." His smile was calm, unreadable, his gaze held mine.

I opened the phone. Punched in my aunt's number. It rang twice, then her answering machine kicked on. Torrance watched. "It's me," I said before the message finished. I paused, heard the tone, hoped Torrance didn't. "No. I didn't forget to make dinner reservations for tomorrow night. I told you I would . . . Okay. See you then."

I hit END, handed the phone to Torrance, wondering if he would push RECALL to see the number. He put the phone in his pocket, and I breathed an inward sigh of relief. "Ready to go back to the Hall?"

"If you are."

I wasn't. I had no wish to see crime scene tape still strung up, in places I'd considered safe all these years.

9

As I expected, there was no peace from the media. They were on the steps of the Hall of Justice when we returned, their vans double-parked. We entered through a side door, having to show our IDs to the officers posted there. Every exit, we found, was guarded in the same manner, not a soul getting in without an ID, and everyone who wasn't a uniformed cop passing through the metal detectors. If that didn't bring reality crashing home, Scolari's picture posted at every workstation did.

Torrance and I kept our thoughts to ourselves, neither of us needing a reminder of the horrific events of the day. Silently we entered Homicide, and I wondered how I would gain three minutes to myself in order to return Scolari's page. What I didn't expect was the answer to be napping at my desk in the otherwise vacated office.

"Reid? What are you doing here?"

Bettencourt opened his eyes and took in the pair of us watching him. "Waiting for you. I was, uh . . ." He brushed a lock of hair from his forehead. Very cute. Too bad the rest of the package didn't match. "I wanted you to know I was thinking about you."

"Thank you," I said, very much aware of Torrance's presence beside me.

"Actually, I figured you could use some company right about now. One of your SWAT guys was in my office when he got paged. I heard what happened." He rose and stretched his arms.

"Yes." My mind raced to analyze how I could take this situation—Reid's presence—and make it work to my advantage. "If it was Scolari, he wasn't in there."

"How are you holding up?" he asked, almost hesitantly. He shoved his hands in his pants pockets, once again reminding me of that little-boy look. He appeared very innocent. He was good in the acting department.

"I don't know." I knew then what I needed to do. I glanced at Torrance, who seemed unmoved by our touching scene, as though he saw through me. That of course was nothing unusual, but it made me wonder about him even more. "Can we have a few minutes?" I asked him.

"I'll be outside in the hall."

Torrance shut the door behind him, and for a moment I thought about confiding in Reid about Scolari paging me. His concern was endearing, though I didn't doubt for a moment it was a show. He was a DA's investigator and part of the special homicide team investigating Patricia's death, so his job was on the side of the prosecution. Like Torrance, he'd look at the circumstantial facts, which at the moment were overwhelmingly against Scolari. And who knew if his overpossessiveness would get in the way? I was being watched enough as it was. "I'm glad you're here," I said, taking the seat he'd vacated on my arrival.

He reached out, took my hand. "Maybe we can go out tonight, talk about it. What you're going through can't be pleasant."

"Worse than you can imagine," I said, ignoring his invitation.

"Look. Those property clerks . . . Paolini . . . Well, after I spoke to Torrance on the phone this afternoon, I agree with him that Paolini might have set this whole thing up, killing the property clerks and destroying the evidence in his case."

"I know. I'd rather not talk about it," I said truthfully. "It's too soon."

"I'm sorry." He looked genuinely so, still holding my hand as though he didn't know what to say, and I felt bad. Maybe he wanted to talk, needed to talk, and I was shutting him down. Hell, I was using him. I wanted Torrance out, and it had worked; now I needed Reid out. The question was why? What loyalty did I owe Scolari other than that he was my partner?

He dragged me from the Twin Palms after I'd been shot. At risk to himself.

The least I could do was give him a few moments of my time. If he was innocent, then he deserved my help. If he was guilty . . . then so be it. I'd lead him to Torrance in a set of silver handcuffs.

With my free hand, I fiddled with papers at my desk, my fingers itching to get at the phone. "About tonight. I'd love to go out with you, but I'm afraid there'd be a third wheel. Lieutenant Torrance is keeping me under constant surveillance. He has been since Saturday night when I met you for dinner."

Reid's grip on my hand tightened, his expression tensed. "That's one of the reasons I'm here. Paolini's attorneys have filed an appeal based on Scott Forrest's involvement in his case. The DA sent me here to make sure you were aware—"

"Thanks," I said. "But Torrance already told me. Which is why he's playing pseudo-bodyguard."

"How much of a bodyguard are we talking?" he asked, apparently still not quite understanding what I was telling him.

"He's been staying at my place since—"

"He's sleeping with you?"

"Excuse me?"

"Bad choice of words. I meant, at your house?"

"Yes."

He sat in Scolari's chair, leaned back, crossed his leg over his knee. I don't know why, but I got the idea Reid was regrouping. "Sort of puts a damper on your private life."

"You could say that."

"Look, Kate, I know the timing's bad, what with everything that's been going on, but after our lunch and dinner the other night, I thought maybe . . ."

"I don't think it'll work," I said in all seriousness. We'd had this conversation before. His possessive side was starting to show through again, something he seemed able to hide behind all that charm he oozed. I needed to cut this guy out of my life, and fast. But then I remembered what I had to do, and changed tactics midstream. "Unless you can talk to Torrance. But talk to him outside in the hallway. He's got a thing about not bending the rules in front of officers. With you, he might be more inclined."

"Sort of a man-to-man thing?"

"You got it."

"Anything for you, babe." I didn't bother telling him I wasn't anyone's "babe," especially not his. The moment he exited, shut the door behind him, I reached for the phone, punched in the numbers on the keypad, numbers I knew by heart.

It rang once. "Where are you?" I asked the moment Scolari answered.

"Never mind. What the hell took you so long?"

"I'm being watched closer than the president," I said, my gaze locked on the door. "Why haven't you turned yourself in?"

"Someone out there's serious about this shit, and at the moment, I have no plans to end up in a body bag."

"If you're innocent, they'll protect you."

"I'm more worried about you right now."

"I'm fine. Torrance is watching me."

"You trust him?"

"Shouldn't I?"

"At the moment, don't trust anyone. Just yourself, and your instincts."

"They say you were in the basement today. Just before Martin and Smith were killed."

"How the hell would I have gotten into the Hall without being arrested?"

"They saw you at the morgue."

He didn't try to deny it. "I wanted copies of the autopsies Patricia oversaw the last year."

"Why?" I heard the door open, and saw Reid swinging it wide. Four people were grouped in the doorway behind him, including Torrance. There was Josie Hilliard, wearing a red dress, undoubtedly Dior. Her husband, Evan Hilliard, tanned, white-haired, dark silk suit, no tie, his hand at her elbow as though supporting her in her delicate medicated state. Dex Kermgard brought up the rear. Reid was saying something to Torrance, who was now watching me. I ignored nearly everyone, more interested in what was going on in Torrance's mind. I figured I might as well hold up a flag that said, "Scolari's here, talking to me on his cellular."

"I don't know, yet," Scolari continued, unaware of

my predicament. "But why would anyone kill Patricia unless she knew something? And what could she have known that didn't come in on a gurney?"

I wanted to ask him if she'd mentioned the seeds, if he knew about them, but I didn't dare. "Make it a small. Pepperoni and mushrooms."

"Who's there?" Scolari asked.

"Hold on." I stood just as Mathis and Zim came in through the secretary's office. "You guys interested in some pizza? I'm calling in a phone order."

"Can't," Reid said. "Gotta get back to the office."

"Sure," came Torrance's reply. Mathis shook his head. Zim said nothing.

"Small is fine," I said into the receiver.

"Get the reports. Read them. Let me know." He disconnected.

I hung up, sat back, my chair squeaking. Reid, Mathis, and Zim appeared oblivious to my call. Torrance was a different story. I didn't know whether he believed the pizza thing, but at the moment, I didn't care. I was more interested in the Hilliards' presence. "Mrs. Hilliard," I said, standing. "I wasn't expecting you so soon."

Her face was pale, more so than when I'd seen her earlier, and her red lipstick, the same shade as her dress, made her skin seem ethereal. It was her husband who spoke. "My wife wants it on record that we intend to cooperate with your investigation," he said, "and with Lieutenant Torrance. I understand that he needs to speak with my wife . . . about another matter. But I must ask if we can schedule for a later date. I have a board meeting in fifteen minutes. Several representatives flew in from Arkansas, and are due to leave in two hours. It will be extremely inconvenient to have to reschedule."

The matter of homicide wasn't exactly convenient either, but I kept my remark to myself.

I caught Dex's gaze, the almost imperceptible nod he gave to Evan Hilliard at his comment. I had to reevaluate the man. Gone was Dex's lab coat, in its place a charcoal suit. His stance on the surface casual, feet apart, hands clasped before him, reminded me more of a Secret Service agent guarding an ambassador. I wasn't sure that I was too far off the mark. Dex had a dangerous look about him, reminded me a bit of Zim, someone who thrived on intimidation. I thought of the homicide Dex left the department over, and decided it bore looking into.

"Dexter," Evan Hilliard continued, "has explained the importance of speed in such an investigation."

"It can wait," I said. Only because I needed time to prepare— and think about the latest developments concerning the Hilliards and Dex. Let Torrance think I was working on the Ice Man case. What I really wanted to know was what went on between Josie and the doctor, how Scolari was involved, and why he seemed to harbor such ambivalent feelings toward Dex after all these years. "Why don't we reschedule for, let's say, tomorrow?"

"Tomorrow's fine," Hilliard said, without consulting his wife. "Thank you, Inspector."

"You're welcome."

Torrance accompanied them out, but returned directly. I picked up the phone and called the morgue. "Mary," I said when she answered. "You wouldn't happen to have those reports ready for the last year?"

"I started it, but got sidetracked. Half-done, though. You need it soon?"

"As soon as you can get it to me."

"You got it."

Shipley wandered in, stood next to Zim and Mathis by the coffeepot. "Yo, Torrance, captain's looking for you."

Torrance glanced at his watch, then me. "You gonna be here a few?"

"Yeah, why?"

"I'm not thrilled about you being left alone, after what happened down in Property."

Reid sat on the edge of my desk. "I got a few minutes. I'll wait till you get back."

Torrance nodded, took off.

"Great," I said. "You might as well sign me up for the Federal Witness Protection plan. I've already got a head start on what it feels like."

"And you're gonna need it," Zim said, moving to my desk. "There's gonna be a lot of pissed off cops around here, lookin' for someone to blame."

"For what?" I asked.

"For your investigation being the cause of them gettin' laid off. Or didn't you figure out that's why the Hilliards showed up here? They delivered pink slips to every cop they got workin' security. On the advice from their attorneys. Conflict of interest."

"And I'm somehow responsible?"

Zim picked up a clasp envelope from my desk, Patricia's autopsy photos. "You are, according to the conversation I overheard between Dex Kermgard and Torrance."

I removed the envelope from his hands and placed it in my top drawer. "If you're looking for someone to blame, forget it. I had nothing to do with it."

"Except piss off one of the owners," Zim replied.

"Lay off, Zimwit," Shipley said. "It wasn't her fault."

"Like hell it wasn't."

Mathis opened the door. "Come on, Zim."

Zim hesitated. Mathis motioned for him to follow. Zim gave one last glance at my desk drawer and took off.

"Well, you might as well take advantage of the company," Reid said, rubbing my shoulders. "Damn, you're tense."

I closed my eyes, trying to forget what Zim said. Reid's massage felt wonderful. With fingers like that, maybe I would let him call me "babe." Then again, maybe not.

"I'll take one next," Shipley said.

"Forget it," Reid told him. The moment Torrance returned, Reid stopped his ministrations. "Gotta go," he said. "Pick you up around eight?"

"Eight?" I wondered how I'd get out of this dinner date with any grace. I'd think about that later.

Reid blew me a kiss, then strode from the room.

"Well, back to the grindstone," I said, hauling my thickening briefcase onto my desk and pulling some files from it. I didn't want Torrance to ask about my earlier phone call, the pizza ruse that I was sure he saw right through. Undoubtedly the only reason he said nothing was Reid's presence, and now Shipley's. Discretion was second nature to a man like Torrance.

He pulled the chair from Scolari's desk, sat. I flipped through some of the Slasher files, unable to focus on a thing with him hovering in silence beside me. Perhaps it was guilt over my call with Scolari, but I couldn't stand it any longer. Finally I put down my file and swiveled my chair around to face him. "You know, I'd probably get more work done if you weren't sitting there watching my every move. It's disconcerting, to say the least."

He folded his arms, leaned back in the chair. "I need to go to my office and take care of a few things."

"Feel free." I indicated the open door.

"But I wouldn't want to miss the pizza. I can wait ten minutes if you can."

Great. "If you insist."

"You ordered pizza?" Shipley asked. The extra twenty pounds around his middle gave evidence to his love of food.

"Sorry," I told him. "Didn't know you'd be here. I only ordered a small." Ever conscious of the clock ticking away, I turned back to my files, wondering what Torrance would do once he confirmed the pizza wasn't coming.

I'd cross that bridge when I came to it. I attempted to concentrate on my cases once more.

But I couldn't concentrate. I heard Torrance pick up the phone, pressing buttons, silence. Voice mail? The sound of him hitting another button, ACCESS, ERASE, or SAVE, I didn't know. Didn't care. After a few minutes of that, I recalled the message I was waiting for myself. The one from the lady at the Twin Palms.

I picked up my own phone. My hand shook, my pulse quickened. In my head, I heard Martin's last words before his death . . .

I punched in my access code. The nasal voice of Squeaky Kincaid came on, almost a relief, and I took a breath to steady my nerves. How long would it be before I erased the horror of hearing Martin's murder?

"Hey, this is, uh, Squeaky? I been tryin' to get hold of yer partner. Inspector Scolari? I got that info for him. He knows what I'm talkin' about. Can ya tell him I'm tryin' to get ahold of him?" Squeaky was a snitch who would sell his mother's soul for a fix of heroin.

Yeah, I'll get right on that. Like I have constant contact with the guy. I erased the message, since there was nothing valuable, no contact number. It did make me think, however. Then I accessed the next message.

"Hi, Inspector?" A woman's soft voice. "You talked to me this morning about Tanya in number eighteen? Well, I don't know if I should say anything, but the evening before she disappeared, I'm certain an officer came to see her. I've seen him here a couple of times before. The night that officer got shot? Down the hall? I saw him here then. He asked me questions. I remember his name, because it was Italian, like mine. Scolari." She disconnected without leaving her name or any number to contact her at.

Scolari? The phone asked me what to do with the message. I saved it, telling myself there were officers and inspectors crawling from the woodwork that fateful night. But what reason would he have to be there on the very day before the victim disappeared? And why no mention of her in his report?

"About that pizza," Torrance said, breaking into my thoughts. He stood.

Just then, Markowski strolled in, carrying a small pizza box from Giovanni's. "Delivery service," he said. "You can save the tip. I'll take a slice for my efforts, though it's probably cold by now. They wouldn't let the poor kid through the perimeter they got set up at every entrance. Lucky thing I happened to be coming in."

"I totally forgot about that when I ordered," I said, taking the box from him, surprised by Scolari's choice of pizza parlors. Giovanni's wasn't exactly cheap. Nor was I in the mood for pizza. Far from it, actually, but if Scolari had gone to the trouble of having it delivered, I could at least pretend to want it.

I opened the lid, the scent of pepperoni drifting up as

Rocky grabbed his slice. When he did, I noticed an edge of blue paper beneath the remainder of the pizza. A note from Scolari? I slammed the lid shut, tucked the box in my brief-case, and to Torrance said, "Okay. I got it. Let's go."

He gave me a strange look, but I ignored him, hop-ing the cheese and oil weren't oozing from the box into my briefcase. "Go where?"

"Your office. You said you needed to take care of a few things." The hook.

His hesitation was palpable. If he insisted on staying here to eat, I'd never get the note out undetected, not in an office filled with a half dozen others present.

I threw the line. "It's Giovanni's." And now the sinker. "We'll never get a slice if we eat it in here."

"After you." On the way to his office, he said, "I'll be honest with you, Gillespie. I didn't think you'd ordered it."

"Who'd you think I was on the phone with?" I asked, attempting to sound innocent, certain I'd failed miserably.

"Scolari," he responded, unlocking his office door. "You can use Mathis's desk."

I set out my pizza box, pulled a dollar from my pocket, waved the bill. "You trust me enough to get a Coke?" There was a machine down the hall. I fully expected him to play the gentleman. He didn't disappoint me.

"We've got a fridge in the back. I'll get you one."

As he headed to the rear of the office, I took a bite, for authenticity's sake. The cheese tasted a bit stale, but the pepperoni covered it. Not up to Giovanni's usual standards, but what the heck, it was free.

I took a second bite, pulled the slip of now greasy paper from beneath the slice.

My throat constricted at the two words. I dropped

the note. Spit out what I could of the pizza. Beige and yellow mush flew onto the box. Most had disintegrated in my mouth.

Your next

The misspelled word taunted me.

Torrance returned. Took one look at my face and rushed over. "What is it?"

I shoved the note his way. I was afraid to swallow. Grabbed the can from him, popped it open. I tilted it and swished the sugary liquid in my mouth.

Torrance grabbed an empty coffee cup from Mathis's desk. Held it to my mouth.

The liquid spewed out, very unladylike. Not that either of us noticed. Instead, our gazes met at the very same time. "Markowski," we said in unison.

We ran from the room, took the stairs, down the hall to Homicide, pushed past a couple of uniformed officers walking the opposite direction. Bursting through the door almost shoulder to shoulder, we looked around for Rocky. Shipley sat at his desk, the phone to his ear. He glanced at us, covered the mouthpiece. "Forget something?"

"Where's Markowski?" I asked.

"Men's room. Dropped his pizza, went for some paper towels to clean it up."

He nodded at the floor by Markowski's desk. The pizza lay there, face-down on the blue-gray carpet. A perfect triangle, minus a bit of cheese, and pepperoni hanging off to one side.

We breathed a sigh of relief.

"You're going to the hospital, the pizza's going to the lab," Torrance said, using paper from the printer to scoop up the slice. "Tell Markowski to scrub his hands good, then put some gloves on before he wipes that up. And save the paper towels. Have him meet me in my office."

"Yes, sir," Shipley said, eyeing me, then the pizza.

Torrance carried the pizza in its paper sling, then took my arm. "Let's go."

I allowed him to lead me from the room, my thoughts in a jumble. If there was something in that pizza, who put it there? My mind whispered Scolari, but I shot down that thought. He wouldn't do that to me. Couldn't.

But someone had put that note in there. If not Scolari, who?

Zim. A bluff. The pizza was fine. He was trying to scare me. Nothing more.

While I conjured up any number of poisons that might be absorbed into my tongue the short time the pizza was in my mouth, Torrance dropped Rocky's slice into the box, shut the lid, bagged the note, placing both in a large file box that he emptied for the purpose.

"I don't trust anyone else to take this. We'll drop it off at the lab on our way to the hospital. If something turns up, they can let the hospital know."

"I'm fine," I said, but the truth was, I wasn't sure. I knew the power of suggestion. As we walked, passing the heavily armed officers who guarded the exit, and after we dropped the pizza off at the lab that adjoined the morgue, my stomach reacted by producing an overload of acid. My heart beat sharp, fast. My throat burned, my eyes watered. By the time we made it to his car, I corrected my earlier assessment. "I'm a mess."

"What's wrong?" He set the file box on the ground, took me by my shoulders, his dark eyes searching mine. "I'll call an ambulance."

"No. It's psychosomatic, I'm sure. We better go."

He held me for a second longer, as though assessing the reliability of my statement. At least, that's what I thought. But for some reason, I had the strange impulse to pull myself against him, let him wrap his arms around me, have a good cry. The moment passed, but the thought didn't die, and I allowed him to open the car door for me, telling myself that if Reid were here, I'd feel the same way. I was merely looking for a good shoulder to lean on. Nothing more.

The drive to the hospital seemed to take forever. I watched the side mirror as we turned onto the freeway. A cream-colored car made the same turn. After that it was a green car. "We're being followed." I pulled my gun from my holster.

Torrance checked the rearview mirror. He picked up the phone and spoke into it. I paid little attention to what he said. The green car turned off, but another one took its place. Point, counterpoint.

"Take this exit," I said. "I don't want them to follow us." When Torrance didn't, I grew suspicious. I thought of all the coincidences in the case, how he was on top of every one of them. "The way I see it, only a few people overheard me order that pizza. You, Mathis, Shipley, Zim. And Bettencourt." Torrance's very presence put him at the top of my list. My heart started triple time. My palms started sweating. I was locked in the car with this man, his vehicle moving at a speed too high for me to jump.

"I was with you the entire time," he said in that implacable voice of his. It only made me suspect him more. My tongue felt dry, like I'd been in the desert for days. "And so were the others."

"You left. And so did they. Everyone except Shipley. Someone tried to poison me."

"Put down the gun, Gillespie."

I looked at the weapon I held. It seemed so foreign. I moved it from my right to my left hand. I had to jump the first chance. "I don't think I will."

We pulled off the freeway. I found the handle. Opened my door. He grabbed me. Twisted, forcing my grip loose. My gun fell to the floorboard. My gaze followed it, assessed the distance.

Remain calm. Get the gun.

He drove with one hand on the wheel, like a maniac, his other wrapped like steel around my wrist. Finally, wheels screeching, he stopped at the back of a building.

Double doors slid open. Two men strode out.

Run.

But I couldn't move. They forced me from the car.

"Why?" I screamed.

Torrance never answered. Just watched from the car as they dragged me away.

A gurney stood just inside the doors. They lifted me onto it while another man strapped me. I felt as if I were sinking in white, the gurney melting around me, paralyzing me. He was having me committed so I couldn't testify.

Nurses hovered over me as the ceiling swam by. Something tearing, then something tight around my arms. I felt cold and wet on my chest, saw them talking, all in white, white and more white. Then shattering pain in my temple, the smell of blood.

Voices around me faded as though I were hearing them from a tunnel. Or entering one, not unlike falling asleep, aware of bits of conversation at a distance. Not really a part of it.

I'd trusted him.

The next thing I knew, I stood over a hospital bed. My brother's. Deathly white. This was how he went. I tried to reach him. And then my father took his place. The machines at work, trying to keep him alive, doctors and nurses working quickly, efficiently. "Heart rate is slowing." *Blip, blip, blip-lip-lip.* "Slowing." Just no tone. I didn't want to hear the tone.

Then I saw Torrance, standing at the head, his hand reaching out. What is he doing here in my father's room? Where's Scolari?

"It's okay," I felt Torrance say through rippling white, his voice turning into a rainbow of color.

When I awoke, I was alone. Enveloped between white walls, white acoustic ceiling, white fluorescent lights. I closed my eyes. I wanted to die.

"Gillespie?"

A voice. Or was I dreaming? I opened my eyes, saw darkness in one corner. Like a bull. Solid, dependable. Ferdinand, the gentle bull in a book my father read to Sean and me. Flowers. He didn't want to fight like the other bulls. He wanted to sit, smell the flowers. No one ever sits to smell the flowers anymore.

The bull moved. Came closer. Taurus. As my vision focused, the darkness took the form of a man. Not Taurus. Torrance.

"Torrance?" My voice sounded raspy, not my own.

"You're awake."

"What happened?"

A white-coated doctor entered, picked up my chart, came over and checked the monitors behind my bed.

"How are we feeling this morning?"

"Morning?"

He smiled and went about his duties with the efficiency of someone who was used to confused patients. I looked at Torrance. Noticed the dark circles beneath his eyes. "How long have I been in here?"

"Since yesterday," he said.

I tried to sit, panicked momentarily that I was paralyzed.

"Can we loosen the straps now?" Torrance asked.

The doctor checked the chart before answering. "It's been over twelve hours. I don't see why not."

He undid the straps and raised the bed for me. "So far, everything looks good, but I think we'll keep you one more night at the minimum, for observation. That's quite a concussion you have."

"Concussion?"

"You tried to run off. Fell. Six stitches," he said, pointing to his own left temple. He took a penlight, shined it into first one and then my other eye. "You'll be dizzy. For the next day or two, I don't want you walking around."

Fragments of my experience floated about in my conscious mind while I tried to piece it all together. I kept thinking mushrooms—who didn't like mushrooms? Everything around me started to move. "Run off?"

"The pizza," Torrance said. "It was drugged."

The pizza. The pizza that Sam sent. The drug in the pizza that Sam sent.

Great. Someone had tried to kill me, and here I was composing nursery rhymes. Exhaustion overtook me. "Tell me later," I said, closing my eyes. "The paint on the walls is starting to melt."

The doctor held my wrist, checked my pulse. "You may still have quite a headache, but by tomorrow, I suspect you won't even know you were under the influence."

No, but Torrance would, and the thought bothered me more than I cared to admit.

10

According to the doctor, I was lucky. Had I not spit out the drug-laden pizza, or rinsed my mouth, I might have OD'd. Apparently, enough had been absorbed through the membranes of my mouth to send me into the state of psychotic paranoia that Torrance now described to me. When I learned how I drew my weapon and tried to jump from the car, I felt sick. My life was spinning out of control. And it wasn't just the drug-laden pizza. I'd lost it at the Twin Palms— and almost shot an innocent woman. I was a psychological mess, even without the drugs in my system.

In that moment, I thought I understood how some cops ended up eating their guns. Had Scolari reached that point, taken out his wife instead? Could he have snapped? Killed the property clerks?

The questions swirled in my head like the hospital walls yesterday when Torrance brought me here. Somehow I had to regain control, recover what I'd lost. I wondered if I ever could.

Torrance watched me carefully, as though checking for signs of flashbacks. As it was, I couldn't be sure that what I was feeling wasn't a part of that process. I wasn't normal. I hated that he had seen me like that, even if my psychosis was drug induced. Still, I wondered how much of it was the drug, and not me. These past few days, the murders, everything had taken their toll, whittling away at my nerve, my resolve, to a point where I didn't know if I could trust myself or even my own instincts anymore.

Again the Twin Palms came to mind, and I thought of the way I drew down on that woman. I felt I was balancing precariously, wondered if, were I ever faced with a real shoot–don't shoot situation, would I make the right decision?

Part of me wanted to tell Torrance about the Twin Palms, gain a modicum of reassurance that what had occurred was normal, not a sign that I was losing it. But I couldn't bring myself to tell him. Not without crying. No way would I ever let Torrance see me do that. It would be the ultimate sign of my weakness, that I'd completely lost control, that no way was I fit to be in Homicide.

"Something on your mind, Inspector?"

I had the distinct impression that he could see into my head, discern my thoughts. Ridiculous, of course, but I couldn't hold his gaze and looked away. I tried to tell myself it was the drug, but shame coursed through me, as though my actions yesterday were my fault. In a way, they were. I'd led everyone down this path.

"I'm sorry," I said, for lack of anything better to say. What could I have said in the face of all I'd done?

"I'm leaving what happened in the car yesterday out of the report."

Relief flooded through me. Still, I was curious. "Why?"

"I don't think it's relevant. You wouldn't have done it otherwise. What is relevant is how that pizza came to be."

The heart monitor bleeped faster. I wanted to yank the offending wires from my chest. As it was, a nurse walked in right then and removed them. "I don't know that part."

"Explain," he said after the nurse left.

I really didn't want to. Because now I had to admit to him that I had been speaking to Scolari. And that Scolari could possibly be the one who sent it. Which meant I also had to admit that he was the most viable suspect. "You were right when—"

A pager went off and it took me a moment to realize it was mine. It was hooked to my fanny pack, slung over the chair Torrance had occupied during my hospital stay. He handed it to me, and I was half-surprised that he didn't read it first. After what happened yesterday, I certainly would have.

I pressed the display. "It's a Berkeley prefix," I said. "But I don't recognize the number."

"You didn't order the pizza, did you."

I noticed he wasn't asking, and shook my head, feeling my brain spin as if I were recovering from a hangover, and feeling as guilty as if I'd laced the pizza myself. I thought about what would've happened had Rocky Markowski eaten that slice he'd dropped. He didn't have the benefit of seeing the note. He probably wouldn't have spit it out.

He would have died.

I palmed the pager. I'd return the call later. "I was talking to Scolari on the phone. But he wouldn't have done that."

Torrance's gaze darkened with an anger I'd never seen before. Not knowing if it was directed at me, I wanted to shrink from it, but I didn't look away. I deserved his censure.

"What concerns me," he said, "is how to do my job

and protect you at the same time. If I were to turn in a full report, you'd be lucky not to be suspended, much less terminated."

Protect me? "Why don't you turn in the report?"

"Because if you're suspended—which you would be—you'd have to surrender your weapon. My conscience won't allow that."

There were those in the department who would debate him even having a conscience. "If I get killed, you mean."

"Other reasons as well," he added.

"Like what?" I wanted to sleep, but what I wanted more was to hear his point of view on this matter. Perhaps I hoped he'd absolve me of guilt.

"You seem to have some as yet unknown connection or link. If you're off the force, you're off the case. If you're off the case, it'll take me that much longer to discover why someone wants you dead."

His reasons were all professional, and I found myself slightly disappointed. "You're using me." I ignored the fact I'd done the same with Reid in the office yesterday when I'd wanted to return Scolari's page.

He folded his arms across his chest, leaned against the wall, once more the emotionless man I'd come to know.

"I take back all the nice things I was thinking about you just seconds ago," I said.

"We were talking about the pizza."

"I was discussing my pager." The pizza was the last thing I wanted to talk about.

"I'm ordering you to tell me."

"Meaning what?" I asked, waiting for him to read me

my Miranda rights. In the paramilitary world of law enforcement, I could be ordered to give a statement. If I refused, I'd be guilty of insubordination. I could be fired. I could also be fired as a result of the statement I gave. But even if I invoked my Miranda rights by refusing to give a statement, under California's Lybarger decision I would have to tell him. What he couldn't do was use my statement against me in a criminal court of law. Unless, of course, he read me my rights. Then I knew I'd be in big trouble. I waited for him to start with "You have the right to remain silent . . ."

"Help me find the answers," Torrance said instead. "About the pizza."

I breathed a sigh of relief, deciding right then that the truth was probably the best defense. Torrance knew the ropes better than I did. If he wasn't reading me my rights, he wasn't interested in hanging me out to dry. "Scolari paged me when we were at coffee after the morgue incident. Back at the office after I sent Reid out to discuss dinner with you, I called the number Scolari left."

"Dinner with Bettencourt was a ruse?"

Not sure if it would make him angrier if I told him it was, I ignored the question, continued on with my story. "Scolari suggested I look at his wife's old autopsies. He didn't know I'd already ordered them. When I saw Reid open the door and the two of you looking at me, I came up with the pizza idea. Scolari never mentioned anything about ordering it. I was as surprised as you were when it came. I figured that'd be the end of it."

"Apparently it wasn't."

"Apparently not, but I do know this. Scolari never goes to Giovanni's for his pizza." I didn't mention that I always ordered from Giovanni's, and that Scolari knew that. Instead I said, "He's a Domino's man through and through."

"The last of the big spenders."

Torrance and I both glanced at the door upon hearing Sergeant Mathis's voice. Mathis leaned into the room, knocking on the door frame. "Sorry to eavesdrop. Mind if I come in?" he asked.

I smiled, and Torrance stood aside. "How's it going?"

"Same. Linda Perkins is out at Gillespie's place, giving me a break. Heard about what happened, so I thought I'd come by." Mathis pulled a small bouquet of mixed flowers from behind him. "For you," he said, handing them to me. "And your apartment's still there, in one piece as far as I can tell through the layer of beer cans from that party we threw last night. Oh, yeah. The dinner you requested? It got cold."

"Very funny. And thanks for the flowers," I said, lifting them to my nose, but smelling little.

"Least I can do. Let's see," he pulled out a paper, read the note. "Your landlord stopped by. Said he and his wife are going to Ohio. They want you to feed Dinky. Pick up the papers. Here's the number where they'll be at." He handed me the note.

"Thanks," I said, and placed it on the bedside table.

"And your aunt called," Mathis said. "I told her you were here. She's planning on visiting you this afternoon, after she picks up your nephew from school. Hope you don't mind?"

"No." Though I did worry about her worrying about me.

Mathis didn't stay long, but before he left he motioned to Torrance that he wanted to speak to him privately, and the two stepped outside. The door stayed open, Torrance never leaving my sight or turning his back to me. If that wasn't a clue that he was taking this body-guard business seriously, then the two uniformed officers standing on either side just outside my hospital door were.

I sat up and swung my feet over the side, intending on using the rest room while he was occupied. I stood, pleased to see my knees didn't buckle. My head started spinning, though, and I felt nauseated. It eventually passed. Torrance watched my every step, as though I might make a mad dash for it in a hospital gown that I had to hold shut in the back. I gave him as sarcastic a smile as I could muster, while grasping said hospital gown closed with an, "Excuse me, won't you?"

I guessed that he'd already determined there were no escape routes out the bathroom, or even out the window, which from what I surmised was several floors up. I shut the bathroom door, then leaned against it, grateful for the moment of privacy it yielded me.

And then I glanced in the mirror. I wanted to groan. It was the only appropriate sound for what stared back at me. My face was pale, my eyes puffy. Half of my hair was plastered to one side of my head, the other half stuck out, and my bangs reminded me of Medusa's snakes. A purple bruise on my right temple accentuated the six neat and very small stitches. All that was needed to complete the effect was a safety pin through my cheek, though I doubted it would help. I'd seen punk rockers at slam con-certs looking better. I splashed water on my face, then my hair, only to discover I had to pat my head dry with paper towels. I wanted a shower, but figured I'd have to forgo that for a later time, and was grateful I had a room with a toilet in it.

Feeling a little better, and trying not to reflect on the number of people who may have seen me in this condition, I wandered back to my bed. I saw that Torrance had closed the door. Even so, I clutched my gown about me in case someone should have the indecency to enter before I was ready. After a couple of minutes, someone knocked. Torrance, I discovered. Mathis was leaving, and he wanted to ask if there was anything that I needed done at my apartment. I told him to feed the cat.

After Mathis's departure, I had a steady stream of visitors. Shipley and Markowski showed up with a get well card and stayed a few minutes. My soul ached at the thought of Markowski being exposed to that pizza, and if truth be told, I was glad when he left. Reid and my aunt wandered in after them. Reid's bouquet of dark red roses dwarfed the flowers that Mathis had brought, and I was glad Mathis wasn't there to see. In the short time I'd been around him, I was beginning to notice he was the sensitive type.

My aunt scuttled about the room, straightening out my clothes, then smoothing my bed sheets before sitting beside me. "Kevin wanted to come, but he has a math test to study for. Oh, and I bought you some makeup, dear. Every one of my friends I know who's been in the hospital says if they had their choice between having good underwear when going in and having makeup with them when going out, they'd pick the makeup every time."

I grimaced inwardly at the amused expression on Torrance's face as he stood behind my aunt, listening.

Reid said, "Since we missed dinner last night, I thought we could try again."

"I'd like that," I said, more to be polite than anything else. I was too tired to think.

Torrance cleared his throat, his expression now serious. "She has a concussion. The doctor doesn't want her going out on her own. And considering what happened, I agree."

"Going out with me is not alone," Reid said. Had I been more energetic, I might have protested. I didn't want anyone telling me what I could and couldn't do. But then it occurred to me that Torrance's objections might be the silver lining I was looking for. I really didn't want to go out with Reid anyway.

"A concussion?" my aunt asked Torrance. "I thought you told me she had food poisoning."

"She fell," Torrance said. "An accident."

"Oh, you poor dear," my aunt said, oblivious to the undertones. "I think the lieutenant is right, you shouldn't go out alone. We can make it a foursome. You can make up for the dinner you promised me in that lounge message I received on my answering machine."

I couldn't help but glance at Torrance this time, at the dirt my aunt added to the pizza mess. His dark brows raised a fraction, undoubtedly to let me know that he had hit redial on his cell phone and found out that my call to her was also false. One more strike against me—and Scolari, I thought—closing my eyes against the weight and pain of it all.

"Why don't we discuss dinner outside," Torrance said.

"Yes. We've tired her," my aunt said. I felt her hand grasp mine, cool and soft to the touch, and I remembered she used to do the same when I was a child, on nights when my father was working swing and midnights. I longed to hear her humming "Claire de Lune." I longed for Sean, for my father, for my lost youth. For that simpler time when my biggest worry was that I had to be in bed by eight.

Reid kissed me on the cheek, dispelling the thought, and my aunt kissed me on my forehead as always, but I didn't open my eyes. They said their good-byes to Torrance, apparently thinking I'd fallen asleep, and soon I heard their footsteps fade from the room. Torrance followed them, and outside my door they made dinner plans for the following night. Torrance returned a few minutes later.

"Personally," I heard him say, "I'd pick the clean underwear."

I looked at him. He had a slight smile on his face, a definite sparkle in his eye. We were alone, and the door was closed. "Since I've seen myself in the mirror, and the doctors, nurses, and everyone else in Emergency yesterday have already seen my underwear, I'm going with the makeup."

"Silk."

"I beg your pardon?"

"I would have pictured you for the silk type. Not cotton."

"Great. You were there, too." I was beyond embarrassment. After the pizza debacle, I didn't think I could sink any lower.

"Actually," he said, "the nurse brought your things in, folded up. I missed that part."

"Thank God for small miracles."

He smiled. A full-blown smile. If we weren't talking about underwear, I might have been moved. As it was, my pager went off again, saving me from the topic of the year. It was that Berkeley number again, and I realized it was just what I needed. To be busy doing something else besides lying here and thinking about my troubles. And silk underwear.

I looked around for a telephone, but didn't see one. "I need to make a call."

"We had the phone removed."

"Why?"

For the millisecond it took him to answer, I imagined they'd removed it because I was a prisoner.

"The ringing disturbed you."

His expression told me there was more, but before I could ask him what he meant, there was a sharp rap on the door, and the nurse bustled in. She picked up my chart. An orderly wheeled a cart past my door, and with it came the sound of vials rattling against each other.

"May I have a telephone?" I asked her as she checked my blood pressure. Perhaps it was the remnants of the drug, but I felt my heart quicken while I waited for her response.

"Your chart says no phone."

Nurse Nightingale from Hell. She wrote down the results on that very chart, and I wanted to rip it from her, read it myself.

"Why not?" I asked, recognizing that what I was feeling was a sense of panic. Why wouldn't anyone let me have a phone? *Was* I a prisoner?

"Well . . ." she began, her gaze catching Torrance's. That little exchange gave me the impression she was waiting for some response or signal from him on what to divulge, but his expression remained as impassive as ever. "You had a bad reaction to it," she finally said. "I'm sure it was because of the drug you ingested—"

"Not intentionally," I felt it necessary to add.

She went right on as though the mere fact was of no

concern to her. "But when the phone rang, well, we had to restrain you. You were a little . . . out of control."

My cheeks and ears heated up, and Torrance looked away as though uncomfortable with my sudden embarrassment.

I wanted to pull the sheet over my head, but the nurse was efficiently shoving a thermometer in my mouth. I was almost grateful, since her action hid the prick of tears in my eyes. I admit now that what I felt was my own sense of failure at my loss of control exposed to all, especially Torrance. As an IA investigator, he was the eyes and ears of the department. I knew he said he wouldn't talk about the drive to the hospital, but what about what he'd seen in the emergency room? Would he reveal what he'd witnessed? At the moment, I didn't have the courage to ask. I barely had time to compose myself before the thermometer beeped. The nurse removed it, and recorded the temperature on my chart.

I closed my eyes, thinking that the walls of my prison were of my own making, constructed by my inadequacies as an investigator. Had I merely been up-front with Torrance, I doubted I would have eaten the pizza. Hell, I would never have pretended to order it. How had everything snowballed to this point?

What must he think of me? I didn't want to ask. But as I lay there, my eyes still closed, I heard him say softly to the retreating nurse, "We would like a phone in here, now."

"I'm sorry, Lieutenant, but the chart—"

"To hell with the chart." His voice, low, even, rang with an authority I knew he possessed but had never heard until now. Surprised, I looked to see him push past the nurse and the two uniformed officers outside my door. A minute later he returned with a phone, which he plugged in. When he rose, he handed it to me.

"Thanks," I said, meeting his gaze, pleased and surprised by his actions.

"You're welcome," he responded quietly.

I don't know why, but when I saw him give me a glimmer of a smile, I wanted to cry all over again. He couldn't take away my pain, fight my demons, but he could do this one small thing. For now, it was enough.

The number on my pager turned out to be Professor Rocklin of UC Berkeley. "I just wanted to give you a progress report," he said. "Hold on a sec."

"Sure," I told him as I clutched the phone. Torrance found the remote control to the TV and started flicking through the channels. Beth Skyler's face filled the screen. "Pharmaceutical giant Montgard, MPR, of Arkansas announces a merger possibility with Hilliard Pharmaceutical . . ." I had a strange sense of déjà vu, and it had nothing to do with her announcement. It was her voice. Before I could pinpoint it, the professor spoke again.

"I've got the report here."

Skyler's voice droned on, ". . . and the search continues for the suspect in the Hall of Justice murders. News at five on Two." Before I had a chance to place why her voice got to me, Torrance switched channels.

"You there?" Professor Rocklin asked.

"Yes," I said, drawing my attention back to the matter at hand.

"Definitely pokeweed."

"You're sure?"

"Positive."

"Thanks." I hung up.

"Anything?" Torrance asked, looking away from his hockey game.

"I don't get it. Why on earth would a dead guy be hiding seven pokeweed seeds in his ring?"

11

Monday morning, while Torrance informed the hospital billing department where to send the papers for worker's comp, I stood beneath a hot spray, hoping that a shower would wash away some of the residue of the past few days. It did little to restore my spirits, but at least my hair was clean and no longer standing on end. The bruise on my temple was another matter, as were the doctor's instructions, "No driving, no exerting yourself, no going up or down stairs by yourself . . ." etc., etc., etc. Had my head not started spinning when I got out of bed, I might have disregarded everything he said. And until he released me, I was on light duty. Desk job. I'd find a way around it, with or without Torrance.

Wrapped in a towel and designer hospital gown, I stepped from the hallway shower past an orderly who politely pretended not to notice, and into my hospital room to find my clothes wrapped neatly in a package from the laundry. I'd completely forgotten about them, but apparently Torrance hadn't. He walked in at that precise moment.

"Thanks," I said, holding up the package. "I'm assuming it was you who sent them out to be washed?"

"Don't have time to get anything clean from your apartment. We need to head straight back to the Hall this morning. I've got a couple interviews I couldn't reschedule."

"Well, thanks," I said.

"Don't mention it."

We stood there looking at each other, and I smiled, waiting for him to leave. I wanted to dress. Didn't think I needed a bodyguard to do it. "The door?" I said, pointing.

He got the hint, and exited.

I dressed, buckled my fannypack around my waist, and realized my gun wasn't in it.

Torrance was waiting down the hall.

"Where's my weapon?" I asked, ignoring the nurses who were insisting I leave in a wheelchair. I wasn't the least bit dizzy.

"In the trunk of my car."

He guided me toward the elevator.

"What now?"

"Now we get down to investigating this mess."

At the car, he returned my weapon. Our gazes met briefly, and I wondered if he had any doubts about letting me carry it. If so, he kept his thoughts to himself.

An hour later we were at the Hall, bagels and fresh coffee in hand. Torrance stationed me at Mathis's desk, where he could watch me through his office window. Mathis was still guarding my apartment, waiting for Scolari to show. I thought about telling them they could save the overtime—Scolari wasn't stupid—but after the pizza fiasco, I didn't really want to bring up his name.

Torrance made a few calls from his office, watching me like a hawk through the glass, and I again had that feeling of being a prisoner. I wasn't altogether wrong, because when I got up to toss my empty coffee cup in the trash, Torrance was out of his chair, through his office door, the phone cord stretched taut.

"Where're you going? You're not dizzy are you?" he asked, covering the mouthpiece with his hand. He eyed the exit as though judging the distance between it and me, and whether or not he could get there before I crashed to the floor should I decide to flee.

I lobbed my coffee cup into the trash, annoyed that my life had come to this. "Just doing my part to keep the environment clean." I returned to my chair, pulled out a desk drawer, and propped up my feet to show my boredom.

Finally he hung up, then went to his file cabinet and opened the top drawer.

I was anxious to get out of the office, but felt funny having to ask him how much longer. I didn't need a chauffeur, but figured he'd be taking this light duty stuff as seriously as the doctor. "Am I getting OT for this?"

He raised his brows.

"No offense," I said, "but I can't go anywhere, or do anything without you. What do you expect me to accomplish?"

"What do you need?" he asked without glancing up.

"My stuff."

He closed the file drawer and faced me. "And then you'll be happy?"

"Infinitely."

"After you," he said, waving his hand toward the door.

Homicide was deserted. On my desk was a large box. There must have been dozens of photocopies stacked inside. I picked up the top sheet.

"What is it?" he asked.

"It's from the Coroner's office. I guess it's those autopsy reports that I ordered from Dr. Mead-Scolari's files."

Torrance picked up the box. "Apparently you'll have something to occupy your time now."

"I guess so," I said, sorting through the files on my desk, looking for the clasp envelope containing Doctor Mead-Scolari's autopsy. I opened the top drawer, certain that's where I'd shoved it, but it wasn't there. I went through all my other drawers. Nor was it in my briefcase. "I can't find the doctor's autopsy."

"I have another copy. You can look over that one."

I grabbed my briefcase, then followed him back to his office. "How long are we going to play ball and chain?"

"You anxious to start working with Zimmerman?"

He had me there. "Not exactly."

"Then consider this a temporary reprieve until you're off light duty."

"How temporary?"

Torrance hefted the box to one arm, held his office door open, allowing me to step through. His phone was ringing on his desk. "I told Andrews I wanted you assigned to me for the next couple of days. He agreed."

"Which makes you my boss."

His eyes fairly sparkled as he dropped the box onto Mathis's desk, then answered his phone.

"I don't find it the least bit amusing," I said. He opened a case file on his desk while he spoke softly into the phone. If he heard me, I had no idea. I followed his example, found myself grateful for the mundane chore of reviewing the doctor's old autopsies. But after a half hour, I changed my mind. Perhaps reviewing the autopsies was too mundane. I'd seen four stabbings in a row. As I picked

up the fifth, a thirty-year-old white female, I thought
about the pizza, and how if not for nearly overdosing
myself, I'd be able to get up and walk away without Torrance acting like an overzealous Secret Service agent.

Who had placed the drug on the pizza? And where?
Suddenly I wondered if anyone had contacted Giovanni's
to see who ordered it. Absently I turned to the next page
on the autopsy report, forgetting why I was reviewing the
thing at all. From the corner of my eye, I saw Torrance
sitting in his glass-enclosed office, conducting his interview with one of the property clerks, who had walked in
right after her coworkers were murdered. The whole
time, Torrance kept close watch over me.

I closed my eyes, blocking him out. Who had
ordered the pizza? Torrance was there, but I couldn't see
him as the enemy. If he was, I was in serious trouble. No,
it had to be someone else, and I reviewed the list of possible suspects in my mind.

Shipley had been sitting across from me that afternoon. He certainly heard my half of the conversation with
Scolari. Reid was there with the Hilliards, who were talking to Torrance, and Reid more than anyone knew I liked
Giovanni's. And I didn't want to forget Markowski, who
brought the pizza in. But he had taken a slice—and would
have eaten it had he not dropped it. Or would he have? I
didn't want to think about that possibility. There was
Zimmerman, of course. The man made my skin crawl,
but that wasn't enough to convict him. Still, Zim had
motive and opportunity. And he was making it clear
something was up by his constant avoidance of working
with me. Not that I was anxious.

I'd seen him lose his temper, and wondered if he had
it in him to shoot someone in a fit of rage. Could he have

spiked the pizza? Working in Property, he certainly had access to any number of drugs.

I had to find out.

I broke the tip of my pencil. I hadn't taken two steps in the direction of the sharpener when Torrance got up, stood in his doorway, and asked, "Something wrong?"

"Just sharpening my pencil." I held it up.

He waited there while I inserted it into the machine. It whirred, and the scent of wood and graphite drifted up. "You're not feeling dizzy?"

"No." I pulled it out, shoved it in again. "Anyone check on who ordered that pizza from Giovanni's yet?"

The sharpener whined. Jerking out the pencil, I touched the tip to my finger.

When he failed to answer, I met his gaze, surprised to see him look away.

"I'd intended to do that once we got back," he finally said.

I couldn't believe it. Had he actually forgotten? Or was there something more? I blew on the pencil point, not wanting to give away just how much my thoughts were churning. I made no reply. I couldn't find my voice.

Torrance returned to his office and his interview, and I returned to my seat at Mathis's desk. I started writing notes on the last Coroner's case I'd read. "No unusual findings." I underlined it twice, then picked up the next report, which dropped from my shaking hand. As I watched the report float to the floor, I realized I was angry.

Even frightened.

I wanted to know why he hadn't checked with Giovanni's. A weekend had gone by, and it bothered me that he'd let something like that slip past. In the back of my mind was the vague memory of my ride to the hospital, and my suspicion that Torrance had heard me "order" my pizza.

What an elaborate ruse to poison me, then faithfully stand guard over my hospital bed. Was that why I was obsessed with this need to get to Giovanni's and discover who had placed the order? Was I worried that it was Torrance who didn't want me to find out?

Ridiculous. The man had no motive.

But there were plenty of others who did, and I knew what I needed to do. I was going to Giovanni's, and I wasn't about to wait for Torrance or anyone else.

I exited, hearing Torrance's "damn it" echoing after me as I darted around the corner and down the hall, only to stop short when I saw Zim deep in conversation with my ex. They stood outside the men's room. Reid had his hand on the door as though about to enter, or leave. I'd always been under the impression that Reid and Zim disliked each other, and I couldn't help wonder what the two seemed to find of common interest on such a chance meeting.

Reid looked up and saw me. "Kate? Wait up."

I pretended not to hear, continued on, but he caught up with me as Zim took off down the hallway and around the corner.

"I've been looking for you," he said.

Something in his expression set my senses on alert. The hallway was entirely too quiet, and I didn't want to be here alone with him. Turning on my heel, I started back toward IA.

He followed, grabbed my arm, turned me toward him. "Why won't you stop and talk to me?"

"Let go of my arm, Reid."

"Not until I get some answers."

"What do you want? A blow-by-blow account since I came home from the hospital? I'm busy. We're no longer married." I yanked my arm from his grasp and entered IA. Torrance wasn't in his office. He must have gone off in the opposite direction. "What were you and Zim talking about?"

Reid hesitated, glanced at Torrance's vacated desk. "An old homicide case. Nothing important."

Suddenly the door flew open. Torrance stormed in. "Leave," he told Bettencourt.

Whatever protest Reid had been about to give faded at the sight of Torrance's deadly calm. "I'll call you later, Kate," he said, never looking at me once.

I wasn't sure what Torrance had witnessed in the hallway. A muscle in his jaw ticked, his dark eyes unreadable.

I sat, took a sudden interest in the nap of the gray carpet, feeling as guilty as a child caught stealing. Finally I lifted my gaze to Torrance's, waiting for his lecture. What I saw surprised me, and I thought perhaps I was mistaken.

A man like Torrance didn't wear his emotions on his face, allowing others to be privy, but I could have sworn what I saw there was disappointment—no, fear.

"Ignoring the fact that we have two dead officers, and you have a concussion, what the doctor said made no sense to you?"

"I'm fine."

He closed the distance between us. He leaned down and gripped the wooden arms of my chair, his face mere inches from mine. His dark eyes burned into me. My pulse thudded several times while I waited for him to speak. It took every effort on my part not to back away. Not that I had anywhere to go. I stared into my lap.

"Where did you think you were going?"

"Out."

"Right now, you can be partnered with me, or with Zimmerman. If you're with me, you stay with me. No exceptions."

"Understood."

When I gathered the courage to look him in the eye, his gaze dropped to my mouth. I could feel his breath on my lips, he was so close. The seconds ticked by.

"If you try that again," he said, his voice deceptively soft, "I'll handcuff you to the goddamn chair." Then he walked past me into his office.

I sat there for a good five minutes, not doubting for a second that given the slightest provocation, Torrance would do exactly as he had threatened. I thought about the way he looked at my mouth. "Definitely not gay," I quipped to the empty room.

When I dared glance into his office, I wondered if I'd lost the last of my good sense by taking off. I wanted to discuss Zim's and Reid's meeting. Wasn't sure how to bring it up, since it fell into the realm of two-guys-talking-about-nothing-in-particular, which meant I was reading something into nothing.

"Let's go," Torrance said from his doorway. His voice, while understandably terse, held none of his earlier anger.

"Go where?" I asked, surprised he was still speaking to me.

"Giovanni's."

So much for my earlier speculation that he didn't want me to find out who had ordered the pizza.

The restaurant was crowded with the usual lunch rush as the manager led us into his cramped office that doubled as a storeroom for canned goods.

"I could pull up the computer tapes for that day. See when a small pepperoni was ordered, and who was working delivery," he told us.

"How long will that take?" I asked.

"Depends on the time frame, and how many orders I'm sifting through. We're talking phone orders only?"

"Anything to go," I said.

"I could have it for you by this evening."

"That will be fine," Torrance responded. He stood and shook the manager's hand.

"You don't think it was one of my people, do you?"

"No," Torrance and I said emphatically.

The young man's face flooded with relief. "I'll get right on it."

"We'd appreciate it," Torrance replied.

In the car, I thanked him.

"For what?"

"I don't know. I guess I felt sort of helpless. Not knowing. Not doing anything about this."

"Cops are like that," he said, pulling out of the parking lot. "But it's probably my fault. I should have done this sooner."

"Well, it's done now." I glanced at the digital clock on the dash. "It's after three. I want to go home, change clothes."

We were almost to the Bay Bridge when Torrance snapped his pager from his belt, then took a moment to read it. "Looks like your comfort will have to wait a few. We're wanted elsewhere."

"For what?"

"Josephine Hilliard is requesting our presence."

And as he made an illegal U-turn, I wondered how I had forgotten about the woman who was allegedly Dr. Patricia Mead-Scolari's lover.

12

I wasn't prepared to interview Josephine Hilliard, but I didn't want her or Torrance to know. On the way over, I grilled him about why he'd kept his knowledge about Mrs. Hilliard's relationship with the doctor to himself.

"It wasn't something you needed to know," he told me.

"Excuse me?" I said. "My partner's suspected of killing his wife, and you arbitrarily decided I don't need to know?" I couldn't keep the sarcasm from my voice. "You taking lessons from the CIA now? Sorry, ma'am, if we told you, we'd have to kill you?"

Torrance threw me a dark look.

I chose to ignore it and plunged right on. "Did it occur to you that I might be able to help? That I might know him better than you? That maybe, *maybe*, I might be able to make—"

He slammed the brakes and pulled to the side of the road. "Look, Gillespie," he said, his fingers gripping the steering wheel, his gaze angry. "At the time I made that decision, I felt it was in the department's best interest. We had to know what Scolari knew of his wife's relationship, and if he'd ever told you."

"In other words, you were looking for more motive. You were using me to see if you could pin more motive on him."

"I was conducting an investigation."

"Did Reid know?"

"Yes."

"And Shipley? Markowski?" I asked, recalling a portion of their conversation one morning, and the silence that followed once they realized I'd overheard them. At the time, I hadn't paid much attention, though now it was clear they'd been discussing Scolari and his wife. *Wouldn't you do the same if you found out your wife . . . was gay.* I'd assumed it was the typical male bonding, we-don't-tell-those-jokes-in-front-of-females thing. Now it smacked of the can't-tell-her-because-she's-female-therefore-not-as-good-an-investigator syndrome.

"Yes," he said, even quieter than before.

Several swear words in connection with Torrance's name hovered on the tip of my tongue, the least of which could bring me under charges of insubordination. "Mrs. Hilliard awaits," I said instead.

Torrance looked straight ahead, said nothing. A cable car rumbled up the hill, the operator ringing the bell when it approached the intersection. After it passed, Torrance signaled, and drove back into traffic.

Eight minutes later we were parked in front of Hilliard Pharmaceutical's executive offices, and I promised myself then and there that I'd have to come up with a line of questioning that made her—and Torrance—believe I knew what I was talking about. I didn't see that convincing Mrs. Hilliard would be a problem. Torrance was a different matter entirely, and I wasn't sure why it was important that he be included in my charade of wits. Surely I didn't consider him a threat? Not to me, at least. To Scolari? That had to be it.

Josephine Hilliard's hilltop office overlooked the bay,

which this afternoon appeared calm despite the increasing wind.

"Come in," she told us from behind her mahogany desk. "Please, have a seat."

She indicated two leather armchairs placed with a view to the floor-to-ceiling windows. In the distance, a half dozen or so pelicans circled over the bay, their wings flashing silver in the sunlight.

Torrance and I both entered and sat, ignoring the picturesque scene.

"May I get you a drink?" She crossed the room, her footfall silent on the thick white carpet. She opened an armoire made of the same polished wood as her desk. There was enough liquor inside the thing to supply an entire shift party, though I doubted any cops I knew would appreciate the quality labels on her bottles.

"Uh, no thanks," I said.

Torrance shook his head.

"Well, then." She poured herself a vodka and tonic, smiled, returned to her desk, and sat. "What can I do for you?"

"You called us," I reminded her.

"You did want to interview me?"

"Of course."

"I have . . ." she looked at the watch dangling from the gold band on her wrist, "approximately fifty-five minutes before I'm due in another meeting."

"What exactly do you know about the last occupants of the building next to your storage warehouse?" I asked her. Sounded good.

"Actually, nothing."

"Nothing?" So much for my intelligent line of questioning. I needed to regroup, and so pulled out my small notebook from my pocket. "Do you know who would know?" I asked, jotting her answer down as though I found it of great importance.

"Dexter. If you like, I can call him up here."

I flipped back a few pages to my earlier notes—to when Dexter Kermgard let Scolari and me into the building on the day we found the Ice Man. "Earthquake '89— two tenants—leather goods, export," was what I had written. Scrawled beneath that, in Scolari's writing, was "Hx—DK." He'd underlined "Hx" three times. Doodling, or some fleeting thought? Dex, I realized. We'd been talking about Dexter Kermgard's history, not the building's. I remembered Scolari's attitude toward Dex. And his intimation that Dex's past with the department was far more checkered than Dex would have anyone believe. Scolari had taken my notebook, presumably to write notes about the extension cord. At the time, I figured he was merely avoiding having to speak to Dex. Now I wondered if he had written this for his benefit, or mine.

After making a note to myself to look up Dex's case involving the homicide in Narcotics, I glanced at Torrance. He gave no indication of whether or not he cared if Mrs. Hilliard asked Dex to come in. I did. "Yes. I wouldn't mind talking to him. That would be fine."

She called her secretary to make the arrangements, and said it would be several minutes, as he had to drive in from the north office.

"Great. In the meantime, is there anything at all you can tell us about the body we found? Any suspicions? Theories?" In the years I'd been a cop, this sort of open-ended question either netted me far-fetched bullshit or nothing at all. Every once in a while, however, I got lucky. The key was to not rush the interviewee. Let them fill the

gap of silence. Six seconds was usually all it took. I
counted.

Hilliard shook her head.

I waited. Two seconds to go.

"No," she finally said. "It was a total surprise." She
lifted her drink to her lips.

Maybe she needed a more direct approach. "Could it
be related to Hilliard Pharmaceutical?"

Her glass nearly slipped from her hands, and a bit of
vodka and tonic sloshed, but didn't spill. "How clumsy of
me. I probably shouldn't be drinking at all. Not with the
pills I'm taking."

I underlined "Hilliard" in my notes and wrote,
"Connection?" I was curious about her reaction, but
knew better than to push the issue. I didn't want her to
throw us out of her office. I smiled, then turned to Torrance, "I don't really have any more questions until Mister Kermgard arrives. Unless there was something you
needed to speak with Mrs. Hilliard about?"

"Actually, there is," he said.

I wasn't sure, but just before he pulled out his own
notebook, from the corner of my eye I thought I saw
Josephine Hilliard breathe a sigh of relief. "Mrs. Hilliard,"
he continued. "What I'm about to ask you is of a sensitive
nature, and I want you to understand, I don't mean to
offend. However, it's imperative that you be entirely
truthful with me."

"Of course," she said, relaxing into her desk chair
once more.

"What, exactly, was your relationship with Doctor
Mead-Scolari?"

Josephine Hilliard picked up a sterling lighter, and
then a cigarette from a mahogany box on her desk. For

several seconds she didn't move, speak, or seemingly even take a breath. Just stared at the two items in her hands. "Where exactly will this information go?" she finally asked.

"At the moment, it's confidential. But if it is pertinent to our investigation, it could end up in the report, and possibly even be brought out at the trial—should we eventually arrest a suspect."

"I see." She lit the cigarette, inhaled once, then set it in a crystal ashtray, watching the smoke drift up.

We waited. Outside, the bay shimmered gray as the sun descended into the four o'clock fog bank rolling in from the Pacific.

"Why must you know?" she finally asked.

"I believe it may have something to do with why the doctor was killed."

"We were very close . . . friends."

"How close, Mrs. Hilliard?"

She pressed her lips together, glanced over at the neat bottles of booze lined up in her liquor cabinet, then said, "We were lovers."

"Who knew about this?" Torrance's voice was soft, full of understanding. I looked over at him and saw his face was filled with concern, as though he knew what it was like. I wondered if he did.

"At first, no one," she answered. "Patricia wanted it that way. And so did I."

"And then?"

"She wanted to tell her husband. I told her I didn't think it was a good idea. He didn't seem like the type that would take such news in a calm manner."

She was right about that.

Hilliard took another drag from her cigarette, then

stubbed it out in the ashtray. "I was the one who told her that she should just ask for a divorce. Not reveal our relationship. I told her that, in time, he'd get over her, and then it wouldn't . . ." She cleared her throat. "Well, it wouldn't be such a blow to his ego. Patricia told me he had a temper, and frankly, it worried me."

She eyed the liquor cabinet again, and this time temptation won out. She got up and mixed herself another drink. Torrance and I said nothing. After she took a fortifying sip, she continued. "If you want a theory on that murder, Inspector," she said, her gaze directed at me, "I think he did it. I think she told him, and he killed her for it. The night she was murdered, she called me, and told me that she wasn't sure if she should meet with him. She was afraid."

The intercom on her desk buzzed, and she answered it. Apparently, Dexter had arrived and was waiting outside. She took another drink, then looked Torrance directly in the eye. "As far as anyone here knows, the doctor and I were merely close friends. I'd just as soon keep it that way."

Torrance nodded to her as the door burst open, slammed against the wall. Her husband entered, impeccably dressed in a gray silk suit, black turtleneck, and black tasseled loafers. His tanned face set off his white hair and mustache to perfection.

"Josie, what the goddamn hell do you think you're doing?" He stormed past us to her desk, slapped a newspaper on it. "For Christ's sake. I leave town for one night—"

"We have guests," Josephine said, cutting him off. She stood, waving her hand toward us. "Of course you remember Inspector Gillespie and Lieutenant Torrance?"

He turned and faced us, his apparent anger masked
with a look of polite neutrality, reminding me of that
night we'd first met at the rain forest fund-raiser given by
Paolini. I'd overheard him and Paolini speaking on the
balcony about Paolini's associate, Antonio Foust. But
the moment they noticed I was listening, they changed
the subject. I never did find out why they brought up
Foust's name. Nor had I actually ever met Foust face-to-
face, but I was told he was there. I'd gathered my final evidence at that party to put Paolini away, and whatever he
and Hilliard had discussed remained a secret.

Evan Hilliard shook hands with both of us, then said
to his wife, "I need to speak with you the moment you're
free." Before leaving, Evan picked up the newspaper and
tucked it under his arm. I caught a glimpse of the heading on the newsprint, enough to see that he carried a section of the *Chronicle*. The word MERGER was just visible,
and I recalled Skyler's announcement of the merger on
Channel Two News. Had his wife made a premature
announcement while he was gone? And why would it
matter?

Not thirty seconds after he exited, the door was
swung open again, this time by Dex, his face bent over a
clipboard filled with papers.

"About the rain forest report to Montgard . . ." He
looked up, saw me, then smiled. "Ka— Inspector Gillespie." He held the clipboard against his chest. "What can
I do for you?"

"I was hoping you might tell us about the storage
building?" I asked. "What you know of it?"

His fingers started a cadence on the back of the clipboard. "Not much more than I already told you. The
building was procured for us by a Realtor. As far as I knew,

it was already divided in half, and since we didn't need the other half, we employed a property management company to rent it out. Wells and Stern, I believe. I'm sure they'd have records on the renters."

I jotted it down in my notebook, then asked Torrance, "You got anything?"

"Not at the moment."

"That should do it," I said, glancing at my watch. It was ten after four. I wanted to get home, shower, and sprawl out on my couch. Alone. Torrance and I stood. "We'll get back to you if there are further questions."

"Yes, do," Josephine said, looking distinctly relieved that we were leaving.

Torrance and I moved past Dex. "Good-bye, Inspectors," he said.

Torrance opened the door.

"There is one thing," I said, turning back. "You wouldn't happen to know who it is we found in your warehouse?"

Dex met my gaze head-on. As a cop he'd have been intimidating. He was still so now. "Not the faintest."

"If you should think of something, either of you, call."

Dex glanced at his watch. "If you'll excuse me, I'm late." He rushed past us and out the door.

Torrance and I left as well, and just before I closed the door behind us, I caught a glimpse of Josephine Hilliard draining her drink. "What do you think?" I asked Torrance in the elevator.

"I think Mrs. Hilliard knows something she'd rather we knew nothing about."

"My thoughts exactly. I'm even more curious about what her husband was so ticked off about. He looked

ready to strangle her. Something about the merger.
Might be worth picking up a copy of the *Chronicle* to find
out."

"Damn," Torrance replied once we were outside.

I glanced at him, and he nodded to the car. The right
rear tire. Flat.

A group of kids were watching us from the end of the
street. When they saw us looking, they took off running.
Torrance crouched to inspect the tire. "Slashed," he said,
running his finger over the cut in the black sidewall.

"I wonder if those were our culprits," I said, nodding
toward the corner.

Torrance popped the trunk and pulled out the spare.
Normally we'd call for someone from the Corp yard to do
it, but neither of us felt like waiting around. It was easier
to do it ourselves.

While Torrance changed the tire, I telephoned the
Hall to see if Giovanni's had called back with info on who
had ordered the pizza.

"Anything?" Torrance asked after I disconnected.

"So far, nothing. The manager has two more tapes to
look up." I watched him tighten the lug nuts. Cars zipped
past on the street beside us. "What do you know about
Dex Kermgard's history with the PD?"

"About what everyone else does," he said with a final
twist of the tire iron. He threw it into the trunk, then
hefted the flat tire in after it. "Something on your mind?"

I showed him the bit Scolari had left in my notebook.
He eyed the paper while he wiped the grime from his
hands on a couple of napkins I'd dug out of the glove box.

"We can look up the case when we get back," he said.
"See if there's any relevance."

At the Hall, Torrance pulled the case from the

archives in IA. "Look it over while I go wash up."

I opened the black binder and read the report. It was not your basic officer-involved shooting IA investigation. And I did a double-take when I found out just who Dex's partner was: Scolari. Dex claimed that he and Scolari were en route to meet with a snitch, and the snitch pulled a gun on them. Dex fired twice, according to the report. The question of guilt arose when the slugs pulled from the dead snitch didn't match. Both were thirty-eight calibers, but a ballistics test showed they were from different guns.

According to Dex's initial report, Scolari was right there with him, but Dex later recanted, stating that everything happened so fast, he was confused, and maybe he only shot once.

But two rounds had been fired from his weapon.

Scolari maintained that he came up after the shooting, never saw it, but heard two shots. There were no rounds missing from Scolari's weapon, a forty caliber, which incidentally was not his normal duty weapon. Like everyone else, back then he carried a thirty-eight, but had reported it stolen from his vehicle the night before. That report was attached, along with photos from the theft report, showing the broken wing window.

"So far it looks like a thorough investigation," Torrance said.

"So far. But I can't help wonder at Scolari's missing thirty-eight. The way he acted when we ran into Dex at the warehouse that afternoon makes me wonder if he doesn't think Dex was somehow responsible for the theft of his weapon. Like maybe this whole thing was a setup gone bad."

"You mean like Dex almost got caught."

"Precisely," I said, turning the page. "But how is it there were two rounds missing from his gun, and only one matched the bullet found in the dead guy?"

I stopped cold when I saw who the witness had been who had verified Dex's initial report. "Antonio Foust," I said, pointing to the name on the narrative continuation. "What are the odds that a guy like Foust just happened to be standing there to see the whole thing?"

"Makes you wonder if he didn't put that extra slug in the guy."

"Doesn't it, though."

I stared at the names, wondering about the implication of what I was seeing. Scolari was Dex's partner?

I remembered the way Scolari avoided him at the warehouse. He'd seemed tense in Dex's presence. Why?

And what connection did Foust have? Apparently, back then he was more of a bit player. Not well known in the crime world. "Were you aware that Dex Kermgard and Scolari were partners?" I asked Torrance.

"From what I recall, it was a short-lived partnership. About three, four months tops. After the shooting, Scolari was temporarily reassigned to Property. He blamed Kermgard for the transfer, and as you know, Dex Kermgard quit. I was a rookie at the time, too busy trying to keep my head above water to pay attention to who was partnered with whom."

"I had no idea," I said. "But when Scolari saw Dex out at the warehouse, it was definitely apparent that he held some sort of grudge. What about, I don't know."

"Could have been the transfer to Property. A step down, a blow to the ego."

"Maybe."

13

It took a good hour to get to my place, but I hardly noticed. I was daydreaming of sleeping in my own bed, maybe having Thai food delivered in. We were pulling up in front of my apartment when Torrance spoke. "Any thoughts on where you want to go to eat dinner?"

"What?" I shook thoughts of TV and microwave popcorn from my head to concentrate on what he was saying.

"You're home. You promised Bettencourt dinner. He made arrangements for tonight. I figured you'd want to change."

I looked down at the slacks I was wearing, having nearly forgotten that I hadn't changed since the hospital. And then it struck me what he'd said. Dinner with Bettencourt. I didn't want to go to dinner with my ex. Not tonight or any other night. "I've changed my mind," I said. "I want to stay home."

"Then you want me to tell him this dinner thing was all a sham?"

Reid would blow up if he suspected a thing. Never mind that I wished I could take it all back. "No, dinner's fine."

We entered my apartment to find Mathis sitting at the kitchen table, reading the newspaper, Dinky purring away in his lap. As soon as the cat saw me he rose, then meowed loudly.

I scooped the tabby up and nuzzled my face against his silky fur. "Hello, Dinky. I missed you."

"I missed you too, sweetie," Mathis said with a grin. He folded up the paper, gave us a quick rundown of the day's happenings, which consisted of two phone calls from solicitors—I didn't want one hundred free rolls of film, or a ten dollar coupon good on the Home Shopping Network, did I? Then with a quick good-bye, he left.

I showered, then changed in my room into an emerald green silk dress that hit just above my knees. I wasn't the vain sort, but as I surveyed my reflection, I wondered if I hadn't chosen that particular dress in hopes of eliciting a compliment out of Torrance.

When I emerged, he looked at his watch. "Not bad. Only ten minutes before we're due to leave."

"Nice dress" would have worked. Aloud I said, "You're going?"

"So is your aunt. She wanted a foursome, if you recall."

"I forgot," I said.

"Apparently so." Still no mention of the dress.

Tonight was going to be the date from hell.

I seriously considered claiming illness, a flashback from the pizza, anything—until I saw my aunt's face as Reid escorted her into my apartment. This was the woman who had tucked me into bed on those nights my father had worked swing shifts. She was the one who picked up the pieces of our lives after my mother ran off with her lover. It was my aunt's shoulder I cried on when Sean died. I couldn't let her down. She was clearly delighted about going out, and I told myself for her I would do this.

Torrance played chauffeur, with my aunt riding shot-gun, while Reid and I occupied the backseat. After a friendly debate among the four of us, we ended up at Berkeley's Fish Grotto, a restaurant just off University and Interstate 80.

The lobby area was thick with people, which meant we'd have a good wait. While Reid gave his name to the hostess, my aunt visited the ladies' room. Torrance and I jostled our way through the crowd, hoping to find a seat. I led the way. A woman, clearly drunk, stumbled, knock-ing me against Torrance. He caught me, and held me a second too long.

"Are you okay?" he asked.

I caught my breath, amazed that my stomach swirled at the simple touch of his mouth against my ear. I turned suddenly, faced him, oblivious of the people trying to guide the woman out.

Torrance's gaze met mine, but before I could decide if my imagination was working overtime and that this was nothing more than him acting the gentleman to a lady in distress, Reid stepped up, and whatever possibility that something might happen was gone.

Reid looked from me to Torrance, and I gathered that he thought he'd missed something. "I didn't buy you that, did I?" Reid asked, nodding to the dress I'd taken such pains with.

"No." I knew exactly what he was doing. Trying to show that he had prior claims on me.

"You should have worn that red dress I gave you last Christmas instead."

The hostess called our names and seated us, allowing me to conveniently ignore him.

Reid and Torrance opted for lobster and steak, respectively, while my aunt and I went for the cioppino, the best in the Bay Area.

"This smells heavenly," my aunt said once our dinner was served. The aroma of spices, tomato base, and seafood wafted up from our bowls. "I certainly hope no one gets food poisoning like you, dear," she added, with a wink in my direction.

"They're pretty scrupulous here," I said.

"Well, if I were you, I certainly wouldn't go back to that pizza parlor. Did they ever find out what it was that went bad?"

Reid, Torrance, and I exchanged glances. "Not yet," I replied. "How's your cioppino?"

"Excellent. So tell me, Lieutenant. Is it true the department believes that Sam Scolari is the SoMa Slasher?

"He's not the Slasher," I said.

"Well, surely you don't think he killed his wife?" she asked Torrance.

"It's still under investigation," he replied diplomatically.

Reid tapped his fingers on the table. Figuring he felt left out, and wanting to change the subject from Scolari to anything else, I said, "Reid's working some interesting cases at the DA's office."

"Oh?" my aunt said.

"Nothing, really," Reid said, giving her a small smile. He seemed to like being center of attention.

"Have you finished with the embezzlement at Hilliard Pharmaceutical?" I asked.

He rose suddenly, pinning his narrowed gaze on me. "That case is confidential." His response shocked me.

Reid never had a problem discussing cases in front of my aunt before. In fact, he relished it.

"Since when?" I asked.

"Do you know," Torrance said to my aunt, "I've never had cioppino before. What is it? A stew?"

I could have kissed him for changing the subject. Aunt Molly pushed her bowl across the table to him. "I suppose that's exactly what it is. A seafood stew. Dip your bread into it. I guarantee you won't be disappointed."

He did, then tasted it. "Not bad. I wish I'd ordered it myself."

"Excuse me," Reid said tersely, then left in the direction of the men's room.

He hadn't been gone five seconds when my aunt leaned across the table to me and whispered loud enough for Torrance, seated beside her, to hear: "I hope you're not planning on getting back together with Reid. I really don't think he's your type, dear. Now, Lieutenant Torrance—"

"Aunt Molly," I interjected. I smiled at her, hoping she'd drop the subject.

She completely ignored me. "Are you married, Lieutenant?"

"Uh, no, ma'am," he replied, clearly amused.

Great, I thought. This one I'd never live down.

"Well, do you like high school football? My nephew's quite good."

"I've been known to attend a game or two."

Aunt Molly kicked me under the table and raised her eyebrows, her actions not missed by Torrance. The waiter's arrival with our cheesecake and then Reid's return put a stop to that conversation, and I prayed she'd have the sense not to continue it. Ever.

"What were you talking about?" Reid asked.

"Nothing," I said. I gave him my sweetest smile. And ignored him.

Aunt Molly didn't, however. "I was merely asking the lieutenant if he had a family," she said, full of innocence.

This appeared to mollify him for the time being, but as the evening progressed, I knew without a doubt that I should never have agreed to this date. As possessive as Reid was, we'd never have a future together. Nor was it fair of me to string him along. I didn't want to deal with the fallout, and for some reason my mind conjured up thoughts of Reid stalking me to coerce me to go out with him again.

I had no idea if Reid sensed anything, but I knew I had to somehow end things between us, fast. Thankfully, by the time we all returned to my apartment, my aunt had convinced Reid that he hadn't experienced life until he'd learned to play canasta. Reid excused himself to use the bathroom. When he returned several minutes later, my aunt dealt the cards, I poured the drinks, and he became embroiled in learning the game. I wondered if he thought the way to me was through my aunt.

Torrance disappeared into my bedroom shortly thereafter to use the phone. The call took a long time, but he eventually emerged to work on reports in the kitchen, not imbibing at all, while the three of us sat in the living room.

Reid and my aunt were into their second game; I was into my third drink, trying not to think about Torrance, when his cellular rang. I heard him speaking softly for several minutes, and then louder, "I'll talk to her about it, then get back to you right away. I don't know. Give me a few minutes."

I looked up as Torrance entered. "I need to speak to you about something," he said, his expression unreadable.

I stood and started for the kitchen.

He glanced at my aunt and said, "This is better discussed in private."

"The bedroom?" I responded, curious. It was either that or the porch.

He followed me in. "We won't be more than a few minutes," he told Bettencourt and my aunt.

"Does police work never end?" my aunt asked Reid.

"Hardly," he said. "Now, refresh my memory. What card is it I want to get?"

I shut the door behind us, confident that my aunt would keep Reid perfect company for the next couple of minutes.

Torrance put his finger to his lips, whispered, "Your aunt," then motioned me away from the door. "I need to make sure we're not overheard." He led me into the bathroom, then shut that door as well.

"What is it?"

He didn't answer. Not at first. He simply looked at me, his gaze dark, dangerous. Finally he said, "That was Mathis checking in. He said they got a lead on the pizza."

"And?"

He reached out, brushed a strand of hair from my face, his touch lingering on my ear. I thought of how he'd caught me in the restaurant, held me, his whisper. His finger trailed down my neck, and then along the edge of my dress.

"What are you doing?" I asked.

"Are you and Bettencourt . . . ?"

He never finished. He didn't need to. I knew what he was asking. He stepped closer until we were a hairsbreadth apart, yet still not touching. Heat emanated from his body.

"No." My voice cracked, and I wasn't sure if he heard me. I shook my head and said slightly louder, "No."

Then his mouth crashed against mine. His tongue sought its way inside, his kiss deep, swift, his fingers entwined in my hair, preventing me from moving away. "God, I've wanted you from the moment you sat in my car that night," he whispered against my lips, his body pressing into mine. A shiver swept through me. "Tell me you don't want me. Tell me . . . and I'll let you go."

He waited. I felt his heart pounding against mine. I couldn't answer, couldn't find the breath to speak.

"Tell me."

"I can't," I said.

He kissed the bruise on my temple, then paused to look at me. This time when his lips touched mine, he lifted me until I was sitting on the edge of the sink. The paradox of the cold porcelain through the silk of my dress and the heat of him against me was delirious and erotic. I didn't think more than a minute passed, and I found myself wishing my aunt and Reid were anywhere but here. I wanted more. But this was not the time or place, and so I reached up and put my fingers to his mouth.

He pulled back, looking at me. I sensed he was disappointed. In me? Himself?

"You were talking about the pizza," I reminded him.

"Was I?" He kissed me again, softly, slowly. Finally he drew away, but it seemed forever before either of us caught our breath.

"The pizza?" I managed.

He searched my face. "The pizza order to Giovanni's

was called in. The phone number left with the cashier was from the Hall of Justice."

"Where in the Hall of Justice?"

"Homicide. It was your number."

I think I stared at him for a full ten seconds "That doesn't mean anything."

"No. It means only that someone knew your number, and left it as the callback number for the pizza order."

"Someone as in Scolari?"

"I didn't say that."

"But you thought it."

"That's my job. To think of all possibilities." He was quiet a moment, then, "Are you okay?"

With what? I wanted to ask. With this latest news he'd just dropped on me? With the idea we'd almost had sex on my sink? "Yeah. Fine."

Whether he believed me or not I don't know, because he regarded me for quite some time without saying a word. He started to turn away, stopped suddenly, hauled me against him, and kissed me again. Then he turned to go, and breathless, I watched him leave, listening to the soft click of the bedroom door as he closed it on his way out.

This man was spending the night. Did that mean we'd sleep together? I picked up my hairbrush off the mirrored tray on my dresser. I stroked the brush through my shoulder-length dark brown hair, examining my reflection, finding no evidence of our quick rendezvous written in my brown eyes. As I set down my hairbrush, I noticed the mirrored tray it sat upon had been moved. There was an edge of oval, dust free—not more than a quarter of an inch, as though someone had lifted it and tried to replace it.

Had I moved it when I picked up the brush? I looked around the room, unable to convince myself it was merely my imagination. My underwear drawer had a bit of white sticking out, preventing it from closing completely. I opened it. Everything was still folded, but shoved forward as though someone had reached toward the back. Then I noticed the closet, open, shoe box lids slightly askew. I'd straightened every one of those a few days ago while trying to avoid the very man I'd just kissed in my bathroom.

My head started hammering. Slow down. Think. Mathis, cross-dresser? No one was here when we went out. Scolari? Searching for what? Who else? Reid had been in here. Torrance. Me. I couldn't very well go out and say, hey, who the hell was digging through my room. Well, I could, but Reid would explode, either at the suggestion it was him or the idea that someone had been in my room. I'd wait to tell Torrance in private, after Reid and my aunt left.

Torrance had returned to the kitchen and his laptop, picking up where he'd left off as though nothing was out of the ordinary. Reid and my aunt were still engrossed in their game, and at first Ried didn't appear to have even missed me. But after several minutes I couldn't help but notice the way he studiously avoided looking at me, or even speaking to me. I was glad. I could tell he was steaming and I had no desire to get into it with him. Reid wasn't the sort who would overlook his ex-wife kissing another man beneath his very nose. Come to think of it, I wasn't sure I would either. I wasn't exactly proud of myself at that moment. I picked up my drink, promptly drained it, then poured another.

Twenty minutes later there was a knock at the door. "Damn it," Torrance said, slamming his laptop shut. His actions surprised me, since rarely did he show any sort of emotion. He got up, answered the door. Mathis walked in.

"Guess I'm your baby-sitter tonight," Mathis said to me.

Reid and my aunt wrapped up their game, oblivious to my turmoil. "Are you switching places now?" I asked in as casual a voice as I could manage.

"Something came up," Torrance said.

Really? I thought.

"Speaking of baby-sitters," my aunt said. "I better get home to Kevin. Her glance strayed from me to Torrance, then back. Had she suspected our tryst in the bathroom? I threw her a dark look, willing her not to say anything more. For once she complied.

Reid helped her on with her jacket. "I think that's my cue." He came up to me and gave me a perfunctory kiss on the cheek. "Call if you need anything." His tone was cold, unconvincing

"Thanks. I will." It was the best I could do under the circumstances. Confusion reigned as Reid and my aunt left, and I watched Torrance pack up his gear.

"The couch?" Mathis said.

I pulled myself together, picking up the sheets that Torrance folded every morning and placed on a shelf beneath the telephone stand. "Yes. I'll get you some fresh sheets." In the bedroom, I tossed the old sheets on the bed, then pulled another set from the top shelf of my closet. When I turned, Torrance was standing there. I wanted to tell him about the things being misplaced. I wanted to know about his intentions toward me.

"I'll talk to you in the morning," he said.

I tried to read something in his words, his stance, his expression. Just once, I wanted him to give me some clue as to what he was thinking. "Yeah, sure," I said, holding the sheets in front of me like a shield. At the same time, I reminded myself why I'd been so adamant about not dating within the department. It wasn't something I'd experienced any success at.

My first attempt had been with a guy I'd dated in the Academy. At our graduation, I was surprised when he never introduced me to his parents. I took it upon myself to do so, only to have them politely introduce me to the young woman seated next to them. His fiancée.

My fault, I figured. The guy wasn't mature enough. Strike one.

The second cop I dated was a good ten years older than my twenty-five years. Much more mature. What I didn't know was that our idea of shift partners differed. While I was working swings, he was supposed to be at home, sleeping. Alone. One afternoon I showed up unexpectedly, only to find him in bed with the woman he worked with on day shift. Strike two.

I had no wish to do it a third time—Reid was bad enough, and he wasn't even a cop. I couldn't stand the awkwardness when things didn't turn out the way I thought they were supposed to. And I hated how the entire department seemed to know about it before I did.

Torrance stood there a moment longer, as though waiting for me to say something more, then turned to leave.

I followed him out, and handed the sheets to Mathis, who, thank God, appeared not to notice the tension emanating from me. Perhaps I was becoming as adept as Torrance at hiding my feelings.

"See ya, Mathis," he said, dropping his laptop into his briefcase, then heading out the door.

It shut behind him, and I stood there staring at the empty kitchen, when Mathis said, "That a report he left behind?"

A black three-ring binder lay on the table, and I hurried over, picked up the thing. Before I even thought about what I was doing, I opened the door and stepped out to the porch. Torrance was near the bottom of the steps.

"You forgot a case file," I called out.

He glanced over his shoulder. "I left it for you," he said without stopping.

"Can you at least tell me what's going on?"

This time he stopped. His hand on the railing, he turned and regarded me as though what he was about to say weighed heavily on him. "I'm not even sure myself."

We stood there in silence for several moments. Finally I descended. "What happened up there in the bathroom—"

"I can assure you, I've never done anything remotely close to what occurred up there before."

What on earth did he mean by that? "Why are you leaving?" I asked instead.

His expression shuttered, and he looked away. "I was afraid I'd end up sleeping with you," came his quiet reply. "I've never allowed that to happen before, to sleep with a woman . . ."

Oh, God. The rumors. Torrid Torrance. I wasn't sure if I could take the truth at the moment. "Tell me you're not saying what I think you're saying."

"Which would be . . ."

"Tell me you're not gay."

He stood one step below me, nearly eye to eye, and

so close, I could feel his warm breath on my face. He lifted my chin with his finger. "Is that what you think?" he asked, his voice deceptively soft.

When I didn't respond, he moved even closer, wrapping his arm around my waist, pressing himself into my thigh.

Okay, that answered that question.

"Like you," he said, stepping back, allowing the cold air to rush between us, "I don't date cops, which was what I was trying to tell you. Nor do I give a damn what others in the department think about me. And before you ask, I'm not bi, either."

His admission about dating surprised me, mostly because it meant he was aware of my private life. "I've never really done anything like that before," I said. "Dating someone, and then, well, what happened in the bathroom."

"I figured the date was made under duress," he said, and I had to do a double take at the sparkle in his eyes. Then again, knowing Torrance, it was probably the reflection from the porch light.

The insecurity caused by his departure and Mathis's sudden arrival returned, and I hugged the thick binder to my chest. "So, you're leaving?"

This time his gaze darkened considerably. "My duty is to protect you. I called Mathis, because I knew if I had to spend one more night with you, I wouldn't be able to avoid sleeping with you."

"And that's bad?"

"I told Mathis something came up, and we needed to change hours. Besides, my ego couldn't take it if you turned me down. So, I took you aside to tell you about the change in plans, but—"

"Temptation won out?"

His electric smile went straight to my heart. I was amazed at the transformation to his usually serious features. "Something like that," he said.

"So, go tell Mathis to take a hike."

"Wish I could. But I can't sleep with you and watch you at the same time."

"I'll install a mirror on the ceiling."

"A very tempting offer, Inspector," he said, reaching up to brush his fingertips across my cheek. "Now get inside, before I change my mind."

He gave me a gentle push up the steps. He waited until I reached the top. "And to think all this time," he said, "I thought you were uncomfortable because I worked in IA."

"Management Control," I corrected, wishing he hadn't reminded me of where he worked.

"Goodnight, Kate," he called out as he headed around the corner.

"Goodnight . . . Mike." He left before I remembered to tell him about the things in my room being moved.

Mathis was already snoring on the couch when I returned inside, so I locked up and wandered into my bedroom, wondering how I was going to be able to sleep without knowing who had been in my room, and why. Falling into the bed, I glanced at the binder he'd left me. I opened it, and all thoughts of anyone invading my bedroom fled at the sight of what I held.

Sam Scolari's complete case file.

14

I tried calling Torrance twice to tell him someone had been in my room. No answer. Finally I paged him to call me, then got back to the case file. I had so many conflicting thoughts as I looked through it. Why had Torrance left it? Did he believe Scolari was innocent? Or did he want me to realize Scolari was guilty?

The file was thick. It was late.

Start at the beginning.

But that was stuff I knew. I was there at the scene. Saw it all, I flipped through several sections until I came to the interviews done in the Management Control office. Mine I ignored, turning pages until I got to Mary's. I scanned over her report of the doctor's alleged affair with Josie Hilliard, and Mary's statement that Patricia was doing cancer research for Hilliard Pharmaceutical. My eyes drifted closed. Forcing them open, I focused on the word "research," realizing I'd read that line three times, now.

I wanted to know what evidence they had against Scolari, but I couldn't stay awake. Careful not to disturb the sleeping Mathis, I made myself a cup of tea, then reviewed the reports relating to the evidence collection and Torrance's notes on that. The list was long, not unusual in a murder case. Still, I thought, grabbing a sheet of paper to make my own notes, I'd never expected so much of it to be overwhelmingly against Scolari, even if it was all circumstantial.

The blood type in the Range Rover came back to Patricia. Expected. Scolari's thumbprint in Patricia's blood on the inside passenger door handle. Undoubtedly a simple explanation. A cigarette butt found in the parking lot matched Scolari's brand. Anyone could have dropped it.

I turned the page. Scolari's fingerprints found on the counter at the Chinese restaurant that abutted the parking lot. It was no secret they were meeting for dinner.

I went over the list of trace evidence, fibers, debris found on the seats and floorboards. I read over each item carefully, hoping that something would jump out, lead to some as yet unknown suspect. Nothing. I turned the page, and nearly choked on my tea.

A smeared, bloody palm print on the dash—the blood type matched Scolari's, not his wife's. There were also the items taken from the search warrant on Scolari's apartment—items including bloody clothes found stuffed in the bottom of his closet. All of it his wife's blood.

Scolari had told me she was already dead when he found her, and I clearly recall the cut on his hand when I saw him. Perfect explanation. I suppose I never expected there to be quite so much blood. They'd also found a book on his coffee table titled *How to Change Your Identity and Disappear.* A bit on the damning side—especially considering what Scolari had used as a bookmark: a Dear John note from his wife.

I leaned back against the headboard, staring at the cracks in my ceiling. The phone rang. I snatched it up. "Hello?" It came out curt, but what the hell. It was well past midnight.

"You paged?" Torrance.

"I found a few things misplaced in my room. I meant to tell you about it before you left."

"What sort of things?"

"My underwear. My shoes. Girl things. Could it be Mathis? Maybe he's into cross-dressing? Or just being snoopy?" I said. I thought of the flowers he'd brought to me in the hospital. "I don't know. My dresser drawers were gone through. My closet. Nothing missing that I can tell."

"Damn it. I shouldn't have gone to dinner with you."

"You had no way of knowing. Besides, it could have happened before we left, and I didn't notice."

"The one time we leave the place unwatched?"

Neither of us said anything, both mulling over that piece of information. Then he changed the subject.

"What do you think of Scolari's case? I take it you're reading the case file."

"Yeah." It took me a moment to regroup. "I'll admit, it doesn't look good."

"And?"

I looked at my notes. "I don't get a lot of stuff in here. Why would he leave so much evidence behind? The bloody print. The bloody clothes. It doesn't make sense."

"Crime of passion. Panic."

"Bull. Scolari was—is—a trained homicide inspector."

"He was first and foremost a man. His wife was leaving him for a woman. She told him; he snapped."

"Manslaughter," I said.

"Exactly. Bettencourt told me the DA's willing to let him plea if he turns himself in."

"Why'd you leave me the file?" I asked suddenly.

Silence.

My gaze strayed to the bathroom, the memory of our kisses vivid. It clouded my thoughts. Took away my focus. Please don't let that be a part of this.

Finally he answered. "I want your opinion, Kate. Nothing more."

It was enough. It had to be.

The next morning, after a quick stop for a double latte, Mathis drove me to the Hall of Justice, since I was still under doctor's orders not to drive. Sergeant Linda Perkins was watching my place in his absence, and Torrance was having an evidence tech dust my bedroom for prints. If Torrance had told Mathis or Perkins about my bedroom being gone through, neither mentioned it to me.

"You sure that foo-foo stuff's gonna do it?" Mathis asked, referring to my coffee.

I was dead tired after reviewing Scolari's case all night, and had nodded off twice on the way to the coffee shop. "Sure as hell hope so."

Torrance was waiting for us in his office, reviewing some report or another. He looked up as I dumped my things on the nearest desk. Our gazes met briefly, and then nothing. While last night wasn't something I wanted to advertise, some reaction would have been nice. Sleep well? Get a new sink?

Mathis threw his things on his desk, then went out to find some real coffee, preferably something that had stagnated on the bottom of a coffeepot left over from the graveyard shift. I wished him well, then looked about the room for my briefcase and the autopsy files. They'd been moved. Where, I hadn't a clue.

There was nothing for it but to make first contact. I

strode into Torrance's office, leaned against the door frame, opting for the ultracool whatever-happened-between-us-last-night-is-no-big-deal pose. "Where's my stuff ?"

It was a totally wasted move. He never looked up. "On the table. You'll be working in here with me."

Had I bothered glancing a little farther into his office, I might have seen everything spread out on the table against the far wall. He'd even moved a chair in.

He flipped a page, still no eye contact.

I started out to get my latte, then thought better of it. He might be able to pretend nothing happened last night, but I couldn't. "This is precisely why I don't date in the department," I said.

He lowered the report, glanced out his window into the office beyond, then at me. "Why is that, Gillespie?"

I stared in disbelief. "Last night it was 'Kate.' How can you sit there and look at me as though nothing happened? It was less than twelve hours ago. Or have you forgotten?"

He got up, closed the door, stood inches away from me. "Hardly."

"Then what?"

"What do you want me to do?"

"Anything. I don't care. Just don't sit there with that damned implacable . . ." I realized then how foolish I sounded. Worse yet, I felt my eyes welling up. I hated crying in front of male cops. It made me feel so inferior. "I can't believe I'm doing this."

I tried to leave. His hand covered mine on the knob, stopping me. Outside, we heard a door open. Mathis with his coffee. Torrance pulled the cord, lowered the blinds over the window.

"What?" he asked softly.

I couldn't look at him. Instead, I stared up at the fluorescent lights, having read somewhere that your tears, if not too far gone, might drain back into the ducts. Fat chance. "Everything's wrong," I said. "People are dead, my partner's a suspect, and I'm a damned emotional wreck."

"I'm sorry."

"For what?" This time I looked at him and was surprised to see his face filled with anguish.

"For last night," he said, stroking the stitches in my temple with his thumb. "I shouldn't have taken advantage of your emotional state."

"I was a willing participant. Or hadn't you noticed?"

"Trust me," he said, leaning his face toward mine. "I noticed."

I pushed him away, though it was tempting not to. "This is the problem."

He looked confused.

"We're behind closed doors, and it's okay to pretend we know each other. Open the blinds, and we're strangers again. I don't like it."

His expression darkened. "And you think I do? For Christ's sake, Kate. Do you have any idea what it's like to walk down the hallway and see friends you've known for years avoid you because you work in IA? Because you were instrumental in investigating a fellow officer's illegal misconduct that resulted in suspension, termination, whatever? I'm the enemy. Never mind that the officer shouldn't have stolen those drugs, or raped that hooker. You don't want to be on this side of the fence. I don't want that for you."

"It's my life. My decision."

He brushed the tears from my eyes. "You have enough problems without the added burden of everyone wondering if you're a snitch for IA."

I hated that he was right. "Then what? Go on pretending nothing happened?"

"I can't do that any more than you can. What I can do is suggest that we be friends. Let's get through this investigation first, before we venture elsewhere."

"What if my sink gets stopped up in the middle of the night?" It was out before I could stop myself.

His gaze held mine. "Heaven help the man that stands between me and my pipe wrench."

I wish I could say Torrance's response eased my mind. But he was dead-on when he thought my being linked romantically with him would be a burden. Peer pressure in the department was astronomical, to say the least, and if I was going to expose myself to something of that nature, then I had better be certain that a relationship with Torrance was what I wanted.

Before either of us could fantasize more about such double entendres, his secretary knocked on the door, advising him that he was due in a meeting with the special homicide team. Mathis was to be my pseudo–baby-sitter, in case I had any dizzy spells, while Torrance and the others went over the latest in the doctor's murder. Unfortunately, Torrance took the Mead-Scolari case file, which meant I would have to finish reviewing it at a later date.

"You're not going to faint on me?" Mathis asked, coming in the office and opening the blinds.

"Hardly. I haven't felt lightheaded since we left the hospital."

"What're you working on?"

I pulled myself together, dismissed all thoughts of

Torrance, erotic or otherwise, from my mind. "Good question," I said, eyeing my things, which Torrance had set up for me on the worktable. Not that there were a lot of choices on what I could do.

I stared at the box labeled "Morgue," trying to remember why I'd even started going over them. So many things had happened since then.

Scolari. He'd said something on the phone about the autopsies. What was it? That if I reviewed the cases, I'd figure out that he wasn't the SoMa Slasher. "I'm reading about dead bodies," I told Mathis.

"I'd tell ya, have fun, but that goes without saying for you homicide types," he said, making himself at home behind Torrance's desk.

"I wouldn't want to corner the market on fun. Sure you don't want to join me?"

"Uh, no. Don't think so." He opened a *People* magazine—something I doubted he'd do were Torrance not occupied elsewhere.

The notes I had on the few cases I'd already reviewed told me little, but I figured I might as well go back at it. That settled, I started separating the cases into stacks of male, female. After that, I sorted through the female, taking anything that looked remotely like a Slasher case.

It took about a half an hour to go through them, but in the end I was left with a more manageable seven cases that met my profile. Reviewing those took more time, since I went over every detail and took copious notes. Five were confirmed SoMa Slasher cases, which I had been investigating anyway. One had no bearing whatsoever, a suicide by knife. I tossed it back in the box with the others. The seventh case, however, made me sit up. Her middle name was Tanya—Christy Tanya McAllen—and I thought of the Tanya reported murdered at the Twin Palms. Yet it wasn't merely the coincidence of the name that caught my eye.

I compared it with the notes from my other cases. "I can't believe it," I whispered after reading McAllen's report over again.

"Find something?" Mathis asked, looking up from his magazine.

"Maybe." The MO was so close, I couldn't figure out how anyone in Homicide had missed it. Of course, it was possible that it wasn't a Slasher case—it might have been coincidentally similar, or the real Slasher had copycatted that homicide. But I didn't think so. I wheeled my chair over to the desk and picked up the phone, calling Gypsy's office in Homicide.

Rocky Markowski answered. "Hey, Gillespie," he said. "How's it going?"

"Never better. Gypsy around?"

"She stepped out a minute. Told me to answer her phone, or else. Said she was expecting a call. What's up?"

"You know who's working the McAllen case? Happened about a year ago."

"Seems to me I recall Zimwit working on that right before he got transferred out."

"Who got it when he left?"

"Good question. Hold on, Gypsy's back. . . . Hey, Gyps. McAllen? Year ago."

"Case number, Rocky," I heard Gypsy say.

I read it off to him, and he repeated it.

The clicking of a keyboard, several moments of silence, then from Markowski, "You sure?"

"Says so right there," came Gypsy's reply.

"No shit." To me Rocky said, "Looks like it was assigned to you."

"What?"

"Sure as shit. Says so in the log. Went to Zim, then when he transferred out, you inherited it."

"No way," I said.

"It happens. Hold on, let me see if I can find it." He was gone a couple of minutes, searching, while I pondered how a whole homicide could have been misplaced for a year. Had Zimmerman purposefully not given it to me? Could that be why he'd been avoiding me all this time? Because he knew if I was looking into the Slasher cases, I'd turn up this one and uncover what he'd done? "Nope, not there. Maybe check with Records."

"Thanks." I disconnected, called Zimmerman's office down in Property. "McAllen," I demanded when he answered.

"What about her?"

"You were supposed to turn that case over to me. What the hell did you do with it?"

"Gave it to you. Why?"

"It doesn't bother you that no one's looked into her case in over a year?"

"Hey, look, Gillespie. I interviewed the girl's boyfriend. He was too stupid to commit the crime and lie about it. He had an airtight alibi. There weren't any further leads, case closed. I can't be bothered by somethin' that ain't my business anymore. It ain't my fault if you misplaced it."

I slammed the phone. I knew I couldn't prove that he'd purposefully sabotaged me, since it would be his word against mine. If he had any idea the case might be related to the Slasher cases, would he have kept it from

me? Could he have realized what he held? The Slasher
had yet to be dubbed that for another six months down
the road.

The important thing was that I'd found it, and now I
had to play catch-up. What if there was some clue that
would tie together the other cases?

What if there was some clue that would have prevented the other six murders?

I could only hope that Zimmerman wasn't so egotis-
tical as to destroy everything in it. Still, there was part of
it that even he would have a hard time doing away with. I
picked up the phone once more, punched in the number.

"Records, Allison speaking."

Hearing her voice stopped me cold. I glanced at
Mathis, then stopped myself from asking Allison if she'd
heard from Scolari—definitely not the thing to do with
IA sitting right there. "Yeah, this is Gillespie from Homicide. I need a case pulled, ASAP." I read her the number,
furious over Zimmerman's deceit, yet excited by the
prospect that I was holding the autopsy from a potential
Slasher case that had occurred a good several months
before our first documented case. I wanted to confirm it
by reading the police report. And I wanted to see why no
connection had been made.

"Hate to interrupt your literary break, Sarge," I said
to Mathis as I cradled the phone to my ear, "but I need to
pick up a case from Records."

He tossed the magazine onto the desk.

"Promise I won't faint," I said. "You can stay here."

"Don't think so."

In Records, I waited in line like every other officer,
while Mathis stood next to me, looking like he'd trade in
his star for a chance to strike up a conversation with a tall,

blond officer reading a report by the window. We had a saying in the women's locker room: If a guy looked too good to be true, he probably was. Mathis fit that description, and so did the guy he was staring at.

"For Pete's sake. Go talk to him," I said.

"Torrance'll kill me if I let you out of my sight."

"I promise I won't move from this line. If I go down, call 911. How far can help be?"

He seemed to think about it for all of three seconds before he wandered over. He was still there, talking, five minutes later when my turn came up. "Gillespie, Homicide," I told the clerk at the window.

"Oh, Allison said you'd be coming by. Hold on. I'll get her." She left. Another clerk wandered up, asked if I'd been helped, then asked the next person in line to step forward. A few moments later Allison wandered up with a binder, which she dropped on the counter.

"Isn't there a copy of this up in your office?" she asked.

"One would think so. How long till I can get a complete copy of this?"

"You mean right now?" she asked, as though I were cutting into her coffee break.

I opened it and flipped through the pages. For a homicide file, it was pretty thin. Apparently not that much follow-up had been done on it. I could only hope that while Zimmerman had it, he'd followed up on all the leads—assuming there were any leads to follow.

"Do me a favor," I said, closing the binder and giving it to her. "Make me a copy of the original case report and any supplementals, then get me the rest as soon as you can."

When Allison returned with the copies, I glanced at

Mathis to make sure he was still occupied. He was, and looking radiant for it. I leaned over the counter. "You hear from Sam?" I asked.

She, too, glanced over at Mathis. "Uh, no. Not in the last day or two."

Her answer shocked me, but I kept the surprise from my voice, having learned during my first interview with Allison how easily she was distracted. "Had he ever mentioned to you that he was considering leaving the department?"

"I feel like I'm betraying him."

"I'm his partner," I said, reaching out, placing my hand over hers. "I'm trying to help him."

"Well," she said, curling the edge of my report. Today her long fingernails and matching lipstick were blood red. "He did talk about just getting away from it all. You know, one day get in the car, keep driving, never look back?"

Hadn't everyone entertained that thought? "When was this?"

"I dunno. Maybe a couple of weeks ago? I remember it, because we were meeting at that weird bookstore for coffee. The one that sells all those spy books? They make great espresso."

I doubted Scolari went there for the coffee. Like Mathis, he was the bottom-of-the-pot sort of guy. The longer it stagnated, the better Scolari liked it.

Mathis, glancing my way, didn't look like he was in any hurry. "What was Sam doing at that bookstore?"

"He talked about going into the PI business. Said he needed information."

Scolari hated private investigators. Thought they were all wannabe cops. "So, how is Sam doing?" I asked in as casual a manner as I could under the circumstances.

"Pretty good, I guess. He didn't really say. He only called long enough to ask about a report."

"Which one?"

"This one." She patted the McAllen binder.

I practically dragged Mathis from the room.

"You couldn't wait five minutes?"

"No."

"But—"

"It wouldn't work out anyway. You're IA; he's patrol," I said. Sounded good to me.

"What's got your goose?"

I held up the McAllen report. "I need to go out on some contacts."

"Not without permission from Torrance, you don't. And I doubt he'll be available for the next hour or so. You're on light duty, that means you stay inside."

"Where's his meeting at?"

"Down the hall," he said, nodding at a conference room.

"Come on."

Mathis hurried after me, but hesitated at the entrance. "You sure you want to interrupt this?"

I opened the door and peeked in to see Torrance, my ex, our current DA, Lieutenant Andrews, and some of the heavy department brass in deep conference apparently plotting the best way to bring in Scolari. After reading what little I had out of the Mead-Scolari homicide file, I couldn't blame them. "No need to interrupt them, if you're going to take me," I whispered over my shoulder.

"Not unless Mike gives the okay."

Finally Torrance looked up, saw me. I waved the

report slightly, but he shook his head as though to say, "Not now, later." Good enough. At least I tried.

Backing out, I closed the door. "Okay. We got our permission."

"I don't know . . ."

"You can take me or I can ditch you."

"Mike's my boss."

I patted him on the shoulder. "He'll get over it."

Mathis rolled his eyes, muttered something about women, then followed me to the elevator and the garage.

We sat in his car while I scanned the report, immediately discovering why the McAllen case hadn't been looked upon as a potential Slasher case. McAllen hadn't died right away.

And she knew her attacker.

15

Torrance might end up being ticked off at Mathis, but he was going to murder me. It couldn't be helped, and at least I was taking my bodyguard with me, though I doubted Torrance would see it that way. McAllen had been dead over a year—she could wait a couple of hours more, at least till Torrance got out of his meeting. There was also the matter that Scolari was following this same trail, and that being so, we stood a chance of running into each other. While I took that as a sign of his innocence—he was trying to prove he wasn't the SoMa Slasher—I was pretty certain Torrance wouldn't.

"Can you give me a hint on what we're doing?" Mathis asked, fingertips drumming the steering wheel.

"As soon as I figure it out myself." Scanning the list of witnesses, I picked the first name. Thomas Sherwood.

"Great," he muttered, signaling for a turn onto Seventh. "For the record, I'm doing this under duress."

Reading in the car usually made me sick, as it was doing now, but time was of the essence. Torrance would undoubtedly figure out what had happened and call us back. I wanted to be well away from here when that happened—the better to convince Mathis that we shouldn't return—so I rolled down the window, took in the fresh air, and concentrated on the report.

According to the case file, Christy Tanya McAllen, age 22, had lived a few blocks from the SoMa area with a roommate, Trish Tilden, also 22. Neither showed an address at the Twin Palms. Tilden had found McAllen in a parking lot a few blocks away from the Gold Ox bar. Someone heard her screaming hysterically and placed an anonymous 911 call. The responding officer reported that McAllen was still alive at his arrival. When he asked, "Who did this to you? Do you know who did this to you?" McAllen indicated yes, but the officer couldn't understand the name. Tilden, however, told the officer that McAllen's boyfriend, Thomas "Spider" Sherwood, was "really creepy," and she suspected him since they'd just had a fight. Spider Sherwood's address was listed at the Twin Palms. From my visit there earlier in the week, I knew he no longer lived there. I ran a check on him, got his current address, and gave it to Mathis.

I went through the report again. Allison had included the supplemental report from Zimmerman as well. In it was his interview with Sherwood, and the supposed airtight alibi Zim had told me about. Sherwood was allegedly playing in a band at the Gold Ox bar at the time.

In my opinion, when it came to homicide there was no such thing as an airtight alibi.

"Here it is," Mathis said, pulling in front of a mom and pop store. The apartment entrance was around the back.

The place wasn't as seedy as the Twin Palms, but it ran a close second. I climbed the stairs to the second floor and knocked on Sherwood's door at the end of the hall. The man who answered looked like he just woke up, even though he was dressed in Levi's, worn at the knees, dingy T-shirt, and black leather vest. If I had to hazard a guess, he changed his clothes about as often as he washed his hair, which at the moment was pulled back in a ponytail.

"Thomas Sherwood?"

"Yeah," he said, tucking his T-shirt into his jeans. There was a black widow spider tattooed on his neck.

"Inspector Gillespie," I said, showing him my star. "And this is Sergeant Mathis. We would like to speak to you about Christy McAllen?"

"Shit."

Shit? There's a response I'd expect after a year of no contacts in his girlfriend's death. "Mind if we come in?"

"Uh," he looked over his shoulder as if assessing what he might have left out that would be incriminating.

"We're only interested in speaking to you about Christy. Nothing else."

"Uh, yeah, okay. Let me just clear off the table, I had a little company last night."

He made a beeline for the coffee table, a piece of plywood mounted on cinder blocks. He lifted a mirror covered with white filmy powder, razor blade, and a straw, which Mathis and I chose to ignore. "My old lady's asleep in the bedroom," he said, nodding toward a mattress on the floor situated on one side of the room. A tapestry hung from the ceiling, one corner flung over a chair, allowing us to see into the "bedroom."

He deposited the mirror on the chair, then lowered the tapestry, blocking our view of his contraband and his bedmate. I was curious as to how long he'd grieved, if at all, before acquiring his latest love.

"You can sit down, if you want."

Mathis and I glanced around, and both shook our heads. The couch, when new, might have been off-white, but now was mottled more shades of gray than I knew existed. There was no kitchen, or bathroom, merely a sink in one corner next to the window that overlooked a neon sign for the market below. "Can we interest you in some coffee?" I asked instead, envisioning the clean Formica tabletop of a coffee shop as far from this apartment as possible.

"Actually, I just made a pot." He laughed, a sound reminding me more of a burned-out surfer than a rocker with the moniker of "Spider." I recalled Zimmerman saying something about the guy being stupid, and figured he was right. He nodded toward the pot. "You want some?"

Eyeing the dishes in the sink and the cockroaches on the wall behind it, I decided to risk offending him, even though I doubted he was sharp enough to be offended. "No, you go ahead," I said. "I'm not sure we'll be here that long."

He poured his coffee into a Styrofoam cup. Maybe he was sharper than he looked.

"Mr. Sherwood—"

"You can call me Spider."

"I realize it's been a while, but we really need to ask you about Christy."

"Yeah," he said, with that laugh. "I was wondering if you guys were ever going to get around to it."

"You seemed a bit put off," I said. He looked blank. "Upset at our arrival?"

"Oh," he said, sinking into the couch and propping his feet on the table. "I guess I'd kinda forgotten about her. Sort of a downer to be reminded first thing in the morning of your dead girlfriend."

"Isn't it, though." Having forgotten a notebook, I folded my report and turned it over to write on the back.

Mathis fell into the role of casual observer, and I hoped if there was anything to be discovered on the walls or tables that might help us, he'd discover it. Had Scolari been here with me, I wouldn't have given it a second thought. When we left, he would have come out with information on the guy's Social Security status, any unborn children, and a complete medical history. "Can you tell me anything about that night? Anything that might help at all?"

"No. I wasn't there. I was playing in a band. I'm a drummer, ya know."

"Really? Where at?"

"Well, right now, nowhere, but then, I was playing in a band at this bar. The Gold Ox."

"Do you remember what time?"

"Yeah. We had a pretty long gig there—well, till that night." He laughed again. I wanted to shake him. "Three sets a night. First one started at nine. We played till closing with a half-hour break at eleven and twelve-thirty."

"You go anywhere during your second break?" I asked, noting that McAllen's roommate had called 911 around twelve forty-five. That would certainly give him time and opportunity.

"Not that night. I met this chick. We, uh, did it in my car."

I'd heard that story before. Was this the airtight alibi Zim had reported? "Anyone see you?"

"Yeah, her boyfriend. He broke my nose. You shoulda seen the owner. He was pissed 'cause his bartender left." He grinned. "We, uh, sort of turned it into a barroom brawl, 'cause the guy followed me in. Broke a table after we went inside. The owner called the police. That was our last gig there."

I hated to think Zim was right. Not too many holes in that alibi. Still . . . "You remember the girl's name?"

"Yeah. She's sleeping in my bed. You want me to get her?"

I turned to the list of witnesses. Tory Greene. "Yes," I said. "Do that."

It took him a while to wake her. Tory looked like a cranker, the sort that would hang out with a rock and roll guy—overly thin, jeans that fit like a second skin, crop-topped tee, and no bra. At least her wavy blond hair was clean. After the cursory questions, she verified the report she'd given Zimmerman, and there was little else I could ask her. I left them my card, telling them if they thought of anything to call me.

As Mathis and I were leaving, I paused. I had almost forgotten to ask the magic question. "Either of you have any idea who might have killed Christy?"

Sherwood shook his head. Tory, whom I'd dismissed as being clueless, said, "If anyone knows, her roommate does."

"Why do you say that?"

"'Cause she quit working at the Ox right after the murder. Said she didn't want to be the next victim."

Her statement hit me like a ton of bricks. In the car, I looked for any reference in the report that might confirm this. Everything alluded to her believing that the killer was the victim's boyfriend, Spider, yet it was quite apparent that he couldn't be the suspect. Even Zimmerman would have picked up on something like that.

I read the roommate's statement again, and saw that she had in fact told the officer that other than Spider Sherwood, she didn't know who might have killed McAllen.

"You see anything in there that might lead to something?" I asked Mathis.

"Not unless you can get roaches to talk. And we need to check in with Torrance."

"We need to find the roommate."

Before he could protest, my pager went off. I knew when I picked it up who it was from. Pressing the button, I read, RETURN TO BRYANT STREET CODE TWO. I knew better than to ignore Torrance's page, but wasn't about to return to the Hall of Justice. I told Mathis to drive to McAllen's old address, then pulled out my cellular and called Torrance.

"Where are you?" Torrance answered sharply. I was glad I was on the phone, blocks away from the PD.

"What's up?" I asked in as neutral a voice as I could manage. "I got a page, but it didn't come through all the way. I think my battery's going dead."

"Cut the crap, Gillespie."

"You don't need to worry. Mathis is with me."

"I'll deal with him later. Now tell me what the hell is going on."

"I found another Slasher case. I tried to tell you, but—"

"Get back here, now. You're on light duty."

"I feel fine." It was hard, under the circumstances, to not read underlying emotions into his voice. He was being a good supervisor, was all. At least, that was what I told myself. And I was being a good cop with a good lead, which meant that sometimes our pagers and cellulars were more of an inconvenience. "I don't know if it's safe to talk on an unsecured line," I said. "I'll call you from a land line."

"Damn it, Gillespie—"

The term "Management Control" took on a new meaning, and I wondered if that was what they had in mind when they changed the name from Internal Affairs. I turned off the power to the phone, then changed my pager to silent alert. If I was going to ignore it, I didn't want Mathis to end up having to report the number of times he heard the thing go off in case Torrance decided to open a "management control" investigation.

Unfortunately, what I didn't count on was Mathis being paged by Torrance. He read the page, his expression telling me he wasn't pleased by what it said. "We gotta go back, Gillespie. Sorry."

"We're almost there," I said, looking at the address on the street sign. Fourteen-hundred block. McAllen's building was in the fifteen-hundred block.

"I'm about that far away from being transferred back to patrol on midnights. I gotta call him."

"You can't call him a block up the road?"

When Mathis hesitated, I knew I had him. "Just drive to her apartment. You can be talking to Torrance on the phone while I knock on one door. One, that's it. I promise."

"One, Gillespie."

I crossed my heart.

"Hell," he said, pulling out into traffic. "You know how long it's been since I worked patrol? I don't even have a uniform that fits."

"Yeah, but that cute guy you were talking to works patrol." He stopped in front of McAllen's building, a blue and white Victorian-style home converted into a four-plex. "Here. Use my phone." I'd locked it, and figured I'd have about a minute before Mathis came after. Jumping out of the car, I ran up the three steps. Didn't feel

dizzy at all. The place was nice in comparison to the last
address we'd been to, and I wondered about McAllen's
relationship with Spider Sherwood. The two neighbor-
hoods didn't seem to fit, but I suppose there was no
accounting for taste when it came to falling for potential
rock stars.

McAllen and Tilden had lived in number two. I
knocked there, and a man answered, telling me that he'd
moved in shortly after the murder. He didn't know where
Tilden lived, but suggested I check with the woman in
number three upstairs, as they had been friends.

I was halfway up the steps when I heard Mathis's car
door open and then close. I hurried on, rapping sharply
on number three. He caught up to me, took me by the
hand, and started to lead me away. "You said one contact.
You got one. Now be a good girl and get back in the car.
That's an order from Torrance. And he says if you don't,
I'm to hand off you to the door of the car."

"One more minute?"

"No." His grip on my wrist tightened.

"Fine. You win."

"You bet I do."

We started down the steps when the door opened. A
large, square-shouldered woman, mid-forties, short
brown hair, gazed from me to Mathis, then down to his
hand clasped around my wrist. She could have been a
linebacker for the Forty-Niners.

"You okay?" she asked, sounding every bit like she'd
trounce Mathis should my answer be no.

I glanced at Mathis, who sighed in resignation, then
muttered, "I hate midnights."

"I'll be quick." He let go, and I returned to her door.
"I'm Inspector Gillespie, Homicide," I said. "This is my,

uh, partner, Sergeant Mathis. And I'm fine, thanks."

She relaxed her stance, then opened the door wider. "What can I do for you?"

"I was wondering if you could tell us anything about your former neighbors? Christy McAllen or Trish Tilden?"

"Sure. You want to come in?" She stepped aside, allowing us both to enter. She identified herself as Reba Fairbanks. Her apartment was clean and neat, and I doubted there was a roach within walking distance. "Can I get you anything to drink?"

Mathis gave a pointed look at his watch.

"No, thanks, we're sort of in a hurry. What can you tell us about them?"

"Not a lot. I looked after their cat while they were away. Still got it," she said, nodding to the calico sprawled out on the windowsill. "Trish left it here when she moved. That's her there in the photo. With Christy." She pointed to a photo on a bookshelf. Reba Fairbanks was standing between two shorter women, both with long dark hair, similar height and build.

"Who's who?" I asked.

"Trish is on the left. She's the pretty one. Christy's on my right. Nice girl till she got mixed up with that Spider guy. He's the one started calling her Tanya. Said it sounded more rock and roll."

"Do you know where Trish went?"

"No, but I've got a message number. There was a private investigator here earlier. I already gave it to him."

"The PI. Do you recall his name?"

"He didn't say. Just flashed some ID. I can tell you what he looks like, though." She proceeded to describe Scolari to a tee. Mathis and I exchanged glances. "I'll get that number. It's in my phone book," she said, retrieving her purse from her dinette table. "She gave it to me when I agreed to take care of her cat. Said if something happened, and I couldn't do it, call, and she'd get back to me. It was supposed to be temporary, but she hasn't come back for it."

Reba gave me the number, and I noted it had no area code but had a city prefix, which meant Trish was still in the vicinity—well, at least her message taker was, assuming the number was still valid. I asked to use the phone, called, and got an answering machine with a man's voice recorded on it. I left a message asking Trish to call me, then rejoined Mathis and Reba.

"I know you've probably gone over this before with the other inspectors," I said to Reba, "but can you tell me what happened the night of the murder?"

"I'm not sure if it's anything important. I mean, I didn't see anybody or anything."

"Not a problem. Just tell me what you remember."

She rubbed her chin. "The only thing significant is that Trish called me from work. Asked me to come pick her up. No explanation. Might have been around nine." At the first break. "I get there, wondering what's up, 'cause she's sitting in her car, making out with some guy. At least I think so, till I walk right up to the window, about to knock. I wasn't exactly thrilled." She opened her purse and pulled out a pack of Marlboros. "Mind if I smoke?"

"Go ahead."

She lit the cigarette, took a long drag, then blew a plume of smoke to the side. "Like I said, I think I see Trish in this car, then suddenly, Trish calls out from behind me. So I go, 'What the hell's going on?' and she goes, 'I'm quitting.'

"That's it. No explanation." She sucked in a lungful of smoke, speaking as she exhaled. "So I'm pulling out of the parking lot, and I go, 'What about your car?' She says something about Christy and her boyfriend going at it. She says they'd gotten in a fight during the first break, and now that they were making up, she didn't have the heart to interrupt them.

"I'll tell you what," Reba said, flicking her ashes into a glass ashtray. "If it was me, I would have booted Christy's ass right out of the car."

"So what happened after that?"

"Trish went to the car, said something to Christy, and then I took her home. Later, she's telling me about someone putting something in her drink. Never did find out what that was all about. Anyway, about two, three hours later, Trish gets a call. It's Christy from the bar, crying, because she finds her dimwit boyfriend of three months making out with some barfly. Trish tells her to forget him and come home, because she needs her car back. I think she was getting ready to take off for a few days."

"Why do you say that?"

"Well, she was packing a suitcase. So I give Trish a ride to the Ox. We found the car a couple of blocks away from the bar, but not Christy. We circled the area where we found the car. About halfway around the block, Trish saw her lying in some parking lot. She started screaming. Hysterical."

"Prior to that night, did Christy ever give any indication that she was being stalked?"

"No, not her. But the way Trish was carrying on, I figured she was." The woman stared at her cigarette. "She kept saying over and over, 'It could have been me. Oh, God, it could have been me.'" She exhaled.

I gave her a moment to compose herself. "Why do you think she said that?"

"To me it was pretty obvious. If you look at that picture of them, you'll see why. And that night, Christy was driving Trish's car and wearing Trish's coat."

16

"You're off the SoMa Slasher case," Torrance told me when I got back to the office. His calm voice belied the fury in his eyes.

I'd made great strides on what had at one time appeared to be a case with a near-zero solvability factor, and I wasn't about to let him take that away from me. He picked up a report and started reading it. Placing both my hands on the edge of his desk I leaned in close until he had no choice but to acknowledge me. "This is *my* case. I won't give it to someone else. Do you realize that the first victim may have been a case of mistaken identity? She knew her attacker. The—"

"Forget it, Gillespie. You're on administrative leave, starting now."

"You can't do that."

"I can and will. Look at you. You've got six stitches in your head. The doctor said light duty and you chose to ignore him. What if an incident occurred—"

"I'm fine."

Our gazes locked, and I knew he wasn't going to back down. Finally I turned away, grabbed my purse, not willing to let him see how mad I was. Before he could stop me, I was out the door.

"Gillespie!"

Ignoring him, I continued on down the hall and around the corner.

He had no choice but to follow me. "Where do you think you're going?"

I stopped to face him, at this point not caring that he saw my anger. "The ladies' room. Do you plan on following me there, too?" Without waiting for an answer, I pushed open the ladies' room door and stormed in. Dropping my purse on the counter below the mirror, I strode to the sink, turned on the faucet, then drenched my face in cold water—another trick I'd learned to stop any tears before they started. I wouldn't give him the satisfaction.

When the door opened behind me, I whirled around, ready to lay into him for following. "How dare—" It wasn't Torrance at all. It was Leslie O'Keefe, my friend from the Domestic Violence detail. I think she was as shocked as I.

"You okay?"

"I'm fine." Water dripped down my face and onto my neck. After a moment she grabbed a couple of paper towels and handed them to me. I plastered them onto my face, turning away to hide my misery. Leslie and I had gone to the Academy together, and had remained friends ever since. She probably knew me better than anyone in the department. Right now, however, I didn't want to explain the intricacies of my problems to her.

"This have anything to do with the lieutenant watching the bathroom door like a hawk?"

"Yep."

"Anything you want to talk about?"

"Nope."

"Hey, Kate. It's me, Les."

Slowly I lowered the wet towels and looked at her in

the mirror. Les stared right back, her stance telling me she wasn't going anywhere until she knew I was fine. Sometimes friends were a pain in the rear, and right now I knew she was going to be that type of friend. "I'm ticked off," I said, crumpling up the paper towels and tossing them into the trash.

"No kidding."

"They would never do this to me if I were a man."

"Do what?"

"Act as if I can't take care of myself." I tried the looking-up-into-the-ceiling trick, but the tears still came, so I turned the water back on.

"I doubt anyone thinks that."

"Oh, bull," I said, splashing the cold water onto my face until I thought I could control my emotions. "I can't do anything, go anywhere, use the damn bathroom without someone holding my hand."

She held out more paper towels. "Has it occurred to you that maybe they don't want you to end up like Martin and Smith?"

"What if it were reversed? What if I were the suspect and Scolari were here? You think Torrance would be standing outside the door, waiting? Of course not."

"He wouldn't need to. He could walk right in with him. Like I'm doing with you."

"Okay. Bad example."

"Look, Kate. I know you're upset about Scolari. We all are. But you can't let it get to you. It'll eat you alive. Channel that anger into your case. Solve it. Prove Scolari's not the Slasher, like you told everyone you were going to do."

"Nice thought, but they took me off the case."

"What do you mean?"

"Torrance put me on AL." I lifted my hair, showed her my stitches, and told her about my stunt with Mathis and how I ignored Torrance's orders to return. By the time I finished, my paper towels were in shreds, but my tears were gone, my anger dissipated. "Torrance's idea of light duty doesn't match mine."

Les pulled a lipstick from her purse, applied it, but I could see her wheels turning. "Okay," she said a moment later, handing me the tube. My face was pretty much washed out, no pun intended, so I applied a coat to my lips. "Apparently Torrance thinks you need to be watched closer than he can do while you're working, light duty or not."

"So," I said, handing the lipstick back.

"So, you need to make him realize otherwise." She eyed me in the mirror. "At least your stitches are right at your hairline. You know, that color looks better on you than me."

"How?"

"Skin tone. Except for the bruise."

"No, how do I convince him otherwise?"

Her smile was reminiscent of our academy days, and the nights we spent talking about anything and everything but police work. "If you're on administrative leave, you're not on duty. Period."

It took me a moment to figure out what she was saying, then it struck me. "You're an angel, Les." I hugged her.

"I know. Just remember, I didn't tell you."

"Don't worry."

She brushed her hair, headed for the door, pushed it open, and looked out. "You get my message about the tickets for your aunt?"

"Tickets?"

"The Forty-Niner tickets your aunt wanted me to pick up for your nephew's birthday? I left a message on your voice mail. Remember?"

"Voice mail. Yeah," I said, suddenly recalling that her message had come just before Martin's did on the afternoon he was killed in Property. She gave me a strange look, and I added, "My mind was elsewhere. Of course I got your message. I know Aunt Molly will be thrilled. Thanks."

"Any time. By the way, he's still there." Then she was gone, leaving me there to ponder my next step.

One glance in the mirror told me that it would take more than a shade of red on my lips to undo the damage, mostly because my hair hung in wet strands down either side of my face.

Brushing my hair out, then tucking it behind my ears, I exited the rest room feeling confident. As expected, Torrance was right there. I swept past him to the elevators.

"Where do you think you're going?" he demanded.

"Macy's."

"You're kidding, right?"

"Do I look like I'm kidding?" I stopped in front of the elevator, trying my best to ignore him.

"You may not care about your life, but I do."

"Oh, I care. But there's more than just my life at stake," I said, punching the DOWN button. "My partner's life. He's out there somewhere, because someone's blaming him for a murder he says he didn't commit—not to mention the accusation of him being the SoMa Slasher. If he were your partner, wouldn't you want to know? Now, if you don't mind, I seem to have plenty of free time on my hands. I have some shopping to do."

The elevator door opened. I waited a palpable moment for him to say something. When he didn't, I stepped on.

The door started to shut.

At the last moment, he stopped it with his hand. "What do you want?"

"To work the Slasher case my way."

"Fine."

I didn't move.

"There's something else?" he asked.

"Since everyone seems to think the Slasher murdered Doctor Mead-Scolari, I want to be included in that investigation as well."

"I already let you look at the file."

"Not enough. I want in. Every meeting, every report. All the way."

He gave it several seconds of thought, then stepped aside, still holding the door open. "Consider yourself anointed."

"Thank you."

"There will be ground rules."

"Naturally."

"I am your only backup. You go nowhere without me."

"An inconvenience, but I'll manage. Anything else?"

"I want to be apprised of everything you discover as well."

"Deal."

We returned to his office, and without another word he gave me everything he had on Patricia Mead-Scolari's murder, including the autopsy I still hadn't been able to locate, then sat at his desk, regarding me. Knowing better than to try to guess his feelings on the matter—if I had to, I'd say he wasn't pleased—I removed the autopsy report from the binder, and put the remainder aside. "Why do you want to do this?" he asked.

His question surprised me. "He's my partner."

"And you think he'd do the same for you?"

I thought about saying yes, but in truth, I had no idea, even though he'd saved my life at the Twin Palms. "I don't know."

There comes a time for every couple when disenchantment sets in. The first disappointment, first fight, whatever. I felt that we had reached that point, Torrance and I—although I doubted that our rendezvous on my sink constituted a true relationship, or made us a real couple. Regardless, I felt the strain between us, undoubtedly caused by his belief in Scolari's guilt, and my unwavering conviction, at least verbally, of Scolari's innocence.

Torrance returned to his work, and so did I. I knew I was missing something simple from the autopsies, and lined the Slasher cases side by side with the doctor's and with McAllen's. I took a tablet, divided it into columns, and listed each of the obvious traits as well as the dates of each murder. Nothing stood out the first time around. The second time, I stopped on McAllen's case. The date. How had I missed it? January twenty-fourth. The night I'd been shot. I stared, unbelieving.

I wanted to tell Torrance what I'd found, but I heard him pick up his phone and ask to speak with Captain Griffin, his boss.

"Just wanted you to know that I've asked Inspector Gillespie to join the Mead-Scolari task force," he said. Silence, then, "No, sir. I believe she'll be an asset."

He hung up and said, "He feels you'll be a risk, because you're too close to Scolari."

"What do you think?" I asked without turning

around. I could see his reflection in one of several framed certificates on the wall. He sat with hands clasped before him, steepled fingers tap-tapping.

"Exactly what I told the captain," he finally said. "Don't let me down."

This last was said so quietly, I barely heard. I swiveled my chair to face him, weighing whether or not to tell him what I'd just learned. Then I said, "I think I have the proof that Scolari's not the Slasher."

"And that would be?"

I held up the McAllen autopsy. "If my theory proves correct, this is a Slasher case that we missed." I handed it to him. "Look at the date."

"Wasn't that the night you were shot at the Twin Palms?"

"Yes," I said, surprised that the date stood out in his mind.

"Scolari was with you."

"Exactly."

He returned the autopsy to me. "Get me more facts, a tighter case." Then he nodded, picked up a report, his actions dismissing me.

I decided then and there that Torrance was a man I would never understand. Now, however, was not the time to dwell on it, and I pulled out the autopsy photo packets from each case, spreading them on the table. There were several in each packet, but I concentrated on the neck shots, since that was the Slasher's MO.

Looking at the photos reminded me of a conversation I'd overheard as a rookie. Two officers on my shift discussing a throat slashing they'd responded to, one saying something about the suspect cutting a second smile on the victim. At the time I thought it macabre. Still did.

But seeing the photos spread out before me, the gaping wounds cleansed of blood, I knew exactly what he meant.

And that was when I realized what I'd missed. The location and severity of the entrance wounds and exit wounds. In black and white.

Ask any cop what it's like to fit the missing puzzle pieces, and they'll tell you that's the thing that keeps them coming back for more. I felt that excitement as I scanned each of the reports, starting with McAllen's. Nothing was going to stop me now.

Nothing except a page from Scolari.

17

I wasn't sure what Scolari's motivation was. At the moment I didn't care. "What do you make of this?" I asked Torrance, showing him Scolari's page, telling me to go to the Gold Ox.

"Why the Gold Ox?"

"The autopsy I just showed you, McAllen. She was killed in a parking lot a couple of blocks away from the Ox." I gave him the particulars on the report.

"How is it that no one made the connection?"

"The case was in limbo for a year. I think it was overlooked because right before the victim died, she led the officer to believe that she knew her attacker. It didn't fit the profile, and there wasn't another Slasher case until six months later."

"So for the past six months, Scolari says nothing and suddenly this case takes top billing?"

"Look. I'm not Scolari's keeper. I don't know why he never mentioned this to me before. But he is now. And I intend to find out why. The question I have for you is, are you coming along?"

The sun had disappeared behind the fog bank, and a light drizzle was falling when we pulled out of the parking garage. Torrance was driving. We were probably about a block from the Ox when Torrance nodded at the gray pickup in front of him. "Isn't that Dex Kermgard?"

"Looks like him. Let's follow."

The pickup turned right, and then made a left. We dropped a couple of cars back when it became apparent that he was heading straight for the Wharf area.

"A man on a mission," Torrance said, commenting on the way Dex was driving, weaving in and out of traffic.

I didn't think he was trying to lose us—assuming he saw us at all—for the mere fact he didn't turn onto one of the side streets. "Hot date?"

"With who?"

We found out soon enough. He managed to find a parking space, then walked about half a block to the Buena Vista, a bar immortalized for its Irish coffee by the late *San Francisco Chronicle* columnist Herb Caen. We parked farther up the road, away from his car, and quite illegally, leaving the radio's mike over the rearview mirror to ward off the parking patrol, who were known for eating their young.

As we approached I asked, "How do you want to do this? Walk in, see who he's meeting? Or pretend we chanced on him coming here for a drink?"

Torrance looked at his watch. "Three-thirty. Too early for us to get off and imbibe. Guess we go for the former." He pushed open the door, then stood aside for me to enter.

Frequented by locals and tourists alike, the bar was crowded, all the tables taken even at this hour. We found Dex standing at the end of the long polished-wood bar, apparently ordering a drink. As we headed that way, he turned and saw us, his expression never wavering. Behind him, at the table in the corner, sat Nick Paolini, and a man who seemed familiar. I couldn't place him at the moment. We approached the table.

Paolini stood, his gray silk suit impeccable. He was a smooth talker, very formal, and when he wanted he could turn on the charm. He reminded me of the glamorous crooks portrayed in the *Godfather* movies. Al Pacino with tattoos. "Inspector Gillespie. I understand you are assigned to Homicide now."

"Yes. Funny I should run into you. I have a few things I need to discuss."

His dark brows raised a fraction. "I admit to a fascination for your new assignment, and would love to stay, but Tony and I are late for a very important meeting." Tony? Of course. Antonio Foust. I glanced at Foust, who stood, and without a word, turned toward the door. With that, the pair wove their way through the myriad of chairs, tables, people, then out the door. Not once did they acknowledge Dex's presence, which I found more odd than their "chance" meeting here in the first place.

"Hello, Dex," I said, eyeing him.

"Kate." He nodded in greeting to Torrance.

"You here to meet Paolini?"

"Actually, I'm waiting for Josie." He looked at his watch. "She's late. Buy you a drink?"

"Sure," I said. "Coffee, black." Torrance declined the offer.

Dex went to the bar to order, and I sat in the chair Paolini had vacated. Six empty glass mugs littered the table, giving testament that Paolini and Foust had probably sat there awhile, drinking. Torrance took a seat, keeping an eye on the window and the door while I watched Dex.

"You don't really expect me to believe you weren't

here to meet with Paolini?" I asked him when he brought my coffee. I didn't drink it.

"I suppose you'll believe what you want."

"I read the old IA reports about the informant and the missing drug money. What's with you and Foust?"

"You have that conversation with Scolari, too? He was there."

"Really?"

"You read the report. You know that one of the slugs dug out of the dirtbag's heart was never identified. Maybe you ought to ask Scolari what the hell he did with that old thirty-eight he used to carry back then. You think it was stolen like he said? Or conveniently lost?"

"You're saying Scolari killed the guy?"

"I'm saying I'm grateful I'm alive. Just like it says in the IA. But you might want to ask Scolari how he put his wife through medical school."

I crossed my arms, leaned back, tried not to show my surprise. "Why do I think you're trying to distract me from the real issue? That you were here to meet with Paolini?"

"Look, Inspector. I'm here to meet with Josephine Hilliard. By coincidence, Paolini and Foust happened to be sitting here when I arrived. You ask Paolini, he'll tell you. I haven't spoken to him in years. But don't take my word for it. You wait long enough, you can ask Mrs. Hilliard herself. She's getting out of that cab now." He tilted his head to the window, where out in the street, sure enough, Josie Hilliard was exiting a Yellow Cab.

Dex's gaze held mine. "Any more questions, Inspector?"

"For now, no," I said, rising. I had enough to think about, and we still needed to get to the Gold Ox. "I'll be in touch."

"I'm sure you will."

Once the door closed behind us, I said, "I'd like to know who's lying. Scolari did report his gun missing the night before the shooting. Which was why he was cleared." I thought about what Dex implied, that Scolari had faked the theft, then lied about the shooting. "Had it occurred to me sooner that that was Foust, I might have asked him about Dex's shooting. I thought he looked familiar, but couldn't place why."

"You think he would have told you the truth?"

"Never hurts to ask."

We entered the Gold Ox, stepping into a long, narrow room lit by amber-hued lights that helped to camouflage the peeling paint. The Ox was everything the Buena Vista wasn't. Typical beer signs littered the wall to our right, the bar ran along to our left. A man, stout, liftylsh, with brown hair that looked like it came out of a spray can, stood behind the counter, wiping the wood surface down with a towel. At the far end sat a woman, thin, red nose, sagging features of a classic alcoholic, sipping on something clear from a tall glass. Farther down, through an opening in the wall, I caught a glimpse of what appeared to be another room, perhaps the dance floor where Spider Sherwood had played in the band.

The woman looked up, her gaze lingering on Torrance a moment before settling on me, and then just as quickly dismissed us.

"Something I can get fer ya?" the bartender asked.

I was about to pull my star when Torrance stopped me. "Do you have a telephone?" he asked.

"Down there, next to the rest rooms," he said, nodding past the dance floor to a narrow, dim hallway.

"Thanks."

We strolled over, not in any great hurry. "Why no ID?" I asked Torrance when we were out of earshot.

"Just a feeling."

He poked his head out the back door, then checked the men's room while I looked into the women's room. Nothing but a single toilet, sink, and warped faux marble wall paneling. No sign of Scolari or an ambush. Not that I expected Scolari to be present.

I let the door swing shut. "Empty."

"Same here."

We leaned against the wall by the phone. Torrance called his desk. After two minutes we wandered back to the bar, taking a seat.

The woman eyed us with a glazed curiosity. "What are you guys? Like the potty police?"

At first I thought she'd made us, which surprised me—her slow, deliberate voice told me she'd been drinking the afternoon away. But then she continued on. "I mean, you walk right in, and without even buying a drink, you check the goddamn rest rooms out. Figure ya gotta be from the Department of Health, the way yer all dressed. What'dya think, Joe?"

Joe the bartender made a sound that could have been a sign of agreement. He straightened out some glasses, then looked over at us.

So remind me never to wear tan wool slacks and blazer with a white blouse to a dive bar.

"Buy you a drink?" Torrance asked.

I shrugged.

"Two margaritas," he ordered. "Over ice."

Without a word the bartender polished up a couple of glasses, filled them with ice, tequila, and margarita mix.

He stirred them, dropped a quarter of lime in each, then slid them toward us.

Torrance laid a twenty on the counter. I waited to see if he was really going to drink. Lifting the glass to his lips, he took a long sip. No doubt about it. I did the same, curious.

"You work here long?" Torrance asked.

"Twelve years. Own the place," Joe said, running the towel over the drip marks left while concocting our drinks.

Torrance drank some more. "That you?" he asked, pointing to a framed photograph on a shelf behind the bar.

The owner turned, gave a thorough appraisal of the picture of a much younger version of himself standing next to a yellow race car. His chest swelled with pride, "Sure is. Used to be pretty damn good. Got that trophy up there at Sears Point, Came in second," he said, returning to his polishing and polishing, glasses clinking as he returned them to their shelves. "That was my last race. My wife didn't want me ending up dead."

For the next several minutes they discussed racing while I nursed my drink.

"How's business been these past few months?" Torrance asked during a lull.

"Not bad."

"Hasn't sloughed off any with all that SoMa Slasher stuff you hear in the news?"

"People get immune to hearin' 'bout it."

"You here that night the first one got killed?"

"You two PIs?" he queried, looking us over. I took a long sip. Everyone knew cops didn't drink on duty.

"Why do you ask?" Torrance countered.

"The way I see it, the cops ain't done shit. And there's already been one PI here the last week. Who hired you?"

"We're looking into Christy McAllen's death."

He wiped down the counter again, avoiding our gaze. "I thought you were lookin' into the SoMa Slasher stuff."

Torrance swirled his drink, then sipped. "Read it in the paper. Might be related."

"No kiddin'?" he said, tossing the towel over his shoulder, then picking up a couple of bottles from the counter behind him. "Don't know nothin' about it."

Torrance lifted his glass as if to say, You're up.

Although Joe's back was to us, from the angle where I sat, I had a clear view of his actions. He proceeded to pour whiskey from a generic bottle into a Seagram's bottle, then did the same with generic gin into a Tanqueray bottle. Despite that I wasn't experienced enough with gin to distinguish real Tanqueray from lighter fluid, I knew any agent from Alcoholic Beverage Control would have a field day inspecting this place.

"Hey, what's the name of that friend of ours that works for the ABC?" I asked Torrance, nodding toward Joe. The bartender looked up, his gaze catching mine in the mirror. He seemed to be waiting for Torrance's answer, as though to ensure I wasn't bluffing. I kicked Torrance's shin.

"Henry," he said quickly. I should have kicked him harder. There was a Henry Weinhard clock on the wall almost eye level with the bartender's face.

"Yeah. Henry. How's he doing, anyway?"

"Not bad. Wife and kids are doing pretty good, too."

The bartender still watching, I gave my best Mona Lisa smile.

"Maybe I remember somethin' after all," Joe said.

"You'll have to give me a minute. A lot happened that night, what with my bartender skippin' out for some family emergency. Left me stranded on a Friday night. I was busier than hell."

Funny how some details such as a murder got pushed to the wayside while the fact he had to work a little harder on a particular day of the week was still at the forefront of his memory. "Really?" I queried. I loved that word. People usually felt compelled to comment.

"Yeah. I just haven't thought about it since then," he added, as though he realized what his earlier remark had sounded like. "My waitress, Trish, she quit that night," he said, picking up a jar of maraschino cherries. He twisted off the top, then dumped them into a small container next to the green olives. The sweet-smelling syrup splashed onto the counter, but he didn't seem to notice.

"Anyway, I was pissed. It's after nine, and we're busier than hell. Trish comes waltzin' into my storeroom, and announces she's leaving as soon as her ride gets there. I'm tryin' to talk her out of it, but she don't listen. Out she goes, tellin' me if I want to know what's goin' on, I should ask my bartender. Then, 'bout two hours later, some idiot from this band I hired gets in a fight with someone else. Got caught screwin' some guy's chick, and gets his nose rearranged with one of my tables. I call the cops, and my bartender announces he's takin' off for some freakin' family emergency. In the meantime, my bouncer's missin' in action, and I have to haul these two goons out by myself, and nearly get run over by Trish's Volkswagen that's screechin' from the parkin' lot like a rat after cheese. Probably why the engine died."

"Pardon?"

"The way she took off. Car started sputtering 'bout a

block down the road. Watched her coast for another block after that."

I thought of the proximity of the phone booths to the other murders. Wondered if anyone checked the car angle. Car tampered with, breaks down, victim calls for help. "Did you see who was driving it?"

"I figured Trish was."

"But didn't she say she had called for a ride home?"

He paused. "Yeah. She did. But it was definitely her car."

"You know her roommate at all? The girl that got killed?"

"Met her once or twice. Trish mentioned somethin' about her datin' that drummer. The one who got his nose broke."

"Was Christy there that night?"

"Christy?"

"Trish's roommate. She might have gone by 'Tanya.'"

He wiped the cherry juice from the counter. "Like I said, my bartender, Eric Lange, up and left me that night right after Trish left, and I wasn't exactly worried about who the hell was drivin' the car. I suppose it could've been her, but truthfully, I was too pissed to care."

18

The bar owner left us to ourselves once he finished his tale, saying he didn't remember much else. But at least his story seemed to coincide with that of the rocker boyfriend and the neighbor. I was curious about the bartender that night, the one who left on a family emergency. Trish had gone to the trouble of mentioning him to the owner when she quit. It couldn't hurt to talk to him as well, and I wondered if Zim had mentioned him in the report. I didn't recall seeing his name.

"You think Scolari ever intended to show?" Torrance asked outside the bar. Light emanating from the neon Gold Ox sign did little to penetrate the thick gray mist that had smothered the street now that the sun was gone.

"Not a chance. Scolari would know I'd never come alone. My guess is that he's trying to prove he's not the Slasher by getting me to solve the case."

"Where to now?"

"Grab a bite, then home, James." I had no desire to return to the Hall and look at dead bodies that could wait until tomorrow, and so we went to dinner at a Greek restaurant not too far from the Hall.

Torrance apparently was a regular there. After dinner the owner's wife brought him a plate of still-warm baklava. "For you, Mike," she said in a thick Greek accent. She leaned down and whispered a little too loud, "It's about time you bring a beautiful woman in here with you."

I pretended not to hear, but after she returned to the kitchen, I could no longer hide my amusement. "Come here often, do you?"

He was clearly embarrassed, which I found endearing, because it was so at odds with the man I thought I knew. He left a generous tip, and we were soon on our way back to Berkeley.

At my apartment, however, I had forgotten that Torrance was insistent on playing bodyguard. Apparently, Linda Perkins had errands to run and couldn't stay in his stead, and he didn't believe me when I told him that I hadn't felt the least bit dizzy since we left the hospital. Even after I mentioned that my health was perfect, he pointed out that there were the death threats, and Scolari was still at large. Great.

I locked the door behind Linda, listening to her footfall as she descended the wooden stairs outside. After the last creak of the last step, I knew she had rounded the corner and was now headed down the moss-covered brick walkway. Suddenly I was very much aware of the man standing in my apartment, and the fact that we were alone.

We stared at each other for several moments.

I knew what I wanted him to do, what I wanted to do.

"Sheets?" he asked.

"Sheets?" I shook myself. Moved past him to get the sheets from my room. When I handed them over, our fingers touched. My pulse raced.

He stood stock-still, his gaze held mine.

"Need . . . anything else?" I finally asked.

"Yes."

I waited. The refrigerator hummed. The clock ticked on the wall.

"Go to bed, Gillespie."

It wasn't until I got into my room and shut the door that I realized it was only eight-thirty. I rarely went to bed before ten or eleven, but there was no way on earth I was leaving this room. Taking rejection well was not one of my stronger attributes, and at the moment, I liked that we parted on the ambiguity of it being bedtime, no matter that he was the one who did the dismissing, so to speak. It wasn't rejection. He'd told me once before that he had a job to do, and couldn't do it if we were in bed together.

Not rejection at all.

Worked for me.

I took stock of my bedroom. Everything was in its place. I started wondering who had searched through my things earlier. I could certainly go out and ask Torrance his opinion. Good excuse. But I was too chicken. I didn't want him to think I was looking for a reason to speak with him. Not that I needed a reason.

But who *had* searched my room? Scolari? He'd broken in once before. But what could he possibly have been searching for? Mathis? I suppose he could have done it before we returned to the apartment the night we all went to dinner. Perhaps I didn't notice right off. Reid? He'd come in to use the bathroom. I could well imagine him looking for some clue that I was dating another man. I could handle that—didn't like it, but at least he was a known entity.

The only other possibility was Torrance. He'd been in here ostensibly to speak on the phone in private. Yet I clearly recalled seeing him later that night using his cell phone in the kitchen. Had he truly wanted privacy, he would've taken his phone onto the porch, closed the door.

I sank to my bed. Eight thirty-five. Sleep eluded me—no surprise there—and I looked around for something to occupy the next few hours. Cleaning was out. My eye caught on several magazines stacked by my nightstand. Picking one at random, *Newsweek*, I opened it, flipping through the pages. A photograph of a shriveled corpse, very brown, preserved, caught my eye. Homicide being my business, I was instantly intrigued.

Apparently, the man had been an ancient traveler found frozen in the Swiss Alps. Switzerland and Italy both claimed the corpse, and the relics with it, including a pouch of seeds. They surmised the ancient guy was a hunter-gatherer, on his way to who knew where. Probably on his way to get to the other side of the mountain.

The article was fascinating and even ironic in the similarity to my current John Doe, the Ice Man. Two dead men, one centuries old, one modern. Both frozen solid. Both alone, unidentified. Both with seeds, I realized, although the ancient guy had several hundred as opposed to my John Doe, who had seven tucked—hidden?—in his ring.

I wondered if there was any way to tell exactly how long my Ice Man had been dead. A month? More?

At least they had that. My John Doe was still nameless, no known occupation, and I seriously doubted he was on his way to plant those seeds anywhere.

Why would someone kill for them? What was so important about pokeweed seeds? Did Scolari's wife discover something when she did the autopsy on the Ice Man? Had she told Scolari? Was it possible those seven tiny seeds were the connection to each of the other murders? The doctor's, Martin's and Smith's . . . and my attempted poisoning?

I took out a pen and piece of stationery from the nightstand. In the center I sketched a coin-sized circle, and wrote SEEDS in the middle. From there I drew lines radiating out from the circle, like spider legs. At the end of each line I drew another circle for each of the victims. The drawing looked more like a rendering of Itsy Bitsy Spider with shoes, but then, art was never my specialty. Brainstorming murders was.

In the first circle, I wrote "Ice Man," the first known victim that started this. In the next circle, I wrote "Doctor." Martin and Smith followed. And finally myself—so my spider was missing a couple of legs.

The seeds seemed to have a connection to everything. I needed to find out why.

And how?

Okay. That was temporarily out. Look at suspects. I wrote Scolari's name on the left. He was in his wife's car the night she was murdered. He was seen down in Property. Rhetorically speaking, bodies littered his trail. The only homicide I couldn't place him as a suspect at was that of the Ice Man.

I tapped my pen on the Ice Man circle, drew a line from there and wrote "Paolini." Then I wrote "Hilliard Rx" and drew another line from there to Ice Man. Hilliard rented the facility to Paolini, which earned them a connecting line to each other, forming a triangle. I drew a line from Paolini to Martin and Smith. Paolini's evidence was at stake. What I couldn't do was connect him to Doctor Mead-Scolari's murder. But she knew about the seeds, even if she didn't know *what* they were. The seeds were in Hilliard's building and she knew that, therefore a line connecting Hilliard to the doctor's death.

Hilliard.

Paolini.

Scolari.

My drawing was starting to look like some complex chemical solution in a chemistry book. Atoms linked to each other.

Link. Missing link.

MO of the doctor's death.

The Slasher victims were not linked in any way to any of these deaths but Patricia's. Her killer had copied the MO. Why? Obvious. Whoever killed her wanted us to think it was the Slasher. I'd figured this out from the entrance and exit wounds on the autopsy photos. Scolari paging me to go to the Gold Ox had distracted me. I had yet to tell Torrance what I'd discovered.

I fell back onto my pillow. I didn't really know what part Scolari played in all this. He was adamant that he wasn't the SoMa Slasher. I knew he wasn't.

But had he killed his wife? Did he know something about those seeds that I was missing?

I lay there several more minutes, contemplating any other possibilities regarding the doctor's murder. Nothing came to mind, and I knew I needed to tell Torrance about the autopsy photos. My aunt always said while doing a jigsaw puzzle when you couldn't find the pivotal piece, "A fresh eye always helps." Torrance would be my fresh eye.

I got up, padded to the door. My hand on the knob, I opened it, paused on the threshold at the sight of Torrance in the kitchen speaking softly to Mathis. I wasn't aware Mathis had arrived, and as I watched, I saw Torrance grab his jacket and exit the kitchen door, leaving Mathis behind.

I stepped back into the bedroom, closing the door before Mathis noticed. So Torrance was skipping out. No big deal.

My list could wait until morning. But as I stripped to a T-shirt and slipped between the sheets, I realized I was curiously disappointed. I wasn't sure how long I remained awake thinking about it, hours it seemed. Although rain was predicted for the night, moonlight angled in through the bedroom window, and the last thing I remembered before drifting off was turning on my side, catching a glimpse of the bathroom sink, and recalling in minute detail the feel of cool porcelain against my skin.

A creak in the floor woke me.

My eyes flew open to stygian black. My heart thudded against my sternum. Pulse pounded in my ears.

Outside, a gale whipped the trees, rain slashed against the windows. The wind. Imagination. Then I saw my bedroom door.

Ajar.

Darkness moved at my side. Large, male. A hand clamped over my mouth.

Every muscle in my body tensed. I twisted away, clawed at my captor. He pulled me against him. His whiskers scraped my cheek as he spoke. "Not a sound." Then I felt the cold steel of a gun against my bare thigh.

I froze. My thoughts and the world went spinning. In the millisecond it took to right itself, I realized the gun wasn't pointed at me but at my bedroom door. And it wasn't only my heart thudding out of control, but also that of the bare-chested man holding me. Torrance.

When he apparently assured himself that I was calm, fully awake, and in charge of my faculties, he lowered his hand. "Someone's in," he whispered. The wind whistled beneath the eaves, branches banged on the side of the house.

"Where's Mathis?"

"Should be on his way back to the city, left about an hour ago. Where's your weapon?"

"Kitchen."

"So's the intruder. You got a way out?"

I pointed to the bathroom window. Torrance rose from the bed, his departure leaving me cold. I watched as he edged toward the door, his gun held close. Combat ready.

He covered the portal, ready to shoot. I untangled my bare legs from the sheets and got out of bed. On afterthought, I stuffed my pillows beneath the blankets, then hurried into the bathroom to open the window.

Torrance backed his way after me. Seconds ticked by. Winter dampness had taken its toll on the peeling paint and wood frame window. Leaning into it, I shoved harder. Open. I climbed through, stepped onto the two-foot-wide ledge of slippery terra-cotta tiled roof. Torrance followed.

Rain pelted me, soaked my T-shirt through. To our right the roof continued toward the front of the house. To our left, just past the window, the roofline ended abruptly. Below us was the brick pathway that ran alongside the house.

Two muffled gunshots sent me scrambling from the ledge. Torrance as well. He dropped to the ground and reached up. I hung for a moment, feeling his arms come around my legs. I landed on cold, wet bricks.

Another gunshot. The fence board splintered beside us. Torrance grabbed my hand and pulled me to the front of the house. We flew up the driveway.

Lights around us came on. My neighbors would undoubtedly call 911. In minutes, the cops would be here. I didn't know if we had minutes. I glanced over my shoulder. I doubted we'd be able to get into Torrance's car, even start it in time.

"This way," I said, tugging him toward a neighbor's yard about three houses up. Art never locked his garage door, no matter how often I lectured him on it. I only prayed he hadn't changed his habits. Our best chance lay in keeping out of sight until the cops got there. The suspects wouldn't risk getting caught. I hoped.

The garage door was open. We rushed in. Torrance pushed it closed, locked it. We sank to the floor.

Footfall pounding. A shout. Car doors slamming. A moment later, the rev of an engine, tires squealing.

Finally all was quiet.

Our labored breathing was the only sound. I leaned my head back and closed my eyes. The rush of adrenaline finally caught up to me. I started shivering.

Torrance drew me to his side, wrapping his arm around me. It did little to dispel the cold. At last, the blessed sound of a siren in the distance. We didn't move until the flashing red and blue of the patrol car briefly lit the garage through the window as it passed.

Torrance ran his hand up the wall near the door, found the light switch, turned it on, eyed my wet T-shirt. "I'd offer you my coat, if I had one."

"And deprive the patrol officers of something to talk about at briefing?"

His glance strayed down, lingering about the edge of the shirt, which hit the top of my thighs. "They'll be discussing this in the locker room, if you step out like that."

"Suggestions?"

"You know your neighbor very well?"

"Well enough."

Art Harrelson had one of the few garages in the area that wasn't detached from the house. One wall was covered with hand tools, neatly arranged on Peg-Board, along with a good amount of fishing equipment, poles, and the like at one end. No jacket. Not even a towel.

"I'm gossip fodder," I said.

Suddenly the door to the house flew open.

Torrance and I whirled about to see my white-haired, walrus-mustachioed neighbor pointing a shotgun at us.

"Hi, Art."

"Kate?" he asked, his craggy face a mixture of relief and confusion. "What the dag-nabbit are you doin' here? And who is he?" he asked, swinging the shotgun at Torrance now that he'd apparently assured himself I was not the threat.

"This is Lieutenant Torrance. He, um, works with me."

"You're not in any danger?" he asked, never removing his gaze from Torrance.

"Not now. The lieutenant saved me," I said, thinking how ridiculous it must sound, considering the way we were dressed. Or undressed. "Someone broke into my apartment. We had to climb out the window."

Harrelson lowered the shotgun. "Heard the commotion. Then when I heard you two in here, I figured someone was breaking in, and I wasn't about to wait for them damned cops to find 'em. Well, you better come in, put something on before you go out and get wet again."

We followed him into his kitchen. He put away the shotgun, put on some water, then set out a couple of mugs and tea bags. He handed me the phone. "You better call the police department, or you'll have them boys wondering what the heck's goin' on out there. I'll get you some dry clothes."

I called, explained to the dispatcher what happened, and within two minutes there was a knock at Harrelson's front door.

"Hold on," Harrelson called out. "Here you go, Kate. Brought you a flannel shirt 'n some socks. You go on into the bathroom and change. There's clean towels hanging on the wall. I'll get the door."

He handed the items to me, ushering me off to the bathroom. "Got one for you, too, lieutenant," I heard him say. There was another knock, then, "Hold on."

Had someone not taken a couple potshots at me, I might have been more embarrassed at the view I must have presented. I pulled off my wet T-shirt, toweled down, then slipped on the warm, soft red flannel shirt, which hit me midthigh, and then the socks. I quickly ran my fingers through my hair, trying to improve the drowned rat appearance—strictly for the Berkeley police, I told myself.

There was little else I could do without a shower and a blow dryer, so I stepped out to face the cops.

Torrance sat at the kitchen table wearing a similar blue flannel shirt, unbuttoned. He looked up at me, his expression cold, forbidding. Two uniformed officers sat across from him, while Harrelson offered tea. The officers saw me, and rose. "You're Kate Gillespie?" one asked.

"Yes."

"You know anything about the man we found lying at the bottom of your stairs?"

19

What man?" I asked, my gaze locking with Torrance's.

"Mathis," he said quietly.

I sank into a chair, glancing at the officer. "Is he okay?"

"We've called an ambulance, ma'am. My partner's with him now. And the sergeant. He was breathing when we got there."

"Was he shot?" Seconds ticked by.

"We're not sure. A neighbor reported hearing a shot. We got a 911 call. When we found him, there was a pair of black leather gloves lying next to him. Men's gloves. Figured they might have been his."

"I don't think he had any gloves on," Torrance replied. "At least not when he left."

I closed my eyes, replaying the events, trying to recount the shots I'd heard. Three. Two in my house, one as we fled. Was Mathis shot in the house?

The officer's radio crackled, but I didn't hear what was said. Someone grasped my hand. Warmth suffused my cold skin. I opened my eyes to see Torrance watching me closely. "They've finished checking your apartment. It's clear."

I said nothing.

"Let's go see Mathis."

I nodded, and he drew me to my feet.

Harrelson threw a raincoat over my shoulders, told me not to worry about his things. No rush. Somehow I thanked him, as did Torrance, and we followed the officer out the door. Three patrol cars as well as an ambulance were parked out front between my house and Harrelson's, turning the quiet, tree-lined street into a spectacle of red and blue lights. Despite the rain sluicing down, neighbors stood on their porches or on the sidewalk, watching the activity as though it were a sideshow at the circus. I wanted to scream at everyone to go back inside. Give us some privacy. I didn't. Merely allowed Torrance to draw me by my hand down the street to the ambulance.

Mathis was on the gurney, covered by a yellow water-proof, disposable tarp. His face was pale, his eyes closed. The EMTs were wheeling him to the back of the ambulance. Together they lifted and swung the gurney in, the wheels collapsing.

"How is he?" Torrance asked one of the attendants. He still held my hand, his grip tightening while he waited for the immediate prognosis.

"Stable. You know what happened? Did he fall?"

"He wasn't shot?" Torrance asked.

"Not that we can tell. At the moment, he's uncon-scious. Possibly a blow to the head, judging by the lump on the back of his skull. Small cut. Heads bleed a lot. Thought he might have taken a tumble down those wet steps in the back."

Torrance's grip on my hand relaxed. At the same time, I exhaled in relief.

Mathis groaned.

Torrance asked if he could speak to him. The attendant said yes, and Torrance climbed into the back. "Hey, buddy. You playing slip 'n' slide on the steps?"

Whatever Mathis said, I couldn't hear. Torrance had to lean closer, his ear next to the sergeant's mouth.

Torrance patted him on the shoulder. "We'll follow you in a flash."

When he hopped down, he drew me away. "Hit from behind. Never saw him."

I knew he was thinking Scolari did it.

The ambulance left without lights or siren, which was another sign that Mathis would be fine. I told myself to relax. I couldn't. Someone had invaded my most private space. Once again, officers plied me with questions while I stood in the rain dressed in a coat and wet socks.

"I've asked them to send evidence techs out here to dust the apartment," Torrance told me after the last question was asked and answered.

"You can take the place apart board by board. I don't care, as long as I get a hot shower, some clothes, and a place to sleep. Just let me get some things, and I'll turn the place over to whoever you want."

He hesitated.

"For Christ's sake," I said, my anger surfacing. "You think I don't know what to touch or not touch? Or are you worried that I'll disturb any precious evidence that Scolari might have left?"

"I'm sorry." He told the officers to allow me in, and I ignored the fact that I had to ask permission to get into my own place. I told myself that he was simply worried about Mathis. The man was his partner, after all.

When I entered my bedroom, everything seemed in order. Until I took a closer look at my bed. The pillows I'd covered with blankets were pulled out. I picked up

one, saw nothing but a single feather floating down.
Which meant there was a hole in the ticking. On closer
examination, I realized there were four holes. Two
entrance, two exit on the other side. And on the mattress
as well. I didn't bother looking beneath the bed to see if
the rounds had pierced the hardwood flooring. Instead, I
called my landlord. There was no answer, and then I
remembered Mathis telling me when I was in the hospital
that they were visiting relatives in Ohio. I only hoped
they didn't return to find their kitchen sink had two new
drain holes.

It didn't take me long to put on some jeans, a sweater,
dry socks, and soft leather boots, then gather a few things
and throw them into a garment bag. I thought about taking a shower, but didn't want to do so with officers waiting outside my bathroom door, anxious for me to finish so
they could examine and dust the windowsill. Besides that,
the steam was bound to take forever to evaporate, which
would make dusting near impossible. As I started out of
the bedroom, I remembered the list I'd been making of
victims and possible connections to the case. One of the
evidence techs was waiting with a very annoyed look on
his face. I felt like telling him my taxes paid his salary. I'd
heard it enough. I stopped myself, for the simple reason it
wasn't a good idea to tick off the people throwing around
the black dust. I'd been to scenes where that happened,
saw the damage they could do by *accidentally* spilling
graphite, or dusting things that didn't need dusting. Not
a pretty sight.

"Sorry, guys, let me look in one more place." I
checked behind the nightstand, found the list I'd made,
stuffed it into my pocket. "Thanks." And I was out of
there.

Torrance stood guard in the kitchen, dressed once more in his own shirt. His dark slacks were still wet. His jacket hung over the chair, right where he'd left it before this latest nightmare started. As I approached, he handed me my purse. "Anything missing?"

I opened it, glanced in, saw my weapon. The rest was incidental, since I knew this was no random cat burglar that happened upon my place. "Doesn't look like it. But there are a few new holes in my pillows."

"I've called one of our teams in. They're going to stay here until Berkeley's finished collecting evidence. We'll come back tomorrow for anything else you need. Do you have any idea how the suspect gained entry?"

"Are you saying you don't?" I didn't mention that he was the one who was supposed to be standing guard.

"I have a theory. One you don't want to hear."

I waited.

"Scolari hid somewhere. Waited for the opportunity, which happened when I relieved Mathis after I got back tonight."

"That's ridiculous. Scolari wouldn't do this."

"Regardless, someone has, and you're not staying." He held the door open, his actions telling me he would consider no other options.

"For the record, I'm leaving because someone is try-ing to kill me—*someone*, not Scolari. And I'm tired of being uprooted."

"And I'm not?"

"Point taken," I said.

We drove to the hospital, checked in on Mathis, and learned his only injury was the blow to his head. He hadn't seen who hit him. After being reassured by the doctor that he suffered from a concussion but otherwise seemed fine, we left. Neither of us spoke on the drive back to the city. My guess was that, like me, Torrance was busy trying to figure out what had happened and how it was possible. I thought about Scolari's page, telling us to head to the Gold Ox, the bar where McAllen had spent her last night. We crossed the Bay Bridge, and at first I thought we were headed to the Hall of Justice. There was a cot in the locker room as well as showers. But Torrance took the financial district exit instead.

As we passed the pyramid-shaped TransAmerica building, I glanced over at him. "Where are you taking me?"

He signaled for a left turn. "You do want to sleep tonight, don't you?" He pulled into the parking garage below the Holiday Inn at the edge of Chinatown. He parked, popped the trunk, got out.

I followed suit. "The Holiday Inn? You're kidding."

"My place is too small, and it doesn't have room service. You have any better ideas?" He pulled an overnight case from his trunk.

"Not a one." Besides, it beat Motel 6.

At the front desk he requested one room, two double beds, got the government rate, and within minutes we were stepping off the elevator onto the fifth floor into a room with a view of Portsmouth Square, and beyond that, Chinatown.

He turned the lock, put on the safety latch, then threw his bag on the bed by the door. "You want to shower first?"

"Sure." I took my duffel bag into the bathroom, shutting myself in. I'd long ago stopped shivering, but my skin was thoroughly cold, and I stood a long time under the hot spray of the shower, too tired and numb to think about anything but the feel of the heat penetrating my body.

Thawed, I toweled off, pulled on my sweats, brushed my teeth, then vacated the bathroom. While Torrance showered, I combed my hair, shut off the lamp, climbed into the bed near the window.

I drifted off, vaguely aware of the bathroom door opening, light spilling into the room. "Thanks for catching me," I said. "When we jumped from the roof."

"Thank you," I thought he said. Thank you for what? I fell asleep before an answer came to mind.

The following morning I awoke to see Torrance hidden behind the *Chronicle* in the armchair by the window. He turned the page, lowered the paper a few inches, and I found myself fascinated by the planes of his unshaven face. I watched him for a few minutes, trying to understand what made him tick. I wasn't sure if I'd ever understand him, or if I ever wanted to. The man was IA, and if I associated with him in any way after this nightmare came to a close, I would be branding myself. There was enough pressure being the only female homicide inspector without that added burden. Yet the fact that he knew it, had even pointed it out, said much for him as a man.

If I were a better person, I wouldn't care what others thought, the IA/Management Control label be damned. I wanted him in bed, but I wasn't willing to pay the price, and he knew that. Apparently, he wasn't willing to pay the price either. He'd demonstrated a stronger resolve than mine on several occasions. Last night included. I knew few men who wouldn't have taken advantage of the situation of complete privacy in a girl's apartment. Or a hotel room.

The bruise to my ego made me wonder if I wasn't good enough, sexy enough for Torrid Torrance. Then I recalled the moment he stepped from the shower last night, and thanked me—after I thanked him for catching me. I couldn't help my small smile at the view he must have had, me wearing nothing but a wet T-shirt while hanging above him from a roof. I couldn't help thinking we had as strange a relationship as any. Pantyhose, bathroom sinks, and tiled roofs on rainy nights.

He glanced over. "Sleep well?"

"Yeah." I sat up, took a moment to acclimate myself and rearrange my thoughts. The drapes were wide open, revealing a blue sky filled with puffy cumulus clouds. In the square below, a few men played chess on boards built into the table. Normalcy. "You hear how Mathis is doing?"

"He'll be released soon. Doing fine."

"Good."

"Breakfast? We have about forty-five minutes. The Mead-Scolari task force is meeting this morning."

"Bagel."

"No latte?"

"That goes without saying."

He picked up the phone, placed an order to room service while I dragged myself into the bathroom to dress. Only the rumpled bed beside mine gave evidence that the man had actually slept a wink. When I came out he nodded to the *Chronicle*. "I saved that for you."

I picked up the newsprint and looked at it.

"You said you wanted to see what Evan Hilliard was so upset about. Second page at the bottom."

I opened the paper. He tapped a small article announcing that Montgard Pharmaceutical Research of Arkansas was buying Hilliard Pharmaceutical. "I don't get it," I said. "Why would he be upset about that?"

"Good question."

The article went on to explain that Montgard became interested in Hilliard Pharmaceutical after Hilliard discovered some rare plants in the rain forests of Central America that held the potential cure of a number of cancers and other maladies. No news there. What caught my interest was the mention that further forays into the jungle for more of the same proved impossible, because that particular rain forest where the plants had been found was destroyed.

"Did you read this about the rain forest?" I asked.

"Yes."

"I'm seeing major dollar signs here," I said. "Money motive."

He leaned back in his chair, regarding me. "I'm listening."

"Let's say this miracle plant does what they say it does." I folded the newspaper and tossed it onto the table. "What if someone thought those little seeds found with the Ice Man were, oh, the last remaining seeds of this so-called plant?"

"I suppose it would make those seeds invaluable."

"And Ice Man had them. Someone killed for them."

"The same someone who shot at us last night?" he asked.

I thought of the bullet holes in my bed. Of Mathis injured, in the hospital. "I don't know."

The task force was seated when we arrived, and I stepped in, carrying my stacks of homicide binders, photos, and autopsy reports. Everyone's gaze seemed locked on my actions. Torrance drew an extra chair for me, placing it beside his own. Sitting in the back of the room, watching, was the Chief of Police—as if there weren't enough pressure on me.

"As you know, Inspector Gillespie has been asked to be a part of this team," Torrance announced quietly. No one said anything, and he went on to brief everyone about last night's incident. "At this time, we're not sure who is responsible. Gillespie, however, does have a new theory to present regarding the case. Inspector?"

Their gazes shifted to me once more. I felt like an academy graduate at my first oral board to become an officer. Just be yourself, my father had told me back then. I started with the homicide of the frozen John Doe, then proceeded on with the details of each case, including my findings from the comparisons of the autopsy photos. I'd sent them to forensics. Dr. Meyers verified my suspicions, and now it was up to me to convince everyone here.

"There are, of course, similarities in the MO of the doctor's homicide, but the differences are too great to be ignored." I passed around the autopsy photos of the Slasher victims, as well as the doctor's autopsy photos, explaining my findings. "Look at the entrance wounds in comparison to the exit wounds. Doctor Mead-Scolari's wounds are indicative of a serrated knife—unlike the smooth-bladed knife wounds found on the other Slasher victims."

One by one, they examined the photos. When all were done, Reid took a second look, lined each up side by side, just as I had done yesterday. "Forgive me if I don't understand how this relates, Inspector," he said. I wondered if his formal tone had to do with his boss's presence, or with our faux date the other night. "So he changed knives."

"A possibility," I conceded. "But he also changed hands. Each of the Slasher victims was killed by someone more than likely holding the knife in their left hand, and holding the victim from behind. Patricia's, Doctor Mead-Scolari's entrance wound is located on the left side of her neck, and proceeds to her right. It appears the suspect used his right hand to slit her throat, not his left."

"You're not telling us anything we didn't already know," Reid said. "Besides, Scolari could have done it to throw us off the trail."

Andrews cleared his throat. "Let her finish, Bettencourt."

"That is not the only thing, merely the most obvious. If you look closely, you will see that in all but Patricia Mead-Scolari's case, the carotid artery on the right is untouched, but on the left it is nicked enough to let the victim bleed out. In Patricia's case, both carotids are slashed completely, meaning a fast death. Whoever killed her was in a hurry."

"Your theory?" Andrews asked.

"In the Slasher cases, the suspect wanted to *see* his victims die. Undoubtedly the nick on the carotid was done purposefully to prolong the moment of death and to intensify his gratification when that moment finally came." I passed around the autopsy reports of the known Slasher cases, holding on to the newly discovered case of Christy Tanya McAllen. They looked at them in turn, while I gave McAllen's report to Torrance to examine, then pass on.

"This, gentlemen," I said, opting to sound as formal as my ex, "is a case I researched and pulled for an example. You can see by the MO, the injuries recorded, as well as the photos, that it can be nothing but a Slasher case."

"Which proves what?" Lieutenant Andrews asked.

"That Sam Scolari is not the Slasher."

There was some murmuring, but then silence. The only sound was that of my pulse in my ears while they waited for me to continue. I looked at Torrance. His gaze met mine, but he said nothing, merely handed it to Rocky Markowski on his right.

Rocky looked at it, then Shipley. He passed it to Reid, who made a show of thoroughly examining it. "So it's maybe a Slasher case," Reid said.

"Look at the date, gentleman," Torrance said quietly, never taking his gaze from me.

"January twenty-fourth. What about it?" Reid asked.

When we were married, he hadn't remembered my birthday. It didn't surprise me that this date held no particular meaning for him.

Lieutenant Andrews had the report now. His dark brows raised a fraction. "Good work, Gillespie."

"What the hell are you talking about?" the DA asked.

Andrews handed him the report. "If this is a Slasher case, and all these women here were killed by the Slasher," he said, nodding at the photos spread across the table, "then Scolari was with Gillespie the night this girl was killed."

The chief, who'd not said a word until now, leaned forward. "How do you know?" he asked.

"That was the night Gillespie was shot. Scolari was with her the entire time," Andrews said.

Pandemonium broke out. The chief sat back in relief, undoubtedly with the thought that his political career was saved. One didn't run for mayor with rogue cops on the lam for murder. The only one who wasn't moved by the announcement was Torrance.

"Allow me to play devil's advocate," he said.

Voices died. All waited.

My heart sank. I felt a sense of betrayal. Despite that I had a fair idea of what he was about to say—I would have said the same myself—it didn't change the fact that I wanted his support.

"By all appearances, Inspector Gillespie, you have proved that Scolari is not the Slasher." He paused, allowing this to sink in. "What you have yet to prove is that he's innocent of killing his wife."

It took every effort to appear neutral to such an announcement. Any nuance of emotion on my part would be like a drop of blood in a shark tank just before a feeding frenzy.

The chief gripped the arms of his chair, apparently seeing his political chances fading before his eyes. My own hopes dashed, I didn't care.

Still, I tried to salvage what was left of my career as a homicide inspector. "We are missing the point. It's not about Scolari, it's about something else, entirely. Maybe even the seeds found with the frozen homicide victim."

"How do we know that?" Reid asked.

"What seeds?" the DA asked.

I explained about the seeds the doctor had found, and their history so far. "Professor Rocklin seemed pretty certain the seeds were from the pokeweed plant."

"What's a pokeweed?" Markowski asked.

"Some tuber rooted plant indigenous to just about everywhere," I said.

"What's your theory on this pokeweed?" Andrews asked me.

"I think someone thought these pokeweed seeds were the real thing. The rare rain forest seeds that cured cancer. They probably thought they were getting away with the loot."

"Someone killed the guy, but didn't find the seeds?" Shipley supplied.

"Something like that. And if so, then they killed the frozen John Doe, Doctor Mead-Scolari, then Martin and Smith in Property." I paused, allowing this to sink in. "Assuming these cases are related, which we can't be certain of, what would be Scolari's motive?"

"The murder of his wife," Reid said.

"He killed and froze the John Doe to cover for a murder he had yet to commit?"

Reid tipped back in his chair, shrugged. "Maybe the John Doe case isn't related. But Scolari saw the opportunity to use the homicide to his advantage. Everything after that had something to do with covering up the evidence in his wife's case. I'd think the murders of Smith and Martin would be proof of that."

"And what about Paolini?" I asked, standing, both palms flat on the table. I hated Reid's nonchalance. "You were all so damn sure Paolini was responsible. That he had it done to destroy his case to win a dismissal. Or have you forgotten the death threats he made? The attempt on my life the night Christy McAllen was killed?"

"What about the pizza?" Lieutenant Andrews asked. "Are you saying Paolini sent that?"

I took a deep breath, realizing I couldn't win this argument. Not without further proof. I swept up my photos and reports. "I may be the only one here who believes Scolari is innocent. Someone else, Paolini, or who knows, is behind this."

"Scolari skipped town, for God's sake," Reid pointed out. Now he was angry. Suddenly I wasn't sure I knew or wanted to know his motivation. I thought of his conversation with Zim that I'd witnessed. The missing autopsy photos. I was suspicious.

"Did he?" I asked, stacking my reports. I looked Reid in the eye, then each of the men at the table. Except Torrance. "All I know is that someone killed Scolari's wife, and he thinks he's being blamed for it. Come to think of it, he is being blamed. Now, if we're finished . . . ?" I may have crossed the political line, but I wasn't brash enough to walk out with the chief present.

Andrews nodded, as did the deputy chief. I think they wanted me out of there as much as I wanted to go.

Torrance rose with me, but was stopped by the deputy chief. "Lieutenant? A minute of your time?"

"Wait for me outside the door," Torrance said. "You can pick up your reports later."

I walked from the room empty-handed, only too glad to leave.

"Do you think this is wise? What in the hell . . ." I heard the deputy chief say before I closed the door. I didn't bother to eavesdrop. I didn't want to know what was being said. I didn't want to know if Torrance agreed with what I knew was their opinion on this case. That my being there was a mistake. That I refused to face the facts.

That Sam Scolari was guilty of murder.

20

About three minutes passed while I waited in the deserted hallway. How easy it would be to walk away from it all. Leave everything and not come back. Leave Torrance's unnerving presence.

Was I mad at him about the case, or about the fact that twice now, when the opportunity had presented itself, he'd refused to take advantage of me? This morning I'd tried to rationalize his objectivity to my being female, but I had to face it—I wanted him in bed. Or on the sink, the roof, in the shower, or anywhere else we had a moment of privacy. I wasn't sure why I was being so emotional. I knew, had we jumped into bed together last night in my apartment, we might both be dead.

The door opened beside me, Torrance joined me in the hallway.

"So, I'm off the task force?" I asked as we strode down the hall. Bringing up sex at this moment was probably not a great idea.

"Let's just say you passed the Burning Bridges 101 course with flying colors. I wouldn't look into promoting any time soon. Especially if you're right about Scolari."

"I can't believe I'm hearing this," I said, lengthening my pace to keep up with him. It should have given me a clue that now was not the time for this discussion either, but I tend to be blindsided by my own ire. "You'd think I was a pariah for believing my partner is innocent."

"It's more that people don't like being proved they're wrong."

"You included?"

He halted. Before I realized what was happening, he pulled me through the closest available door, which happened to be to the men's room.

A uniformed officer stood at the sink, washing his hands.

"Get out," Torrance ordered.

The officer glanced at me and hurried out, wet hands dripping.

Torrance locked the door behind him, then turned to me, his gaze filled with all the fury I'd felt moments before. While it occurred to me that what I was seeing was undoubtedly rare, witnessed by a select few, I wished myself anywhere but here.

Forced to stay, I wanted to diffuse this. "I know—"

He reached up, and it took all my resolve not to flinch as he held my chin so that I had no choice but to look him in the eye. "What happened in there," he said, his voice tight, "I'd do it again—I did it because I believe in you. I believe in your right to think your partner is innocent no matter how guilty I believe him. I want you to be right, goddammit. I want to see the look on your face when you prove them all wrong, but not—" he broke off. He cleared his throat, took a breath, apparently forcing himself to relax. His gaze went to the stitches at my temple. "Not at the expense of your life."

He turned away from me, reaching for the dead bolt. "I'm sorry."

He paused. I couldn't see his face, but from the tension in his shoulders, I guessed that his admission, and lack of control, cost him plenty. I touched his shoulder. "I'm sorry," I said again.

He didn't turn. "When this is over, and our emotions aren't . . ."

He never finished. Merely opened the door and strode from the room. I stared at the space he'd vacated, wondering what he'd been about to say. I thought about what he had said, and wondered how was I supposed to interpret that?

Telling myself that he was as screwed up as I—and once again vowing never to date within the department—I followed him out, nearly running into Markowski and Shipley, who were carting my reports and binders with them.

Markowski glanced up at the door. "They oughta put them universal signs up. For people who can't read."

"Screw yourself, Rocky," I said, not caring what it looked like or how I sounded. I moved past him to where Torrance waited at the corner, his face a mask of indifference. Apparently, he wasn't about to let me out of his sight, no matter how much he wanted to.

Markowski and Shipley followed us into Torrance's office. "Good job on the Slasher case," Shipley said, dropping the binders on my work table.

"Yeah," Rocky said, giving me a pat on the back. I was almost touched by their delayed show of support. Where the hell were their voices fifteen minutes ago? "Now all you gotta do is prove Scolari didn't kill his wife. Think you're up to it?"

"Of course," I said. I wished.

Torrance indicated the men should be seated, and when Lieutenant Andrews wandered in a moment later, I realized they'd arranged some sort of mini task force themselves.

"Regardless of where our loyalties are," Torrance said, keeping his gaze from mine, "I think it's apparent that until the Mead-Scolari case is solved, as well as the murders of Smith and Martin, this organization will suffer. Andrews agrees with me that we need to make this a top priority, without the interference of the DA's office, or any other political party's influence." Translation: my ex, the DA, and the Chief of Police.

Lieutenant Andrews said, "I think, now that we are fairly certain that Scolari is not the Slasher, we need to focus less on those cases and more on what brought this all to a head. The death of his wife. Even so," he looked right at me, "we need to remember that he is still a suspect. And unpredictable. Therefore, what I suggest is that we divide and conquer. I'd like to see us each concentrate on a different aspect of the case, continuing to meet and analyze as necessary."

"How's that different from what we're already doing?" Markowski asked Andrews.

"It's really not, except that, as Torrance explained, we're leaving certain factions out. They will continue to run their investigation as they see fit, but we will be answering to our own entity. You need approval, you come to me, not the task force. Just remember, if my head rolls, it rolls downhill. That warning aside, let's get back to business. Okay," Andrews said, looking at his notes from the earlier meeting. "Markowski and Shipley. You two continue on with the Martin, Smith homicides. But forward your report to Gillespie. Gillespie, I want you off the Slasher case."

I leaned forward to protest, but he put his hand up, stopped me. "You've done a hell of a job. It won't go unrecognized. But now that you've presented us with the new leads, I'm turning it over to Zimmerman. He's still temporarily assigned to the Homicide detail to work on that case alone. Full-time."

I wanted to tell him that had Zimmerman not tried to sabotage my career in the first place, the Slasher case might have been solved long ago. It was at a breaking point. The solvability factor had shot sky high from the near zero percent Zim had left it at. "You can't give it to Zimmerman," I said.

"Why not?"

Anything I said would sound like whining, pure and simple. I couldn't prove he'd purposefully lost the case, it was his word against mine. And I didn't doubt that if I looked, I'd find some record of it in the papers he'd turned over to me when I transferred into homicide. "Because I'm that close to solving it," I said. Great answer.

"Consider yourself temporarily assigned to Management Control," Andrews replied. "You can work most of that sitting in this office with Torrance. After last night, I'm not sure I want you running around the city following up on leads that may or may not go somewhere. Unless you think the Slasher is the one who showed up at your place last night?"

"No."

"Okay. Then it's settled. Turn over everything you have to Zimmerman. From this point on, you'll be concentrating on Patricia Mead-Scolari, and this seed theory of yours."

"I don't get it," Shipley said. "Why would someone kill over a few seeds?"

"Maybe it's seeds from some prizewinning rosebush. Like the stud services of the Triple Crown winner," Rocky said. "Couple spurts of semen worth millions."

"Sorta like yours, Markowski?" Shipley quipped.

I had a feeling that Rocky wasn't far off in his analogy, but doubted I'd find the answer in any mail-order seed catalogue.

Andrews ignored their wisecracks. "Go with it," he told me. "I also think you should explore the doctor's connection to them. We need a complete profile." He jotted down a few notes. "I want a daily report. Keep in touch with each other, and keep your egos out. And Gillespie. I think after last night, it goes without saying that you don't go anywhere without a backup, regardless of whatever else is going on."

Torrance's phone rang, and he answered. "It's Berkeley PD," he said, covering the mouthpiece. We listened to one side of the conversation, which informed us of nothing, Torrance's expression not giving anything away. He hung up, looking straight at me. "They put a rush on the print they found on your windowsill. Ran it through ALPS." ALPS was the Automated Latent Print System.

"Did they get a hit?" I asked with far more calm than I felt.

"Yes."

My heart sped up a notch in anticipation of his answer.

"It came back to Antonio Foust."

I'd wanted so much for Scolari not to be involved, it took a moment for his words to sink in. For me to realize he hadn't said, "Sam Scolari."

"Holy shit," Rocky said.

"Foust?" I repeated, stunned.

"Yes."

I swallowed. Antonio Foust. Nick Paolini's hit man.

21

Foust's presence in my house made a lot more sense than anything else so far. Granted, I wasn't pleased about being the target of death threats or attempts, but at least he was a known entity. What the hit didn't explain was if anything else we'd examined had any relation. Where the hell did Scolari fit into this?

"Shoots the seed theory right down the toilet," Shipley said.

"Maybe not," Rocky countered. "What if Paolini has an interest in the seeds? If there's money involved, he's there. Why else send his hit man out?"

"Which means Foust killed the doctor? She had an interest in the seeds. She found them," Shipley said.

"Not Foust's style," Andrews said.

We all knew Foust was suspected of several hits, including the attempt on my life that night at the Twin Palms, but nothing was ever proven. What was hard to believe was that he'd left a print to begin with. The man was a professional. But then, I wondered if perhaps Mathis had interrupted him. Surprised him, perhaps made him lose the gloves in the first place. Which meant he'd taken Mathis out on his way up. Apparently before he'd put the gloves on?

"Now what?" I asked.

"Now we continue on with what we we're doing," Andrews said. "Only, with a lot more care. I think we can safely conclude that Foust is not the Slasher. And that Paolini still wants you dead, Gillespie. Makes sense, with his appeal on the calendar. From what Bettencourt told me this morning, his case is being heard tomorrow. In light of the evidence being destroyed before his appeal could be heard, they expect a full dismissal."

"Of course," I said, "we need to look at the possibility that Foust took out Smith and Martin to gain Paolini's freedom."

"Good point, Gillespie. Check into it." Andrews said. He looked at his watch, then at Torrance. "Mind if I have a minute of your time?"

We vacated the office while he and Torrance remained behind in a closed-door discussion.

Shipley paced while Rocky balled up scrap paper, tossing wads of it into the wastebasket beside Mathis's desk. He paused before making his second shot. "So, what's with you and Torrance?" he asked.

"What do you mean?"

"After you left, the deputy chief ripped into him for letting you run the show for the task force. Thought Torrance was gonna toss his badge on the table."

I must have stared at Rocky for several seconds. "Why?"

"Why d'ya think? Torrance was telling the man to screw himself if he took you off the task force—not that the guy had a clue. It was classic." He lobbed another paper ball. Missed.

My glance strayed to the window of Torrance's office, to the back of his head as he listened to whatever it was that Andrews was telling him. "What'd the deputy chief say?"

"Never got a chance. The chief told him to shut the hell up, and for Torrance to get with Andrews and fix this thing fast. Of course, you shoulda seen the DA's face when he realized he was being left outta the game."

He tossed a few more wadded paper balls. "So, you 'n Torrance an item?"

"No."

Shipley paced the room, giving no indication the matter concerned him at all. Finally he stopped, turned to Rocky, and asked, "What'dya think?"

"About what?"

"About Foust doing Martin and Smith."

"Right up his alley. Not that it bodes well for Gillespie. You aren't going home soon, are you?" he asked me.

"No," I said. The way things were progressing, I wasn't sure if I'd ever get back home.

"Where you staying at?"

I was prevented from answering Markowski, because Andrews exited Torrance's office, telling him, "Let's get moving. We've got a lot of evidence to sort through."

Markowski made one last pitch. It hit the edge of the wastebasket, then dropped in. "He scores!"

"In his dreams," Shipley said, pushing him from the room.

Swiveling around in my chair, I looked in Torrance's door. He sat at his desk, his chin resting on steepled fingers. His shoulders rose and fell with an inward sigh, and I wondered if he wished he'd never become involved with me and this nightmare of a case. And if he wanted to go home. When had he last seen his own house?

"Dollar for your thoughts," I called out from where I sat.

He turned toward me, schooling his features into a

facade of granite. "Isn't it 'a penny for your thoughts'?"

"Inflation."

I won a glimmer of a smile, and I thought, I know where your fissures are. The knowledge did me little good, since Torrance had made it clear by his lack of . . . attention during potentially intimate moments that we were a professional team only. After that, who knew? It was something I couldn't dwell on. Not if I wanted to concentrate on my cases.

"I was thinking about Paolini and where he comes into this," Torrance said. "I think we need to discuss our options."

"Options to what?" I queried, moving into his office.

"Is he connected to the doctor's death? Is that why you're being made into a target? This case is becoming more complicated by the minute."

"I was a target before she got killed. Only they missed."

"Maybe we need to go back to the basics."

I pulled a chair to his desk and sat opposite him. "Such as start at the beginning."

"I'm listening."

"Good, because I'm not quite sure where the beginning is." I leaned back, propping one foot on my knee. "If we start with Paolini, we'd go back a year ago to when I got shot at the Twin Palms Motel. Which was also the night of the first known Slasher case. I can't imagine they're related, because we didn't know I would ever be investigating the SoMa Slasher."

"Coincidence, then?"

"Has to be. I started a chart at home, listing the suspects, victims, trying to sort through this, see what was related." I dug it out of my pocket and unfolded it.

Torrance got up. On the wall to the left of the door was a dry erase board. He took a red marker and uncapped it. The marker's strong odor like nail polish filled the room.

As I read off each of the victims, he listed them down the left side of the board: Ice Man, Patricia Mead-Scolari, Martin/Smith, and myself. Beneath each name he drew horizontal lines that ran the entire length of the board. Then he drew vertical lines down to form a grid of squares like a giant tic-tac-toe game, but with four squares across and down instead of three.

While I looked at the board, Torrance poked his head out the door that led to his secretary's office, asking her to bring us a couple cups of coffee, and real half-and-half, if possible. He returned to the board. "Anything else?"

"I'm working on it. Let me get a boost of caffeine." We waited for the coffee, which his secretary brewed fresh, then brought a few minutes later.

We both stared at the board, sipping our coffee. The process seemed right, but we were still missing our suspects.

"I guess what we need to do is start making a connection," I said. "So far the common thread in all these cases appears to be these seeds. If the seeds were a suspect, we could put an X in every box."

Torrance took me literally, writing the word "Seeds" on the top left, over the first vertical row of boxes. Then he put an X in the boxes beside Ice Man, Mead-Scolari, and Martin/Smith, as well as the one beside my name. The curse of the deadly seeds. It sounded like a Nancy Drew mystery title.

"Definite link," he said, standing back to look at the vertical row of Xs beside each victim.

"Okay. What else? Ice Man was found in the warehouse, so we need the Paolini connection."

He wrote "Paolini/Foust" at the top, over the next vertical row. Paolini got an X in the Ice Man and Martin/Smith boxes, as well as in my square.

"Scolari," I offered next, though I hated saying it.

Torrance wordlessly added Scolari's name, then poised his marker over the row of boxes beside the Ice Man.

"No. No connection."

He hesitated over the square beside Mead-Scolari's name.

"Yes," I said quietly.

He drew a red X there, then moved down to Martin/Smith.

"Yes."

My name.

I said nothing.

He put an X there as well.

I wanted to tell him to erase the last, that Scolari wouldn't try to kill me. "Hilliard Pharmaceutical," I said. "They owned the building."

"A company as a suspect?"

"You have seeds."

He waited.

"Okay, Evan Hilliard."

He wrote the name at the top. Hilliard got an X beside Ice Man and Mead-Scolari.

"Josephine Hilliard."

He added another row. Again, an X beside Ice Man and Mead-Scolari's name. We stood back and looked.

"Well," Torrance asked. "What does it tell you?"

"Looks like Scolari won the vote."

"Let's wait for the absentee ballots."

I liked Torrance a lot in that one moment. Even so, I regarded the vertical row of Xs below Scolari's name. On the off chance he was guilty, the connection was clear. But what if Paolini was guilty? If so, I could only connect him to two cases. Ice Man, and Martin and Smith. It was the seeds that made no sense. What could Paolini want with them? I stood, looking at all the names. My focus kept returning to Paolini. "Why would he kill the doctor?"

"Who?"

"Paolini. I mean, I can almost understand him placing a hit on Martin and Smith, and possibly the Ice Man for the warehouse connection."

"But perhaps that's merely coincidence. How long has it been since Paolini's organization leased that warehouse? And how long was the body there?"

"We have no way of knowing. The pathologist can only give an estimate of the length of time the body was dead at the time it was frozen." I paced the length of his desk, thinking. The key to it all was up there, I was sure. "The Ice Man," I said, stopping in front of the dry erase board and tapping the area beside his name. "His case started the ball rolling when the seeds were found on his corpse. He's the one."

"So you think you can tie Patricia's murder to his, or to Paolini?"

"Not unless we get him identified." I thought of the article Torrance had pointed out to me in the *Chronicle*, the same article that seemed to have gotten Evan Hilliard so upset that afternoon he stormed into Josephine's office with his newspaper. Why would an announcement of their merger with the Arkansas-based Montgard Pharmaceutical make him mad? "Hold on a sec." I picked up the phone and dialed Shipley's desk.

"What's up?" he asked.

"Do me a favor. Get with Missing Persons, have them do a check in Arkansas, see if they have any missing persons who might match our frozen John Doe."

"Arkansas?"

"A hunch."

"Okay."

That done, I returned my attention back to our list.

"You know that article you showed me this morning in the *Chronicle*?" I asked, eyeing the column where "Hilliard" was written, with Xs beside the Ice Man and Dr. Mead-Scolari rows.

"About the merger?"

Meeting Torrance's gaze, I nodded. "I don't know the first thing about pharmaceutical companies, but I'm thinking that maybe talking with the Hilliards isn't enough."

"What do you have in mind, Inspector?"

"A search warrant."

It took about half an hour to dictate the warrant, which I gave to Gypsy to transcribe. She knew all the verbiage to put in between the important stuff regarding what we were looking for: documents, computer files, anything that showed the doctor may have been killed due to her research or knowledge in the company, or activities involving one Nicholas Paolini. Were Mead-Scolari not dead, it might be more difficult to obtain, especially considering laws on confidentiality. Of course, finding a prior homicide victim in a warehouse owned by Hilliard Pharmaceutical helped our case as well, despite no other connection being noted or known.

In truth, we were going in blind, not having any clue

what we were looking for. That was often the way with search warrants. You went in, turned the place upside-down, then came out with bits and pieces you hoped would materialize into evidence of significance.

Gypsy handed us the transcribed warrant a little over two hours later. My intention was to "walk the warrant through," which meant skipping the usual routine of having the documents reviewed by the DA's office first, instead taking it straight to a judge for a signature.

Hoping to avoid running into anyone, particularly from the DA's office, Torrance and I took the stairs to the second floor. When we exited the stairwell, I saw my ex at the opposite end of the hall, his back to us, in private conversation with a dark-haired woman of short stature, wearing a yellow business suit.

Reid glanced around, and I caught a glimpse of the woman's face. When he leaned down and kissed her, I bristled.

Beth Skyler. Channel Two News.

Suddenly my missed Napa trip came to mind, calling Reid that morning at his hotel room, hearing *her* voice, and him telling me he was watching the news.

Skyler did the evening news only.

"That son of a bitch," I whispered. A moment later Reid and Skyler took off in separate directions. I moved back into the stairwell, not wanting to be seen.

Torrance remained where he was, regarding me intently. "I thought it was over between you."

"It is."

"Really?" He started toward the judge's chambers. "We better get this signed."

"It's not what you think," I said, catching up to him.

He waited for me to clue him in.

"The night that Patricia was killed, I was pretty sure someone leaked her murder to the press."

"How did you come to that conclusion?"

"By the questions Skyler was asking me. Things we wouldn't have released. You read the article the next day, saw the news. You can draw your own conclusions from what you saw."

"What would be his motivation?"

"Politics? Sex? Money? With Reid, who knows."

We turned the corner, en route to the judge's chambers, and ran straight into Reid. He acted cool toward me, speaking only with Torrance. "The DA's on my butt, Mike," he said. "Wants to know how soon we're gonna wrap this thing up."

"The crystal ball's in the repair shop, Bettencourt," Torrance said, guiding me on toward the judge's chambers, holding the door open for me.

I passed through, since I had the warrant. He stayed behind to continue his conversation with Reid, a stalling tactic, since neither of us wanted him to know we had a search warrant. The way Reid was eyeing me, however, gave me the feeling that Torrance's efforts would be wasted. Once Reid found out, we couldn't exactly tell him to back off. Not when he was assigned to the task force. There was also the little matter of bypassing the DA's office in preparing the warrant. In a high-profile case such as this, feathers would be more than ruffled.

I hoped to see Judge Gehrhardt, but was shown to Judge Earling's chambers instead. Earling was notorious for doing things by the book. He wore wire-rimmed spectacles and was still dressed in his black judge's robe.

All he needed was a powdered wig covering his already white hair to complete the effect of a nineteenth-century hanging judge. Judge Earling's problem was that he was hanging the wrong people. Word on the street had it that if you were guilty, you wanted Earling and no jury. Cops avoided him like stale doughnuts dunked in sour milk.

"DA go over this?" he asked, scratching his gray goatee while he pored over the first page.

"Uh, no, Your Honor. We have a bit of a time dilemma."

"Hmm, wouldn't think you'd take a chance in a case like this." He turned the second page, running his finger down the lines of legal prose, rapidly mumbling the words written so that he sounded something like an auctioneer without a microphone. "Everything looks okay so far. You've verified the address and such?"

"Yes, sir," I said, just as his gaze strayed past me. I hoped whoever he was looking at was Torrance by himself.

"Ah, Reid Bettencourt," the judge said, looking over the top of his spectacles. "I understand you're on the task force. Your boss let you pass a warrant through without reading it first?"

Reid gave Torrance a dark look. "What warrant?"

Judge Earling flipped back to the first page as though to refresh his memory on what he was reading. "To Hilliard Pharmaceutical regarding the Mead-Scolari matter."

I stared straight at the warrant, avoiding Reid's gaze completely. If Judge Earling wanted to be his typical stubborn self, he could refuse to sign it, thereby forcing us to go through the DA's office. That spelled another delay, undoubtedly until tomorrow.

"I'm certain Lieutenant Andrews called the DA's office about this," I said. "In fact, I naturally assumed that's why Investigator Bettencourt was down here—because the DA sent him."

Now it was up to Reid. He could be a jerk, tell Earling I was full of it, or go along, then take us for whatever we had outside the door. And if he did, I was going to hang him for his tête-à-tête with Skyler. Ah, what the hell, I'd do it now.

I met Reid's gaze and smiled sweetly while Torrance regarded us. When the judge wasn't looking, I mouthed two words to Reid. *Beth Skyler.*

I could almost see his wheels turning. Several seconds of silence, as his expression told me, *You'll pay, somehow;* then, "Yes, Your Honor."

"Very well." The judge finished reading, signed his name, had me initial a minor change regarding the date being wrong on the fifth page, and we were off.

"I can't believe you did this," Reid said as we strode down the hall to the elevators. "You drew up a warrant without informing the task force?" He stopped and wedged his way around us, blocking the UP button.

We were to meet Markowski and Shipley in Homicide, then head straight for Hilliard Pharmaceutical. It was a low-risk warrant, no SWAT team, since Hilliard Pharmaceutical was considered a safe business and there was very little chance of our being shot upon entry. I only hoped it stayed that way once we found whatever it was we were looking for. Not that we didn't take precautions.

First, however, I intended to confront my ex. "So, how long have you and the Channel Two newsgirl been dating? Certainly not *before* the Napa trip?" I didn't mention the leak for the simple reason I was saving that trump card.

"Kiss my—"

"Enough." Torrance stepped between us.

"I demand to know why I wasn't included in this warrant." Reid's face started turning red. He was ticked.

He deserved it.

Torrance answered. "You may not believe us, but if we were to call your office, go through the usual routine, we'd be another two hours. With elections coming up next year, the DA would want to handle it himself, and he's a busy man. No way would he let a deputy handle it, maybe steal a moment of glory right before campaign season starts."

That was at least part of the truth. Suddenly I wondered if the elections weren't part of what was behind the leak. A political motive. I could accept that, whether I liked it or not. It fit Reid.

"What?" Reid countered. "You think you guys can write a warrant faster than us?"

"Of course not," I lied. If we turned this into an us-against-them thing, nothing would be accomplished. "All Torrance is saying is that we got a good lead and ran with it. We tried to get ahold of you, but you weren't there, and you know that Arlington isn't available, so it seemed simpler to do it ourselves."

Arlington was a deputy DA who worked primarily with the Homicide detail. Under normal circumstances he would have sat in on the task force, had the DA not been concerned with Arlington running for his position next year.

"Lieutenant?"

A short, stocky female officer waved at Torrance from the lobby of the second floor, the gear on her Sam Brown jangling and squeaking with her movement. Torrance glanced at me, then Reid, as though worried we might go at each other's throats if he left us alone.

"Don't worry about me," I said.

He approached the brown-haired woman, but stood where he could keep an eye on us. She was the crime scene technician who had gone out, dusted for prints, and taken photos after the murders in Property. Since coming to Homicide, I knew just about every technician.

The thought nagged at me, but before I could place why, Reid said, "You doing him?"

"*What?*" I whipped my head around, unable to believe he'd said that. Another reason not to sleep with someone within these hallowed halls.

"You heard me."

"I'd tell you to go screw yourself, but that's apparently part of your problem."

"I take it that means yes."

"No, it doesn't mean yes. And if it did, I sure as hell wouldn't tell you."

"I'm sorry. It was just that I thought we might have something special between us."

"Special? This from the man who was just kissing a reporter in the hallway? The same reporter who was in his room in Napa?"

"A chance meeting."

"How convenient I was late."

"I guess I got jealous. Something about the way Torrance looked at you when you were down in Earling's chambers just now."

I couldn't believe how easily he lied. And then I thought about what he said, getting jealous. He might have laughed had he realized how many times Torrance and I should have slept together, but didn't. Besides, Torrance was coming back, and I had no wish to continue the conversation.

"Ready?" Torrance asked.

I nodded.

He asked Reid, "Are you coming with us?"

"Yes," Reid announced. If Torrance read the loud *No!* in my eyes, he chose to ignore it. Reid's apology to me hadn't been sincere. I doubted there was a sincere cell in his body.

"We'll meet in the garage in a half hour," Torrance told him. We left him standing in the hallway.

Back in Torrance's office, without going into minute detail, I told him about Reid assuming the injured lover's role. "He acted like he was jealous."

"Maybe he was."

"More than likely he was overcompensating for his rendezvous with Skyler. He had to be worried about the press leak."

"Any speculation?"

"I hate to think his motivation was anything more than trading a scoop for sex. But who knows? He and Zim were thick as thieves the other day in the hall. Reid said they were talking about an old homicide."

"Unusual?"

"Other than Reid and Zim hating each other, no. But it was more Reid's expression when he saw me."

"Maybe they *were* talking about an old homicide." He patted the thick black three-ring binder on his desk. Dex Kermgard's IA file. "We overlooked one minor detail. One of the investigating officers in the case was Zim."

"This is taking coincidence a bit far."

"My thoughts exactly."

I looked up at the dry erase board. "Maybe we need to enlarge our pool of suspects. Add Dex Kermgard."

"What would be his motivation?"

"He's dirty on the murder of the snitch. Which makes him connected to Paolini and Foust somehow. And he knows this building, the exits, the procedures. He could easily get in or out."

"You're thinking the murders in Property?"

"Absolutely."

"Definitely something to think about. In the meantime, we have a warrant to serve."

That settled, we got together our mini task force plus Reid. He rode with Shipley and Markowski while I rode with Torrance to Hilliard Pharmaceutical's main facility, where we intended to serve the warrant.

It was a little after five when we arrived at the pharmaceutical building. We managed to get security to let us in by showing our stars and ID cards while keeping mum about the search warrant. I didn't want anyone tipping the Hilliards off, and perhaps allowing any evidence to be destroyed. Once we were in, the guard at the front desk—full-time, not a moonlighting SFPD officer—refused to let us go a step farther until he contacted Evan Hilliard, who apparently was still in his office.

The guard punched a number on the phone while he kept his eye on us. Tall, heavy, mid-forties, he looked like a recent ex-smoker, because he was going through gum like it was a wonder drug. He'd chew a stick for a few minutes, then turn and spit it into the garbage, like someone spitting tobacco juice into a spittoon. A minute went by while he waited on hold, and soon he was unwrapping a new piece, shoving it into his mouth.

"Yep. They're here now," he said into the phone. "Yep. Can do."

He hung up, then led us into a room off the main entryway that was set up as a waiting area, with several low-back armchairs in a dusty rose, a few silk philodendron plants, and the requisite weeping fig tree, also in silk. Two paintings, pastel blue, pink, and lavender splotches, completed the "soft room" effect, a term we at the PD use for an interview room where we interrogate witnesses as opposed to suspects. Unlike our rooms, however, this had windows across the front through which one could view the lobby and the elevator just off it.

After about fifteen minutes I began to pace the confines, the warrant rolled up in my hand like a diploma about to be handed out. After the fourth time across the room, I happened to glance up just as Dexter Kermgard stepped off the elevator with several white-coated, cerebral looking men. I pictured them calling up each other in the morning with, "Which pocket protector are you wearing today?" The notion made me think of Scolari— it was the sort of comment he would make.

Dex did not fit the pocket protector role. I too easily pictured him in the bodyguard role. Mafia. Paolini. I thought about Dex's shooting. The drug case. Ties to organized crime? Neither Paolini nor Foust were big names in those days, but they were up-and-coming in the world of crime, establishing a trade.

Dex had retired long before the rumors started to circulate that some officers were suspected of being on Paolini's payroll.

Still, Dex had been a friend of my father. Not that I ever saw Dex again after the shooting scandal—except for my brother's funeral. But now that I thought about it, Dex never came to my father's funeral.

And what about the way Scolari had acted toward Dex?

Dex happened to look up, and saw me watching him.

He halted in his tracks. One of the other lab workers bumped into him and Dex's clipboard crashed to the floor, papers flying on impact.

I stepped out. "Dex?"

He glanced up in the midst of retrieving his clipboard and papers. His coworkers stood there like robots, totally oblivious to a real-life predicament. When he stood, they all started forward again, lending further credence to my suspicions of artificial intelligence.

I offered my most solicitous smile, but found myself at a loss as to what to do. Dex was an enigma. Now, after having read the IA report on his homicide case, I was even less sure about him than before. I needed his help to get past the watch dog at the front desk and into the doctor's office. Half our battle might be over, just being inside Hilliard Pharmaceutical, but it did little good if we didn't know which floor or which room.

Perhaps if I brought up his friendship with my father? No, with Dex, I figured it was best to get straight to the point. "Listen, Dex, I was wondering if you'd do us a favor?"

There was a flicker of something in his gaze, something indecipherable. He didn't comment, merely waited for me to continue.

"I need to get into Dr. Mead-Scolari's office."

You could have heard a search warrant drop in the ensuing silence. As it was, I kept that particular document curled behind my back.

He looked into the room, saw the others waiting, watching. Finally he said, "Officially or unofficially?"

Now, there was a strange response. "Does it matter?"

"Officially, I don't have a key. You'll have to wait."

"Unofficially, then."

His smile was slight, almost nonexistent. "Follow me."

I walked beside Dex to the elevator, beckoning for the others to follow. The door opened and we all stepped in. "How did people around here take the news of the doctor's demise?" I asked.

"Actually, very few people were aware she worked here."

"Really?"

"Yes. It was all hush-hush. Whatever it was about, Mrs. Hilliard wanted it kept quiet." He hesitated, lowered his voice despite that we were now enclosed in the elevator, out of earshot of his coworkers. My companions did a great job of pretending interest in the paneling on the elevator walls. "If you want my opinion, there were two reasons besides the very obvious one of Josephine's addiction."

"Addiction?"

"Cocaine."

If there was cocaine involved, then Paolini was probably connected. "You're certain?"

"Look at her eyes the next time you see her."

"What are the other two reasons?"

"The first, of course, was to protect Mrs. Hilliard's reputation. Her alternative lifestyle."

"What was the second reason?"

The elevator door slid open. He took me by my arm, guiding me a few steps away from the group. "The merger, of course. That sort of thing might be okay here in San Francisco, but I guarantee, the moment Mrs. Hilliard's, er, lifestyle got out to the stockholders of Montgard Pharmaceutical, they'd balk."

Undoubtedly Dex was right. Montgard operated their main offices in the state of Arkansas, right in the midst of the Bible Belt. Suddenly I recalled the words of the doctor's secretary, Mary, and how she mentioned that Patricia Mead-Scolari wanted to come out of the closet.

Two motives popped up time and again in homicide, and they were both staring me in the face right now. The first, passion, included everything from love to hate. The second, money, was a definite biggie.

As a suspect, Scolari had a motive that fell into the first category, because of his wife's relationship with Josephine. The Hilliards, however, now fit the second half of the motive theory. Money. A multimillion-dollar merger offered plenty of motivation. Couple that with Hilliard's wife undoubtedly not wanting it announced to the world what she did behind closed doors, and you could add a dollop of passion to the list.

Dex led us past a wide open space filled with a dozen desks, announcing the accounting department as though giving us a tour. We continued on down a hallway, and he stopped in front of an unmarked door on our right. "Here it is," he said. "Dr. Mead-Scolari's office."

Here it is, I echoed silently. Now all I had to do was get in and find the proof.

22

I watched Dexter Kermgard fiddle with the keys, trying to fit one in the lock. With a sense of déjà vu I was reminded of that first afternoon we'd met at the warehouse. With Scolari. I wondered where he was now. What he was thinking. I also wondered if there was anything I could have said or done that first day that might have changed the course of events. I'd recognized Scolari's depression, worried about it even. What if I'd looked for him harder? Made more of an effort than simply waiting for him to call?

A blanket of guilt descended over me, but not, I realized, from my inactions on that particular night.

I was thinking about Scolari as though he'd killed his wife. As though he were guilty.

I wondered if he was.

Footsteps echoed down the hallway. Not a casual pace, but a determined, get-the-hell-out-of-my-way stride. Josephine Hilliard approached, a look of fury upon her face.

So much for the unofficial route.

"What is going on here, Dexter?" she asked in her cultured voice. No one was fooled by her tone. If looks could kill, we'd be riddled with bullets.

"This is Inspector Gillespie, and these officers—"

"I know who this is. I asked what are you doing?"

"They want to see the doctor's research office."

"Impossible.

"But—"

"Mister Kermgard," she said, looking solely at me now, "has made a terrible mistake. This office is off-limits to the public."

"We aren't the public," I said, noting her pupils, dilated, almost to the point of completely obliterating the blue of her irises.

"Be that as it may . . ."

"Have I introduced you to Reid Bettencourt?" I asked sweetly. "He's from the District Attorney's office." Nice and vague. Let her think he's an attorney. I held out the search warrant. Even though we were within our legal rights, it helped when all parties cooperated.

Reid nodded at her. "You may want to read this," he said. "In fact, have your legal department look it over if you want."

Good boy, I thought. Not that it made up for anything, but Reid was no fool.

She looked at the document, her hand shaking slightly. I doubt she saw a word written there. "It will take some time to get them here. I'll have to ask you to wait. I need to call my husband."

"The waiting is over, Mrs. Hilliard," I said. "We are going in, and we are doing it now—with or without your cooperation. The choice is yours."

"You mean you'd break down the door?" she asked.

"If necessary," I said, letting her believe what she would. If this were a drug bust, we'd simply handcuff everyone, then force the door. Unfortunately, the public took a dim view when the same thing was done to white-collar types. They too easily identified with them. "Do I need to call a team to bring in a battering ram?"

She curled the document in her fist. "Didn't Mister Kermgard tell you he does not have a key?"

"He did." I waited.

She reached into the pocket of her pleated wool trousers and pulled out a key on a small ring, which she gave to Dexter. As he was about to turn the lock, she stayed his hand. "I insist that we be present."

"Not a problem," I said, generous in my victory. "As long as you don't touch anything."

When she let loose of Dexter's hand, he swung open the door. We stepped into a brightly lit white-walled room covered with posters of jungles and rain forests. Other than the posters, it looked like any other office— two desks, a computer, low cabinets circling the circumference, the countertops covered with papers, books, that sort of thing. Nothing said, *Look at me. I'm the reason you're here.* Not that I expected it to, especially after I'd picked up a sheet of computer paper full of scientific garble and tried to read it.

Josephine took the phone and punched in a three-digit number. "Evan. The police are here. In Patricia's office . . . They have a warrant." Her face crumpled. "What was I supposed to do?" She turned her back, listened, nodded. "Okay."

I directed Shipley and Markowski to search the counters and cabinets, while Bettencourt and Torrance started on the desks.

"What exactly did the doctor do for you?" I asked Josephine after she hung up.

"Research."

"Wasn't she a pathologist?"

"For the simple reason her husband insisted," she said with some disdain. "It wasn't what she wanted to do. I gave her the opportunity she deserved."

I sorted through the in-basket. Everything looked foreign, and I wondered if I'd ever be able to determine anything from this venture. "What sort of opportunity?"

"She wanted to go back to school. Further her education and do something that would help the living. Not the dead. I think she was tired of all the bodies."

Scolari's wife unhappy as a pathologist? Possible, I supposed. Books on varying subjects lined one shelf. The titles ranged from the massive hardback edition of the *Physician's Desk Reference* to a well worn, dog-eared, paperback version of *A Woman's Guide to Holistic Herbs*. I pulled out the books one by one, flipped through them, looking for anything, finding nothing.

"Oh, I am sorry." We all stopped to see a tiny woman of Asian descent, perhaps fifty, maybe more, standing in the doorway. Behind her was a cart with a trash can and cleaning supplies. "I know no one is to be here," she said. "I thought maybe you want me to clean?"

"No," Josephine said. "These are the police. They've come to search it. We don't need it cleaned."

"I close it?" The woman backed into the hall.

"Later," Mrs. Hilliard said, her facade of polite culture slipping completely.

"You were saying the doctor was unhappy," I reminded her, looking up from my perusal of *Holistic Herbs*.

She eyed Bettencourt, who had sat down at the computer and was typing something into the keyboard. I don't know why, but I did, too. I wasn't sure if I wanted him there.

"Mrs. Hilliard?"

It took a moment for her to return her attention to our conversation. "She wanted to be a pioneer. I let her use the facilities to research her options for the future, nothing more. As far as what she did, I had no idea. We never discussed it."

From the corner of my eye, I saw Torrance pause at her declaration. It stopped me as well. "Are you saying she wasn't on your payroll?"

She moved closer to me, lowering her voice. "I allowed her entrance as a favor, Inspector. In truth, she sat at that desk, searched the Internet for something, God knows what, and I sat there," she said, pointing to the chair where Rocky Markowski perched while he pored over papers he'd dug from the wastebasket. "We talked. That's it."

"She didn't work for you?"

"No, Inspector. She didn't. We were simply friends."

My guess was that she thought Dex wasn't aware of their relationship. Well, let her have her veil of secrecy, I thought, continuing my search. I was more interested in whether her husband knew who her bedmate was. Then again, it wouldn't hurt to get a copy of employment records. If I found that the doctor was on her payroll, as I believed, that would go a long way to prove the theory brought to mind by Dex—that Josephine was hiding her sexual preference because of the possible merger.

What I needed to do was get to the accounting department down the hall. It being an open area, it wouldn't be difficult to get into. Unfortunately, our warrant didn't exactly cover the accounting records, its scope being more the work the doctor was doing at Hilliard Pharmaceutical. But then, who the hell could understand the legal crap written there? "Other documents" could loosely be translated as accounting records, and I decided to let Josephine believe that—should she balk at my requesting the records. But that was down the line. We had to finish searching the doctor's office first, and the way things appeared, we could be there all night. I looked at my watch. Quarter after six. Torrance and Shipley were digging through boxes of printed documents.

"You find anything in the computer?" I asked Betten-court.

"She's got some lock on it. I'm trying to figure out the password."

"Have Markowski look at it." I should have done that in the first place. Rocky was the closest thing we had to a computer expert, which wasn't saying a lot, but at least it eased my mind about Reid having access to it.

"I can do this." Reid's gaze locked with mine in challenge. I pictured him driving the Lexus, kissing Beth Skyler. I knew with a certainty he'd taken her to Napa, and I wondered where he'd gotten the money. Had *she* paid him? I supposed that was a distinct possibility.

"Rocky," I said, never taking my eye off my ex. "The keyboard."

"This is not your investigation," Reid said. He continued typing.

I wanted to rip the keyboard from beneath his fingers. Cognizant of the many sets of eyes trained on the two of us, I decided to end this battle quickly. I was at his side, laid the herb book on top of the monitor with all the casualness I could muster. I put my hand on his shoulder, leaned down, whispered so that there was absolutely no doubt as to what he thought I suspected between him and Skyler.

"Press leak."

Reid stiffened and his face turned red. Without further argument, he rose.

Rocky took his place and fiddled with the keyboard.

Finished with the books, I moved on to other stacks of papers, ignoring Reid as best I could in so small a space. "I suppose what we need to do is box this stuff. Take it with us. Do you have anything we can use, Mrs. Hilliard?"

"I would think you'd come prepared, Inspector."

"Oh, I'm plenty prepared. All I need to do is call for more officers. We can have a slew of them in about five minutes." I glanced at the clock. "Maybe sooner."

"Dexter," came a deep voice from the hallway, "see if you can find the inspectors some boxes."

I looked up to see Evan Hilliard standing in the hallway, watching us.

Dex was out in a flash, probably glad to escape his boss's icy demeanor.

"Is there anything else you care for, Inspector?" he asked me.

I took the moment to appear deep in thought. "The other documents," I said.

"What other documents?" Evan Hilliard replied.

"May I?" I took the search warrant from Josephine, turned to the page that I knew read like something in a foreign language but had the words "other documents" listed amongst the booty we were looking for. "Right here. I need to see your accounting department. Verify the doctor's employment status."

Evan eyed his wife, then the computer, where Rocky diligently worked, still with no success. It could have been my imagination, but it seemed as though he was trying to tell her something. "It's down the hall. I'll show you."

I followed Hilliard while Torrance, a very curious

look on his face, accompanied us. He knew the ropes, knew I was full of it but, thankfully, said nothing.

Hilliard led us into the heart of the accounting office, turned on a computer, typed in a password—at least I assumed it was a password—then opened several files on the screen trying to get to the one he needed. "I'll print a list of every employee. It shouldn't take more than a few minutes." He tapped away at the keys. "There. It'll come out on that printer over there," he said.

He sat back in his chair, regarding me. "I was trying to remember where we'd met before. It was at the fund-raiser, wasn't it? For the rain forests."

"Yes."

"You were, I believe, the lovely woman I saw on Nicholas Paolini's arm. Basic black gown, ruby earrings."

"You have a good memory."

"Only when it comes to beautiful women." He scored points for that one, but I didn't let it go to my head. "So tell me," he continued, "was your presence that night as official as it is now? Or was it a date?"

I merely smiled.

He nodded in acquiescence. "Of course, you don't discuss your cases."

"Nor my private life."

"Touché." He smiled in return.

"Do you mind if I ask you a personal question?" Turnabout was fair play.

"And if I choose not to discuss my private life?"

"I indicate that in my report."

"I hope you don't mind if I reserve the right not to answer, should I incriminate myself."

"Are you aware of your wife's . . . associations?"

"Please be specific."

"Her affairs? Coke addiction?

A look of weariness settled over him. He indicated I should take a seat. Torrance, ever the chameleon, had long since faded into the background.

"Do you believe in the sanctity of marriage, Inspector?" He continued on without waiting for my response, which was probably just as well. Having been married to Reid, my answer would have been a resounding no. "My wife has a number of faults, but I married her for better or for worse. I have worked hard to keep our marriage intact, not always successfully. I'm sure you realize that she is almost assuredly under the influence at this very moment. I have tried everything. Narcotics Anonymous, Betty Ford . . . she will be fine for a while, but I can't watch her twenty-four hours a day."

"You have no idea where she gets her cocaine?"

He shrugged. "I doubt it matters. The night I met you, the rain forest fund raiser, I believe that was where she was introduced to the drug."

"Paolini."

"Perhaps. I am well aware of the results of your operation that night, as is anyone who reads the paper or watches the news. He was arrested for dealing cocaine, and my wife, after associating with him closely on that fund-raiser, is now a coke addict."

I silently conceded the point, but let him continue.

"Since then, things have been difficult. She is not the woman I married. We sleep in separate rooms. She's had affairs—"

"Do you know with whom?"

His smile did not reach his eyes. "Yes."

I waited. The printer droned on, the paper fed into it, spewed out the other end.

"Most recently . . ." He covered his eyes as though the thought hurt him, might make him cry. Was that how Scolari felt? "I'm sorry," he said, looking up, his eyes glassy. He twisted the gold band on his finger, and said, "Dexter Kermgard."

The surprise I felt must have shown on my face, because he said, "I know you must think me a fool for letting the man continue working here."

"Um, no, I could never presume to tell you how to run your business." Now, there was a cliché if I ever heard one.

"Kermgard was instrumental in building our business. I'm sure you're well aware of the officers he hired for security. It was he who introduced Nicholas Paolini to me and my wife. Unfortunately, none of us knew of Paolini's, shall we say, underworld dealings? By then, it was too late. But it was that very thing that sent our stocks soaring. Had she not met Paolini and gotten caught up in this rain forest thing, our scientists would never have made the discovery. Well, that is history, water under the bridge."

In that respect he was right. I wanted to know if he knew about Patricia's affair. Nothing like kicking a man when he was down. "Can you tell me about your wife's relationship with Doctor Mead-Scolari?"

"They had the same interests. Rain forests."

"What sort of friends were they?"

"I suppose they were close."

"How close?"

"Is there somewhere you're leading with this?"

Bluntness had its advantages. "Were you aware your wife was sleeping with the doctor?"

His hand gripped the arms of the chair. "That's ridiculous. Who told you that?"

"My source is not relevant."

Evan stood, his chair rolled back, hit the desk behind him. "Inspector Gillespie. I suggest you gather what you came for, then leave. Now, if you don't mind, I'll return to the doctor's office. I trust your men have done nothing illegal in my absence?"

No, I've pretty much covered that base myself. "They're very trustworthy."

I watched him weave through the office, past chairs, desks, workstations.

"What do you think?" I asked Torrance once Hilliard was out of earshot.

"Other than your knack for bringing out the very best in people?"

"Just men."

"I'd say he had no idea his wife was sleeping with the doctor." He nodded toward the printer. "I'm curious about these so-called other documents."

"You think of a better way to get these files?"

"Another search warrant."

"And risk the wait involved, chance they might erase something? Like the doctor's name?" I scooted my chair over to the printer, lifted the sheets in the READY tray, scanned the names.

"You realize that if you find anything of value, it goes out the window in a court trial?"

"Of course. But it's better to know and pretend you don't, than to never know."

"You don't think he led us here too easily?"

Before I could ponder that question, we were interrupted.

"Excuse please?" came a soft voice. The cleaning woman had crept up on us like a cat in the night.

I glanced at Torrance with a sort of and-you-call-

yourself-a-bodyguard? look, before turning my attention
to the cleaning woman.

She smiled shyly. "You are police?"

"Yes."

"We talk?"

"Okay." I waved to a chair. She refused my offer, but
I stayed seated for the simple fact I'd tower over her if I
stood. "What can I do for you?"

"My son is working here," she said, her face beaming
with pride. "He bring me here from China. He is important. Work in lab. He is making very good money, but I
take this job to be near him." She nodded, and I smiled,
hoping to imply that I agreed with her about her son. "He
is very upset when the doctor die. She is very great
woman, he say."

"Really?" I said, wondering if there was a point. I
didn't want to be rude, but I figured I had about five minutes to get what I was looking for before Hilliard figured
out that "other documents" was about as questionable as
one could get. I scanned the list of names, attempting to
appear interested in the woman at the same time.

"She do great things someday. She ask him about
things I do not understand. Cancer?"

"Yes . . ." I said, running my finger down the printout
that was alphabetized by last names. H, I, J, K, King,
Kendall, Larrimore, Lynch, Marvin . . .

"The night she die, I see her. I see her every night in
her office. She very nice to me."

Her words caught me off guard, and I learned two
things in that moment. One, the name Mead-Scolari was
not on this payroll list. Two, never overlook diminutive
cleaning women who are trying to tell you something.
"You saw her that night?"

She nodded. "Every night, I clean her office, while she work. But not that night. I come, but Mrs. Hilliard is there, and she make me go," she said, nodding her head with emphasis. "They argue, argue."

"Did you hear about what?"

"I tried not to. My son, he would be very displeased. He say his job important, and to not make Mrs. Hilliard mad. He say she is different, but I tell him I want to be near him. I stay."

"Go on."

"She was mad at the doctor. Very, very mad. She tell the doctor not to tell anyone what she find in her book and her computer. She tell the doctor it will ruin everything."

"What will ruin everything?"

"The seeds."

23

The cleaning lady's statement, delivered in her tiny voice, about knocked me from my chair.

"Seeds?" I repeated.

She nodded.

"What seeds?"

With a shrug she said, "That is all I hear."

I wrote down her name and phone number. After thanking her, I collected my employment records, and with Torrance at my heels flew back to the room. Searching the doctor's office seemed more important than ever. Somehow I had to discover what was so damn important about those seven pokeweed seeds.

Biding my time and biting my tongue were difficult during the meticulous, and therefore slow, search through the papers and belongings of the doctor. I wanted to ask about the seeds, but didn't want to reveal their importance. Dex stood in the corner, the silent observer of all the activity around him, which included constant swearing on Markowski's part while he tried to gain access to Patricia's main files. The computer was a linked PC, having its own hard drive but still connected to other computers in the building.

We'd boxed most of the papers and books. "How much longer?" I asked Rocky.

He rubbed the back of his neck in contemplation. "Hard to say."

"Can't we take it with us?"

"No!" Josephine cried. She stood over him, her hand on the computer. "I will not allow you to remove this from the premises."

"You don't have a choice," I said. While the employment records were questionable, and even tainted considering the bit of white lying it took to get them, we were within our full rights to take the computer. "This falls under the scope of the doctor's personal records and files," I said. "If we can't gain access to it here, we'll take it with us."

"Evan," she said. He didn't answer her, his expression closed, and I wondered if he was thinking about my accusations that his wife had slept with a woman. She frantically turned to Kermgard. "Oh, for God's sake, Dexter! Do something."

"They have a warrant, Mrs. Hilliard."

"They want to take the PC. Tell them why they can't."

"It contains materials, documents that are classified," Dex answered.

"Classified?" I echoed somewhat sardonically. "Are we working for the government now?"

"Classified to the pharmaceutical business," Dex said calmly. "If some of these projects were to get out, if other companies were to learn of them, we could lose millions."

I found Dex's use of the word "we" interesting, especially in light of Hilliard's revelation about his wife's affair with Dex.

"Millions?" I said.

Hilliard answered. "The attempt has already been

made. Which is why my wife is taking precautions."

"Being as we aren't a pharmaceutical company, I wouldn't worry too much," I said. "We have no interest in new recipes for aspirin."

Hilliard nodded and said, "My wife tends to get emotionally involved."

Josephine refused to let go of the monitor. "This has nothing to do with emotions, Evan—"

Hilliard took her by the shoulders and gently pulled her away. Her fingers slid across the top of the monitor, grabbing like a lifeline the *Holistic Herbs* paperback that I'd left on it.

"Give them the code," Hilliard said.

She started crying, shook her head, hugged the book to her chest like a mother would a baby.

Hilliard drew her from the room. "I'll talk to her," he said.

"The book." I held out my hand.

They hesitated by the door. He looked at her, brushed the tears from her eyes. "Josie?"

Sobbing, she handed him the book, and he gave it to me.

"Pack it up," I told Markowski, tossing the paperback into a box filled with other books. It was seven o'clock. High time we left. I wanted dinner, and caffeine, though not in that order.

It took us about ten minutes to gather up the last few items, then carry everything to the cars. On our way out we passed a door, ajar. I heard Evan speaking to his wife. "What was Patricia really doing here?" he asked.

I paused, but Evan saw me. He closed the door, preventing me from hearing anything further, and so I moved on.

The easy part was done. Now we had to sort through

everything at the office, attempt to determine what if anything had value to our case. My money was on the computer. Why else would Josephine guard it like a lioness watching over her cub?

We turned the conference room into our headquarters, dumping the boxes onto the long table. Each of us, excluding Rocky, took a box and started wading through the material. After picking up another sheet that described the process of cell division, I was beginning to think that Rocky had the easy job, trying to come up with a way to get into the doctor's computer files. Before he disappeared with the computer, he told me he'd found some documents among Patricia's things that had to do with the company's finances. "They're in the red," he said. "Apparently, they need this merger, big time."

Which meant the money motive was making its way back to the top.

At 0200 hours we were on our second pot of coffee, down to the last box, and still no one had found anything of significance.

"What do you make of all this?" Bettencourt asked, leaning back in the chair, propping his feet on the table. His question was directed to the room in general, so I didn't have to answer him. I didn't want him here, and thought of everything I had told him through the course of this investigation. What had he passed on to Skyler? I wanted to believe that the kiss I'd witnessed between Reid and Beth Skyler outside the judge's chambers was innocent, unrelated to this case.

Shipley poured Torrance some coffee, then emptied the pot into his own Styrofoam cup. "You mean, other than the doctor could've been a brain surgeon but decided to earn her living cutting up dead bodies?" He dumped some creamer in, then stirred it. "I'd say she was doing something with all this, but God only knows what."

"Cancer research," I said. The day finally caught up with me, and I took a seat at the table, unable to stand a second longer.

"You figured that out from this?" Shipley asked, holding up a sheet of paper that might as well have been written in Greek. Maybe it was.

"Mary told me."

"And she knew because . . ."

"Because Patricia told her."

Shipley looked at the sheet with a renewed interest that passed quickly enough the moment he apparently figured it still wouldn't make sense to him. "I'll take your word on it." He dug out the employment records from the box. "What're you planning on doing with that?"

"I was looking to see if the doctor was listed on there."

"You think Scolari's on here?" Shipley asked.

"Patricia?" I clarified. "Not under M. Didn't get to check under S. I was interrupted."

"Here's Markowski. His wife must've bled him dry in his divorce for him to take a second job. Shit, half the department worked for Hilliard Pharmaceutical at one time or another." He chuckled, turning the pages. "S, Scolari. Sam. No Patricia. How long you figure they leave the names on here? Didn't think Sam still worked there."

"Who knows. You guys want more coffee?" I asked, eyeing the empty pot. Considering the layoffs, I wasn't sure I wanted anyone to dwell on the employment list, not until I had a chance to mull it over myself.

Shipley, however, had other ideas, and started from

the first page. "No, thanks," he said. "This is too good. Didn't know some of these guys—"

"Let me see that." Reid reached over, tried to take the papers from Shipley.

"Not a chance," Shipley said, backing away. He scanned the names on the first sheet. "Did you know Charlie Adkins works there? Least he did before the chief put the nix on it." He flipped through more pages. "Ho, Bettencourt. Needed a little cash, did you?"

"None of your goddamned business," Reid said.

Torrance and I exchanged glances. I had no idea Reid had joined the ranks of Hilliard, and I was surprised by his almost violent reaction. "What are you doing for them?" I asked, curious if he was merely worried about someone thinking his finances were in disarray. Which they were.

"Same as everyone else you know there," he replied. "Working security."

I wasn't sure how the DA's office handled it when their investigators wanted extra work, but every cop at SFPD who wanted a second job had to get clearance through the chief's office, allegedly to prevent unethical situations or conflict of interest—such as investigating a homicide at Hilliard Pharmaceutical while being employed there. "Didn't you say you were working an embezzlement case at Hilliard? I'd think you'd have brought this up before now."

"Jesus, Kate," he said, jumping to his feet. His chair tipped precariously. "And you wonder why we got divorced?" He stormed from the room.

Actually, not at all.

"What's with him?" Shipley asked.

That I did wonder about.

Torrance watched the door, a thoughtful look upon his face. "I think we need to address this issue of Bettencourt working an embezzlement case while employed by Hilliard Pharmaceutical."

Shipley gave a low whistle. "I'm not hearing this. Pretend I'm not here."

Ignoring him, I said, "I have no idea if the dates coincide, or how involved he is. I do wonder about the money."

"Money?" This from Torrance.

Shipley no longer pretended disinterest.

"Have you noticed the new car?"

"They make loans," Shipley pointed out.

"For some people. Not for Reid. His credit was a mess when we married, it was worse after our divorce."

"Inheritance?" Shipley asked.

"No."

Shipley nodded toward the employment records. "A second job, apparently."

"Or selling a news story," Torrance suggested.

"A news story?" Shipley looked from Torrance to me. "What're you talking about?"

"About Beth Skyler," I said. "He's been on somewhat intimate terms with her, and the night of Patricia's murder, Skyler was there asking questions that someone had to have fed her."

"The son of a bitch."

"The question is, is he doing it for money or sex?"

The conference room door swung open and Rocky entered, carrying the computer with him.

"Well, I've done what I can," he said, looking anything but the bearer of glad tidings.

"This is one of those good news, bad news things,

isn't it?" I asked.

"Sorry. Every file's been erased."

That night, or rather early that morning, I lay in the still dark of the hotel room, thinking about the computer. Moonlight spilled through the window, lighting the carpet below with its soft glow.

Erased. Rocky's voice echoed in my head. I'd been unable to sleep.

I'd managed to pin all my hopes on that box of modern technology. I wondered who had deleted the files. Evan Hilliard had accessed the computer in accounting. Could he have done it? I hadn't paid that much attention to the keys he pressed. Didn't think he had time, though I suppose it was possible. And what about Reid, the way he reacted when I pulled him from the computer, and later when we learned he was employed at Hilliard Pharmaceutical? He'd never mentioned it before, which I found curious though not all that unusual. It wasn't as if Reid and I had spent hours going over each facet of our private lives since our divorce.

At the moment, it didn't really matter. Whatever had been on the hard drive was now gone, a forgotten bit of memory never to be seen again.

Or was I mistaken?

I didn't know anything about computers, but I knew someone who did. Rising, I switched on the light, dug for my phone book in my purse. My childhood sweetheart worked for the Department of Justice. Bill Moore and I kept in touch over the years, mostly by phone. I was very happy for him, he was very happy for me, but our lives never meshed. City girl, country boy, we drifted apart. He'd married, had a wife, two kids, did the dad routine, made big bucks working for Microsoft. Then, when I thought he'd forgotten his country roots, he gave up the job to work as a computer expert at DOJ, all so he could live in the foothills of Sacramento and raise horses. Big loss for Microsoft, major boon to law enforcement.

"What are you doing?" Torrance asked from his bed, his eyes closed against the lamplight.

"Calling a friend of mine who works at DOJ. This guy makes Rocky's computer skills look like mine." I found the number and picked up the phone.

Torrance glanced at the clock. "You do realize it's three-twenty?"

I dropped the phone in the cradle. Bill wouldn't mind. His wife might. "Damn."

"At least wait till seven," he said, rolling over so his back was to the light—and to me.

His pajamas, flannel, had a sharp crease in them, and I wondered if he wore them strictly for my benefit. Putting my phone book aside, I turned out the light, nestled beneath the covers, and stared out the window into what was left of the night. "What do you normally wear to bed?" I asked, regretting my impulsive question the moment it left my mouth.

"Nothing."

I took a deep breath. I'd always wondered what it meant to be sexually frustrated. Now I knew.

Naturally, Torrance was dressed by the time I opened my eyes. He was not, however, reading the paper, but watching me from his chair at the table. I sat up, rubbing my neck.

"Here," he said, handing me a latte delivered from room service. It was warm, though not as warm as I liked it. "We need to get moving. Big day."

"Got it all planned, do you?"

"The afternoon, at least. Paolini's case is this afternoon."

I didn't move. I'd purposefully put it from my mind. I'd had to. I thought of the threats, all designed to keep me from testifying in this case. And now, today was the day. All I had to do was walk in, swear to tell the truth, testify, then wait. Wait to see if someone—Paolini—would make good on the threats.

"I'll be damned if I let that happen."

Torrance gave me an odd look at my comment.

"The threats," I clarified. "Why should I wait? I say, find a way to bring Paolini in and confront him now."

"Makes you wonder why someone at the DA's office didn't think of that."

"Doesn't it, though. The question now is, what charges?"

"I'm sure if we look hard enough, we'll find something," Torrance said.

A few phone calls later, I had what we needed. "A speeding ticket," I said after I'd hung up. "He hasn't paid it yet, and it's past due."

"That's it?"

"It was the best they could do, considering. Vice is going to tail him. They owe me for playing a hooker for them on a sting a couple of months ago."

After taking a few sips of lukewarm espresso and steamed milk, I dragged myself into the bathroom to shower. I glanced at my garment bag. What to wear while interviewing a mobster? I decided on jeans, sweater—and boots in case the crap got too deep to wade in. Brushing my wet hair, I looked in the mirror. The bruise on my temple had faded considerably, now a shade of yellow-purple. I belatedly wondered if Paolini wasn't behind the poisoned pizza caper. I'd have to remember to ask, then decided I was being overly optimistic if I expected him to answer about anything.

"Ready or not, Paolini, here we come."

At precisely nine, Torrance and I, acting as backup in addition to the four Vice officers, watched from our own vehicle as Paolini's black limousine pulled up in front of the Olympic Club. I thought of Reid, stopping to talk to someone in a black limo outside the PD. The city was full of black limos, and I had no way of knowing if that particular limo happened to be Paolini's. But I intended to ask.

The arrest went without incident, Paolini accepting the trumped-up charge of failure to pay a traffic fine, undoubtedly because he knew that by the time the booking was filled out, his lawyer would already be there and he'd be a free man. He was searched, and brought in by the Vice detail.

At the jail we secured our weapons in the gun locker. The custody officers had already moved Paolini into an interview room.

I had my feelings about facing Paolini, the man suspected of placing the hit on me at the Twin Palms. I wasn't afraid, but neither was I comfortable with it. I wanted a clear head, and thinking about the night I was shot did little to help.

With Torrance at my side, however, I felt a slight degree of comfort. Especially once I stifled the outlandish thought that Paolini had put the jail guards on his payroll somehow. It could happen, and it had happened, but I couldn't go through this interview worrying about it.

Paolini smiled when I entered the room. He unnerved me still, and I wondered if his looks didn't play a part in that. He was tall, thin, olive-complected. His narrow face and aquiline nose were strikingly handsome. Seeing him this close was like stepping back in time to the night we attended the Save the Rain Forest dinner together. Instead of a tux, however, he now wore a pink Ralph Lauren polo shirt and tan slacks neatly pressed. He sat on one side of the table, barely sparing Torrance a glance, and appearing for all the world as though we were calling for tea. "Inspector Gillespie. So nice of you to visit. And you brought your friend."

"Such a pleasure to see you again, too," I said. Two things I knew from countless jailhouse interviews were, never show fear and don't let them get the upper hand in the conversation. Paolini would take advantage of both. "We're not here to play good cop, bad cop. We want some answers."

"And perhaps I can give them to you," he said, still with a smile. "My attorney is on his way. I feel magnanimous in that I am to be released soon."

I bet you do. "Tell me about the warehouse owned by Hilliard Pharmaceutical."

He looked mildly confused. I gave him the address.

"Oh, yes. An import/export business. Until the unfortunate matter with the on-site manager."

"The money laundering scheme disguised as a Save the Rain Forest fund-raiser dinner," I supplied.

"So the police tell me."

Aside from the money and drugs we'd confiscated, for which his case was on appeal, he'd skated on the money laundering charges, garnering a one-year sentence. But there was still the dead body to be reckoned with. "You aren't aware of the freezer left there?"

"We had no freezer, Inspector. Who is your friend?" he asked, nodding to Torrance, who leaned against the door, strong, silent, arms crossed, very much the body-guard.

"Lieutenant Torrance from IA."

"Found yourself in a bit of trouble?"

I hid my exasperation at Paolini's attempt to steer the conversation. "There was a body in the freezer."

"Inspector Gillespie. I do hope you are not blaming me for a body you found?"

"I don't know who to blame. I was hoping you could shed some light on the matter."

"If I could help you, I would. But I don't know much of what's gone on in the outside world this past year. What sort of trouble have you gotten yourself into?" he asked, eyeing Torrance.

"You're saying you have no idea a body was found in your warehouse?"

"None."

Okay, let's move on to Reid Bettencourt."

"The DA investigator?"

"Yes."

Paolini waited.

I had nothing solid, but I forged ahead. "You were seen talking to him."

"And?"

"And I want to know why."

"Perhaps it would be best if you asked him."

"I'm asking you."

I waited several seconds. He remained silent, smiled.

"Very well," I conceded. "Phone threats."

"I have received none."

I wanted to wipe that smirk right off his face. Was it a guilty smirk, or the type all ex-cons gave to cops who come to question them? It bothered me that I couldn't tell. "Do you deny that you've had someone calling me over the last year, making threats that if I testified at your trial, you'd kill me?"

He steepled his fingers, placed the tips at his mouth, his expression serious. "Why would I bother?"

"Because you believed I might be intimidated by threats?"

Suddenly he laughed. "Inspector Gillespie. Why would I threaten you, and not the officers who were listening on the wire? Were they not also a part of that case?"

They were, and he had a point, though a minor one. They could only testify to what they heard, and I failed to see how that could make him innocent. I *was* receiving death threats about his case. "Okay, let's say you didn't order one of your men to do this. How do you explain the hit on the two property clerks, and the destruction of the evidence in your case?"

"An unfortunate incident with fortunate results."

I shot from my chair, slamming my hands onto the table. My face was inches from his, and I expected to feel Torrance grab my shoulder, restrain me. It occurred to me he might have to restrain himself. "Two innocent people are dead because of that. They had families. Grandchildren."

He stared a moment, then gave an apologetic smile. "You'll have to forgive me. What I said was tactless." The smile vanished, and he continued, "But I did not have those men killed. My attorney promised me that I'd be getting off on a . . . technicality. How else did you think we were granted a retrial?"

"You tell me."

"The lab worker who tested the drugs was dirty. He

could very well have switched the product, tainted the evidence. Or hadn't you heard he was arrested for falsifying evidence and being under the influence of the very drugs he was testing?"

Taking a breath, I sat and leaned back in my chair. It suddenly occurred to me that Paolini might be behind the corruption and arrest of Scott Forrest, the lab tech. His arrest had produced a domino effect throughout the city.

Paolini's case was tainted by Forrest, which meant Paolini would win his appeal on the drug charges, undoubtedly get credit for time served on the money laundering charge if not be totally acquitted on that as well. He'd be released in a heartbeat.

Unless we could get him on witness intimidation—me.

Despite my false bravado, I had to admit I was somewhat intimidated. I suppose it came from being shot at close quarters. Even so, I would never let him see it.

"You expect me to believe you're innocent?" I asked slowly, evenly, not willing to give an inch. "You know very well I was shot outside one of your drug runner's motel rooms a year ago. I've lived with constant threats of death. Someone almost made good on it the other night. Someone you know quite well."

He never blinked.

"Antonio Foust," I announced.

His gaze widened almost imperceptibly. His jaw clenched. "Inspector Gillespie," he began, his voice low, tinged with anger, his gaze cutting into mine. "It appears I have been made the fool."

"And how is that?" I asked, hiding my surprise at his reaction. I would have expected the earlier smirk, not this bridled anger.

"You have proof that Tony tried to kill you?"

"His fingerprint in my house."

"A print?"

"Not to mention a couple bullet holes in my bed. Or isn't that enough?"

Paolini stared at his hands on the table before him, palms up. "What happened to you a year ago, at the Twin Palms . . . I was most sorry to hear." His gaze met mine once more, the anger diminished. "I liked you. Had I not, you would never have gotten the information you had. You would never have gotten so close. But I was not responsible. I had no idea until the news made it to me through the usual channels.

"And as I said earlier, I did not order the threats on your life. I did not kill, nor did I order anyone to kill the two men who worked for your department. I am a businessman. Perhaps unscrupulous at times, but not to the point of killing innocent people."

"And if you didn't do it, who did? And why?"

"The why of it is easy. To set me up, of course."

"Come again?"

"My dear Inspector. If I am found guilty of murdering your two officers, possibly receiving the death penalty, there is one person who stands to gain everything."

"And that would be?"

The anger returned to his eyes. A vein on his temple pulsed. "Antonio Foust."

24

W hat's this about Bettencourt?" Torrance asked after we left the jail.

"I saw him talking to someone in a limo. It was purely a guess."

"Apparently an accurate one."

"Right now, I'm more interested in what Paolini had to say about Foust. Do you believe him?"

The heels of my boots clicked across the floor, echoing to the end of the hall. Several staccato beats later, he answered. "What he's saying makes sense."

"Sense? How does a man guilty of the crimes Paolini's committed make a claim that he doesn't kill innocent people?"

"Think about the known hits. True, never proved, but what kind of people were they?"

Torrance was right. If Paolini hadn't had them killed—*allegedly*, I forced myself to add—they undoubtedly would have killed him or someone else. It didn't excuse the man. But it did make sense. So did the fact that his case was bound to be dismissed on the basis that the lab tech, Forrest, was dirty. Every other case that had made it to retrial because of the same reason had been dismissed.

I needed to think about this logically. "Okay. Foust

makes the phone threats the moment Paolini is in jail, perhaps at first with his blessings, until Paolini's released. Later, Foust learns his boss's case is up for appeal, and concocts this plan to set him up? This is ridiculous," I said, frustrated. I was having a difficult time changing my mind about Paolini's guilt after so long. I bore a scar on my shoulder, for God's sake. Who shot me? Was it, as Paolini had said, an unknown person? Did he really have no knowledge?

I supposed it was possible. And for the moment, water under the bridge. I stopped in the middle of the hallway and looked at Torrance. "If what he is saying is true, then Foust has been planning this for a long time. Months."

"And why is that so hard to believe? Especially when you consider how much money is at stake? Paolini's net worth probably exceeds the city's annual budget. Foust had a taste of it, taking control in Paolini's absence," Torrance responded, guiding me on toward the elevator. He played the devil's advocate so well. "Foust is as much of a crook as Paolini, perhaps more so. He's a known murderer. A hit man. He's—"

Torrance stopped short when I placed my hand on his shoulder. Perhaps it was this talk about Foust, but I'd suddenly recalled the moment yesterday when we were waiting by the elevator, when one of the crime scene investigators, Rebecca, had called out to Torrance. Her presence had spurred something in my mind, but I'd been distracted by Reid and his affair with Skyler. "I need to see photographs of all the CSIs," I said. "Now."

"Why?"

"I'll tell you when we get there."

Scores of photos lined the hallways throughout the

floors of the police department, the uniforms and hair-styles changing over the years, as well as the film. Black-and-white at first, now color. I knew there was a recent photo of the crime scene investigators on the wall outside their office, along with several other similar framed photos of their predecessors. It was something we all did every few years or so. One of the few times we put on our class A uniforms when there wasn't a cop funeral to go to.

I found the picture, stopped before it.

"What are you looking for?" Torrance asked. "Maybe I can help."

"I don't think so." I knew I wouldn't find who I was looking for, but searched the photo anyway. I didn't see the face, no one similar. No one who could have been there. "The afternoon that Martin and Smith were killed," I said, going over the photos once more, "I ran into someone on the staircase by the Property room. Kicked something. He was kneeling down near his brief-case, and I was so busy chasing after someone I thought was Zimmerman, I didn't see him there at first."

"Who?"

"The man on the stairs." We returned to my office, and Torrance patiently waited for me to explain. "He was wearing a uniform, the coverall type. I assumed he was an evidence tech, and I didn't stop to check."

I looked Torrance in the eye. "I think it was Foust. When we were in the Buena Vista, I thought he looked familiar and couldn't place why. It was the first time I'd actually seen the man face-to-face. Now I'm just about certain that he's the man I saw on the steps that day. I didn't see him full on, but now that I know there's no evidence techs that even look like him, I know I have to be right."

I closed my eyes, trying to bring him into focus. I could see him there, hear the clatter of whatever it was I kicked sliding across the landing. A gun? Had I kicked a gun?

The horror of that afternoon came back, and then the realization that had I been a minute later, I too might have been killed.

Opening my eyes, I looked at Torrance with renewed determination. The silence in the room overwhelmed me. "Foust was trying to kill me because I saw him on the steps. That's why he came to my apartment."

I took a breath. My hands shook, and I felt like I couldn't move.

"You okay?" Torrance asked.

"Yeah, fine," I said. I wasn't really, but just then Rocky walked in, and I didn't feel like explaining how I really felt.

Torrance didn't look as if he believed me.

I ignored him and turned my attention to Rocky, who appeared to be waiting for me.

Rocky cleared his throat. "Um, I was wondering about the computer."

After meeting with Paolini, I'd completely forgotten about it. "I plan on taking it to Agent Moore at DOJ. I'll let you know the moment we learn anything."

I picked up the phone and called my friend.

"Bill? Hi, it's Kate."

"What's up? You decided after all these months you want to leave your job, move to the valley and be near me?"

"You and your wife?"

"She's an understanding woman."

"Listen," I said, cutting the chitchat short. "I've got a hard drive that's been erased. I was wondering if you could take a look. See if anything can be recovered on it."

"Give it a try. What's it for?"

"Homicide case. We're looking for anything that might help. Last resort sort of thing."

"Bring it by. I'll get right on it."

Sacramento was a little over two hours away, and Torrance and I left immediately. He drove. About ten minutes into the drive, he said, "You want to talk about it?"

"About what?"

"Foust."

"No." I couldn't, for the simple reason that the man I'd blamed for the past year, Paolini, appeared innocent. My life should be getting back to normal once Foust was arrested. Why didn't I feel the least bit elated?

I knew why. Essentially, I'd cleared Scolari in two murder cases. He wasn't the SoMa Slasher, and he wasn't the cop killer. But he was still a suspect in his wife's case. I wanted him to come forward, clear himself. I deserved that much, didn't I?

"Pretty country," Torrance said. We were just east of Fairfield, and the green rolling hills this time of year always reminded me of photos of Ireland.

I nodded, grateful that he was allowing me my peace, and for the rest of the trip we discussed what it would be like to live in the country.

We made good time, arriving at the Department of Justice a little after two. Typical of government buildings, it was multistoried, square, and not particularly an architectural masterpiece. The few trees scattered across the small patches of lawn out front helped to soften it, however. Torrance held open the heavy glass door, allowing me to step in. I carried the computer, letting go only long enough to show my ID for clearance. Until it was in my friend's hands, I would not feel comfortable.

Moore's office was cluttered with books, keyboards, and power strips on the countertops, blank monitors mounted on the walls, everything waiting to be plugged into whatever computer Moore happened to be working on.

He took the computer, flipped it over, eyed the jack, plugged it into a power strip below one suspended monitor, then turned everything on. The monitor lit up like a TV screen.

"You want to wait?"

"How long will it take?"

"Well, if it's on a—"

"So I can understand, Bill," I interjected. He had a tendency to go off the deep end when it came to computer techno-talk, a small reason our romance never took off. I never knew what he was talking about.

"Depends on how the files were deleted. If there's anything left, I'll find it."

"Where's the closest place to eat?" Torrance asked.

"Cafeteria, upstairs," he said, plugging in a keyboard. "But if I were you, I'd hit the deli around the corner. You can walk."

We opted for the deli, and started that way. My pager went off before we ever made it.

"It's Shipley," I said, recognizing my office number and his call sign directly after.

Torrance gave me his phone.

I called the office. "Shipley?"

"Might have an ID on your John Doe," Shipley said. "Thought you'd want to know."

"Who is it?"

"We're waiting for dental records to confirm. But it might be a guy named Chester Lynch, a PI out of Arkansas hired by Montgard Pharmaceutical. I was wondering how you knew."

"Because Arkansas happens to be the home of Montgard Pharmaceutical, the company that's trying to merge with Hilliard Pharmaceutical. Now that I think about it, I'm pretty certain that I saw the name Lynch on Hilliard's employment records. Do me a favor. Check it now, just to verify."

"Hold on."

I heard the rustle of papers in the background.

"Yep. Chester Lynch," he confirmed.

"Thanks."

Torrance and I decided to skip lunch after that piece of news. I didn't want the computer out of my sight.

We returned to Agent Moore's office, and he glanced up. "Not very challenging," he said. "Lucky for you, whoever erased this didn't use any type of high-level I've recovered most of what was there."

"Meaning what?" I asked.

"Thought you didn't want to know the technical stuff," he teased.

I didn't, but figured it might give me a clue as to who erased the data. "Humor me. In terms I can understand."

"The info was stored on a F.A.T. partition. Simply put, when it was erased, it wasn't truly deleted, merely hidden from view. It's recoverable up until the time that data gets written on top of it. Which is why I couldn't get all of it. There's a lot of"—he lifted a sheet from the printer—"cold remedies, drugs. The other stuff looks like accounting info."

"Is this pretty basic? This F.A.T. partition thing?" I asked, wondering why Rocky hadn't thought of it, for all he was supposed to know about computers.

"For this type of system it is. Now, if you need to

recover anything below what I've done, you'll have to take it to the NSA, uh, National Security Agency," he clarified when he saw my look of confusion. "They can recover up to seven layers, last I heard. That's a little beyond my expertise."

I looked over what was being printed. "You know who to get ahold of, should I need it?"

"Just call."

"There is one more thing. Do you have any idea when it was erased?"

"That's easy enough to determine." He typed some commands on the keyboard, looked at the monitor, and said, "Looks like the majority of it was yesterday, between 1800 and 1830 hours."

Right around the time we were there. Evan Hilliard had printed up the employee records. Was it possible he had erased the files while I looked on, oblivious? Patricia's computer was networked. His wife was desperate to keep us from taking it. Then again, Rocky was also on the computer at that time. Wouldn't he have discovered something? And what about Reid? He was also at the keyboard, though I didn't pay attention to the time. Both Rocky and Reid had been employed by Hilliard Pharmaceutical, but that didn't mean they were loyal to the company. Besides, what would their motive be? Money, I thought, recalling Reid's reaction when Shipley had pointed out his name on the Hilliard Pharmaceutical employment list.

We were out of there in half an hour, Torrance carrying the computer. I carried an inch-thick stack of newly printed documents, as well as copies of the disks that Bill had made of what was recovered. I hoped it would turn out to be a worthwhile trip.

Torrance drove while I looked over the papers. Everything was happening so fast, I couldn't concentrate. Worse, I was getting carsick. I never could read in the car; I don't know why I bothered trying.

"Find anything?" Torrance asked.

"No. Not yet." I put the papers aside. "I need to eat."

"You want to stop?"

"No. Let's get back to the Hall. We've got a ton of work to sort through."

The four of us, Torrance, Shipley, Markowski, and I, sat in the conference room going over the doctor's papers one by one. A pizza sat untouched in the center of the table. Some joker had ordered it and sent it up. I didn't know if I'd ever be able to eat one again. Torrance had sent his secretary to pick up sandwiches from the deli across the street, but they had yet to arrive.

"Any of this make sense to you?" Rocky asked.

"Nothing," I said, going over the last sheet in my stack. We'd divided the papers between us. I handed mine to Torrance before I took those that Shipley had already looked at.

An hour later I was going over a paper that read like a recipe from a chemistry book. A chemical name stood out. Methylenedioxy methamphetamine. MDMA. Ecstasy, or XTC as it was known on the streets. I supposed Patricia might have had it on her computer at Hilliard Pharmaceutical for the simple reason she'd been involved in the autopsies of several individuals who had this particular compound in their bloodstreams at the time of death.

Unfortunately, I couldn't ask her, and I couldn't see what relevance MDMA had to the seeds.

The sandwiches arrived, but my appetite had fled. I wanted this over and done with. The private investigator had apparently found these seeds, and had been killed because of them. I was certain Patricia had been killed for the same reason. Now all I had to do was figure out what that reason was.

"Why do you suppose this is here?" Rocky asked sometime later. "This whole paper's about it. Reads like some documentary. You figure it's a like a chemotherapy drug? It talks about rain forests and cancer."

"Cancer?" I took the paper from him. "Project Green," I read aloud from the heading.

The sheet fluttered in my fingers, and I laid it on the table. The first paragraph appeared to discuss the disappearing rain forests, and the untapped but threatened potential to find new cures. Hilliard Pharmaceutical had funded a team of scientists to scour one particular part of the rain forest, bringing home samples of plants, seeds, leaves, and bark before that area of the rain forest had been obliterated. Project Green.

Certain seed samples had shown great promise in halting the spread of cancer, even AIDS. The samples were all that was left, unless the seeds from the pods could be grown, or identical species could be located in other forests around the world. So far nothing had been found.

That was nothing new, and I skimmed over the words, moving on to the portion that mentioned investors. "Hello," I said.

"What?"

"Project Green was funded by the Save the Rain Forest Foundation."

"Come again?" Shipley asked.

"Paolini's pet project. Apparently he was an original

investor." Evan Hilliard had hinted as much. But this paper proved it.

"The project that got Hilliard the big break? Sent its stocks soaring?"

"The same. Maybe Paolini used the Hilliards to transport cocaine."

My gaze returned to the paragraph about the seed pods, and I thought of the *Holistic Herbs* paperback book.

Hilliard Pharmaceutical was becoming a major force in the pharmaceutical world, with the potential of introducing a vast line of cancer drugs. A new cancer cure was big business. But why would this PI, Chester Lynch, feel the need to smuggle the seeds out? Especially when we had it on authority that the seeds he had were nothing? Had someone switched them? Made Lynch think they were the rare rain forest seeds?

"I think we need to talk with Evan Hilliard again," I said.

"Good luck," Shipley responded. "You're deluding yourself if you think the Hilliards are gonna let you within ten feet of their office building."

"It's not his office building I want. We need to get into the warehouse."

"Warehouse?" Rocky asked.

"Hilliard Pharmaceutical's storage facility. Patricia must have found some properties in those seeds. I have a feeling that she stumbled on them accidentally." I explained about the conversation overheard between Josephine Hilliard and Patricia, and how Josephine was upset at what Patricia had found pertaining to the seeds.

"A cleaning lady heard them talking about seeds, and you wanna look at files?" Rocky asked. "What files?"

"Project Green files."

"Why?"

I held up the paper. "Someone tried to erase this from the doctor's computer. At first glance, it looks like nothing. Another look at the documentary making the news."

They all sat at attention. "Go on," Torrance said.

"Until now, we could never tie the evidence together. Chester Lynch, Montgard's PI, gets ahold of these seeds, learns something's up at Hilliard Pharmaceutical that maybe goes with his investigation, maybe not. Whatever. He was killed with these seven seeds in his possession, then dumped on the other side of the warehouse. My guess is that he was looking for something in there. Undoubtedly the very thing we pulled up on Patricia's computer. When we were at Hilliard's office, both he and Dex alluded to information being leaked out about some major pharmaceutical secret. They even confirmed it had happened in the past. I'm wondering if this Chester Lynch wasn't the source of the leak. What if Montgard Pharmaceutical hired him to investigate Hilliard before the merger was finalized?"

"And someone at Hilliard Pharmaceutical finds out about it, and has him taken out?" Torrance asked.

"Exactly." I looked at Shipley. "Have you found anything out from your sources at Montgard Pharmaceutical yet?"

"No. No one admits knowing Lynch. I'm still waiting to hear from the head honcho, who's due back from the Bahamas this afternoon. Second honeymoon, or something like that. His secretary told me she'd have him call the moment he gets in."

"How does your PI tie into Patricia's death?" Rocky asked.

"He's killed. Patricia does his autopsy. She finds the seeds, maybe knows what they are, maybe not. Even so, she ends up dead a few days later. I, for one, have a hard time believing her death is a coincidence. Which makes me think we've been looking at this thing from the wrong angle all along."

"So you're saying Scolari killed the PI *and* his wife?" Rocky asked.

For all Rocky's investigative skills, he could be dense at times. "Let's pretend for one minute that Scolari's innocent. If so, then someone killed the doctor for what she knew," I said, picking up the *Holistic Herbs* book from the box it sat in. I flipped through the index and found Pokeweed, then turned to that page. "Or what they *thought* she knew. And what we do know from the cleaning lady is that she was talking about those seeds the night she died."

"So what'dya suggest?" Shipley asked

"We search Hilliard Pharmaceutical's file storage. See if we can find something to back up this paper," I said, slapping the book to the table. "Then we confront the Hilliards."

"Christ Almighty," Rocky said, sinking into his chair. "You got any idea how many files there are in that warehouse?"

Torrance pulled his pager from his belt, pressed the button, read it. "They've just arrested Scolari."

Everyone looked at me. I stared at Torrance in disbelief. My throat tightened, but somehow I managed to speak anyway. "Where? What happened?"

"I don't have all the details, except that they're bringing him into the jail now.

* * *

Scolari looked like hell. His short gray hair hung limply over his forehead. Dark circles framed his eyes, and his unshaven cheeks were sunken as though he hadn't eaten in days. He didn't seem to notice us as we entered the booking area.

I recognized the transporting officer, Robertson, from the afternoon we'd found the John Doe out at the warehouse. He was the one who reminded me of my brother. He looked up from his paperwork, saw Torrance, and said, "We read him his rights like you asked, but he said he wants to talk to his attorney."

"Thanks," Torrance said.

Not sure I heard correctly, I glanced at Torrance. "You knew they were bringing him in?" I asked in disbelief. The fact he was IA—and I was not—spread clear and wide like a chasm between us.

"Hey, you mind gettin' these cuffs off me?" I heard Scolari order.

I stormed past Torrance to the jailer, a short woman, heavyset, with blond hair. "I'll handle the booking," I said.

She opened the cell door, and I stepped in.

"Gillespie," was all Scolari said.

As I looked at Scolari, I wasn't sure who I was more angry at. Scolari for running off at the height of the investigation and putting me through this, or Torrance for neglecting to tell me Scolari was about to be arrested. "Put him in an interview room," I told the jailer.

She shrugged, drawing Scolari, still handcuffed, from the cell, then heading down the hall to an interview room. I started to follow them when Torrance stopped me.

"I didn't think you needed the added worry. I didn't tell you because I felt it best."

"An IA thing, undoubtedly," I said. "And for your

info, I have never stopped worrying about him. But that's beside the point. We had a deal. You reneged on your promise."

"I made a mistake."

"So did I, Lieutenant." Then I walked off.

In the interview room, the jailer had removed Scolari's cuffs, and Scolari rubbed at the red indentations on his wrists. I knew that Torrance was seated outside, watching and listening through the two-way mirror. I suppose I should have been grateful that he at least gave me this much leeway.

I pulled up a chair opposite Scolari's. He eyed me. "You didn't hear the officer? I invoked," he said, referring to his right to remain silent.

"Really? Well, let me tell you something, Scolari. I don't have time for your games right now, so cut the crap and tell me what's going on."

He tapped a cadence on the scarred table. "There's nothing to tell."

"Nothing to tell?" I laughed. The stress of the past two weeks finally took its toll on me. I slid my chair back, and stood so that I looked down at him. "If you want to rot in prison, that's your problem, but how dare you bring me into this. How dare you put me in danger, then sit there and have the gall to tell me that there is nothing to tell."

"Look, Kate, I'm sorry. I made a mistake."

"A mistake? What is that? A catchall phrase for guys that screw with my life?" I said it before I thought better of it. If Torrance got extra meaning out of it, then so be it.

"Who're you pissed off at?"

Scolari could always read me so well. Not that I was being subtle. "Right now, you," I replied. I wasn't about to go into my troubles with Torrance. Not while he watched. And not that it was any of Scolari's business.

"I said I was sorry."

"I don't want your apology. I want an explanation. You can start with whatever is going on at Hilliard Pharmaceutical."

"What about the Slasher?"

"What about him?"

"That's why I sent you to the Ox. I was trying to prove I wasn't the Slasher. Figured since no one else was looking for him, and the press was pointing fingers, I better clear my name."

"Silly me. And here I was twiddling my thumbs the whole time. I can't believe you—"

"Eric Lange," he interjected. "The bartender at the Gold Ox had a thing for McAllen's roommate. I think he killed McAllen by mistake."

"And you're sure it's Lange?" I recalled the name. The owner had mentioned him.

"Positive. I got it straight from Trish. Her neighbor gave me the number she'd left."

I looked at the mirrored window, unable to make out the vague images past our reflections. "Someone want to call Zim and give him that info?"

"Zim?" Scolari asked. "I thought you were handling the Slasher cases."

"Was. I'm investigating your wife's murder."

He turned away, stared at the wall. A vein in his temple pulsed. "My lawyer's en route to post bail."

When he wouldn't meet my gaze, it suddenly occurred to me what he'd done. What he'd been doing all along. "I don't believe it," I said, my temper flaring. I paced the room, trying to calm myself. "You've been spoon-feeding me this SoMa Slasher stuff, stringing me along just like everyone else. I expected you of all people to be different."

"I don't know what you're talking about, Gillespie."

"Oh, bull, Scolari," I said, stopping in front of him, the table between us. "You could have picked up the phone any time, told me that information. All of it. But you didn't."

He looked at me, his expression guarded. "You don't know what you're talking about."

I leaned over until I was inches from his face. "You were trying to distract me from your wife's murder. The question is, why?"

His gaze held mine for several interminable seconds. Finally he uttered, too soft for the microphone to pick up, "Because I want to kill the son of a bitch that killed my wife."

"Forget it, Scolari." I remained where I was, still leaning on the table. "I'll put a hold on your booking. I'll call the judge, get your bail raised. I'm not going to let you screw up what's left of your life. Now tell me what the hell is going on."

He crossed his arms over his chest, closing himself from me. I waited. Nothing.

I turned away, walked toward the door, and pulled it open.

"Fine . . ." he said.

His pause told me a caveat was next. I remained where I was.

"Me and you, Gillespie. No recording equipment. No witnesses behind the window."

"I don't know if they'll let me do that."

"No deal, then."

"I'll ask." I closed the door behind me. Torrance stood as I approached. Andrews had joined him, and I nodded in greeting. "Well?"

"There's no confidentiality here," Torrance said. "You'll be ordered to report everything he tells you."

"I'm sure Scolari is well aware of that."

He looked at Scolari through the window, and nodded. "All right. We have to meet with the DA anyway for the search warrant at Hilliard's warehouse." He handed me a small notebook and pen.

I took it. "I'll let you know when I'm done." I intended to keep all our dealings purely business from now on. I wouldn't let my personal life interfere with my work again. But after they left, and as I took a seat across from Scolari, waiting for him to begin his statement, I realized the naiveté of my thoughts. Everything about this case was personal. "Go ahead," I said, noting the time at the top of the page.

Scolari cleared his throat, glanced out the window. "They're gone?" he asked, his voice shaky.

I nodded.

"What do you want to know?"

"Why you didn't tell me about Patricia and Josephine Hilliard," I said.

"I didn't tell you because it wasn't your business or anyone else's."

"So what happened?"

"We, um, hadn't slept together in three years. You know, she gave me the 'I'm trying to find myself' speech. Suddenly she wants a divorce. The night I gave her the car, she told me she was seeing Josie Hilliard. I blew a gasket. That was it."

"That was it?"

"Until I met with Squeaky Kincaid that night. He told me he thought the cocaine and dirty XTC was coming from Hilliard Pharmaceutical's lab. He said that Dex Kermgard had a deal with Nick Paolini at one time, using Hilliard Pharmaceutical's research trips to the rain forests to transport his coke back to the States. They called it Project Green. It was a sweet deal until you popped Paolini, putting an end to everyone's profits. That's when Dex came up with the idea of selling XTC. Everything he needed was right there in the labs. He didn't need Paolini at all."

I told him about the document on Patricia's computer relating to the research trips to the rain forest, and the XTC.

"That just proves what I'm saying," he replied. "That Dex killed her. He must've found out that she knew about Project Green, and the XTC."

"So Paolini wasn't in it?"

"Not this time. Dex probably figured he was too hot. Which he was."

"What about Foust?"

"What about him?"

I told him about the attempts on my life. The shootings, and Mathis ending up in the hospital.

"You're thinking Dex put a hit on you because you were too close?"

"That's one possibility. Paolini says he knew nothing about it. But I happen to think it's more that Foust thought I could ID him at the homicides in Property. And the threats are real. Foust is still out there."

Scolari stared at his haggard reflection, and nodded. "Dex and Foust go way back. Dex is dirty. No doubt about it," he said, more to himself than to me. He tore his gaze from the mirror and looked directly at me. "Patricia called me from her office at Hilliard Pharmaceutical the night she was killed. She was upset. She said she had something to tell me, and wanted to meet a half hour earlier, in the same parking lot where she was killed."

"Do you know what it was she wanted to talk about?"

"She said she'd been made a fool of, that Josie had used her. And Dex was behind it."

"Evan Hilliard said Dex and Josie were having an affair," I told him, but I don't know if he heard me.

He had a faraway look, his eyes glassy with unshed tears. "I got there, and it was raining. Her lights were on, so I figured she'd just pulled in. She was driving the Range Rover I gave her." Scolari's voice broke. He turned away, brushed at his eyes. "I opened the door. She was— I—God, I just wanted to hold her one last time. Say goodbye," he whispered.

For several seconds he said nothing. A jail door clanged shut down the hall. A jangle of keys, then heavy footsteps passed by outside. He looked at me, said, "I locked the door, Kate. I was going to make sure nothing was disturbed."

"Why didn't you stick around? Call?"

"Because I wanted to find the bastard that did it. I knew how it would look—like I did it. I was covered in her blood. I had a pocketknife on my belt . . ."

I searched his face, saw nothing to indicate he was lying. Scolari might be a damn good poker player, but no one could fake the raw emotion of hurt he openly displayed on his face.

"I believe you, Sam."

"So now what?" he asked, a look of relief coming over him. "The killer's still out there, and I'm in here."

"Who killed her?"

His lips pressed together in a thin line. Hatred filled his gaze. "Dex was using Josie. I think he convinced her to hook up with my wife, use this rain forest thing that Patricia was so into to get close to her, find out what she knew about the XTC autopsies. She found part of that Project Green document, and told me that Dex was worried that his cocaine trafficking, and his connection with Foust, and the XTC could somehow be traced back to him at Hilliard Pharmaceutical."

"That would explain why Dex would kill the PI," I said.

"PI?"

"The Ice Man. Hired by Montgard to look into Hilliard's activities, or so we believe."

"What makes you say Dex killed him?"

"You recall when he let us into the warehouse? He knew that we were looking for the juice that ran the freezer before we even asked. If Patricia told you Dex was worried, I'll lay odds that Dex thought the PI was investigating him for his illicit drug activities."

What I had yet to discover, however, was why the PI was also carrying the so-called garden variety seeds that Patricia had argued about with Josie Hilliard the night of her murder. If they were so common, why kill over them? "I'll let you know what I find out," I said, rising. "Thanks, Sam."

"What're you going to do?"

"Wait for the warrant to be finished, and get the proof I need."

I returned to my office, knowing Torrance wouldn't be there waiting but feeling strange without him there. He had no reason, with Scolari in custody. His IA job was done. Things were back to normal, or would be once

Foust was arrested. Rocky sat at his desk, pecking at the typewriter with two fingers.

The lack of Torrance's presence at my side left me feeling naked. Like the feeling you get the very first time you skinny-dip. Free, yet edgy. I wondered if he was glad to get away, then forced the thought from my mind. I needed to concentrate on what I knew about this case, coupled with what Scolari had told me. I was certain the seeds still played an important part, and the fact they were garden variety set my wheels spinning. I thought of the article in the *Chronicle*, and the discovery of the potential cancer cure in the rain forest. I thought of Montgard of Arkansas, and their interest in purchasing the company. And Evan Hilliard's anger at his wife for making the premature announcement. I thought of the seeds in the PI's ring.

Suddenly I knew why he had those seeds. And what he intended on doing with them.

Now all I had to do was prove it.

I called the DA's office and got ahold of Reid. I wanted to ask him about his contact with Paolini, but needed to know the status of the warrant, and figured it was best not to get Reid on the defensive right now.

"They're signing it now," he said. "Five minutes, tops, and they're done."

"Is Andrews there?"

"Yeah. You want to talk with him?"

"Ask if the warrant team is ready to go. I have a couple of calls I need to make, and I don't want to do it until they're in place."

Reid must have covered the phone. I heard muffled conversation, and then Reid came back on. "He says go ahead. They'll be in place in about five minutes."

"Thanks."

I telephoned Hilliard Pharmaceutical, and got voice mail for both Josie and Evan Hilliard. I left the same message on both, about Project Green, then tried Dex. He answered on the third ring. I asked if he could get ahold of Josie or Evan. "It's important."

"I'll be seeing them both in the next few minutes," he said. "Is there something I can do for you?"

"I need to know about Project Green."

"Can't say that I'm familiar with it. Would you like me to have the Hilliards return your call?"

"Yes. Please." I hung up, figuring I had about fifteen minutes to get out to the warehouse.

"What was that all about?" Rocky asked, looking up from his keyboard.

"Setting the trap for the killer," I said. "I have a feeling someone might not like it if they think I know about Project Green."

"Do you?"

Before I could reply, my phone rang. I answered with a curt, "Gillespie, Homicide detail," hoping it was word that the warrant team was in place.

"Kate?"

It was Reid. "I spoke with Paolini," I said before he could get a word in edgewise. "He told me to talk to you about why you were seen with him."

There was a long moment of silence, then, "An old case. It has nothing to do with you."

"I'd like to—"

"Dexter Kermgard just called."

"About what?"

"He told me that Josie Hilliard was very upset. Apparently he told her you were inquiring into something called Project Green? He thinks she's going to destroy some files in the warehouse."

"Why did he call you?"

Hesitation. Then, "I don't know. And there's been a snag in the warrant. They got the address wrong. Someone put the main facility down instead of the warehouse. The judge won't sign until it's corrected."

I glanced up at the clock. I was running out of time.

"What are you planning on doing?" he asked.

"I want to make sure that warehouse is secured until the warrant's done."

"You need backup. I'll go with you."

"The warrant team should already be there, waiting. And I've got backup here," I said, watching Rocky type away. "Is Andrews still there?"

"No."

"Thanks."

I hung up, tapping my fingers on the phone. Why had Dex called Reid? I found that extremely strange. Since Andrews hadn't returned yet, I called Torrance. No answer.

Should I wait for Torrance? I knew what he'd say. Wait until the warrant's done. Technically speaking, he was no longer my ball and chain. Once again he was IA, and I was an inspector working a case. He was investigating my partner, and I was investigating a murder.

As far as backup, Rocky was it. But then I wondered why it hadn't occurred to him that the doctor's files on the hard drive could be so easily recovered. Bill Moore made it sound like this F.A.T. partition was basic knowledge. Something that Rocky should have known, with all the computer schools the department had sent him to. Why, then, couldn't Rocky bring up the files? I glanced at the clock. I needed to get to the warehouse.

"Let's go, Rocky."

"Where?"

"Hilliard Pharmaceutical's file storage warehouse. Josephine Hilliard's supposed to be en route to destroy some files. I want to stop her."

"Maybe you better run it by Andrews," Rocky said.

"I would if he were here. There isn't time. I'll call him from the car. Let him know we're doing a Code Five." Rocky seemed to relax when I mentioned the Code Five, a term used for standing by, watching at a safe distance. "Besides, the warrant team should already be waiting there."

"Yeah, okay," he said, grabbing his shoulder holster from his top drawer and slipping it on.

25

I drove. Rocky rode shotgun. He gripped the dash, his right foot stomped on a phantom brake pedal. "Jesus, Gillespie, you trying to qualify for Sears Point?"

The light at Montgomery and Broadway cycled to yellow. I floored through it. "I want this Project Green file," I said, not so lucky at the next signal. Red.

"So she destroys the file, what's it gonna prove?"

"The million-dollar question," I said, switching lanes. Someone honked behind me. "My guess is murder."

"You're never gonna make it through," he said, nodding toward the next intersection.

Sure enough, as I neared, the light changed to red. I slammed to a stop. "Come on, come on." I tapped my fingers on the steering wheel. Watched the cross traffic go by. I thought about my conversation with Sam, and told Rocky about it.

"Which means Scolari should've put in for overtime. He gave you the Slasher on a silver platter."

"No, don't you see? He drew this thing out. He knew about it back when all this started with his wife. He was trying to distract me."

"From what?"

"From his wife's murder. He doesn't want us near Hilliard Pharmaceutical."

Rocky looked skeptical, but I let it go. Now I only hoped I could get to Hilliard Pharmaceutical before Josephine did.

"Make a right here," Rocky said, pointing to an alley. "We can cut off some of that commuter traffic."

I whipped the wheel around, pulling into the alley. My rear wheels skidded slightly as I dodged a garbage can someone had knocked over. I hit it anyway. It bounced off the front bumper with a hollow clatter that sounded like a drum encore in a rock concert.

Rocky looked over his shoulder. "They should've made it flat on one side to begin with. So it wouldn't roll into the middle of the alley."

I braked to a stop at the next street, glanced both ways, then shot across the moment it was clear. "You think Hilliard could have erased those files from the accounting office?" I asked.

"Possible. Then again, maybe me or Bettencourt did it accidentally. Hard to say."

"You know what a F.A.T. partition is?" I asked suddenly.

"Yeah, why?"

"My friend over at DOJ says that's what the data on the computer was stored on. It wasn't really erased."

"I guess it didn't occur to me."

I wondered if that was true, that he merely hadn't thought of it, but our arrival at the Hilliard warehouse kept me from pressing the issue.

Josephine Hilliard's Lincoln was parked out front, and I pulled in behind it.

"Where the hell's the warrant team?" Rocky asked.

"Good question," I said, pulling out the cell phone. I called our office, surprised to hear Torrance answer. "Is Andrews there?" I asked.

"He's in the judge's chambers getting the warrant. Where are you?"

"With Rocky."

"And Rocky would be . . . ?"

"With me?"

Silence.

"We're at the warehouse."

"Damn it, Gillespie—"

"There wasn't time to explain. We looked around the office, but no one was there. I knew the warrant team was supposed to be here."

"Explain what?"

"That Dexter Kermgard called Reid," I replied. "He said Josephine was en route to the warehouse to study the Project Green file. Which presents a slight problem."

"What?"

"I think we beat the warrant team here."

"*Gillespie*—"

"We need to contain the scene."

"Key word being *contain*, Gillespie. Don't play hero."

"Gotta go."

Rocky eyed me. "Who was that?"

"Torrance. Who else?"

"Bet you'll be glad when they catch Foust and you can go home, alone."

"Immensely," I said, trying to envision my couch as it was meant to be, without sheets on it. All that came to mind was the bathroom sink. I wondered if I'd ever be able to brush my teeth without thinking about Torrance kissing me there. "Let's go. I want to see what's going on."

I dropped the cell phone onto the seat and grabbed my radio. Rocky and I exited the car. The door to the warehouse wasn't quite shut. We looked at each other, and Rocky shrugged as though to say, what the hell, he never had a choice.

Entering without the warrant presented a problem, but I justified it in my mind with the knowledge that Josephine might be destroying evidence. Exigency of circumstances.

The moment I opened the door, I saw Josephine on the moving ladder in the back, pulling a file box from the top shelf. A large red container was at her feet. Gasoline. There were two more containers on the floor. Halting in my tracks, I put up my hand, motioning for Rocky to stop. We backed out, and I shut the door softly. "She's going to torch the place," I whispered. "We need to call for fire." I keyed my portable, but Dispatch couldn't copy over the static.

"I'll call from the car," Rocky said.

I handed him my radio. Rocky returned to the car. Suddenly I heard a crash inside. I pulled open the door wide enough to peek in. I saw a file box on the floor, papers scattered everywhere. Josephine lifted a second file box from the top shelf. Looking for something? The Project Green file?

I glanced back at Rocky, wondering what was keeping him. He was still talking. When I returned my attention to Josephine, I caught a movement through a space in the shelf. Dex, his weapon in his left hand, edged his way toward Josephine from the next aisle over.

"Oh, no," I muttered. I waved at Rocky. He looked up, and I mouthed, "Dex." He nodded, but I don't think he understood, since I saw his eyes widen as I drew my semiauto. Phone in hand, he nearly fell from the car in his rush to get to me.

"What the hell is going on?"

"Dex's inside. He might be after Josephine Hilliard."

"Yeah? Well, I got even worse news. The warrant team went out to the original address on the warrant. They got sent to the main facility. Torrance is en route now. He says the best they can do is send a radio car our way."

"Great." I couldn't very well ignore the situation within. I raised my hand to knock.

"What are you doing?"

"Maybe saving Josie Hilliard's life," I said. Rapping my knuckles on the door, I waited about two seconds, then opened it, keeping my gun hidden against my right side. "Mrs. Hilliard?" I called out.

I didn't move from the doorway, my only safety zone. Nor did she move from the top of the ladder. The gasoline smell was overpowering, and I realized she had either knocked the container over or dumped it on purpose. In her right hand she held a thick file folder, in her left was a small silver object. I wasn't close enough to see, but when she pushed up on the top with her thumb, I knew what it was. The sterling lighter. The one I'd seen on her desk.

She saw me, and held out the lighter.

"Put it down," I said. "The whole place will go."

"Why didn't I think of that," Josephine replied, giving a slight smile. She cocked her head to one side.

I started to ask her why, but then it hit me. "This is because of the merger, isn't it?"

"Of course. We'll lose everything when they find out."

Behind me, I heard Rocky calling for backup. Dex had yet to make himself known. And until he did, I wasn't about to move from my spot.

"Maybe there's another way you can resolve this," I told her, falling back on my Hostage Negotiation training. I figured I was dealing with a woman who felt she was at the end of her rope. I needed to keep her talking. If she stopped, it would give her time to think. And what I didn't want her to think about was lighting a fire.

"There's no other way," she said. "Everything I have is in this business."

"Then why destroy it?"

"Because if they find it, it's over."

"Find what?" I asked, although I knew. Project Green.

She shook her head, but before she could answer, Dex slipped between the wall and the shelf at the far end. "Hello, Kate," he said, his weapon held low.

My heart pounded as I drew down on Dex. I knew I'd do what it took to protect and survive. But who was I protecting here? Was Dex trying to stop her? Or was he setting me up? "Put your weapon away, Dex," I said, partly for Rocky's benefit. Although Dex had yet to point it at me, I didn't want Rocky stepping in without knowing what was going on. In fact, I didn't want him in at all, since I wasn't sure how Dex would react. Or Josephine, for that matter. Both were protecting their slice of the pie. They were like two animals that when cornered, would fight.

I heard Rocky utter a soft, "Oh, shit," then, "Kermgard's here. He's armed." Apparently, Rocky was giving a play-by-play on the cellular.

"Not a chance, Kate," Dex said in reply to my order.

"Me and Josie got some unfinished business. Give me the file, Josie."

She flipped open the top of the lighter.

"Dex!" I called out. "Can't you smell the gas?"

"Then get out of here, and you won't get hurt."

Behind me, I heard Rocky clear his throat. "Um, Torrance says out. Now."

I pretended not to hear. "Josie, don't do it. Nothing is solved this way."

Dex closed the short distance between them and stepped on the ladder. It rolled a few inches and Josie fell against the shelf behind her, trying to catch her balance. The empty gas can clattered to the ground. I jumped at the echo.

"I've soaked every one of these boxes with gas," she said, holding the lighter up as proof. "I'll take you with me."

"Dex," I said, "put the gun down, come out with me. It's not worth it. You know what happened to Estrada." Ricky Estrada, now retired, fired on an arson suspect who pointed a gun at him. The spark from his weapon, or a ricocheting bullet, no one quite knew for sure, ignited the gasoline. Estrada walked out of there resembling a roasted marshmallow with half a mustache. "He was lucky," I said. "You might not be."

I saw Dex's gaze flick to the empty gas can on the ground. He stepped off the ladder. "And if that file makes it out of here, it won't matter."

"So you go down for a little drug running," I said. Now was not the time to point out that I knew he'd murdered the PI. "You know you can make a deal with the DA. Testify against Paolini."

"An ex-cop in prison?" he said. "I don't think so. Give me the file, Josie."

Josephine backed against the shelves, lifting the lighter higher. A flick of her thumb, and it was lit.

"You want this, Dex?" she cried. "No one is getting this. No one."

I felt helpless, yet curious as to why Josephine and Dex were pitted against each other. I could smell the gas, though not as strong now.

"Put it down," I shouted, eyeing the inch-high wavering flame in her left hand. It was precisely at that moment that I realized what I had overlooked regarding this entire case. It wasn't about Project Green. Not totally. And Scolari was wrong about Dex. Dex and Josephine were both left-handed. Patricia was killed by a right-handed suspect.

I took a step in, but the sound of a car door slamming made me pause. Undoubtedly Torrance.

"Oh, shit . . ."

I ignored Rocky's expletive, figuring Torrance was finally here. Especially after seeing the look on Dex's face as he glanced our way. But in the millisecond it took all this to register, I realized Torrance could never have made it here so fast, even going Code Three, with lights and sirens.

I sensed Rocky's chest at my back, then he grasped my shoulder. At the same time, I saw Dex about to speak, then shut his mouth, a look of confusion on his face. Even Josephine stared.

"Rocky?" I asked in rising panic. I started to turn.

The shock of cold metal on my neck stopped me.

"Sorry, Gillespie," Rocky said.

"What are you doing?"

But Rocky didn't answer.

"Your weapon, Inspector."

Evan Hilliard relieved me of my weapon. "Now the two of you turn around, slowly," he said to Rocky and me. We did, and I saw Hilliard pointing my nine millimeter at us. The left pocket of his suit coat hung with the weight of what I assumed was Rocky's weapon. Rocky wasn't the sort to let down his guard, and I wondered how Hilliard had managed to get the take on him. Me, I knew. I had been wrapped up in trying to get Dex and Josie to give up.

Hilliard motioned to Dex. "Very slowly put your gun on the ground," he said as Dex bent his knees, reaching downward. "Let go, nice and easy," he said, nodding. "Stand up. Slide it to me with your foot. All the way."

Dex shoved his firearm with the toe of his shoe. It rattled across the floor, sliding beneath the ladder. Hilliard eyed it, apparently figuring it was out of reach for the moment.

"Back to the other side of the ladder," Hilliard told us. "Right there in the corner. Perfect."

"What's perfect?" I asked, noting the look of calculation in his eyes.

"How my lovely wife killed everyone in her quest to save her company from her drug-running boyfriend."

"For God's sake, Evan," Josephine cried as she descended the ladder. "I never intended to kill anyone."

"Such a waste of life," he replied, paying little heed to her outburst. "And all to prevent a scandal over Project Green. Into the corner, Josephine. With the others." He shook his head at me. "And here I figured you thought her little affair with Inspector Scolari's wife was at the bottom of it."

Dex tensed beside me, but he remained silent.

Hilliard, keeping his weapon trained on us, grabbed a file box with one hand and pulled it from its shelf. Papers flew everywhere as he tossed the box in the air. He never took his gaze from us, and all we could do was watch while he pulled a second box and repeated his actions. Time, I told myself. We needed time. Help was on the way.

But I didn't hear any sirens. Nothing to indicate we were the focus of rescue efforts yet. Hilliard threw a third box into the pile before us, then picked up one of the containers of gas, spilling the contents onto our death pyre. The smell of fuel assaulted my nostrils. My thoughts fragmented. Shards of fear sliced through me.

"You won't get away with this," I said, vaguely aware of Dex standing next to me, Rocky and Josephine in the corner beside us. We were trapped.

"Your lighter." He reached over the pile of papers toward his wife.

She didn't move.

He aimed the gun at her, his jaw clenching.

Josephine crumpled into a heap on the floor. The lighter as well as her coveted folder slipped from her grasp. Papers drifted about her.

Hilliard leveled his pistol on me. "Pick up the lighter. Or be the first to go."

"Isn't that the file you're looking for?" I asked, nodding to the Project Green papers.

He merely smiled.

"Of course," I said. "You must already have a copy. How else could you prove the desperation of your wife to go to such extremes? Accidentally torch the building?"

His smile thinned, and he motioned for me to get the lighter.

I picked it up. And saw Dex's gun beneath the ladder. I could have easily tossed the lighter to Hilliard. Instead, I worked my way around the gas-soaked files toward him. "That's why you had Dex kill that PI," I said. "You told him that Project Green was a record of his drug running, and the PI had read it."

"The lighter, please."

I held it out. Enticing. I needed to get to the ladder. "But you knew the PI was only interested in the seeds."

"Seeds?" Dex asked. A look of surprise, then sudden understanding came over him. He glared at Hilliard. "You told me he was looking into the drugs, the XTC coming from the lab."

"Did I?"

"You son of a bitch. You set me up."

"You screwed my wife."

Dex charged him.

Hilliard raised my nine millimeter. Pointed it at Dex. He fired.

Dex's body jerked back. My ears rang. Josie cried out.

Blood stained the pristine white shoulder of Dex's lab coat. Hilliard fired again. Dex fell to the ground. "That's for turning my company into an illicit drug haven."

Everyone stared at Hilliard, too shocked to move. Everyone except me. I wanted to get out of there alive. "It was always about the seeds," I said, taking a step closer. "Project Green was your way of keeping Dex in line. But you told Josie a different story. That Project Green would ruin your company. But it was always the seeds, wasn't it?"

Hilliard's eyes glittered triumphantly.

"You killed Patricia because she found out what they were. What you were trying to do."

Keep Hilliard talking. Play to his ego. "You knew

Paolini and Dex were running drugs. You knew the only way to get out from under their control, to get your wife back, was to sell your failing company," I said, judging the distance between me and the ladder. Just a few more feet. "How fortunate you found these seeds from the rain forest. Sent your stocks soaring. Set the pharmaceutical world abuzz."

"And it worked," he said.

"Of course it did," I said, still holding out the lighter. I took another step, as though I were about to hand it to him. "Montgard makes synthetic cancer drugs. They wanted to buy your company. Have access to the seeds."

"To destroy them," Hilliard said.

"Which would have suited you fine, until the PI discovered something even more perverse," I said, edging closer. "The seeds they wanted so badly were nothing. That's when you set up Dex. Told him the PI was looking into his drug operation. You couldn't let him report back to Montgard. Not when they were about to pay millions for something you could buy at the local nursery. Pokeweed. An herbal cancer remedy. Very slick. How did you fool everyone?"

"I used Montgard's own synthetic drugs in my studies to skew the results. With a little computer work and a few pokeweed seeds in a strange pod from the rain forest, it wasn't difficult."

As he spoke, Josephine sobbed and reached out to Dex's still form. "Why? Why?"

Hilliard smiled at his wife's distress. "Why? Look around you, Josie. Why did Dex convince you to come in here and destroy these files? He was using you to destroy evidence of his two-bit drug trafficking."

I took a couple more steps while his attention was

diverted to his wife. I held out the lighter, intending to throw it at him, then dive for the gun.

"Good-bye, Josie," he said, kicking over the remaining gas container. The top fell off and gasoline poured from the opening.

"You sent the pizza," I said quickly. Keep him talking. I needed to get the gun. But he never took his eyes off his wife. "How?" I demanded.

He spared me a glance. "Money buys more than happiness." And then he shoved the gas can with his foot. If he was aiming for his wife, he missed. The container spun toward me. Gas flew out like blades from a helicopter. I felt the liquid hit my right leg, soaking into my jeans. He aimed the gun at Josephine.

"No," she sobbed. "Don't."

Dex groaned.

"The lighter," I shouted, attempting to draw his attention. I threw it at his face. He ducked as it flew past him. At the same time, I saw a flash beside me. The gas ignited. Ripped across the floor. How? The lighter lay twenty feet away on the floor. But a wall of flames roared up, separating Hilliard and me from the others. Rocky jerked Josephine away. She screamed for Dex.

Hilliard grabbed my arm and held the gun to my head. "It's a shame I left my knife at home. I'd take as much pleasure in slitting your throat as I did my wife's lover's."

"How very clever of you to make it look like a Slasher case, and throw everyone off," I said, aware of the roar of fire, the heat, the smoke.

He sighed. "Now I'll be forced to play the grieving widower."

"From a jail cell."

He drew me back, his mouth against my ear. "I'll take you to hell with me first."

"Not this time," I said. I jabbed him with my elbow and twisted, nearly falling over Dex's legs. I glanced down, saw Dex lying there, face ashen, his life's blood spreading across the white concrete. Flames licked at his hand. A disposable lighter lay at his fingertips. Dex had started the fire?

Rocky stood on the other side of the pyre in the corner with Josie. An inferno raged up the shelves on my left. The air seemed to vibrate around us. Hilliard thrust me toward the flames. He came after me. I rolled to the side. Groped beneath the ladder for Dex's gun. Found it. I flipped to my back. Screamed as Hilliard dove for me. I fired twice. Hilliard's face twisted in pain. He stumbled back, fell to the floor. I kicked his weapon into the flames. Kept my own trained at his chest.

Through the gathering haze, I saw Rocky and Josephine pressed into the corner, the fire closing in on them. I had to get them out. But how? Sunlight poured in through the ceiling-high windows, illuminating the smoke-shrouded sprinklers that should have gone off, but didn't.

My gaze swung to the ladder.

It stood like a silver beacon at the edge of the flames. Only Hilliard blocked my way. He saw the direction of my gaze.

He struggled to his feet. Hurled himself onto the ladder.

The fire blazed across his back. His scream pierced the air.

The image burned into my memory. Helpless. I was helpless. A file box fell from the shelf. Sparks flew out as it hit the ground.

"Kate, get back!" Rocky called out.

I took a deep breath, jumped over the smoldering box. I grabbed the ladder. The metal seared my palms. I couldn't move it.

The brake. I tried to dislodge Hilliard's body.

I rammed my boot heel into him. Tried to push him off. He slipped a step, his head bounced on the metal. I heard a *whoosh*. Blue-yellow fire engulfed my foot. I struck him again. He fell to the ground.

I kicked at the brake. Tugging my sleeves over my hands, I pulled the ladder, swung it around, shoved it through the inferno near the wall.

"Here!" I heard a yell. Then pounding. Footfall.

I grabbed Dex's arms and scrambled back toward the door. Heat. Unbearable. My right leg looked like a Roman candle. Kicking, I dropped to the floor, ripped at the buttons on my jeans.

Crack.

I stared in horror at the shelves beside me, now a wall of flames. They wavered, then crashed. I rolled to the wall. Pain shot through my leg.

"Kate!"

Rain pelted.

Then blackness.

26

The telephone," a woman's voice said. I opened my eyes to see Nightingale, Nurse from Hell, standing in my doorway saying something about the phone. Yeah, yeah, I thought. Can't have a phone. Been there, done that. I'd hallucinated everything. It was all one drug-induced nightmare from eating pizza.

"I'll get it in a minute." Torrance stood beside my bed, a soft smile playing at his lips. "Didn't I tell you not to play hero?"

Yep. Definitely hallucinating.

"I'll be right back," he told me.

He moved past Iron Nurse into the hallway. She came in, picked up the chart, consulted her watch, wrote something down. "You should be out of here soon," she said, replacing the chart.

I closed my eyes. Maybe I'd dream something better this time.

"Kate? You awake?"

Sam entered and stood next to my bed. The nurse wrapped a blood-pressure cuff around my arm.

"Hi," I said. Actually, "croaked" would be a more apt description. My throat felt dry, swollen.

He took my bandaged hand. Held it a little too tight. "We have to stop meeting like this."

"How'd you get here?" I asked, then coughed at the effort of talking. Sam poured me some water from a small plastic pink pitcher into a matching cup.

"Everything's cleared," he said while I drank. "Almost."

"Almost?"

"We'll talk later." He nodded toward the nurse and started to pull away.

"No," I said, grasping at his fingers. "I want to know."

I shifted in my bed, trying to sit up, but stopped at the intense pain on my right ankle. I wore a hospital gown and was covered with a light blanket. Lifting it, I saw my leg was bandaged clear up the calf. "Great."

"You were lucky you were wearing boots," the nurse said efficiently. She removed the blood pressure cuff. "Otherwise the burn would be much worse. A year, maybe two, you probably won't even see the scar."

"You okay?" Sam asked.

"Yeah. Fine. I'll live," I said, the pain already subsiding.

"Rocky got it worse," Sam said.

"What happened?"

"Broke his leg on the way down."

"Josephine?"

His face darkened, and I wished I'd kept my mouth shut. "She's fine. A little smoke inhalation, nothing serious. DA's going to file on her. Once they figure out exactly what charges."

"Arson?" I suggested.

"Maybe. Conspiracy and fraud, definitely. Hilliard was DOA."

"Dex?"

"ICU. You saved his life."

I took another drink, wetting my dry throat, then let out a sigh. "And what about you?"

"Me?" He shrugged. "I have a feeling the DA's gonna drop everything. It doesn't matter. I'm pulling out anyway."

"What do you mean?" I asked, alarmed. I couldn't imagine Homicide without Sam. He'd always been there, as constant as the points on our gold stars.

"Retire."

"But—"

"Too much happened, Kate. I need a break. Figured I'd go into the detective business."

"PI? You?" I didn't know a private investigator in the city that Sam respected. Which is not to say there weren't any good ones. That was just Sam's opinion.

"Didn't do half-bad looking for the Slasher."

"You broke the law."

He grinned. "That's the beauty of it. What are they gonna do? Put me on midnights?"

"They'll throw your sorry butt in jail."

"You worry too much. It'll be perfect. I can make my own hours and smoke in the car if I want to."

He leaned down, kissed my cheek. "You did good, Kate. Better than any partner I've ever had."

Rocky Markowski hobbled in on crutches, a sheepish look on his face as he held out a pen. "Sorry I screwed up on the computer, Kate. I've had my mind on other stuff. My wife and I, well, she wanted me to move back in, then she didn't. The stress is gettin' to me."

"Don't worry about it," I said.

"Put something nice on my cast?"

"See ya next fall?"

"Funny. Don't forget I know things about you."

I took the pen. Rocky sat on the side of the bed, lifting his casted leg up. I signed my name, then drew a heart around it.

"That'll start some rumors," he said, smiling. He reached over and tousled my hair. "I'm proud of you."

"Thanks."

Rocky slid off, gathering his crutches. "Scolari's gonna drive me home. I'll see you at work."

Sam kissed my forehead. "Wash your face before you leave. You got black smudges all over it." He indicated for Rocky to exit. "Come on, Gimpy," he said as they stepped through the door.

"You shoulda seen Torrance giving her mouth-to-mouth."

"Shut up, Markowski," Sam said.

Mouth-to-mouth? "What are you talking about, Rocky?" I asked.

"You were out cold. Smoke inhalation. He dragged you out, gave you mouth-to-mouth." He smiled. "You and me got to ride to the hospital together. Same ambulance. You don't remember?"

I shook my head as Sam nudged him from the room. I watched them head past the nurses' station, thinking about Torrance. He'd saved my life. Again. But now it was over.

It occurred to me that Torrance and I had reached a turning point in our relationship. The case was finished, and once our wounds were licked we could all return to our regular duties. I would go back to investigating homicides, and Torrance would go back to investigating cops.

The stigma of his job still weighed on me.

We'd weathered the storm in Sam's case, but what was next? Would I be able to take the pressure from those of my peers who looked down on Torrance for what he did? Was I strong enough?

Throwing back the covers, I sat up and eyed the bandage on my right leg. After this last week, I'd proved myself strong enough for anything. At the moment, however, I felt anything but brave. In fact, I deserved the right to be chicken, and on that note I decided I was getting out of there before Torrance returned. Swinging my legs over the side, I stood, and holding the back of my gown closed, stepped into the rest room, locking the door behind me. After using the head, then washing my soot-covered face, I exited, looking around for my clothes. A wardrobe stood to the left of the bed, and I opened it to find my belongings stuffed in a plastic courtesy bag. I pulled open the strings, and my nostrils flared at the distinct reek from my wet, smoky things, none of them wearable.

I tossed them back in the corner, then turned around, only to find Torrance watching me from the doorway. His collar was open, his tie missing. He regarded me with that closed look of his, while the quiet of the room settled around me until all I heard was my own breathing. I stared into his face, noting the smudges of soot I hadn't seen earlier. I tried to picture him giving me mouth-to-mouth. All I could think about was when he'd kissed me in my bathroom.

"Been to any good fires lately?" I asked.

"One."

I wanted him to smile, frown, anything. Maybe I was worrying about my peers for nothing. Maybe he was through with me. Maybe what happened in my bathroom was already dismissed from his mind. A onetime loss of sanity. A matter of convenience.

"I spoke with the doctor," he finally said.

"I'm going to live?"

"Apparently." He strode in carrying a Macy's bag, leaving me no choice but to face him and the future. "Figured you'd want some clothes to go home in."

"Thanks." I pulled out a pair of jeans, soft, faded, size ten, the same brand I'd lost in the fire. There was also a cotton sweater, as well as one smaller bag remaining. I reached in to get it, but he put his hand on mine and stopped me.

"I know your aunt said makeup was the thing to have in the hospital."

"So you bought some?" I asked.

He gave me that enigmatic stare I'd come to love—and hate. When he removed his hand, I peeked into the bag, finding silk panties and a matching bra. Emerald green.

His dark eyes held a questioning look, and for the moment, I was able to forget we had separate lives.

A portion of the author's royalties will be donated to COPS in memory of the men and women who have given their lives in the line of duty. COPS provides resources to assist in the rebuilding of the lives of surviving families of law enforcement officers killed in the line of duty.

ACKNOWLEDGMENTS

A number of officers and investigators assisted with my technical questions in my endeavor to make this an accurate yet entertaining and purely fictional portrayal of police life. Any errors are strictly mine.

Thanks to: Lieutenant John R. Hennessey, SFPD; Inspector Anthony J. Camilleri Jr., SFPD; Inspector Bill Kidd, SFPD; Assistant Chief Investigator Charles LaMorte, San Francisco Office of the District Attorney; Graham A. Cowley, Investigator San Francisco Medical Examiner's Office, Alan Pringle, Investigator San Francisco Medical Examiner's Office.

Special thanks to fellow hostage negotiator, Inspector Peter R. Maloney, SFPD, for introducing me to all the right people.

When I started this manuscript, there were no female homicide inspectors at SFPD, so I created Kate Gillespie, their first. Prior to the publication of this book, Inspector Sergeant Holly C. Pera became SFPD's first female homicide inspector, and according to those men that she would soon be working with in the Homicide detail, she was well deserving of the position. Any similarities Holly might bear to Kate, including her wit, charm, and brains, are purely coincidental.

Also on a more local level, thanks to: Lieutenant Garold Murray, LPD; Lieutenant David Main, LPD; Lieutenant Ron Tobeck, LPD; Sergeant Frank Grenko,

LPD; Officer Bobby Amin, LPD; Investigator John Bell, SJDA's office.

On the technical aspect of writing, I would like to thank Catherine Coulter and her reference to *Amadeus*, which made it all clear for me. And thank you to Georgia Bockoven for introducing me to Catherine and for always saying "when" and not "if." Thanks to Susan Crosby for reminding me that I could write.

Thanks to Marcy Posner of William Morris, Robin Stamm of HarperCollins (who has a great first name), and of course, Carolyn Marino, also of HarperCollins.

To the wonderful people in my town who make sure my mochas are made to perfection (without which I couldn't have worked the long hours on patrol and stayed up to write this book): the staff at Cottage Bakery and Mocha My Day. Thank you all.

And to Evelyn Herring, and my husband, Gary, for taking such wonderful care of my children so that I could finish this book.